Praise for Emma Miller and her novels

"A warm romance."
—*RT Book Reviews* on *Hannah's Courtship*

"There is warmth to the characters that will leave readers looking forward to seeing more."
—*RT Book Reviews* on *A Match for Addy*

"A captivating story."
—*RT Book Reviews* on *Miriam's Heart*

Praise for Jan Drexler and her novels

"The interaction between family members serves to entertain."
—*RT Book Reviews* on *A Mother for His Children*

"Drexler has delivered a pleasing read with touches of romance, suspense, drama and faith."
—*RT Book Reviews* on *A Home for His Family*

Emma Miller lives quietly in her old farmhouse in rural Delaware. Fortunate enough to be born into a family of strong faith, she grew up on a dairy farm surrounded by loving parents, siblings, grandparents, aunts, uncles and cousins. Emma was educated in local schools and once taught in an Amish schoolhouse. When she's not caring for her large family, reading and writing are her favorite pastimes.

Jan Drexler enjoys living in the Black Hills of South Dakota with her husband of more than thirty years and their four adult children. Intrigued by history and stories from an early age, she loves delving into the world of "what if?" with her characters. If she isn't at her computer giving life to imaginary people, she's probably hiking in the Hills or the Badlands, enjoying the spectacular scenery.

EMMA MILLER

Hannah's Courtship

&

JAN DREXLER

A Mother for His Children

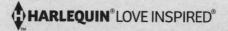

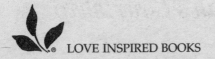 LOVE INSPIRED BOOKS

Recycling programs
for this product may
not exist in your area.

ISBN-13: 978-0-373-83899-8

Hannah's Courtship and A Mother for His Children

Copyright © 2017 by Harlequin Books S.A.

The publisher acknowledges the copyright holders
of the individual works as follows:

Hannah's Courtship
Copyright © 2014 by Emma Miller

A Mother for His Children
Copyright © 2014 by Jan Drexler

www.Harlequin.com

Printed in U.S.A.

CONTENTS

HANNAH'S COURTSHIP

Emma Miller

All these blessings will come on you
and accompany you if you obey the Lord your God.
—*Deuteronomy* 28:2

Chapter One

April
Kent County, Delaware

Heart thumping, Hannah Yoder awoke with a start in her bed, barely catching her Bible before it tumbled off her lap to the floor. Still foggy with sleep, she placed the Good Book safely on the nightstand beside her bed and retrieved the reading glasses that must have fallen when she dozed off. *What time was it?* Glancing at the clock on the mantel over the fireplace, she saw that it was eleven-thirty.

I'm getting old and foolish, she thought, *falling asleep with the propane lamp on.* She never did that. A mother with a houseful of children had to be vigilant against accidental fires…especially when they lived in a two-hundred-year-old house.

And then she remembered that five of her girls were grown and married and the sixth was promised to the community's new preacher. *Where has the time gone? Only yesterday, I was a young woman with a husband and seven beautiful children, and today, I'm widowed and nearly fifty.* In another month, there would be only her youngest daughter, Susanna, and her foster son, Irwin, left to share the big farmhouse.

Nearly midnight and she had to be up by five-thirty… She'd never been one to have trouble sleeping, but maybe the stress of preparing for Rebecca's wedding was affecting her more than she realized. She reached up to turn off the lamp, but then a nagging uneasiness tugged at her and drew her from the bed. The floorboards were cold and she slid her bare feet into a pair of her late husband Jonas's old fleece-lined slippers and reached for her flannel robe.

Something didn't feel right. What had awakened her? Had she had a bad dream? One of her windows was open a crack, letting in a cool, damp breeze, but that wasn't what had raised goose bumps on her arms. No, something was amiss.

She went to the window and stared out into the night. All was quiet in the farmyard. Common sense struggled with maternal instinct. Neither of the dogs had raised the alarm. True, their old sheepdog was somewhat hard of hearing, but Irwin's terrier could hear a mouse squeak in the next county. There was certainly no intruder. What troubled her?

Hannah had always considered herself a calm, rational woman. One couldn't remain sane raising a houseful of children and be prone to nervous fancies. She looked back at her bed, wanting nothing more than to crawl back under the covers and get a good night's sleep. But she knew that she wouldn't get a wink until she'd reassured herself that all was well.

Taking a flashlight from the nightstand, she switched it on. Nothing. Not even a faint glow. The batteries were dead. Again. Hannah sighed, guessing that Susanna had been playing with it.

The propane lamp was attached to the wall, so she took an old-fashioned kerosene lantern from the top of a dresser, lit it and, holding it high, padded into the hall. Quietly, feeling silly, she opened first one door and then the next. There was nothing out of place in the spare bedroom across from hers. No one in the downstairs bathroom. Green eyes peered back at Hannah from the settee in the parlor, and her heart skipped a beat.

Meow!

"Oscar." She let out the breath she'd been unconsciously holding. "Sorry." The glowing green orbs blinked and the tomcat flattened his single remaining ear against his gray head and flicked his long tail back and forth, obviously annoyed at being disturbed when he was on duty.

The landing at the bottom of the main staircase was still, every item in place, the wood gleaming and free of dust. And no wonder, Susanna, the same careless daughter who'd used up the flashlight batteries, had spent all afternoon waxing the floor and furniture, polishing the oak balusters and steps, and sweeping away cobwebs.

A smile curved Hannah's lips. Dear, precious Susanna, born with Down syndrome. Twenty-one and forever a child. Whatever Susanna did, she threw her whole heart and soul into it. That daughter, at least, would remain home with her. In spite of the challenges of mothering a special child, Hannah had always thought of Susanna as God's gift, much more of a blessing than a worry.

The kitchen, warm and cozy from the fire in the

woodstove, was as tidy as Hannah had left it when she'd gone up to bed at nine. Irwin's shoes stood on the steps that led to the back stairway. Hannah opened the door to the staircase and smiled again. From the second floor came the loud, regular buzz of Irwin's snoring. Hannah held the lantern up higher and called softly. "Jeremiah!"

She heard the patter of small feet, and the face of a scruffy terrier appeared at the top of the stairs. "It's all right, Jeremiah," she said, closing the door. If Jeremiah was on guard, no one had come unbidden into the house. She checked the back door, found it locked and retraced her steps to the front room. She'd found nothing to cause her concern, but she still wasn't satisfied.

I'm being ridiculous. "I should just go back to bed," she said, her voice louder than she intended. But she wouldn't be able to sleep until she'd fully investigated the house. She started up to the second floor where Rebecca and Susanna slept. Susanna's room first. Empty, as expected. Susanna had wanted her own bedroom because, in her own words, she was a woman grown. But, usually, she grew lonely at night and crawled into her sister's bed.

The bathroom door stood open, the interior dark. The unused bedrooms presented a wall of closed doors, all latched from the hall side. No problem there. There was only Rebecca's chamber left, where Hannah expected to find both of her girls fast asleep. It was a shame, really, to disturb them by opening the door and shining lamplight into their eyes. She did it anyway.

"Mam?" Rebecca stirred and raised a hand to shield her eyes. "What time is it? Did I oversleep?"

Hannah stepped into the room. Rebecca was alone in the four-poster bed. No Susanna. "Where's your sister?"

she asked, trying to keep the alarm out of her voice. "Where's Susanna?"

"In her bed, I suppose." Rebecca rubbed her eyes with the backs of her hands. "She never came in. I thought—"

"Are you sure?" Hannah raised the lamp to see into the far corners of the room. "She's not in her room."

"Downstairs, maybe? Sometimes she gets hungry and—"

"Not in the bathroom. Not in the kitchen." Hannah suppressed a shiver. "She's not anywhere in the house."

Rebecca scrambled out of bed and found her robe. "I don't think she'd go outside. She's afraid of the dark. She's got to be here. Remember the time we thought she was lost and we found her asleep in the pantry?"

Hannah grimaced. "She was eight years old, and she was only missing for a little while. I went to bed at nine. I don't know how long she's—"

"We'll find her." Rebecca pulled on a pair of black wool stockings and took her sneakers out of a chifforobe. "You check the house again. I'll look in the yard and barns." She turned on a high-powered flashlight. Hannah was glad to know that Rebecca's still had batteries.

Another search of the house, including the rooms over the kitchen, where Irwin slept, proved futile. Anxiously, Hannah stepped out onto the back porch. Rebecca, identified by the bobbing flashlight beam, was just coming out of the barn. "Is she there?" Hannah called.

"Ne." Not Rebecca's normal tone. Her voice was flat.

Hannah's fear flared. Rebecca might not have found Susanna, but she'd discovered something she didn't like.

"What is it?" Hannah demanded, coming down the steps to the back walk. She hurried to the gate, gripping the gatepost to keep her balance. "What's out there?"

"It's what's *not* there, *Mam*. The pony's gone. And Dat's courting buggy."

Hannah stared at her. It was too dark to make out the expression on Rebecca's face, but what she could make out from her tone confirmed Hannah's alarm. Sensible Rebecca was as frightened as she was. "Susanna took the pony and cart," Hannah said.

Rebecca gripped her mother's arm. "Where would she go in the middle of the night?"

Hannah didn't have to think twice. "David's."

David King, the only other person with Down syndrome Susanna had ever met, was the apple of her eye. For months, Susanna had insisted that she *loved* King David, as she called him, and that she was going to marry him.

The Kings didn't live far away, only a quarter of a mile from the end of the lane and to the right, on the opposite side of the county road. But Susanna wasn't allowed to leave the farm alone, and she'd never driven a horse and buggy. Hannah hadn't thought that Susanna could even hitch the pony to the cart. And to be out at night, going down a road that carried trucks and cars? Hannah shuddered, and prayed that God would watch over her.

"We'll find her," Rebecca said. "She's fine. I'm sure of it. We haven't heard any ambulances. You know how the dogs bark when a siren goes off. Wherever she is, Susanna is fine."

"She won't be when I catch up with her," Hannah pronounced. Of all of her girls, Susanna was the last one that she had ever suspected would sneak out at night to see a boy. Johanna, maybe Miriam, or even Leah, but not Susanna. Susanna was an obedient daughter who always followed the rules. It had never been her youngest daughter that had given Hannah her few gray hairs…until now.

"Do you want me to hitch up Blackie?" Rebecca asked. "I'm not dressed, but—"

Hannah set her jaw. "I'm going to walk to the Kings' house."

"In your bathrobe?"

"We have to find her." Hannah tightened the tie on her robe. "Every minute counts, and I trust the Lord will forgive me for my state of undress. Give me your flashlight."

"I should go with you."

"No, you stay here," Hannah told her, taking the flashlight. "Just in case she comes back and I miss her."

"I'll light the lamps in the kitchen." Rebecca went one way. Hannah another.

The dirt farm lane was a long one, and usually Hannah was grateful that her late husband had picked a place where the house was set far back off the road. Tonight, however, she wished it were a shorter driveway. *Oh, Jonas,* she thought. *Why aren't you here with me?* In the five years since a sudden heart attack had taken him from her, she often wished he was still here by her side, but never more so than tonight. She wasn't a weepy woman, but if she had been, she'd be inclined to sit down in the dirt and have a good cry.

She walked quickly, not bothering to call Susanna's name. If she was coming up this lane, with or without the pony and cart, Hannah would have heard her.

Instead, all she heard was the far-off wail of a freight train and the high chirping and deep bass croaks of early spring frogs.

The lights of a car whizzed past Hannah's mailbox. Not far now. The Kings' farm was dark. As with all the Old Order Amish in their community, David's parents didn't have electricity. Hannah had been hoping for the gleam of a kerosene lamp through an uncurtained window, but not a single glimmer showed.

Hannah's anxiety increased with every step. "Susanna," she murmured. "Where are you?" If she wasn't at the Kings' house and she wasn't on the road between here and there, Hannah would have to wake her sons-in-law and maybe send Irwin to the chair shop to use the business phone. Calling the English authorities wasn't a decision to be taken lightly. If an eight-year-old Amish child had been missing at night, it would be considered acceptable. Though Susanna might technically be twenty-one, her maturity level was closer to that of a second-grader.

At the end of the lane, a grove of cedar trees blocked her line of vision on the right. There was no moon tonight, and even with the flashlight, it was difficult to see. Hannah had just turned onto the shoulder of the road when she saw a bobbling light a few hundred feet away. "Susanna?" she called. No answer. Hannah called again. "Susanna!" *Please, God,* she prayed silently. *Let it be her. Let her be safe.*

Whoever it was, they were coming slowly, and Hannah couldn't hear hoof beats or the grate of buggy wheels on the pavement. She hurried toward the light. "Susanna?"

"Mam?"

Relief jolted through Hannah with a physical impact. She broke into a run. "Susanna, are you all right?"

"She's fine!" came a reply in a deep male voice.

"I'm fine."

That was Susanna's voice, but who was with her? Hannah stopped short and aimed the flashlight toward the approaching group: Susanna, short and round, bouncing along in her flat-footed, side-to-side stride and a larger, lumbering figure behind her.

A pickup truck approached, slowed and passed. In the glow of the headlight, Hannah saw a third person, a tall Englisher in a baseball cap leading Hannah's black-and-white pony. No, she decided, not just any Englisher. She recognized that voice. "Albert Hartman? Is that you?" She started toward them again, not running this time, but walking fast.

In another moment, she had her arms around a sobbing Susanna. Her daughter was trying to tell her something, but she quickly dissolved into hysterics. Because Susanna's speech was never clear to begin with, Hannah had trouble understanding what her daughter was trying to tell her.

"Crash," David supplied. He was a young man of few words. "Bam," he said. "Ina ditch."

Hannah gazed over Susanna's head. "Are you hurt, David?" she asked. "What about Taffy? Is the pony—"

"Not a scratch, so far as I can tell. It could have been a lot worse."

Hannah accepted Albert's opinion without hesitation. Not only was he a longtime family friend, but he was a local veterinarian. She turned her attention back to her daughter. "Why did you go out at night?" Hannah demanded. "And what made you take Taffy?"

"Pizza," David said. "We wanted pizza." He shook his head. "*Mam* gonna be mad at me. *Ya.*" He nodded his head. "Really mad."

"I was so worried. Come on," Hannah urged. "Let's get off this road before we're all killed." She held tight to Susanna, unwilling to let her go now that she'd found her. Adrenaline still pumped through Hannah's veins, and she felt vaguely sick to her stomach.

"Good idea," Albert said.

Together, they walked back to Hannah's lane. Once away from the blacktop, she loosened her grip on Susanna's arm and merely held her hand. "Albert," Hannah said, "how did you find them? *Where* did you find them?"

"Half a mile on the other side of the Kings' place," he said. "I was coming back from a call. A cow having twins was in a bit of trouble. Two pretty little heifers, both right as rain once we got their legs untangled and got them delivered. Anyway, I was just on my way home when I saw Jonas's courting buggy in the ditch and these two standing there beside it."

"A car came," Susanna wailed. "It scared Taffy. She jumped in the ditch."

"The buggy rolled over on its side," Albert explained. "A wheel is broken, but the carriage seems okay. I was more concerned for Susanna and David."

"Not David's fault," Susanna stoutly defended. "He drove good. The car beeped and scared Taffy."

Hannah rolled her eyes. "David drove?"

Susanna nodded.

They continued to walk up the long drive. "But, Daughter, you snuck out of the house."

Susanna shook her head. "*Ne.* I didn't."

"You did," Hannah said. "Did David come to the farm and hitch Taffy to the buggy?"

"*Ya,*" Susanna said, but David was shaking his head. "Hush," Susanna ordered, shaking her finger at him. "You *said!*"

Confused, Hannah glanced at Albert, who shrugged. "I couldn't get a straight story out of them, either. They were both crying when I got there. The pony was tangled in the traces."

"It was God's mercy that you found them," Hannah said. The pony belonged to her daughter Miriam, but she stabled it at the home barn so that Rebecca and Hannah had the use of it. They were all very fond of Taffy, and the thought that the animal could have been badly injured or killed by Susanna's carelessness made Hannah angry. "I'm disappointed in you, Susanna," she said sharply. "Very, very disappointed."

Susanna hung her head. Tears ran down her cheeks and she wiped at them with dirty hands, but Hannah wasn't feeling sympathetic.

"What you did was wrong and dangerous," Hannah chided. "You, David or Taffy could have been killed."

"We...we wanted pizza," Susanna mumbled. "You never...never let us go get...get pizza."

"I like pizza," David declared.

The sound of an approaching horse and buggy caught Hannah's attention. "That's got to be Rebecca," she explained to Albert. "Where's your truck?"

"I left it on the side of the road by the buggy."

Hannah nodded. "I can send Charley and Eli to get the buggy in the morning."

"No worry," Albert said. "I called Tony's Towing."

"But that will cost dearly," Hannah said. *Did she even* have *the money for a tow truck?*

"Don't worry about it." Albert gave her a reassuring grin. "Tony owes me for stitching up his Labrador's hind leg last week when he got it caught in the screen door. There won't be a charge. He'll have the buggy back in your barn within the hour."

Rebecca reined in Blackie, and Susanna pulled away from Hannah to run and tell her sister about her adventure. David stood patiently where he was, waiting for Susanna or someone to tell him what to do.

Hannah glanced back at Albert. "You walked right past David's house. Why didn't you leave him there?"

Albert tugged off his ball cap and looked sheepish. "He wouldn't go. Susanna wanted him with her, and I thought maybe you'd be uneasy about me bringing her home alone. You know, how it would look to the community..."

"How it would look? When you saved both of them from who knows what? Albert, you may not be Amish, but we trust you. You'll never know how grateful I am that it was you who came along when I needed you most."

"I suppose it was meant to be," Albert offered slowly. "His plan. I'm just glad I could help."

Rebecca climbed down out of the buggy, and Hannah quickly filled her in on what had happened. "We'll tie Taffy to the back and take her to the barn, and put Susanna to bed," she continued. "Albert and I are going to walk David home—"

"No need for you to put yourself out." Albert started to lead the pony around to the back of the buggy. "I can take David home."

"*Ne,* Albert," Hannah replied. She gave Susanna a gentle push in Rebecca's direction. "I need to come. David's mother has to know what he was up to. I don't think she'll be any more pleased with this night's mischief than I am."

Chapter Two

All I need now is for Bishop Atlee to drive past and see me walking down the road after midnight in my bathrobe and house slippers—accompanied by two men, Hannah thought wryly.

She supposed the wisest thing would have been for her to go back to the house and get dressed, but that would have taken more of Albert's time, and the Yoder family had already put him out a great deal tonight. Her oversize wool scarf and dark blue, ankle-length bathrobe covered more of her than her everyday dresses. She might not be conventionally garbed for an Amish woman, but no one could say she wasn't decently covered.

She was sure that Albert, a Mennonite born-and-bred, with more than the usual allotment of sense for a man, would understand her stretching the rules of proper dress due to the emergency. After all, wasn't Albert practically a member of the family? His nephew, John, was married to her daughter Grace.

Albert had been a friend and veterinarian to the Seven Poplars Amish community for many years, and

as long as Hannah had known him, he'd always treated
her with the greatest respect. To put a fine point on it,
Albert treated her as an equal, as a person with a brain
in her head. She was certain that Albert wouldn't be
ashamed to be seen with her under these circumstances.

It was a short walk from her mailbox to the driveway of the Kings' farmhouse. Only one motor vehicle
passed them, a small car, not the tow truck that Albert
had called to bring the disabled buggy home. She and
Albert kept their pace slow enough for David, who was
often distracted and had to be reminded to stay on the
shoulder. David never did anything quickly, and any
attempt to hurry him would have triggered upset and
possibly tears. Hannah had no wish to deliver him to
his parents in an emotional dither.

Hannah liked David, and she liked his mother and
father. They'd done a good job raising him, and she was
sure that he'd never given them reason to think he'd
sneak out with a girl to go to Dover. Tonight would be
an awakening for the Kings as much as it was for her.
David and Susanna, who had always been obedient,
had suddenly become problem children.

Fifteen minutes later, Hannah and Albert were back
at the spot where Hannah's driveway met the road.
David was safely in the care of his parents, and everyone had agreed that nothing good would come from trying to hash this mess out tonight. Albert had insisted
on walking Hannah home, although that had felt silly.
She was a woman in her late forties, a schoolteacher
and a mother who'd been managing her farm and her
affairs for years. She was certainly capable of following her own lane back to her home without an escort.

"Call me old-fashioned," Albert said, trudging along

beside her. He hadn't been put out by her objection. If anything, he sounded amused. "I just wouldn't feel right if I didn't see you safely to your door." When she didn't answer, he went on. "It's not the same world we grew up in, Hannah. You read the papers. All kinds of craziness going on."

"I try to stay away from the world as much as possible," she replied. It was what her Amish faith taught. *Be not of this world.* The Amish were a people apart, living not so much for today as for their future in heaven.

Albert was a member of the Mennonite Church, another Anabaptist sect that shared a long history with the Amish. The two faiths had separated before they came to America in the eighteenth century. The Amish believed that the Mennonites were too worldly, and Amish founders felt it necessary to remain separate. Today, the Mennonites did charity work with the general public and spread their religion through worldwide missions. The Amish kept to themselves and did not evangelize.

Hannah herself had been born and raised in the more liberal Mennonite faith, but she'd become Amish when she married Jonas Yoder. Although it had cost her dearly, she'd never regretted her decision.

"Wickedness," Albert continued. "Riots, bombings. People using violence against their neighbors."

"I hardly think there's going to be a riot in my farmyard tonight," she teased. "My sister-in-law Martha isn't all that fond of me, but I doubt even she wants to harm me. And my other neighbors are my daughters, my sons-in-law and my grandchildren, so I feel pretty safe."

"You hear stuff on the news every day. I can't help but worry."

"Maybe you should stop listening to the radio and watching television."

"Evil happens."

"Ya," she conceded. "It does. The best we can do is to live according to our conscience, treat one another as the Bible teaches us and pray that God will see to the rest."

"I suppose." Albert was a middling-size man, broad shouldered, with a sturdy body, chestnut-brown hair and a pleasant face. Usually, he walked with a vigorous stride, making him seem younger than his fifty-odd years, but since his father's death two months ago, Albert had lost the spring in his step.

Hannah and most of the Amish community had attended the funeral, and everyone had noted how hard Albert had taken the elderly man's passing. It was natural, she supposed. Albert had never married, and he and his father had lived together ever since Albert had joined the veterinary practice. Maybe Albert was lonely, Hannah thought. John had moved out when he finished building his new house, and now Albert lived alone. His days were full of work, but maybe he missed having someone at the supper table to swap stories with.

"Don't tell me you aren't worried about Susanna," he said. "I know better. You're a woman who's always put her children first. I've always admired that about you, Hannah, that you are such a great mother. And the way your girls turned out proves that you did most things right."

Hannah's throat tightened and she concentrated on the beam of light on the ground in front of them. Rebecca's flashlight was a good one, and it was easy to follow the hard-packed gravel drive. For the first time, she felt a little uncomfortable around Albert. She wasn't used to discussing private matters with outsiders. Although he'd proven himself to be a good friend to both her and her late husband, this subject was awkward. "I do worry about Susanna's future, naturally," she admitted stiffly. "But I have to trust in God's plan for her."

"You think He has a plan for each of us?"

"Of course." She was so surprised that she stopped walking and stared at him. "Don't you?" She knew that Albert was a faithful member of his church, and she'd assumed that he felt the same way.

"Sometimes I think so. But sometimes…"

She heard him exhale slowly.

"Sometimes I wonder if God spoke to me but I didn't listen… If I've waited too late to do what I should have done years ago."

She pressed her hand against her midsection to keep from touching him. Albert was obviously distressed. Had he been one of her children or sons-in-law, she would have reached out to him to touch his shoulder or take his hand, but they were alone. It wasn't proper that she have physical contact with a man not related to her. "In what way?" she asked. "How do you feel that you failed?"

He went on, not directly answering her question. "Getting through college was hard for me. I didn't want to borrow money, so I worked two jobs and attended classes full-time. I never had time for dating. And, then when I got into vet school, it was a struggle for me to keep up my grades."

"And after you graduated? Did you think of marriage then?" Standing outside the circle cast by the flashlight, Albert was a dark, indefinite figure. Hannah knew that she was intruding on his privacy, but out of compassion, she persisted.

"I tried to make up for lost time. I went out with different women, but I was too focused on my veterinary practice. I just wasn't ready to settle down."

"And now you regret not marrying and having children?"

"I think when a man hits fifty, he begins to realize that this is it. His life is more than half over. I've always loved taking care of animals, but there's something missing in my life."

"Have you talked to your preacher about this? Or to John?"

"No."

She and Jonas had wondered why a good man like Albert had never married. Among the Amish, a man or woman remaining single was almost unheard of. She remembered that some time back, before Jonas had died, Albert had kept company with a lady dentist in Dover. The couple had often gone to fund-raiser breakfasts and school auctions together. But, then, Jonas had come home one day and said that the Englisher dentist had married. Not Albert Hartman, but a lawyer.

Not knowing what to say, Hannah walked on a short distance until she came to the edge of the farmyard. "We're here," she said, "and it looks pretty quiet. No rioters." She smiled at him. "I really appreciate what you've done for me—for Susanna—tonight."

He stood there a moment. "I suppose I should get back to the buggy. The tow truck will be there, and the driver might need help loading it." He glanced toward the house. "You can lock up. I'll see that he delivers the buggy. No need for you to wait up."

Hannah found herself yawning. She nodded. Tomorrow was a school day, and she'd have to be up early. Before she left, she'd have to confront Susanna, and she wasn't looking forward to that. "Thanks, again, Albert. I don't know what would have happened if you hadn't helped."

"Don't say another word. Like I said, Hannah, I'm just happy that I came along when I did."

Leaving Albert by the gate, she went into the house. Rebecca and Susanna had already gone up to bed. She returned to her bedroom, removed her robe and slippers, and knelt in prayer. If there was ever a night that she needed to give thanks to God, this was it.

Because it was overcast and threatening to rain when she left home in the morning, Hannah didn't take the shortcut across the pasture to the Seven Poplars School as she usually did. Instead, she hitched up Blackie and drove the family buggy. Teaching twenty-six children in eight grades in one room wasn't easy, but she'd been doing it for five years.

When Jonas had suddenly died of a heart attack, she had not wanted to have to rent out her farmland or sell off any acreage. She'd known that a woman with six girls and no menfolk couldn't make enough off the crops to survive, so she'd convinced Bishop Atlee and the church elders to allow her to take the open schoolteacher's job.

Teachers were usually young single women, but Atlee had thought highly of Jonas, and he'd agreed. Hannah had been thankful to be given the opportunity, and she'd always believed that Atlee Bontrager's decision had been influenced, at least in part, by his fondness and admiration for Jonas.

The school had been a good fit for Hannah. She loved the challenge of teaching, and she loved the children. An added bonus was that being so close to home meant that she could keep a close eye on her own family while working. The pay in the church school wasn't much, but it was enough to provide independence for Hannah and her daughters. Having a steady income was the reason that she'd gone against custom and had remained unmarried after the usual period of mourning had passed.

The day turned out to be an unusually hectic one. She sent Joey Beachy home at noon when he'd thrown up on the playground. She'd asked Irwin, who was Joey's cousin, to walk the child back to the Beachy farm. Naturally, Joey had walked to school that morning, but it had been with his brothers and sisters, and Hannah hadn't felt right sending him home alone. Irwin was delighted. Hannah doubted that she'd see him again until suppertime. Her foster son didn't like school, and ensuring that he received a standard education had been her cross to bear.

She gave a math test to her combined fifth and sixth-graders, and directed rehearsals for the program done every year for parents and friends. Naturally, none of the boys had memorized their parts, and the walk-through for the skit had ended in tears when two sisters each wanted the same role. Hannah was glad that it was a busy day, because it gave her less time to worry about what she would say to David King's parents.

As soon as the last child had departed at the end of the school day, Hannah drove directly to the King house. Though she still had to contend with a tearful

Susanna at home again, it seemed wisest to first discuss the incident with David's mother, Sadie. That way, the two mothers could present a united front. Something had to be done. David and Susanna couldn't go on pretending that they were walking out together.

All the way there, Hannah hoped that Ebben, David's father, would be out of the house. This was women's business, and having Ebben be part of the conversation would make it more awkward for her. Sadie was a good, loving mother and a fine friend. Surely, she and Sadie could put an end to this behavior without harming either of their children.

"Come in, come in." Sadie must have been watching for her because the stocky little woman came out the side door as soon as Hannah drove up the lane. "Ebben!" Sadie called. "Take Hannah's horse." And then to Hannah, "Let Ebben see to him. You come in and have some of the applesauce cake I just took out of the oven."

Sadie's kitchen was smaller than her own, but just as clean. Simple white linen tiebacks hung at the windows, and pale yellow walls brightened the room. A round oak table with four chairs stood in the center of the room. Overhead hung a white kerosene lamp decorated with faded red roses, lit now against the gray afternoon.

"Tea?" Sadie asked. "Or coffee?"

"Coffee, if it's no trouble," Hannah responded.

Sadie bustled around, reminding Hannah of a banty hen in her gray dress, black stockings and white *kapp* and apron. Sadie's clothing still reflected the Amish community that they'd lived in before they'd moved to Delaware. Her *kapp* was sewn slightly different, her skirt and apron were longer and she wore high-topped black leather shoes, rather than the black canvas sneakers most women in Seven Poplars wore in the summer.

Sadie poured the coffee and brought a tiny pottery cream pitcher and matching sugar bowl to the table. She sliced generous pieces of applesauce cake and placed them beside the coffee mugs. "Honey or sugar?" she asked. "I like raw sugar, but Ebben and David do love that honey your Johanna brought us at Christmas."

Hannah was eager to see what David's parents thought about the previous night's misbehavior. Still, it would have been rude to jump right into the subject. First, news of children's and grandchildren's health and activities had to be exchanged, and Hannah had to tell Sadie about the plans for the school picnic. Sadie asked what Hannah was bringing for the shared meal after morning church service on Sunday, and when Hannah said potato salad with peas, Sadie wanted the recipe.

Hannah forced herself to at least appear relaxed, but she couldn't help glancing around. Ebben remained outside, and there was no sign of David. "David's outside with the chickens," Sadie said as she refilled Hannah's coffee cup. "Would you like another piece of cake?" Hannah shook her head. "David loves chickens," Sadie continued. "Ebben says he can coax two eggs a day out of those hens. David's a good boy."

Hannah nodded. "I know he is."

Sadie's right hand trembled as she reached for the sugar. She clenched her fingers into a fist and buried it in the folds of her starched apron. "He's a sweet boy, Hannah, a really gentle soul."

Hannah murmured in agreement. "So is my Susanna."

Sadie knotted her fingers together. Her faded blue

eyes grew misty with tears. "When David was born, the midwife told me that he was a Mongoloid."

Hannah winced. The term was wrong. Ugly. *"Downs,"* she corrected softly. "With Down syndrome. Like my Susanna."

"She wasn't Amish. The midwife. 'He might not live,' she said. 'A lot of times babies like him have a bad heart. It might be a blessing if he did—' My Ebben, he's quiet, like David. But he got so mad at that woman. 'Don't you say that!' he said. 'Don't you say such things about our beautiful son.' And he was beautiful, Hannah. He had this mop of yellow hair, as yellow as May butter, big blue eyes and the sweetest look on his face."

"My husband always said that Susanna was a blessing from God."

Sadie nodded eagerly. "Ebben asked that midwife to leave and not come back. We took David to a baby doctor at a big hospital. He told us that David would grow and learn like any other child. But he never said what a good boy David would be. He's never been willful." She hesitated. "It's why we never thought that David would ever…"

"Sneak out at night?"

"Our older son, now that one. When he was *Rumspringa*—he was a caution. Sowing his wild oats, Ebben always said. And if David wasn't…didn't have Downs, we would have expected him to…"

"But he does. *They* do." Hannah swallowed against the tightness in her throat. "We've always protected Susanna, kept her close. She's afraid of the dark. Running off to buy pizza…" Hannah exhaled softly. "I don't know what to do. They just have this idea that—"

"That they're courting," Sadie finished. "I know. I

know it's crazy, but David is very fond of your Susanna. He talks about her all the time."

"They could have been killed in that buggy accident."

"I know. I couldn't get a wink of sleep last night. David's driven in the field and in the yard, but never a horse on the road. He doesn't understand the danger of motor vehicles. It's a blessing your pony wasn't injured when the buggy went into the ditch."

Both women were quiet for a moment.

"The question is," Hannah said, "what do we do about them? I almost sent her to Brazil to visit Leah and her husband. I thought that maybe a few months away from David and—"

Sadie cut her off absently. "He was sick. When he was little. Cancer. We thought we were going to lose him. But God was good. The doctors…"

She raised her gaze to meet Hannah's. "He can't ever be a father, our David. The doctors said it's impossible. Some boys with his…with Downs… But for certain with David. He'll never be able to…you know."

"Oh." Hannah almost said she was sorry, but was she? Was that a blessing, considering David's difficulty in taking care of his own needs? And why was Sadie sharing that? What did it have to do with Susanna and David sneaking off at night?

"I was just thinking," Sadie said. "Ebben's cousin's daughter Janet, she's slow. Not Downs. Not like Susanna or David. But she can't read, can hardly count to twenty. David can, you know. He can read, too. Easy books and *The Budget*. He loves to read *The Budget* to us in the evenings."

Hannah waited, wondering what Sadie's point was.

"Janet, she got to an age where she wanted to be like her sisters, wanted to walk out with boys and go to the singings and the frolics. And pretty soon, she had herself a beau."

"What did her parents do?"

"They talked to their bishop and their church elders, and they all decided that the best thing to do, considering…"

Hannah shifted in her seat. "Was?"

"To let them get married."

"Get married?" Hannah repeated.

Sadie nodded.

"Are you suggesting that—" Hannah stopped and started again. "Are you saying that you think that David and my daughter—" She took a moment to compose herself. "Sadie, Susanna and David could never be married and live alone. They could never live a *married* life."

Sadie pressed her lips together. "Maybe not the same married life we've had, but…" She looked down at her hands, then back up Hannah. "I'm not saying we should give them permission to court. I just think it's something we need to keep in the back of our minds."

Chapter Three

Albert pulled into the long driveway that led through the trees to his nephew John's new log-cabin-style home. He glanced at his watch as he pulled into a spot in front of the porch. He was right on time.

He'd had a good day, considering that he'd had less sleep last night than usual; by the time he'd returned from the Yoder farm, it had been after two in the morning. Not that he minded. As a matter of fact, he'd enjoyed the little adventure. Of course, he was concerned for Hannah's daughter and her friend. Thankfully, everyone was safe. No harm done.

And his day had turned out to be an easy one. Besides the four routine calls for immunizations, he'd stitched up a pig's snout, and done a physical examination on a nice-looking colt. With the new vet that he and his nephew had hired tending to the small-animal portion of the practice, he was free to spend his time where his heart was, with large-animal cases: cows, horses, pigs, sheep and goats.

John and his wife, Grace, stepped out onto the porch and waved. Albert felt a rush of pride. He'd never fathered a child, but John was as close to being a son as a man could ask for. And the wife he'd chosen, Grace Yoder, had come to the marriage with a bright-eyed little boy who had eased his way into Albert's heart.

Albert walked around the truck, opened the passenger door and let his dog out. From the floor, he took a bag containing a junior-size pair of binoculars he'd found while poking around in his attic. They had been John's when he'd been around Dakota's age, and he thought the boy might like them.

"Come in, Uncle Albert," Grace called. "Supper's ready. My spaghetti and Johanna's yeast rolls. Your favorite." She led them into the house and the dog trotted behind them. "She sent them home with me when I went to pick up 'Kota."

"Where is the little rascal?" Albert looked around. "I brought him these." He held out the binoculars.

"He's not here," Grace explained. "Johanna invited him to stay overnight with Jonah, and I couldn't pry him away."

"He'll be sorry he missed you. But I know he'll love these. I remember when Gramps bought the binoculars for me," John said, taking them from Albert and peering through them. "The two of us used to go bird-watching on Sundays after church."

"I'll just finish up in the kitchen," Grace said with a smile. "You two catch up on vet talk." She hurried away, auburn ponytail swinging behind her.

Albert grinned at John. "I like that girl more every time I see her. You picked a winner. I'm just going to wash up." He pointed toward the half bath in the hall.

John bent to pat the dog's head. "I did, didn't I?" he said. "Grace has made me happy, really happy."

Albert paused at the bathroom door. "You'd have to be crazy if you weren't happy, with her and 'Kota."

Albert entered the small room, switched on the light and closed the door behind him. Funny, he thought as he soaped his hands, how much life there seemed to be inside the walls of this house. He looked into the round mirror. "Love inside these walls," he murmured half under his breath. For days, he'd been looking forward to sharing this evening meal with the three of them. Home was pretty lonely without Pop there now, just him and old Blue and the two cats that had somehow wormed their way into the family.

Blue had been a hard-luck case just like the cats, and had turned out to be one of the best snap decisions he'd ever made. Not a lot of people wanted a three-legged coon hound that couldn't hunt anymore, but he and Blue suited each other just fine. Without Blue... Albert sighed. Dogs had short lives, compared to humans, but most folks couldn't help getting deeply attached to them, and he'd be the first to admit he was guilty.

Grace was still in the kitchen when he joined John at the long pine table in the dining room. As she had predicted, they each had stories of the day's patients and their owners to share. Albert settled into a chair, took a sip from the glass of iced tea John had given him and studied the spacious room.

The log walls, the heavy log beams and wood floors gave the place a real flavor, and Grace and John had furnished it with a mixture of vintage pieces, such as a beautiful refinished icebox and a scarred church pew, mixed with a few antiques. Nothing was fancy. So far as he knew, the young couple didn't own a television. Other than the laptop, which lay on a maple desk in the living room, and electricity, the house could have been from another century.

"So what's this I hear about you coming to the Yoders' rescue last night?" John asked.

"Amish telegraph?" Albert asked with a chuckle.

John laughed. "Johanna told Grace. I can't imagine Susanna and David King out on the road at night with a pony. It's a wonder something worse didn't happen to them."

Albert leaned back in the chair. "I came along at the right time. Whoever ran them into that ditch kept going. But it might teach those kids a lesson and keep them out of worse trouble."

Grace came to the table with individual bowls of garden salad. "Susanna's never done anything like that before. I've never known her to get into any kind of trouble. She's such a sweet girl."

"You think it's serious, David and Susanna?" John asked Grace. "They seem to spend a lot of time together."

"I don't know," she answered.

"It worries Hannah," Albert said. "We got to talk some when we walked David back to his house. You've got to admire Hannah for the job she's done with your sister. It can't have been easy. David's parents, too. From what I've seen of him, he seems like a good boy. But Hannah's alone. She's had to go through all this dating and courtship stuff with all of her girls all by herself since Jonas passed away."

A timer went off in the kitchen. "That's the pasta," Grace explained. "Supper's coming up as soon as I can drain them."

"Is the buggy a total loss?" John asked.

Albert shook his head. "No, not at all. A new axle should fix it good as new. Hannah was fortunate in that, too."

"That's great," John sipped his tea. "Buggies are expensive, and I know the family thinks a lot of that one. Grace said her father brought it from Pennsylvania when he was courting Hannah."

Grace returned with plates of spaghetti, meatballs and sauce, and John jumped up to bring in the bread and butter. Everyone took their seats, they bowed their heads for a silent grace, Amish-style, and then they began to enjoy the delicious meal. It seemed that all three of them had had a good day. Grace had scored well on a test at the community college where she was studying to be a vet tech, and John had successfully delivered a litter of four healthy Cavalier King Charles Spaniels by caesarean section.

As they finished supper, Albert remembered the box of cookies he'd picked up at the German bakery. "Wait right here," he said. "I brought dessert. It won't take a moment to fetch it."

"We won't be able to walk away from the table," Grace teased.

"Then you can just roll me out of the house." Albert got out of his chair. "But I'll bounce down the steps with a grin on my face."

"Uncle Albert, I'll get them." Grace put her hand on his shoulder as she passed him. "You sit. I forgot to pick up the mail, and I have to walk right past your truck. Come on, Blue," she called to the dog. "Want to take a walk?"

John refilled Albert's glass, Albert sat down again

and John shared a joke Milly had told him. Albert laughed so hard he almost choked on his iced tea.

"You're in a good mood tonight," John said thoughtfully. "We've been worried about you since Gramps died. You really haven't seemed like yourself."

"It's not easy losing your father. He had his health problems, and I know he was right with his salvation. But I do miss him every day."

"I miss him, too," John agreed. "Without him—without the two of you—I wouldn't be where I am today. I'd never have gotten through school if—"

"Now, none of that," Albert said, his cheeks flushing with embarrassment. "You would have found your way." Still, John's admission warmed him inside. "You're right, though. I *have* been down in the dumps. Maybe some of it is realizing that when the older generation passes on, I'm suddenly at the top of the hill looking down."

John laughed. "You're what, Uncle Albert? Fifty-five? That's hardly over the hill."

"Fifty-six in July." Albert grimaced. "Sound like I'm eighty-five sometimes, don't I? I should be around Dakota more. Kids keep you young."

John leaned forward. "Have you ever thought about moving in with us? We could build a whole basement suite and even put in a minikitchen, if you don't want to eat with us regularly."

Albert laid his hand over John's. "I have thought about it. I really appreciate the offer, but you and Grace need time and space to build your own family."

John nodded. "You're sure?"

Albert nodded.

"Well, if you ever change your mind, the offer stands.

We'd love to have you here, and it wouldn't hurt to have a built-in babysitter." They both laughed.

"I'll manage on my own just fine," Albert assured him.

"I know you will. I just worry. Maybe you need a hobby. Something to occupy your time when you're not working." John met Albert's gaze. "Because you can't just work, go to church and come here for dinner once a week. You need something more."

"Like what? Playing golf? Jet skiing?"

Again they laughed, because while many men his age might take up either, they weren't and never would be choices Albert would make.

Grace and Blue returned to the house, and then they enjoyed the cookies. It was eight forty-five when Albert drove away. As he turned onto the blacktop, he glanced back at the house. John was right. He had been happier tonight than he'd been since before Pop's health had taken a turn for the worse. It didn't pay for a man to brood on what he didn't have. Maybe John was right; maybe he needed a hobby. He needed something, but that something wasn't moving in with John's family.

He had his work: hard, stressful and challenging. He had friends, John, Grace and Dakota, as well as a great staff. He had his faith, so why did he feel that something was lacking in his life? Was it something—or someone? Maybe fifty-five wasn't over the hill. If he put his mind to it, maybe he could find a way to be happier every day.

He'd actually been thinking about taking up a hobby, of sorts. One of his elderly clients had been the one to plant the seed in his mind and had been generous enough to offer to help get him started. The idea definitely interested him. The thing was, he would need some help.

One person immediately came to mind.

But did he dare ask her?

Hannah let the school children out early on Friday. There were only a few full days left before the end-of-year picnic that marked the beginning of summer vacation. The English public schools ended in June, but Amish children were needed to help with spring planting. The Seven Poplars School began in September and closed at the end of April. Amish students had fewer vacation days during the year so that they could satisfy the state education requirements and still be finished early. For several of Hannah's students, this, their eighth year, would be their last. They would go on to learn a trade and begin their vocational training.

This should have been her foster son, Irwin's, final year of formal schooling, but she had yet to decide if he would be among the graduates. Irwin had never been a scholar. He'd come to her when he was twelve, already far behind his classmates, and each milestone in his education had been a hard-won goal. Hannah wasn't satisfied with Irwin's math skills or his reading comprehension, but she also worried that another year in the back of her classroom would make little difference. Irwin was tired of being shown up by younger students.

Hannah cared deeply about the orphaned boy. Although he had shown little natural ability at caring for animals or general farm work, Irwin had a good heart. She felt instinctively that he needed male guidance to help him develop the skills that would enable him to support himself and, someday, a family.

Hannah supposed that she'd done well enough for her daughters after her husband's passing, but she was beginning to wonder if she would have been wiser to remarry, as everyone had urged her. Few widows in their forties remained single after the customary year of mourning. Maybe she'd been selfish and a little proud to think that she could fill Jonas's shoes. What was the old saying? *A woman might be the heart of the family, but the man was the head.*

After the children had spilled out of the schoolhouse doors and run, walked or ridden their scooter push-bikes home, Hannah packed up to leave. There was plenty to do to prepare the school for the coming celebration, but the weather was so warm, the air so full of spring and the earth so green, Hannah couldn't bear to remain cooped up inside another moment. This was her favorite time of the year, when new life sprang from every inch of field and forest, a time when she felt that anything was possible.

Whistling a spritely tune, a habit for which she had been chastised many times as a child, Hannah walked down the dirt lane, across a clearing and climbed the stile that marked the boundary between her son-in-law Samuel's dairy farm and her own place. What would she do when she got home? Rebecca was at Miriam and Ruth's place and wouldn't be coming home for supper, and Irwin had gone off with his cousins, so it would be just her and Susanna.

When they'd parted after breakfast, Susanna had been unnaturally subdued, still unhappy about the punishment that Hannah had given her after the pizza escapade two days before. She'd forbidden Susanna from seeing David for an entire week.

Hannah had not, however, spoken to Susanna about her visit with David's mother. In fact, she hadn't spoken of it to anyone. Hannah couldn't imagine what Sadie was thinking bringing up the idea of Susanna and David marrying. It was, of course, not possible. David would never learn a trade or how to farm; Susanna was unable to run a household. They certainly couldn't be married.

Hannah pushed the whole idea from her mind, returning to thoughts of her pouting daughter. Susanna hadn't been happy about the forced separation between her and David, but Hannah was determined to be firm. She couldn't allow Susanna to do as she pleased. Her daughter's judgment had been poor, and she had to suffer the consequences. Still, Hannah wasn't angry with her, and she was determined to find something special and fun for the two of them to do together this afternoon.

"*Ne, Mam.* Going to Anna's." Susanna held up a book. "Naomi wants it." She moved to the nearest bookshelf and began to straighten the books. "I will eat supper with Anna. She said."

Hannah didn't know whether to be amused or feel rebuffed. Susanna's reply had been only mildly intoned, but her expression was a stubborn *"So there, Mam!"* It was clear to Hannah that her daughter was still out of sorts with her over the whole David King mishap and was determined to exert her independence. Somehow, in Susanna's mind, sneaking out of the house and the accident with the buggy had been Hannah's fault and not hers.

"I'm the li-bair-ian," Susanna said. "I can't stay here. Have to take the book to Naomi."

Hannah folded her arms. "I see." Clearly, what Grace had said recently was true. Susanna had always developed slower than her sisters, but at almost twenty-one, she had charged headlong into her own form of independence.

When Hannah had turned their unused milk house into a lending library for the local Amish community, she'd suggested that Susanna become the librarian. She'd hoped the responsibility would give Susanna a sense of self-worth. Despite her struggles with the written word, Susanna had taken to the job with great enthusiasm. She could read only a little, and Hannah suspected that much of Susanna's pleasure from the library came from arranging the books by color and requiring users to print their names and the borrowed titles in a large journal.

Susanna and the whole family enjoyed providing suitable books for their neighbors, adults and children alike. But what Hannah hadn't expected was that David King would become an almost daily visitor to Susanna's library, or that the two of them would spend so many hours in the small building laughing and talking together. Hannah was afraid that David was borrowing so many books as an excuse to see Susanna, something definitely against the rules for Amish young people of marriageable age. The trouble was, how did she put an end to an innocent friendship?

"You're walking across the field, aren't you?" Hannah asked, more as a reminder than a question. "You aren't walking down the road?"

"*Ya.* The pasture. I can do it by myself."

"Be home by seven. Ask one of the twins to walk back with you."

"By myself, *Mam*." Susanna threw her a look so much like her sister Johanna's that Hannah smiled.

"All right. By yourself, but be careful, Susanna. No talking to strangers."

Susanna giggled and folded her arms in a mirror image of Hannah. "No strangers in the pasture."

Hannah sighed. "No, I suppose there aren't. But be careful, just the same." Feeling a little out of sorts with herself, Hannah left the library and went back into the house. There, she looked around for something out of place or something that needed doing, but all seemed in order.

The house echoed with emptiness. Chores done, floors scrubbed, dishes washed and put away. Susanna had been busy today, so busy that she'd left nothing for Hannah to do. And with all her children active in their own families, Hannah knew she should have been glad for the peace and quiet. No grandchildren running through the house, no slamming doors, no tracking mud through the kitchen, no supper to cook.

Of course, she would need some sort of supper for herself. Maybe she'd start something that she, Susanna, Rebecca and Irwin could have again tomorrow. Hannah wanted to begin setting out early vegetable plants in the garden, and she wouldn't have time to prepare a big noon meal. She went to the refrigerator, but when she opened it, there was a pot of chicken and dumplings as well as a bowl of coleslaw. A note was propped in front. "Enjoy! Rice pudding on bottom shelf. Love, Johanna."

Hannah sighed. Why did Johanna's thoughtful deed add to her sense of restlessness? Maybe she should walk over to Ruth's and see if she needed help with the twins. Or, perhaps she should check on the chickens to see if

Susanna had remembered to gather the eggs. Taking a basket from a peg on the wall, Hannah went back into the yard.

She was halfway to the chicken house when she heard the sound of a motor vehicle. As she watched, a familiar truck came up the lane and into the yard. Albert pulled to a stop, rolled down the window and smiled.

"Afternoon, Hannah."

"Afternoon, Albert." She walked over to his truck, egg basket on her arm.

"Wondered how the pony was, if you noticed any swelling in his legs or any bruising?"

She shook her head. "*Ne.* The pony is fine, thanks be."

"And Susanna? She's no worse for the tumble?" He tugged at his ball cap and leaned out the window.

"*Ne,* Susanna's good." She chuckled. "Actually, she's not behaving like herself. She's always been the easiest of my children, but recently..." She spread her hands. "I know you don't have children, but..."

"No, I don't, but I think I should have. Sometimes, Hannah, I wonder if..."

"*Ya?*"

He removed his cap and squeezed the brim between his hands, then put it back on his head and tugged it tight. "You sure you don't want me to check that pony out?"

"The pony's fine." First Susanna and now Albert. This was turning into the strangest afternoon, Hannah mused. She liked the man, found his company interesting and felt at ease with him, but she couldn't imagine why he was acting so oddly.

It seemed almost as if Albert wanted to say something but couldn't bring himself to do it. He was like a father to Grace's husband. Was there some trouble with Grace's new family that she didn't know about? Hannah's eyes narrowed. And why was Albert so worried about Susanna? Was there more about Susanna and David than what he'd told her?

"If you've something to tell me," she said. "It's best you just say it instead of beating around the bush."

Albert's earnest face flushed.

Bingo, she thought. But she didn't urge him further. If there was one thing that she'd learned from being a teacher, it was that silence often brought more confessions than demands did.

"There is something I wanted to ask you."

"*Ya,* Albert. What is it?"

He leaned out the window. "Well, I've been doing a lot of thinking about…"

It was all she could do to keep from tapping her foot impatiently. "Yes, Albert?"

"Alpacas," he said.

Chapter Four

Albert raised his gaze to meet Hannah's. He could feel his face growing warm. Being around Hannah Yoder always did that to him. Made him tongue-tied, too.

It wasn't just that Hannah was attractive. She was that and more. Maybe attractive didn't do her justice. Hannah was strikingly handsome, with large brown eyes, a generous mouth and a shapely nose with just a smattering of freckles. Hers wasn't a face a man was likely to forget, no matter his age.

Hannah's creamy skin was as smooth as a baby's, and her hair, what he could see of it, peeking out around her *kapp,* was thick and curly, a soft reddish-brown. She was tall, but not too tall, sturdy, but still graceful. He'd never seen her when she wasn't neat and tidy.

It wasn't just her looks that he liked. Hannah was the sort of woman you expected could take charge if she needed to. Something about her was calming, which didn't make much sense, considering that she always put him off his stride when she was near him. But one thing was certain, she didn't look or act old enough to have grandbabies.

Not that he thought of her as anything but a friend. Their relationship was solidly defined by the rules of what it meant to be Amish and Mennonite. And the fact that they could both acknowledge their friendship and be easy with one another was a tribute to Hannah's respected status among both communities. And, he hoped, to his own.

"Albert?"

Hannah's voice slid through his thoughts like warm maple syrup. She had a way of pronouncing his name that gave it a German lilt, but seemed perfectly natural. He blinked. "Yes, Hannah?"

"Did you say *alpacas?*" Her eyes twinkled, as though she'd heard something amusing but was too kind to laugh at him.

"Ya," he said, falling into the *Deitsch* speech pattern that his family had often used when he was a youngster on the farm. "You've heard of alpacas, haven't you?"

She chuckled. "I have. My friend in Wisconsin raises them. She cards the fleece after she shears it, spins it, and sells the fiber to English women who knit garments out of it. It's much warmer than sheep's wool, too warm for Delaware use. But it's very soft and she gets a good price for it."

"Well," he hesitated, not wanting her to think that he hadn't seriously considered what he was about to propose. "John thinks that I have too much time on my hands," he said. "Since my father…" He took a breath and started again, wondering if coming to Hannah with this scheme had been a big mistake. "The practice keeps me pretty busy, and of course, I'm always welcome at Grace and John's, but…"

She was just looking at him in that patient way of

hers, and he finished in a rush. "John suggested, and I thought it was a good idea, for me to take up a hobby."

She nodded. "I can see where that would make sense, Albert."

Again, he noticed her unique way of saying his name. Hannah's English was flawless, but some words came out with just a hint of German accent.

"And you've been thinking about raising alpacas? Is that what you're saying?" She motioned toward the house. "I've got iced tea chilling in the refrigerator. It's warm this afternoon, and I'm sure you must be thirsty. Would you like some?"

"I would," he answered, getting out of the truck. "That's kind of you. If it's no trouble."

"How much trouble could pouring a glass of tea be?" Hannah led the way toward a picnic table standing in the shade of a tree beside the house. "Have a seat, Albert." He did, and she went into the house through the back door and returned with two glasses of iced tea.

He nodded his thanks, accepted the glass and took a sip of the tea. It was delicious, not too sweet. "Great. Is that mint I taste?"

Hannah's eyes twinkled. "That's Susanna's doing. It does give the tea a refreshing bite, doesn't it?" Hannah sat down across the table from him. He nodded, and then drew the conversation back to his reason for stopping by today. "So I was saying, about the alpacas. As it happens, an acquaintance of mine, another vet over in Talbot County—that's in Maryland—"

Hannah chuckled. "I know where Talbot County is, Albert. Jonas and I bought cows from a farmer there regularly."

"That's right, I remember. Jonas told me that. Anyway, one of this vet's clients, an older man, has a herd of alpacas. Mr. Gephart has had some health problems and he needs to find homes for most of his stock. He's willing to sell me some of his *hembras*—that's what they call the females—at an excellent price if I promise to keep them together. Mr. Gephart has become very fond of them, and he's raised them from *crias*."

"*Crias* are the babies," Hannah said. "I remember my Wisconsin friend mentioning that. She said that they are really cute."

He leaned forward, pleased that Hannah seemed interested in hearing about the alpacas. "One of the females has a *cria*. It's a male, and he's all black. The mother is a rose-gray color, and her name is Estrella. She's gentle and her fleece is especially fine, but she had some problems when the baby was born. She won't be able to have any more little ones, but she's a dominant female, and she'd make an excellent leader for the herd. They live fifteen to twenty years, so she'd produce fleece for a long time. I'm thinking I won't get a male of my own, at least to start with."

"It sounds as if you've made up your mind to start your own herd," she said.

"Pretty much, but here's the thing." He took another swallow of the tea. He'd rehearsed what he would say to Hannah, how he would present his proposal, but his thoughts were all a jumble in his head now. "You know I have that property on Briar Corner Road?" he started slowly. "I've got about seventy acres there. Anyway, that would be a good place for the alpacas if I had fencing and a decent barn, but the place is sort of isolated. There would be no one to keep an eye on them."

"I see your point," she agreed. "Alpacas are a big

investment, and without someone living there, you couldn't be sure that your animals would be safe."

"They're just like any other livestock. They're best kept close. So, what I was wondering is…" He took another drink of tea. "You have this empty second barn and a lot of outbuildings, and you've got first-class fencing. I was hoping that you might consider boarding my alpacas. They wouldn't need much room, five acres at most. And I wouldn't expect you to do the feeding and care. I could come by morning and evening and—"

"Albert." Hannah tilted her head and fixed him with her schoolteacher stare.

"I'm sure we could agree on a fair monthly price. I'd feel so much better about starting the venture if my animals were here." Now that he was on a roll, he just kept going. "Your little stable would make a perfect—"

"Please, stop." She raised a hand, palm up.

He broke off in midsentence, and his expression must have shown his disappointment because she hurried to go on.

"I'm not saying no. What I'm saying is …" She shrugged. "How many times have we had you or John here in the past year to help one of our animals?"

"Not counting the pony?" He paused to consider. "Six, seven times, maybe."

"A lot more than that." She smiled at him. "You've been more than fair with billing us, but still having the proper veterinary care for animals is a big part of our expense." She settled back on the bench and folded her arms. "Why don't we strike a bargain? I'll provide housing and grazing for your alpacas, and you do my veterinary care free of charge for six months? Then we can decide if we want to continue with the arrangement as it is, or make changes."

Relief surged through him. After thinking on the whole idea for a few days, he was really keen on it. It excited him in a way nothing had in a good long while. Mr. Gephart wanted to downsize his herd as soon as possible, and a delay might mean Albert would lose the opportunity. "You'll do it? Without being paid? That hardly seems fair to you—"

She chuckled. "I think I'm in a better place to decide what's fair to me. I like the idea of having animals in those empty stalls. And I have a lot of livestock that need vet care: the pigs, cows, horses. Not to mention the cats people keep dropping off here. Having them neutered or spayed is a drain on my pocketbook, but if I don't have it done, I'd end up buried in hundreds of cats."

He nodded. "I can see your point." Straightening his shoulders, he took another drink of the tea. "I'm thinking of buying seven alpacas to start. Three of the *hembras* are pregnant, and the other females are nearly old enough to—" The word *breed* stuck in his throat and he felt his throat clench.

"It's all right, Albert," Hannah assured him with a sweet, mischievous smile. "I'm a farmer. I understand the process. Unless you're raising the alpacas just as a hobby, you'll want young ones to add to your herd and to sell to help cover expenses."

"Exactly." He drained the last of his tea. "Is it all right if I walk back and take a look at the stable, to see what I'd need to do to bring the animals home?"

"Of course. I'll come with you." Hannah rose and they walked side by side across the yard toward the second, smaller barn and the outbuildings. "There's a small attached pound, a loafing shed and a seven-acre pasture with good grazing, beyond that. As you can see, this field is far back, away from the road."

"It looks perfect."

"I'm fortunate. My son-in-law Charley believes in good fences. I don't know what I'd do without him doing the heavy work on the farm."

"Miriam picked a good husband," Albert agreed. Neither of them mentioned that his nephew, John, had seriously courted Hannah's daughter Miriam, before she'd accepted Charley's offer of marriage. John had been hurt and disappointed at losing Miriam, but that was before he'd met Grace. Now both couples were happily married, and Hannah had the satisfaction of knowing that her Miriam would remain securely in the Amish faith.

"There's no reason for you to stop by every morning," Hannah said as she unlatched the door to the stable. "Our windmill pumps fresh water into the stable and to the trough in the loafing shed. One of us can easily do the first feeding when we tend the other animals. I know that mornings are your busiest time of the day."

"They are," he agreed. "But I wouldn't want to put you out. You're doing me a big favor by letting me keep them here."

"There'll be no talk of favors," she said, smiling so hard that a dimple appeared on her cheek. "We're just old friends, helping each other out."

Hannah showed him the empty small barn with the spacious box stalls, the feed storage area and the door that led into the pound or corral, as horse people liked to refer to it. The stable was as clean as he'd expected.

Alpacas were herd animals so they wouldn't really need individual stalls, but he was glad to see that there were two separate wooden enclosed areas where an injured animal or an expectant female could be cared for. A narrow staircase against one wall led to a half loft overhead.

She pushed open the wide back door. It was built in the old Dutch manner, split, so that the top half could be swung open with the bottom remaining fastened. "You can see what the fence is like from here," she explained.

As he'd expected, Hannah's wooden posts were solid, the stock wire was tight, and the open loafing shed dry and clean. He couldn't have designed anything better for the alpacas if he'd had the time to build out at his farm. Hannah's place was also closer and more convenient to get to. He was sure this would work out fine. "I'll not be a bother to you," he promised.

"I know you won't. But I warn you, you may have to chase off my grandchildren. I think your alpacas are going to be a big hit with them."

"The animals are gentle and sweet-natured," he assured her. "I think that you'll be a fan, too."

As they were leaving the barn, Albert heard the rattle of buggy wheels on the driveway and saw a horse pulling a two-wheel cart coming up the driveway. An Amish woman was driving the open carriage.

Hannah raised her hand to shade her eyes from the late afternoon sun. "Why, that looks like Aunt Jezzy!" she exclaimed. "What a nice surprise."

"I'll be getting back to the office," Albert said. He was a little disappointed. He'd been hoping to talk with Hannah a little longer. He had a lot of questions to ask, like if Hannah had straw for bedding to sell, or if she thought he'd be better off ordering woodchips for the stalls. "I don't want to interfere with your company."

"You'll do no such thing," Hannah said. "Wait right here for a moment until I see if Aunt Jezzy has come on an errand or has time to visit. Don't move an inch, Albert." She hurried over to meet the older woman who'd, until not long ago, been part of her household. Aunt Jezzy had recently married and lived not far from Byler's Store. Today, she didn't have her husband with her; she was alone in the cart.

Hannah greeted her aunt and the two exchanged hugs. They were talking, but they were too far away for Albert to make out what they were saying. Then Hannah turned back and motioned to him. "Aunt Jezzy's come to spend the night with me," she called. "And we'd love it if you'd stay and share supper with us. I've got chicken and dumplings."

Albert's first thought was to refuse. He glanced at his watch. They closed the clinic early on Fridays, and he hadn't had any emergency calls. But surely Hannah was just being polite; she didn't really want him to stay. He couldn't remember anything particular in the refrigerator, but he could always stop and pick up a frozen pizza on the way back to his apartment. "Thanks," he said. "It's kind of you, but I—"

"Homemade coleslaw, some of Anna's yeast rolls and rice pudding with raisins for dessert," Hannah tempted. "Come on, Albert. I know you love chicken and dumplings."

He did. Next to chicken and dumplings, another frozen pizza sounded about as good as a Frisbee with a little ketchup drizzled on it. "You're sure I won't be a bother?" He walked toward them. "I really should…"

"Accept our invitation," Hannah urged. "I know Aunt Jezzy would love to hear about your alpacas."

Albert considered the situation. Jezzy's visit was his good luck. As accepting as the Amish were of him, they had their rules. One was that he couldn't be in a house alone with a woman or a girl of any age. He hadn't seen Susanna or Rebecca around, but having Hannah's aunt present made it perfectly acceptable for him to join them for the evening meal.

"All right," he said, giving in graciously. "I never could pass up a home-cooked meal that I didn't cook." He chuckled. "And I'd walk a mile in bare feet for home-made rice pudding."

Hannah smiled as Albert finished off a second helping of chicken and dumplings. It was always good to have company, and having Aunt Jezzy come by when she did was a delight. It was nice to see a man eat heartily at her table. Hannah guessed that Albert made do for himself with fast food and sandwiches more than he should. At least that's what Grace had shared when she was visiting a few days earlier.

John and I worry about Uncle Albert, Grace had said. *Since John's grandfather passed away, Uncle Albert's all alone in that apartment over the office. He never was much of a cook, according to John, and we're concerned for his health. Sometimes, John says he makes do with bologna-and-cheese sandwiches or just peanut butter and crackers for supper. And he starts work with coffee and a donut.*

Albert's a man who enjoys plain country cooking when it's put in front of him, Hannah thought. She'd believed that Grace's husband, John, had the biggest appetite she'd seen on a normal-size man, but now she knew where John had gotten it. Albert was so polite that he was almost shy. He had to be coaxed to take a decent portion, then seconds, but it was clear he savored every bite. Even Aunt Jezzy took pleasure in watching him enjoy his food.

Aunt Jezzy's husband had gone to visit a dying cousin in Lancaster. She never liked being alone in a house, so she'd hitched up the buggy and come for an overnight visit. Naturally, since neither of them had a telephone in the house, there was no way Aunt Jezzy could let her know she was coming, but she'd been certain of her welcome here.

This afternoon Hannah had been feeling lonely and out of sorts. Then Albert had showed up with his plan for the alpacas, brightening her day. There was no way she could have invited Albert to share her evening meal without anyone else present. It simply wouldn't have been proper. A good Amish woman did not entertain a man without a chaperone.

Then here was Aunt Jezzy, a gift from God, as it were, making it possible for Hannah to invite them both to share the food that her thoughtful daughter had left for her. It just went to prove that the Lord's mercy was unending. She had been feeling sorry for herself, wallowing in self-pity because she had to eat alone, and He had wiped away her gloom in an instant with an unexpected gift of sunshine.

Hannah glanced across the table with a smile. She could see that Albert was enjoying himself as much as she was. With a little urging, he began to explain his plan for raising alpacas; her aunt was fascinated. Aunt Jezzy had always loved animals. Actually, Hannah couldn't think of anything or anyone her aunt-by-marriage didn't like.

Some people thought Jezzy was odd, and she did have some curious habits, such as spinning spoons and turning objects around three times before she could let them rest. But Albert never seemed to notice Aunt Jezzy's endearing little quirks. The three of them weren't halfway through supper when Albert had them laughing so hard with tales from his veterinary practice that she almost dropped her glass.

Not that Albert mentioned any names or repeated anything he shouldn't, but surely it couldn't be a sin to be amused by stories of a man who let his pet pig sleep in a bed in his house and tied a ribbon around its head.

"As I live and breathe," Aunt Jezzy said, wiping her eyes with her napkin. "How could anybody be that silly?"

Chuckling, Hannah rose and went to the refrigerator for the rice pudding. "Are you sure you won't have more coleslaw?" she asked Albert. "And there's more chicken and dumplings in the pot."

"Not another mouthful," Albert protested. "I'll never make it up the stairs to my apartment. I can't tell you how much I've enjoyed myself, being with you two, and sharing your supper. I really appreciate it."

"*Ne, ne,* none of that," Hannah said. "It was our pleasure." The mantel clock chimed, and she glanced up. Was it truly that late? She glanced out the windows to see if she could catch sight of either of her daughters. Of course, it was Susanna she was most concerned about. Rebecca was so busy with wedding plans that she often stayed at one of her sisters' houses until well after dark.

A small concern nagged at Hannah as she served

up generous bowls of the rice pudding. "Would anyone like coffee?" She wondered if it would be an imposition to ask Albert to drive by Anna's and tell Susanna to start for home, if her daughter didn't get home before he left, that was.

But, there was no need. They'd barely started their pudding when the dogs outside began to bark, and Samuel's buggy came into the yard.

Hannah went out onto the back porch. To her surprise, it wasn't Samuel but her daughter Anna who, along with Susanna, was getting down from the buggy. Before Hannah reached the back gate, Susanna handed Anna's little daughter, Rose, down to Anna.

"Mam!" Anna waved. "I hope you don't mind, but I've come to spend the night. I just thought I'd use the excuse of driving Susanna home to take a little vacation."

"Wonderful," Hannah said, smiling back at her. She was always pleased to see Anna. Her daughter's round, pink cheeks glowed with health, and she looked as jolly as ever. Of all her children, Anna and Susanna had always been the easiest to raise.

"Samuel can mind the children tonight," Anna declared. "Baby Rose and I thought it might be fun to surprise you."

"Ya." Susanna giggled. "A surprise for you, *Mam.* I brought Anna and Rose. To sleep with us."

"Wonderful," Hannah said, taking the baby from Anna's arms. "Aunt Jezzy is here to stay the night, too. We'll have our own frolic."

Anna got a bag with their things from the back of the buggy and placed it on the ground. "I'll just unhitch the horse and put him in the barn." She glanced at Albert's truck. "None of your animals are sick, are they?"

"*Ne,* all are fine. Aunt Jezzy and I asked Albert to share supper with us. Grace says he never takes time for a proper meal."

"Good of you, *Mam,* to invite him."

Hannah nuzzled the sweet softness of Rose's neck. "I can't wait to tell you my news." She shifted the baby to her hip. Rose laughed and snatched at Hannah's *kapp* ribbon.

Anna's hearty chuckle echoed through the farmyard. "I warn you. She's teething. Anything she can fit in her mouth, she will. She'll eat your *kapp* if you let her."

Hannah smiled and bounced Rose, and the baby giggled. Could this day get any better? "Albert wants to buy a herd of alpacas, and he's going to keep them here," she told Anna. "We've made a trade. My empty stalls and pasture for his veterinary care."

"Sounds like a good deal to me," Anna said.

"Al-pack-ers?" Susanna asked.

"Alpacas. You'll see." Hannah slipped her free arm around Susanna and hugged her. "I was starting to wonder if you would be home before dark."

"I told you," Susanna said with a determined nod. "I am re-pon-sible."

"Sometimes," Anna teased.

"*Ya,*" Susanna echoed. "Sometimes."

"I'll just be a few minutes," Anna called as she led the horse and buggy away. "And I have news for you, too, *Mam.*"

"Good news I hope?" She didn't want to hear bad news, not tonight, not when everything was going so well.

"Good," Susanna said. "Samuel is building Rose a big girl bed."

Anna shrugged and grinned. "*Ya,* she's right, *Mam.* I think the Lord will send us a new little one to sleep in Rose's cradle before Christmas."

"Truly?" Hannah asked. "You and Samuel are blessed with another child?"

"We are," Anna replied. "And this one feels different." She grinned. "I told Samuel maybe this one will be another little wood chopper."

Chapter Five

With all the women in the house, Hannah fully expected Albert to finish his rice pudding and make his escape, but—surprising her once again—he didn't. And in the hour between Anna and Susanna's arrival and Albert's departure, he told the two of them all about his alpacas, showed everyone pictures of them on his cell phone and bounced Rose on his knee when she became fussy. He even produced a ball of alpaca fleece from his jeans pocket so Susanna could feel how soft it was.

"Albert is nice," Susanna said when his truck pulled out of the yard at seven-thirty. "I'm going to give King David my wool." She held up the fluffy alpaca ball for her mother to see. "Albert said it was mine."

"Of course, you can give it to David, if you want. But maybe you should keep it. Wouldn't it be fun to learn to spin the fleece into yarn?" Hannah was pleased that the Susanna who'd returned with Anna wasn't the sullen girl who, earlier in the day, had strode off across the pasture pouting. Hannah was concerned that David was still on her mind. But, at least this evening, she had her sweet, easygoing daughter back.

"Albert is English, but nice," Susanna declared, scraping her pudding bowl to get the last spoonful of dessert.

"Ne," Anna corrected with a smile. "Albert is a Mennonite like Grace and John. Not Plain, but not English, either."

"And 'Kota." Susanna licked the back of her spoon. "Can I have more?"

Hannah shook her head. "One bowl of rice pudding is plenty. You can have more for breakfast, if you like." Susanna had had supper at Anna and Samuel's table, and Hannah guessed that her daughter had already eaten enough. Like 'Kota and her other young nieces and nephews, Susanna had trouble knowing when to stop eating sweets.

Rose, who'd been toddling around the kitchen, plopped onto her bottom and gave a little wail. Anna put out her arms. "Come here, my dumpling."

"Let me." Aunt Jezzy picked up the baby and settled into the rocking chair with her. Rose fussed for a few moments, and then gave in to the steady movement and the gentle patting on her back and fell asleep. "This one is easily soothed," the older woman pronounced.

Hannah glanced at her granddaughter and smiled. "Like Anna," she said. "You were always a contented baby, Anna."

"Let's hope this next one will be the same," Anna said. "Not like those two boys of mine. I have to keep them busy, else—" She arched her eyebrows and shook her head.

Hannah pulled off her shoes and put them beside Susanna's by the kitchen door. Hearing Anna speak of the twins like that made her feel warm and happy inside. When Samuel, their neighbor, had married Anna, a woman much younger than he was, he'd brought five children to the union. Rose was their first baby together, but to hear Anna tell it, she was the mother of all six. It was a fine match and Samuel obviously loved and adored Anna, despite her plumpness.

Deep in thought, Hannah poured herself a cup of mint tea and sat down at the table across from Anna and Susanna. God's plan for Anna had been the perfect one for her, she thought. He'd truly blessed her with a home and family. But now that all of her daughters but one would soon be settled, Hannah could only hope and pray that He would remember to keep His eye on her special child.

"Why don't we go out onto the front porch, *Mam*," Anna suggested. "It's so warm this evening. And I think it's too early in the year for mosquitoes."

"Ya," Hannah agreed as she stirred sugar into her tea. "There's a nice breeze out there." She reached out to pat Susanna's small hand. "Don't you want to shower and wash your hair?"

Susanna shook her head. "Don't want to go to bed. Want to sit on the front porch with you and Anna and Aunt Jezzy."

"Did I say anything about going to bed?" Hannah asked. "It's early yet. But wouldn't you feel comfy in your nightgown and slippers?"

Susanna grinned broadly, then giggled. "Outside? In my nightgown?"

Anna chuckled. "Why not? There's no one here but us girls tonight. It sounds nice. Maybe I'll put mine on, too."

Susanna's slanting, blue eyes narrowed with suspicion. "Not sleepy."

Anna chuckled and slipped an arm around her sister. "You heard *Mam,* Susanna-Banana. You don't have to go to sleep. But I'm going to wash my hair. If you want, I'll help you wash yours."

"We can have a hair-braiding frolic," Aunt Jezzy suggested. "This little one is fast asleep. Shall I just tuck her into the crib in Hannah's room?"

"*Ya,* if you wouldn't mind," Anna said. "It's what I love about coming home. Plenty of willing hands to take turns holding Rose. And now with the new one coming—"

"New one?" Aunt Jezzy's eyebrows shot up and her crooked smile widened. "I thought you looked particularly glowy, girl." She gently slid Rose's cap off her head and kissed the auburn curls. "I always thought I'd have a baby of my own," she murmured, more to herself than to the others. "But God has taken pity on me and blessed me in my old age with so many great-nieces and great-nephews to love."

Hannah's throat constricted as she thought of how long Aunt Jezzy had lived in the corners of her family's life, first her mother's, then her sister Lovina's and finally here. People had thought her odd, but her new husband didn't care. Who would have ever thought that after so many years a spinster, Aunt Jezzy would take a husband and flourish in her new life as mistress of her own home?

"Can we have popcorn?" Susanna asked.

Anna glanced at her mother, silently asking for permission, and when Hannah nodded, she assured Susanna that she could—as soon as she was showered.

Mollified, Susanna agreed, and the two went off together.

Aunt Jezzy put Rose to bed, and Hannah made a large batch of buttered popcorn. When the girls came back downstairs with wet hair, hairbrushes, combs and bobby pins, Hannah and Aunt Jezzy were already seated on the porch with two large bowls of popcorn and a pitcher of homemade root beer. Both Hannah and her aunt had showered in the downstairs bathroom, put on their own nightgowns and had their wet hair wrapped in towels.

On the porch there was a swing and several rockers, giving the occupants a fine view of the farm. A line of trees across the front of the garden and the distance the house set back from the road made the sitting area private. When Jonas had been alive, they'd often taken their supper on the porch, then relaxed there as the children played on the lawn until bedtime. Hannah loved to sit here in the evenings with the sound of crickets and tree frogs and children's laughter. There was something so peaceful about it, almost like sitting in church and hearing the familiar words of an old hymn.

"Is this a frolic?" Susanna asked as she helped herself to a handful of buttered kernels. "A popcorn frolic?"

"A hair-braiding frolic," Anna said, choosing the wide porch swing. She took the towel off her head and shook out her long strawberry-blond hair, running her fingers through it to make it dry faster.

Motherhood had done little to whittle away Anna's substantial size, Hannah mused. But Aunt Jezzy was right: Anna did glow. She would never have the delicate features or the trim waists of her sisters, but Anna's inner beauty more than made up for it. "What does

Samuel think of your coming child?" Hannah asked. "Is he happy?"

Crimson tinted Anna's plump cheeks. "He thanks God," she said. "We have prayed for another baby."

"I suppose he wants a boy," Aunt Jezzy said. She'd claimed the old green rocker next to Hannah, and motioned Susanna to come sit at her feet. "I'll braid your hair," she offered.

Susanna sat and drew her knees up. The long white nightdress, which belonged to one of her sisters once, more than covered her. Susanna was short, so that it hung below her ankles and dragged behind her when she walked. Hannah had offered to hem it, but Susanna wouldn't hear of it. The sleeping gown was cream-colored flannel, soft to the touch, and although it had no decoration, Susanna loved it so much that she often hid it so that Hannah wouldn't put it in the wash.

The previous afternoon, Hannah had found the garment rolled into a ball and tucked behind a stack of hymnbooks on the attic stairs. Apparently, Susanna had hidden it there several weeks ago and forgotten where she'd put it. She'd been certain that her mother had thrown the nightgown away, and when Hannah had taken it down off the wash line, clean and fresh, and carried it into the house in a basket of laundry, Susanna had been so happy that she'd snatched the gown up and hugged it to her.

My dear little girl. How could David's mother ever think you could be a man's wife? Or think her son could be a husband? David was able to read, but he didn't speak as well as Susanna. It was difficult for Hannah to know if he was more or less capable of caring for himself than Susanna was. David was a sweet boy, certainly. But no one would think of allowing two childlike adults to wed, and that was what Susanna and David were, what they would always be.

"Where are your elastics?" Aunt Jezzy asked Susanna. She glanced at Anna. "Did either of you bring down the rubber bands?"

Susanna giggled and clapped a small hand over her mouth in mock horror. "Forgot. Anna said, 'Susanna-Banana, get the hair ties.' But…" Susanna grimaced. "Forgot."

"Everyone forgets," Aunt Jezzy said. "One day I forgot it was visiting Sunday and got dressed for church."

Susanna giggled again.

"Could you go and get the elastics?" Anna asked. With a nod, Susanna got to her feet and hurried off. Anna glanced at her mother, once her sister was gone. "*Mam,* Susanna said something earlier tonight that troubles me. I don't like the idea of tattling on my little sister, but I think you should know. Susanna told Samuel at the supper table that she and David were courting."

Hannah rolled her eyes. "I know. I don't know how to convince her that it's not true. I keep telling her that she and David are just friends. That she can't court anyone. That I need her here with me, but I don't think she understands."

"She was also talking about getting married." Anna's tone was solemn.

"Well, you told her she wasn't, didn't you?"

"I didn't say anything. I just let it go." Anna pressed her lips together. "I wanted to talk to you to know how you wanted us to handle it."

"You don't see her," Aunt Jezzy mused aloud. "You look, Hannah, but…" She shook her head.

Hannah glanced at Jezzy. "What do you mean?"

"*Atch,* Hannah." She held up a finger, and for a moment an expression as shrewd as that of any of her sister Lovina's played over her soft face. "You do not see that your Susanna has grown into a young woman. You treat her like a child."

"She *is* a child," Hannah protested softly. "She'll always be—"

"*Ne, Mam,*" Anna said gently. "Susanna is no longer a child. She may not be quick about some things, but she feels as deeply as anyone, and whether you like the idea or not, she's convinced she has feelings for David. I think we need to be aware of those feelings and act accordingly."

A cold flood of guilt washed over Hannah as she realized the truth of Anna and Jezzy's words. As she recognized her own denial. If Jonas were here, he'd be so disappointed with her. She glanced from one of them to the other, and her distress must have shown because Anna patted the swing seat beside her.

"Come, sit here, *Mam.*"

Hannah stood, crossed the porch to Anna's side, and sank onto the swing. "If you both thought I wasn't handling the situation with Susanna and David properly, why didn't you or your sisters say something to me earlier?"

Aunt Jezzy passed the hairbrush from hand to hand. "Little lambs will play. You must build tight fences," she murmured.

Hannah looked into Anna's beautiful eyes and read the compassion and love in them. "I have tried to do what's best for Susanna. You know I have."

"This isn't about blame, *Mam*. We're just saying that things have changed. That Susanna is…"

"Growing up." Hannah sighed.

"Yes," Anna agreed, patting her mother's hand. "Which means Susanna should have to follow the same rules about boys like every other girl her age in this community. The same rules we had to follow. We weren't allowed to spend time alone with boys, unchaperoned, and I don't think Susanna should be allowed to, either."

Hannah let Anna's words sink in. What Anna was suggesting was that she was giving Susanna too much freedom. She needed to keep a better eye on her youngest. A tighter rein. And she was probably right. Susanna was quick to move from one interest to the next. One week she would be trying to crochet dishcloths, the next, she would set aside her crochet needle to collect field flowers to dry in books. If Susanna spent less time with David, surely all this would die down. Of course that would mean Hannah would have to give up some of her own freedom. The truth was, she had gotten quite used to coming and going as she pleased more often as her daughters had left the fold one by one. Susanna had begun to show enough maturity to be left home alone and Hannah had allowed it. It was during those hours alone that she suspected Susanna was spending too much unsupervised time with David.

Hannah thought about the conversation she'd had with Albert before he'd left. He'd asked her if she wanted to ride down to the alpaca farm the following day with him. He was eager to tell Mr. Gephart that he'd made arrangements for stabling and that he wanted to finalize the sale. She'd agreed, but now she wondered if it was a good idea. She wouldn't feel comfortable leaving Susanna at home as she usually did, and Albert hadn't included her daughter in the invitation. Maybe it hadn't been wise to say she'd go anyway. Technically, she was a single woman and Albert was a single man. If she was going to hold Susanna to a higher standard, didn't she need to do the same for herself? She hated to go back on her word, but she'd have to tell Albert that she couldn't go when he stopped by for her after lunch.

Susanna's voice drifted through the open front door. She was singing a song, one that boys and girls favored at frolics. She was off-key, as usual, but Hannah had always found that endearing. Even now, Susanna's squeaky little voice triggered emotion in her, bringing a tightness to her chest. "I suppose it's time Susanna and I had a mother-daughter talk," she mused aloud. "But it wouldn't fare to confront her in front of you tonight. I wouldn't want her to think we're ganging up on her." She exhaled. "I'll speak to her about this in the morning."

After breakfast, Hannah followed Susanna outside to tend the chickens. From the barn, she could hear Irwin rattling the lid of the feed bin and calling to the cows. One of his cousins had come home with him and was helping with the chores. Here in the chicken house, there was some privacy.

The hens clucked and milled around, scratching at the kitchen scraps that Susanna tossed to them and snapping up the choice bits. Susanna loved the chickens. Often, Hannah would come out to find Susanna squatting on the ground outside, hugging a hen. She would lay her cheek against the sleek feathers, close her eyes and hum with contentment. The chickens, even the ill-tempered ones, would never peck Susanna.

Large windows filled one wall of the chicken house, making it bright inside. As always, it was clean and smelled of fresh straw. Jonas had believed that animals, even chickens, should live as clean as possible. "Clean water, good food and decent bedding is the best medicine for livestock and poultry," he would say. Hannah had believed him, and she'd never lowered the standards that he'd set.

"Susanna, we have to talk," she said softly. "About something you said yesterday. To Samuel and Anna." Susanna didn't respond, but that didn't mean she wasn't listening. "Did you tell Samuel that you and David were courting?"

"Yes-ter-day?" Susanna nibbled at her lower lip and suddenly became fascinated with a spot of sunshine on the sawdust-covered floor. "King David and me?"

No matter how many times Hannah explained that the young man's name was David King, not King David, Susanna continued to say it her way. And David's habit of wearing a paper crown from Burger King on his head didn't help.

"Susanna. You and David cannot court because you can't get married."

Susanna tilted her head and peered up slyly. "He said."

"Who said?"

"David. He said. He's going to get married." She pointed at herself. "To me."

"I'm sorry, Susanna, but David is wrong."

The door to the chicken house opened and Irwin stuck his head in. "Vernon had to go home. Do I have to clean the chicken house today? Did it last weekend."

"Ya," Hannah said. "Every week, Irwin."

Susanna seized the opportunity to escape. While Hannah was giving Irwin directions, her daughter grabbed the scrap bucket and scooted out the door.

It was a little after one when Albert Hartman drove into the yard. Hannah, Irwin, Rebecca, Aunt Jezzy and Susanna had just finished the noon meal. Rebecca and Hannah had been going over arrangements for Rebecca's upcoming wedding to the new preacher, Caleb Wittner. The banns had already been called twice, and the service would be in May. Usually, weddings were planned for November, after the crops were in, but Caleb was a widower with a young child. Everyone was so pleased that he and Rebecca had chosen each other that people were willing to take a day off from the busy spring planting to witness the ceremony.

Albert pulled his big truck up near the gate closest to the kitchen. Hannah went out, followed closely by Irwin and Susanna. "There's no need for you two to come out," Hannah called over her shoulder. But they didn't return to the house. Instead, they stood on the porch steps and stared as if Albert hadn't driven into their yards dozens of times in the past.

Hannah was slightly piqued. It was a toss-up as to which of them, Irwin or Susanna, was the nosiest. She waved at Albert, sorry that she would have to tell him she couldn't go. Having to refuse his invitation at this point was something of an embarrassment. But she knew she had to do what was right for her family. As she started to walk toward the truck, her grandson 'Kota appeared in the open window in the backseat.

"Are you coming, *Mam?*" he asked excitedly. "I can't wait to see the baby alpaca."

Hannah's heart melted. Grace's son was technically a step-grandchild, but Hannah didn't see it that way. She loved him as much as she did Anna's Rose or Johanna's three, not to mention Ruth's twin boys. "*Mam* can't go," she said. "I've got too much work to do."

"But Mama said you…" His face crinkled with disappointment. "Mama said I could go because you were going."

For an instant, Hannah thought he would burst into tears. Strictly speaking, *Mam* was the name for mother, not grandmother, but 'Kota had copied Grace, and now he called her *Mam,* as her children did.

Albert, who'd gotten out of the truck, glanced at the boy and then back to Hannah. "What did you tell me, Hannah? That I work too hard? Well, the same can be said for you. Come on, go with us. I'm sure Susanna would like to come, as well."

"*Ya,*" Susanna called from the porch. "I want to come."

"Me, too," Irwin chimed in, hands thrust in his pockets. "Can I come?"

"Irwin," Hannah chided. "It isn't polite to invite yourself."

"The more the merrier," Albert insisted. "And it won't take all afternoon. We'll just head over, give the youngsters a chance to see the alpacas and come on home. What do you say, Hannah?"

What could she say? With 'Kota, Susanna and Irwin all staring at her with pleading eyes, she could hardly refuse. "All right," she agreed, good-naturedly. "Let me get my *kapp.* You, too, Susanna. Your good *kapp* and a clean apron."

Minutes later, they were all in Albert's large cab pickup truck, heading west toward Maryland and the alpaca farm.

Chapter Six

"*Mam,* do you want me to start putting the salads into the buggy?" Rebecca asked. "I've put the ice in the coolers."

It was four o'clock on Wednesday afternoon, the day of the school picnic that signaled the end of the school year for Seven Poplars. Tuesday had been the end of classes, but this combined fund-raiser and recognition day was one that parents, students and Hannah always eagerly looked forward to.

"Yes, thank you." Hannah said. "And the pies, too."

Hannah, Johanna, Rebecca and Susanna had been cooking and preparing dishes since early morning. And Hannah was certain that Anna's house had been a hum of activity, as well. Daughters Ruth and Miriam didn't have children in the school, but they'd gone over to help Anna after lunch. Irwin had already been dispatched to assist Miriam's husband, Charley, and Ruth's husband, Eli, in setting up the games and setting out tables for the picnic baskets.

"All done!" Susanna pronounced. A row of misshapen, crumbling whoopie pies lined the kitchen counter. Marshmallow cream filling oozed from between oversize chocolate cookies and dribbled down the cabinet doors to pool on the floor. Susanna's hands and mouth were gooey with marshmallow filling, but she was grinning from ear to ear. "Look, *Mam!*" she urged. "Look at my whoopie pies!"

Johanna and Rebecca exchanged looks, and Rebecca covered her mouth with her hand and coughed to suppress a giggle.

"Gut." Johanna handed her little sister a roll of wax paper. "Do you want me to help you wrap them?"

Susanna shook her head. *"Ne.* I can do it by myself." One by one, she laboriously tore off sheets of wax paper and swaddled the whoopie pies. The results were haphazard, to say the least, but Hannah only smiled and watched as Susanna added several of the sweets to her picnic basket and set the others aside to donate.

The picnic basket auction wouldn't be the only method of raising money that day. Donated pies, cakes and other baked goods were for sale as well as useful items such as buggy wheels, milk buckets, quilts, kitchenware and butter churns. Every penny raised would be put to good use at the school, but the parceling out of choice supper baskets was the prime entertainment of the event. Successes and failures of meals would be talked about for months, perhaps even years, and more than one courtship had started with a heavily laden basket of good food.

Every unmarried woman over the age of sixteen was expected to bring a meal that would be sold to the highest bidder. The custom was that any man could bid, and whoever succeeded in buying the basket would eat supper with the cook. This year, Hannah was preparing

a supper basket. Not that she was looking for a beau.
She'd not met anyone in the county who she could imagine exchanging vows with, but it seemed only fair that
she do her share to support the fund-raiser as the other
widows did.

None of the baskets were labeled, and there was
always a great deal of nosing around so that eligible
men could discover, prior to the auction, who had made
which basket. When a bidder guessed wrong, the onlookers found it hilarious to see a young bachelor having to share supper with someone old enough to be his
grandmother, while the girl he had his eye on spent
time with someone else. But it was always all in good
fun. Frolics were a time for the community to come
together and relax, to share news and renew the ties to
friends and family.

Hannah had intended to pack her meal in a big
egg basket, but the previous night, her mother-in-law,
Lovina, had insisted on taking the basket home to use
herself. The elderly woman, who made her home with
Anna and Samuel, had periods of memory loss and
what the Englishers called dementia. Lovina often believed that her son Jonas, Hannah's late husband, was
still alive. Sometimes, she mistook Samuel for Jonas, a
notion Samuel was too kindhearted to dispute. In any
case, Lovina, who was having a good week, had insisted
that she, too, was going to bring a basket supper to the
school frolic, but wanted her daughter-in-law's basket.
Hannah didn't mind, not even when Lovina sent over
an ancient lidded wicker basket, tied shut with yarn,
for Hannah to use.

The basket Hannah had packed, with its lid tied shut,
obviously belonged to an elderly woman. There was

little chance anyone would be eager to bid on it, but Samuel had already offered to buy it so Hannah would get to share the evening meal with Anna and her family. As for Lovina, she just might get to enjoy someone else's company, and would be glowing like newly churned butter.

"Ready," Susanna declared, lugging her basket toward the kitchen door.

The sound of glass jars clinking caused Hannah to raise an eyebrow. "What did you pack in there besides your whoopie pies?"

"Pickles and peanut butter."

"Peanut-butter-and-pickle sandwiches?" Rebecca asked.

Susanna shook her head. "Jar of peanut butter. Jar of pickles. King David likes peanut butter. And pickles."

"Is he going to bid on your basket?" Johanna asked.

Susanna nodded. Susanna's would probably be the only lunch container with a crooked letter *S* scrawled backward in inkberry juice. Susanna had marked her basket last summer. The red juice had stained the wicker and no amount of scrubbing could remove her initial.

"What are you going to eat with your peanut butter and pickles?" Rebecca opened the refrigerator door, removed several pieces of fried chicken, wrapped them in foil and tucked them into Susanna's basket. "Do you have napkins and knives and forks?"

Susanna eyed the lunch basket warily. "Don't need them."

"Just in case, Susanna-Banana." Rebecca smiled warmly at her younger sister as she added silverware, napkins and two apples to the container. "David might be hungry."

"Maybe," Susanna said grudgingly. "He likes raisins, too. Raisins are good."

"They are good," Hannah agreed. She reached up into a cabinet and found a box of golden raisins. She held them out, and Susanna's mouth puckered. "You know you like raisins, too," Hannah coaxed.

Susanna opened the basket and pushed the raisins inside. Laboriously, she fastened the lid. "Put it in the buggy," she said. "That's enough food. King David likes peanut butter best."

As she watched her daughter trudge out the door, Hannah wondered if it had been a mistake to allow Susanna to put together a supper basket. But where did she draw the line between protecting her daughter and making Susanna's and her own life even more difficult? Refusing Susanna would have been hurtful. Susanna was a part of the community, and it was natural that she'd want to do what other girls did. The trouble was, no matter what Anna and Jezzy said, she wasn't like other girls. And letting her believe that she was might be the cruelest act of all.

Albert parked his truck behind two others along the road near the Seven Poplars schoolhouse. A horse and buggy was just turning into the driveway, and dozens of black buggies were lined up in the field. A sack race was taking place on the far side of the school, and children, mostly Amish, were playing on the swing set and seesaw, and bouncing on a large, black trampoline. Adults stood talking in small groups while young women carried pies to a long table shaded by a white canvas canopy.

Albert wasn't sure why he was here. Well, he *did*

know why. He was here for the good food. And maybe to say hello to Hannah. He just wasn't certain if the decision to come was wise.

Saturday, when they'd gone down to the alpaca farm, it had been Susanna who had invited him to the school picnic. When he'd tried to make an excuse not to come, Hannah had assured him that he'd be welcome and told him that there would be homemade pies for sale as well as jellies, pickles and other home-canned delicacies. She knew his weak spot for home-cooked goodies. He loved pie, and he would walk a mile for real strawberry jam.

It had been a trying day. He'd been called out early that morning to sew up a calf that had been attacked by a stray dog. After that, there had been a young heifer with mastitis and two more urgent cases that had taken up the entire afternoon. Somehow, he'd managed to miss lunch and go all day on three cups of coffee and a stale donut that he'd found in the back of his breadbox.

Seeing the Amish and Mennonite families gathered took Albert back to his own Mennonite childhood. He'd attended a rural schoolhouse only a little larger than this one, and he'd been fortunate enough to grow up in a farming community where most folks didn't count their happiness by how much money they made. He hadn't realized then how fortunate he was or how wealthy he was in the things that mattered. He'd been caught up in dreams of a wider world, and as a teenager, he'd desperately wanted to go to a bigger school, to travel to other parts of the country, to own a television and a truck. Funny, now that he had almost everything he'd ever imagined, those material objects didn't seem as important as he'd expected.

There was something to be said for a slower pace of

life, one in which a man or a woman could live closer to
the land and nearer to God. He remembered telling his
father that if he ever got off the farm, he'd never plow
another row again. But, sometimes, on a warm spring
day, when the air smelled of growing things and the sun
felt warm on his face, his hands itched to wrap around
the handles of a horse-drawn cultivator.

I must be having a midlife crisis, Albert thought. He
considered himself a man of faith. He attended church
and Bible study regularly, and he never failed to pitch
in to raise money for a good cause or to lend a hand
when someone needed it. He never closed his eyes at
night without a period of contemplation and prayer, and
he tried to live according to the principles of his faith.
Still, he was restless.

As much as he loved his work, and as close as he felt
to John and his new family, it wasn't enough. Albert
always felt as if there was something he was supposed
to do that he'd left undone. He'd never considered himself to be a morose person or a selfish one; he hoped he
wasn't being selfish by not being happy with the blessings that God had bestowed on him.

The alpacas, now they were something that got him
excited. He'd had such a good time on Saturday when
he, 'Kota, Hannah, Irwin and Susanna had gone to
make the final arrangements to buy the animals. That
night, he'd lain awake for hours thinking about the smell
of the alpacas, the soft texture of their fleece and the
sounds they made.

A tap on the cab of his truck yanked Albert from his
reverie. He looked over to see Hannah's Irwin grinning
at him. Irwin was a tall, lanky kid with stiff, corn shock
hair, a wide mouth and a plain face. Despite the brief

stint that Irwin had worked at the veterinary clinic that hadn't panned out, Albert liked him. Maybe, he saw something of himself in the boy. Sooner or later, Albert was sure, Irwin would find direction, and then Hannah's patient care and affection would prove worthwhile.

Albert opened the truck door. "Hello, Irwin."

"Hurry up, or you'll miss the supper-basket auction." Irwin pointed. "See. People are gathering around the tables."

"I wasn't planning on bidding." Albert got out of the truck and followed the boy across the grass. "Thought maybe I'd buy a rhubarb pie if there are any for sale."

Irwin waited for him to catch up. "Didn't guess you were. But…" He leaned close and whispered, "Lovina packed her supper in Hannah's basket."

Albert raised his eyebrows.

Irwin grinned. "Food will be good because Anna made it, but Lovina…" He grimaced. "I think Jason Peachy is going to try and win the bid, thinking it's Hannah's. He's got his eye on her. Won't he be surprised when Lovina is who he sits down to supper with?"

Albert knew Jason Peachy, a middle-aged widower with three teenage boys. The man owned a hundred-acre farm over near Black Bottom. Albert didn't have much of an opinion of him. But the man didn't have the best setup for the number of hogs he was raising. He'd built his pigpens in a low spot. Not productive cropland, but not a good place for animals, either.

"I didn't know that Hannah was looking to get married again," Albert commented. As soon as the words were out of his mouth, he wondered why he'd spoken them. It wasn't his concern if Hannah was looking for a husband. Why wouldn't she be? She was still young; she had a lot to offer a man. And it was their way, the Old Order Amish. Frankly, he was surprised she'd stayed single this long.

The teen shrugged. "She'll listen to the bishop sooner or later. He's been telling her she's mourned Jonas too long."

Albert frowned. "The bishop thinks that's *his* business?"

"Everything's his business. He's the bishop. A woman *should* be married."

Something about the careless way the boy was talking about his foster mother rankled Albert, but he held his tongue. He'd known Irwin long enough to realize that he loved Hannah and meant no harm.

"She owns that big farm and she's a good cook," Irwin went on. "Lots of men would want to be her husband, even if she is strong-minded and old."

"Only a fifteen-year-old would call Hannah old," Albert muttered to himself.

Irwin didn't seem to hear or didn't bother to reply. Instead he pointed to a sorry-looking basket at the end of the table. The wicker had seen better days and the catch that held the lid down had broken and was tied with navy blue yarn. *Hannah's,* he mouthed silently and then he motioned toward a knot of young men.

Standing in the center was red-faced, gray-bearded Jason Peachy. He was a short, stocky man wearing a green shirt and black trousers. The man had small, pale blue eyes and his salt-and-pepper brows were thick. The man saw him and turned away.

A group of white *kapps* came into view, chattering women all moving together like a flock of birds. Albert could hear Hannah's distinctive voice in their midst and wondered what she was laughing at. She was a cheerful person, someone whom it was impossible not to have a good time with. He just couldn't see her with a man like Jason Peachy. And he couldn't see her happy with all those pigs. That many were bound to cause a stink, no matter how careful a farmer was to keep his pens clean. No, Jason wasn't the husband for her, and if she asked his opinion, he'd be glad to give it.

Hannah's son-in-law Samuel Mast was holding up a basket. When the crowd didn't quiet down, he urged them to in a good-natured way. Albert liked Samuel. He'd been as surprised as everyone else when Samuel had asked Anna to be his wife. He was some years older than she was, and most folks thought to see him courting Hannah. If Hannah had to remarry, Albert hoped it would be someone like Samuel, someone who could truly appreciate her for the fine woman she was.

"What am I bid for this next supper basket?" Samuel called. He lifted the lid and looked inside, making a show of smelling the delicious food. Albert saw that the basket's handle was wrapped with green willow switches.

One of Zack Byler's sons started the bid off at five dollars. Samuel shook his head, saying that he couldn't think of letting the basket go for such a puny amount. He reminded the crowd that this was a school fundraiser and he was here to accept serious offers. Everyone laughed at the Byler boy as he raised his own bid to ten dollars. Bidding picked up and the basket eventually went to Preacher Caleb for twenty-two dollars.

Albert didn't need Irwin's whisper to tell him that Caleb was Rebecca Yoder's intended. Rebecca would have been heartbroken if anyone else had won her basket. Of course, just the thought that anyone would really challenge Caleb wasn't feasible. The Amish liked a good joke, but they were rarely unkind. The chances were that Samuel had put the Byler boy up to bidding in the first place. But all ended well, and a blushing Rebecca went off happily to share supper with the man who would soon be her husband.

One after another the baskets on the table under the trees were auctioned off. Irwin drifted away with his friends, and Albert's clients, both Amish and English, exchanged greetings with him. Albert was polite, but wasn't feeling as sociable as usual. For some reason his attention remained fixed on the basket Hannah had actually packed.

Samuel kept up a steady patter of auctioneer's jests and taunting, and prices held steady at an average of twenty dollars per supper. Then Samuel produced a basket that appeared as if some child had drawn a snake on it in red poster paint.

"What am I bid for this one?" he asked. Again, he opened the basket, peered inside and pretended to inhale the aromas of wonderful food.

But, to Albert's surprise, no one raised a hand to bid on the sorry little basket. Not a single hand went up. Albert was tempted to offer something, just so that the girl or woman who'd prepared it wouldn't be hurt. Just when he started to move toward the table, the crowd parted and the King boy trudged through to the edge of the table. In one hand, he held a crumpled dollar bill.

"That's mine!" Susanna Yoder cried from the group of women on the far side of the tables. "My basket! Buy that one!"

"Dol-ler," David pronounced. David's father came to

stand beside him and the young man smiled. "Susanna's basket," he said waving the dollar again.

"Make that twenty-one." Ebben King handed his son a larger bill.

"Sold to young David King for twenty-one dollars," Samuel declared.

David seemed frozen to the spot. A wide smile spread across his round face and he nodded. "I bought it," he declared loudly. "My Susanna's basket."

Samuel handed over the basket and David proudly carried it away with a giggling Susanna trailing in his wake.

Albert glanced at Hannah, standing among her daughters. His smile faded as he caught the hint of worry in Hannah's expression. Not much she could do about it, he thought. The two youngsters seemed smitten with each other. But he could understand why Hannah had grave reservations about what might come from Susanna's innocent romance.

"What have we here?" Samuel said, drawing the crowd's attention back to the auction. When Albert looked at the basket he was holding, he saw that it was the battered one with the yarn closing. *Hannah's basket.*

"Fifteen dollars," someone offered.

From the back came another bid. "Seventeen!"

"Eighteen," Samuel's boy, Rudy, called.

"No fair," said an onlooker. "He's too young. Admit it, Samuel. He's bidding for you."

Samuel laughed and shrugged. "I've got to eat, too," he admitted. "And I've got a big family to feed."

Jason Peachy threw up his hand. "Twenty-five dollars!"

Albert's stomach clenched. This wasn't the way it

was supposed to go. Why were men bidding on a supper everyone was supposed to believe belonged to Lovina Yoder? Had Irwin spilled the secret to the whole crowd?

Samuel laughed. "Twenty-five dollars is the bid. Do I hear twenty-six?"

"It's supper," Rudy said, "Not a whole cow."

Laughter followed.

"Twenty-five once," Samuel called. "Twenty-five twice."

Samuel glanced at Jason Peachy. The pig farmer looked as if his prize sow had just taken first place at the Delaware State Fair. Albert couldn't stand it. "Fifty dollars!" he shouted.

"Sold!" Samuel proclaimed.

Chapter Seven

One minute Hannah was standing with her grandchild on her hip, thoroughly enjoying the supper auction, the next, the eyes of the entire community were on her. Jason Peachy was bidding on her supper basket. And from the sly winks Jason threw her way between bids, he was all too aware that it was her basket and not her mother-in-law's.

Hannah retrieved baby Rose's rag doll, catching it just before it fell from the toddler's hand. In an effort to cover her surprise that she'd been caught in her ruse, Hannah gave all her attention to the child. She adjusted the baby's cap and murmured endearingly to her in *Deitsch.*

Hannah was tempted to chuckle. *Jason Peachy was interested in courting her?* Anna met her gaze and glanced away with a suppressed giggle. Anna knew her too well. One exchanged look was all it took for them to each know what the other was thinking.

Jason Peachy. Well, there was a fly in the buttermilk. While she'd been acquainted with Jason for years, Hannah hadn't suspected that he might be sweet on her.

He was a widower and near to her age, but the man had only three teenage sons, which was a small family for an Old Order Amish man. She would have thought he'd be interested in a younger woman than her. Someone who could bear him more children and be up to the tasks of working day and night to keep his household running.

He was a somber man, a farmer and a faithful member of another church district in the county. She'd known his wife, Iris, from a shared quilting project. Sadly, Iris had died of cancer the previous fall and Hannah, along with most of the community, attended her funeral. His farm was near Oak Point School, an area known as Black Bottom—low and woody ground. Hannah's sister-in-law Martha, who kept tabs on all eligible bachelors in the county for her daughter, Dorcas, had remarked recently that Jason Peachy hadn't married until he was in his mid-thirties, which was why he didn't have grown children yet.

Hannah's first thought was that Jason hadn't allowed enough time to pass before looking to remarry, but men were helpless creatures without a wife to tend to their needs. She remembered that Iris had been sick for a long time, and mourning periods were often relaxed when needs were to be met. But what was Martha thinking? Jason was too old and set in his way for Dorcas, who was close in age to Johanna.

Still, Hannah thought, her niece wouldn't be the first young woman to take a husband old enough to be her father. For the Old Order Amish, marriage was considered a practical matter of faith and family as much as a romantic attachment. She'd been fortunate enough to have both in Jonas, but not every woman could expect that. And, poor Dorcas had to marry *someone*.

Jason was a perfectly respectable man, even if he did raise pigs for a living. Pigs were never Hannah's favorite animals, but it would be silly to reject a man because of what livestock he raised. Or so she would reason if she had decided she was ready to remarry, which she hadn't. Or, if she favored Jason Peachy, which she didn't, and wanted to cause even more discord between her and Martha. Why in the name of sweet strawberries hadn't the man had the good sense to bid on Dorcas's basket instead of hers? Surely he knew that Martha had her eye on him; everyone else in the county knew it.

All those thoughts tumbled through her mind in the short time it took Samuel to decide that the bid on her basket was as high as it was going to go and call out "Twenty-five once, twenty-five twice…"

Martha's going to be mad enough to bite green grapes and spit out wasps, Hannah thought as she bounced giggling Rose on her hip and waited to hear Samuel declare, "Sold to Jason Peachy!"

Instead, another voice—Albert Hartman's voice—stunned her by shouting, "Fifty dollars!"

Hannah was so shocked that she nearly dropped Rose. "Here." She pushed the wide-eyed girl into Anna's arms. "Take the baby."

Hannah had never been prone to light-headed nonsense, but suddenly she felt positively giddy. Why had Albert bid on her basket? People would be gossiping about it for months. Then a merry notion came into her head. *Albert's rescued you from Jason Peachy and his pigs.*

Just behind her, Martha remarked sharply in *Deitsch.* "Has Albert Hartman lost his mind? What does he want with Hannah's basket?"

"Mam?" Even sensible Anna was shocked. Her eyes were wider than Rose's. "You can't share supper with Albert. He's not one of us. How would it look?"

Hannah's sense of humor surfaced, and she barely stifled a most improper response. Anna was right, of course. She should have been put out with Albert for getting her in this pickle, but all she could think of was how much more enjoyable sharing supper with him would be than eating with Jason Peachy. She wouldn't have to listen to talk of the price of pork or of Jason's plans for a new sty. She and Albert would sit with Anna and her family and he could tell them about the imminent arrival of the alpacas and discuss the details of settling them in on her property.

"Mam." Two bright splotches of color tinted Anna's cheeks. "People are whispering." She motioned toward the crowd standing near the auction table.

Hannah rolled her eyes. "Nonsense, daughter. Albert was your father's friend and he knows everyone in the community on a first-name basis. He couldn't have guessed it was my basket."

"And why not?" Anna asked. "Everyone else apparently knows, thanks to Irwin's big mouth."

Hannah waved away Anna's intimation. "I'm sure Albert just wanted to support the school." Or had he bought it knowing it was her basket? Knowing he would be able to share supper with her. The notion was not altogether displeasing. In fact, it was deliciously wicked. And then she had a second notion. Who would have thought that her basket would bring more money than any other for the school?

Hochmut, Hannah chided herself. Pride was often the sin of which she'd found herself guilty. But who was she to complain when the children of Seven Poplars would benefit? Albert's fifty dollars would buy good used math books for her eighth-graders, and they were sorely in need of them. The old ones had been used for so long that they were held together with prayer and duct tape. So what if Albert wasn't Amish? It wasn't as if he was asking her to walk out with him. What was one supper on the ground between old friends?

She felt someone staring at her and raised her gaze to collide with Jason's. He was standing at the edge of the cluster of men, arms folded across his ample belly, his sun-burned features creased in disapproval.

Hannah smiled and fluttered her hand in a gesture that she'd seen Aunt Jezzy use a hundred times. It meant, I'm sorry, it's not my fault. Truthfully, what Hannah really wanted to convey was, *Don't frown at me, you old goat. If you wanted my basket that badly, you should have outbid him.*

Lord help me, she thought. *I am truly lacking in charity.*

"*Mam.*" Anna's insistent tone broke through Hannah's musing. "What will Caleb think?"

She pursed her lips. Caleb was the new preacher, and her soon-to-be son-in-law. She certainly didn't want to cause a problem for Rebecca or Caleb. More was expected of the families of the church elders. Certain moral standards had to be upheld for the good of the community. "If Albert's planning to stay for the picnic, we'll eat with you and Samuel and the children," Hannah answered.

All this fuss was probably over nothing. Albert might not have realized that he was supposed to share the meal with her. She chuckled. "Be at ease, daughter. Your husband doesn't look put out," she said quietly to Anna. "And he's our deacon."

Samuel was grinning at Albert as he passed the supper basket. "That will be fifty dollars, hard money."

"Will you take a check?" Albert appeared slightly embarrassed.

Samuel laughed. "I suppose we'll have to." He waved toward Hannah. "I hope you've made enough food. Albert has a reputation for having a big appetite."

"So I've heard." Hannah's giddiness made her heart race, but she smiled at Albert as if he were one of her errant pupils. She could feel all her neighbors looking at her, watching to see how she would react. "Well, Samuel," she called back. "You'd better hope that I've packed enough food, because we're eating with you and Anna. If I didn't, you might have to go hungry."

Samuel laughed.

At least Martha can't say I stole Dorcas's beau, Hannah thought with satisfaction.

A good-natured Amish mason in a Lincoln green, short-sleeved shirt stepped to the front of the onlookers and clapped his big hands together once. "Get on with the auction, Samuel," he urged. "Albert's not the only one who's hungry."

"Ya," Martha urged, tugging a reluctant Dorcas along with her toward the basket table. "I see at least five more supper baskets still waiting to be sold."

Shyly, carrying Hannah's basket in both hands, Albert walked toward her. The women drew aside to let him pass, all eyes on him. Hannah smiled at him. She would not provide the gossips more to whisper about by acting as if she had something to hide.

"What have you done, Albert?" she teased. He grinned, and she decided that he really did have a very pleasant face.

"I hope I didn't upset anyone's buggy." He glanced over his shoulder and lowered his voice conspiratorially. "And I hope Jason doesn't take it to heart, but I didn't get any lunch today, and…and I thought that a homemade supper made by Hannah Yoder was just what I needed."

She arched one eyebrow. "How did you know I made the food inside? It's my mother-in-law's basket."

He grimaced. "Irwin."

"I was afraid of that. Shall we join the family?" She motioned toward Anna. "She and Samuel have laid their picnic supper out in the shade on the far side of the schoolhouse."

"I'd like that," Albert agreed. "I thought we could share with Grace and 'Kota, too. They're here somewhere, and I imagine that they're hungry, too."

"Of course. I think they were already planning to join us." Hannah's smile was genuine. She felt relieved. Albert had known which basket was hers, but he'd only bid on it because he liked her cooking and he wanted to provide for Grace and 'Kota. Not even Bishop Atlee could find fault with an outsider sharing a meal with so many of the family included.

"It was kind of you to contribute so much to our school fund," she said, as she fell into step with him. "And I'll be glad to see my daughter and grandson."

'Kota was her daughter Grace's son by her first marriage, not her grandson by blood, but certainly by heart. Since Grace and Albert's nephew, John, were Mennonite and not Amish, 'Kota didn't attend the Seven Poplars School. Public school wouldn't let out until June, but after that, he'd be spending much of the summer on the farm with Hannah and Susanna while Grace studied for her degree as a veterinary technician at the local college.

"John couldn't make it?" Hannah asked as they rounded the corner of the schoolhouse. She could feel heat in her cheeks, but had no idea why she was blushing.

Albert shook his head. "No. We have a couple of post-op patients at the clinic and he volunteered to stay and watch over them. You know how seriously John takes his work."

"I do," Hannah assured him. She surveyed the three quilts that Anna had spread on the ground earlier. Samuel and Anna's children were there as were Miriam and Charley, sitting among dishes and bowls and plates of food. She'd expected to find Susanna and David, but they were nowhere in sight. "I wonder where Susanna got to?" she murmured. With the auction almost over, other families were gathering to eat on the softball field, under the trees and on the schoolhouse porch.

"I could go and look for them if you like," Albert offered.

"Ne." Hannah shrugged. "I'm sure they're with David's parents. Susanna knows better than to wander off."

Ruth came toward them carrying one of her twin boys. Hannah saw her son-in-law Eli with the other boy coming behind her. "Are you eating with us, too?" Hannah asked.

"Ya. And Johanna and Roland and the children," Ruth said. She nodded a greeting to Albert before glanc-

ing from the supper basket he was carrying to Hannah. "Eli wants to talk to you about Irwin."

Hannah grimaced. "What's he done now?"

Ruth laughed and held up her son for Hannah to nuzzle. "Not a thing. Eli has a new contract and needs help at the shop. He was hoping you could spare Irwin to give him a hand."

"Of course," Hannah answered. "If he can use him. Irwin needs direction." Neither of them was unkind enough to say that the boy wasn't much help on the farm. "I think these two have grown since I've seen them."

"In two days?" Ruth laughed and handed the baby over.

Hannah squeezed him and inhaled the sweet baby scent of her youngest grandson. Ruth had just sewn the twins new baby caps and gowns. They were beautiful babies, but had yet to grow much hair. Hannah thought Luke's might grow in dark like their father's, but Adam was definitely a redhead.

"I heard all about the alpacas," Ruth said to Albert. "It's all my nieces and nephews have been talking about. When are they coming?"

"This weekend, I hope." He placed Hannah's basket on the nearest blanket. "There's Grace." He waved. "Over here, Grace."

She waved back. "Uncle Albert. *Mam.* Hi, everyone!" Grace called as she crossed the schoolyard to join them. 'Kota trailed behind her, but perked up when he saw his cousins. Soon, they were all gathered for a moment of silent thanks before the meal.

Johanna and her husband joined them and their little ones, laughing and talking excitedly, scattered among their cousins. Food was passed around between Hannah's daughters, their husbands and children without regard to whose box, bag or basket it came from. Within minutes, everyone was eating and sharing the week's news, Albert included. Roland was eager to hear about the alpacas and the children kept chiming in, all excited about the arrival at their grandmother's farm of the exotic animals.

Charley brought a folding chair and a desk out of the schoolhouse for Lovina, who appeared with the young man who'd successfully bid on her basket. It was Lydia's eighteen-year-old son, Elmer, much to everyone's delight. Elmer was one of Irwin's cousins, and Irwin took great pleasure in teasing him over his supper partner. No doubt, he'd bid on the basket at Samuel's request. Samuel held Elmer to the bargain until the food was parceled out, then said that he and Irwin were free to go and eat with their friends. The teenagers didn't need to be told twice.

"Don't forget," Eli called after Irwin. "Be at the shop at eight sharp tomorrow morning."

Irwin turned and waved. "*Ya,* I'll be there."

"I'm thinking this might be good for Irwin," Eli said to Hannah. "He seemed interested in assembling the kitchen cabinets when he came by last week."

"It will be a blessing if you can teach him a trade." Hannah munched on a carrot stick that was sweet and crispy. "Maybe woodwork is something he has a feel for."

"He'll find his way," *Grossmama* Lovina injected. "He's young and foolish, but they all are at that age. You should have seen what a woodenhead my Jonas was. And look at him now." Surrounded by family, *Gross-*

mama Lovina was content, even jovial. She smiled and patted Samuel's arm. "A *gut* boy, my Jonas."

Albert glanced questioningly at Hannah.

She leaned close and whispered. "Sometimes Lovina's mind wanders. She thinks Samuel is Jonas. He was her only son, and she has never gotten over his passing."

Albert nodded. "She's right," he agreed. "Jonas was a good man, one of the finest I've ever known."

"He was a good husband and a good father. He would have enjoyed the picnic today." Hannah smiled, feeling nostalgic, but not sad. She really didn't feel so sad anymore. It was true that time healed sorrow. "Jonas never missed a school frolic."

Johanna's Katy sat down beside Hannah. "*Mam* says I can go to school next fall," she announced. "I want to go to school. I want a pink lunchbox."

Hannah smiled at her granddaughter and wiped a smear of baked beans off the child's chin. "Black it will have to be, my sweet, but maybe your mama will find you a pink thermos to go inside."

Katy grinned, then her eyes widened as she caught sight of a pile of treats. "Can I have a popcorn ball?"

"You may." Hannah dug in her basket and came up with six. "Pass them out to the other children," she said. "And if there aren't enough to go around, Aunt Ruth made more. Hers are rainbow-colored."

"Sixteen dollars," *Grossmama* Lovina repeated loudly for the third time. "That Beachy boy paid sixteen dollars for my basket. He didn't know it was mine. Thought he was getting some young gal's." She laughed so hard that she nearly choked on her fried chicken.

Hannah paused, fork in hand, and looked around at her family. She had been truly blessed in her children and their husbands, her grandchildren and her friends. *Thank You, God,* she offered silently. What more could she ask for? Then her gaze drifted to Miriam, who was watching her. There was something in her daughter's eyes that concerned Hannah. Was it worry? Worry for her? Lately, she'd noticed this look on her daughters' faces more often than she cared to admit.

Maybe the bishop and her friends were right. Maybe, so long as she remained single, her daughters felt responsible for her. She didn't want that. It would be natural when and if she reached Lovina's age, but for now, while she was strong, healthy and active, they didn't need to worry about her needs. After Rebecca's wedding, she would stop her dithering and think seriously about remarrying. It was expected of an Amish woman in her position. It was the right thing to do. Surely, there was someone in this community or another with whom she would be content to share the rest of her life. But, she decided finally, she would not leave. Her roots were sunk too deep. She would take a new husband and she would give him the respect and affection he needed, but she would not move away from her children.

She would not.

"Do you think you could?" Albert asked. "Would it be permitted?"

Hannah blinked. Had she been wool-gathering again? "I'm sorry. What did you ask me?"

Albert used a cloth napkin to wipe his mouth. He had such a sincere, kind face. "I was wondering if you would like to come with me to bring the alpacas home."

Hannah didn't have to think before she responded. "I'd like that. You think it will be Saturday?" There were questions she wanted to ask the man who'd raised them, habits and likes and dislikes of individual animals that Albert might not think important. In her experience, each animal was different, and it was most important that the herd leader, the female that Albert had mentioned, be happy in her new home.

"I'm hoping for Saturday, but I'll let you know as soon as I confirm."

"*Ya,* I will come," she said. "I'll bring Susanna, too, if that's all right."

"Of course," Albert said. "I think she had a good time before."

"She did. She had a wonderful time, and so did I," Hannah confessed cheerfully. "She'll be so excited to know we're going with you to pick up the animals." *Me, too,* Hannah thought. Now that the school frolic was almost over, she would have that to look forward to.

Of course, Rebecca's wedding would be a happy day for them all. But the wedding meant a lot to do and many things to plan for. Guests would be coming from out of state to stay with her, and she and the girls would have tons of food to make. Going with Albert to bring home the alpacas, that would be a day of fun with nothing to do but enjoy herself. She couldn't wait

Chapter Eight

Hannah tied her *kapp* strings and picked up her purse. She was so annoyed with Susanna that she had to keep her lips pressed tightly together to keep from saying something that she'd regret. This was the morning that she and Susanna were supposed to ride to Maryland with Albert to pick up the alpacas. Yesterday, Susanna had been so excited about going, but this morning was a different story.

"Susanna," she muttered under her breath. "What am I going to do with you?"

Rebecca was at Anna's making wedding plans. Susanna had gone next door to Ruth's to return a bag of sugar that they'd borrowed earlier in the week. She was supposed to come right back, but instead, she'd apparently met David at the end of the lane. The two of them had gone to Milford in a van with David's mother and older sister. Hannah wouldn't even have known it if Charley hadn't stopped by to tell her.

"Susanna said it would be all right with you," Charley had said. "David said they were going to have pizza."

So much for keeping a tighter rein on her, Hannah thought wryly.

What had Susanna been thinking? If she'd decided that she would rather go and have pizza with David than go to get the alpacas, the right thing would have been to come home and ask permission.

Once again, Hannah felt the weight of being a single parent. "If Jonas were here," she murmured. But that was self-pity. Jonas wasn't here. Her beloved husband had been called home to the Lord, and she'd been left behind. It was her job to make the best of her life and to care for her children, as Jonas would have expected her to. Usually, she did, but she'd hit an unexpected obstacle. What was she going to do with Susanna?

Albert was going to be here any moment. Strictly speaking, it wouldn't be proper for her to go off for the day with Albert without a chaperone. But she'd been looking forward it, and she wanted to help fetch the animals. Between teaching school and her housework, she rarely got a day off to do something fun like this. It wasn't fair that Susanna could spoil her outing.

In the end, she decided to go anyway. Being in a truck with Albert wasn't the same as entertaining him in her home. As long as they were in public, where anyone could see that they weren't misbehaving, she didn't see how it could raise any eyebrows. Jonah had always said, "Misdeeds start in the heart." She was going with a trusted friend to help bring home animals to the farm. If anyone else wanted to think the less of her for it, then that was their affair.

"Where's Susanna?" Albert asked as he opened the truck door for Hannah. "I thought she was coming with us."

Hannah shrugged and gave him a wry look. "So did I, but she's given me the slip again. She went off for the day with David and his parents, something about pizza." She climbed up into the vehicle, and he closed the door behind her.

As he walked back to the driver's side, Albert glanced at the horse trailer he'd borrowed from a client to bring the alpacas home. He had experience in pulling trailers, but not one as large or new as this. He could only imagine what it cost, and it made him a little nervous to be responsible for it. But, he'd been stuck. There was nothing comparable to rent in the area, and his only other solution would have been to pay to have the animals hauled. He'd rather not do that. He didn't want to take any chances with the alpacas' safety, and he knew that he'd be more careful of their well-being than someone being paid to deliver them.

As he got back into the cab, he smiled at Hannah. He was so glad that she was coming, despite her daughter abandoning them. He'd been looking forward to talking with Hannah on the drive, and he was eager to have her participate in the alpaca project at every step. "I had a really good time at the school picnic," he said to her.

She smiled back at him, and he was struck again by what an attractive woman Hannah Yoder was. Her modest green dress, black apron and white *kapp* all appeared freshly washed and ironed. She looked so wholesome. Her hair was rolled into a kind of a bun and tucked up under her *kapp*, but what he could see was a soft, reddish-brown that matched her large, brown, intelligent eyes. Hannah really didn't look a day over thirty-five, although he supposed she had to be closer to his age.

Albert started the truck and carefully pulled the vehicle in a wide circle before exiting the long drive. He didn't say anything until after he pulled out onto the blacktop and drove past the chair shop. "I have to confess, I didn't come to the fund-raiser intending to bid on your basket," he explained. "I was just hoping to get some chicken salad and a sweet to take home."

"A pretty expensive supper it turned out to be." She chuckled. "I'll admit that I was surprised." She glanced at him from under long, thick lashes and he saw the mischief sparkling there. "You surprised a lot of people, Albert. We were the talk of the picnic." She uttered a small sound of amusement. "For about five minutes, until the Beachy boy won my mother-in-law's supper basket. And then the joke was on poor Elmer."

"He was a good sport to bid on her basket. I'm sure someone put him up to it. I hope Lovina wasn't upset that he didn't stay with her for the picnic."

"*Ne,* she wasn't. So long as she has Anna and the children nearby, she's happy."

"She seems content in Anna's household," Albert observed.

One thing that the Amish had in common with his own faith was a strong belief in caring for their own. Among the Mennonites, the elderly—no matter how ill their health—rarely went into nursing care. The Old Order Amish observed the same tradition. He'd never heard of an Amish man or woman being a resident of a nursing home. It made him think of Susanna and others with special needs, and what a good job Hannah had done of making her an integral part of the family.

"*Ya,*" Hannah agreed. "She is. Far happier than she

was when she stayed with me. I don't know why, but the two of us always rubbed each other the wrong way. I tried to respect her and to make allowances for her age and the mental losses she's suffered, and I prayed for God to give me patience—something I've always had in short supply. But I wasn't the girl that Lovina wanted for her son, and she never let me forget it."

"Because you were a convert to the Amish church?" Hannah glanced at him, then away.

He concentrated on the road. "I'm sorry. I didn't mean to pry."

"Ne." She shook her head. "It's no secret in the family, that I was once Mennonite or that Lovina never approved of me. My conversion was so long ago that I sometimes forget myself." She smiled, seeming to have drifted off to a time and place far in the past. "Jonas was strong in his faith. We were very much in love, but there was never a question of his leaving. It would have broken his mother's heart, and his sisters'."

"And you? Was it hard for you to leave your own faith?"

She took a moment to answer, as if she were choosing her words carefully. "It was difficult because my family and his both opposed the match so strongly. But becoming Amish and stepping apart from the English world wasn't as bad as you'd think. Jonas and I were meant to be together, and it was the only way."

"And you've been happy in his church?"

She nodded. "I found a peace here that I never knew before. For me, it was the right choice."

"Did your parents learn to accept your decision?"

She sighed. *"Ne,* they didn't. My father was a leader

in our church, very strict, very much the head of our household. My mother didn't oppose his wishes. He said that if I became Amish, I was dead to them, and I wasn't welcome in their home." Hannah wiped at the corner of her eye, as if she had something in it, but her voice remained soft and clear. "I tried to see my mother when Ruth was a baby and again before she passed away. Both times, someone alerted my father, and he locked the door. I went to the graveyard. He couldn't prevent that, but it was hurtful, not being able to say goodbye."

"And your father? You never made your peace with him?"

She shook her head. "He went on a mission to Northern Canada several years later, and he died of a heart attack." She sighed again. "I pray for them both every night, and I am certain we'll be reunited in heaven."

"Brothers? Sisters?"

"One sister, much older. She's dead, too. My mother was forty-four when I was born. But I can't complain. I was blessed with seven loving daughters, eight including Grace, and they have added to my joy with husbands and children. And I have the whole Seven Poplars Community. Sometimes we rub and pinch each other like a new leather shoe, but they are all family."

"You make me envious when you put it that way." Albert gripped the steering wheel a little tighter as he approached a four-way stop. "I was foolish not to have married when I was a young man. I could have had children of my own."

She chuckled. "When you were a *young* man? You're hardly a graybeard, Albert."

"Fifty-three my last birthday."

She spread her hands. "As I said, no graybeard. And you're right. You should have married. God never intended for men to live alone."

"Or women?"

She laughed. "You have me there. Caught in my own tangle of yarn. But, seriously, Albert, many women would find you attractive. You have a good character. You are respected, and you could provide for a wife and family. You could marry. You could marry a woman who could give you children."

Albert felt the back of his neck growing warm. Why was he talking to Hannah about such personal subjects, and how had they gotten from her conversion to the Amish to his regrets about not having children? He wasn't a man who discussed his personal life. He exhaled slowly. But Hannah was so easy to be with, so easy to talk to, that he'd let down his guard.

"Something I wanted to ask you," he said, abruptly changing the subject as he made a left turn onto a larger road. "At the school picnic, when your little granddaughter said that she wanted a pink lunchbox, you told her that it would have to be black. Do you mind if I ask why? If pink makes a child happy, why shouldn't she be allowed to have it?"

"Maybe that's a question you should be asking Bishop Atlee or my new, soon-to-be son-in-law."

By the animated tone of her voice, Albert knew Hannah wasn't offended. He pressed her. "I'm asking you. Why do you think it would be wrong?"

"It isn't a question of pink or black or of Katy's happiness. Believe me, if Katy gets a new lunchbox for school, she'll be happy. There's nothing wrong with black and it will look just like everyone else's lunchbox at school. Black is Plain. We're plain. If Johanna bought Katy a pink lunchbox, other little girls who didn't have one might feel hurt. The pink lunchbox would make Katy different."

"Better than the other girls?"

"*Ne,* Albert, not better. Just different. Our faith teaches us that what is important is family, community. Like a bee amid thousands in a beehive, we each have a place. We don't need to stand out as individuals. God sees each of us as we truly are, for what we are inside, in our hearts. Katy is a beautiful soul. She doesn't need a pink lunchbox. She is special in His eyes just as she is." Hannah nodded in conviction. "And the pink wouldn't make her happy if it was different. Little girls want to be exactly like their friends and the bigger girls who are there to guide them. It would be no favor to her if we let her think that we would indulge every whim that pops into her head."

Albert mulled over what Hannah had said before speaking. "I see what you're saying, but 'Kota has a superhero on his lunchbox, and I don't see that it has hurt him any."

"That's fine for 'Kota. He goes to school with children who carry all kinds of lunch containers. No one will point him out as different." She smiled. "More than they already do because he is such a kind boy."

"And smart," Albert added. "Top of his class. I wouldn't be surprised to see him in vet school someday."

"If it's what he wants, it would be a good thing," Hannah agreed. "I know John would be pleased."

They drove for several miles in comfortable silence. After a few minutes, Albert said, "There's this place not far ahead. They make really good sausage sandwiches. Would you mind if we stopped there?"

"Don't tell me you missed breakfast again." She chuckled at him.

"I won't." He grinned. "But I will admit to being hungry."

"You're always hungry," she teased. "Of course, we can stop for you to have something."

"They have other stuff," he suggested. "Good coffee and delicious pie."

"Pie and coffee? I think I'd like that."

Albert's grin grew wider.

As they sat in the comfortable booths in the modest restaurant, Hannah found herself chatting away as easily with Albert as she might one of her daughters. Albert was clearly a smart man; he was an animal doctor, after all. But he had common sense and a genuine concern for other people. She hadn't felt this much at ease with a man since Jonas had passed away. Not that a beloved husband and a simple friend of the family could be considered in the same way, but as much as she valued her sons-in-law and other men in the community, Albert was special. He made her laugh, and allowed for her beliefs.

When she accepted his offer to have something to eat at Annie's Sausage Corner, she'd agreed on the condition that she pay for her own food. She didn't have to explain that letting him treat her would be stepping over the line, a line she'd already smudged by coming with him today without a chaperone.

It was cool inside the restaurant. There were few patrons. Hannah thought it must be late for the breakfast crowd and too early for lunch. She ordered iced tea and a slice of blueberry pie with whipped cream. "What time is the farmer expecting us?" she asked after they'd given the waitress their orders.

"He said he would be there all day. I'm supposed to call him fifteen minutes out."

They discussed the feeding schedule for the alpacas, and Albert began to tell her about some of his more interesting animal patients. He'd cared for an armadillo, a deodorized skunk, a mountain lion and a condor with an injured wing. Only the skunk had been his patient here in Delaware. He'd seen the exotic animals when he'd attended veterinary school out west.

"The skunk bit me," he told her. "I find I don't have much sympathy for skunks."

Hannah laughed. "I don't, either. We had one in our henhouse once, and it killed a chicken. Not only that, but we couldn't get the smell out and we had to build a new chicken coop."

The waitress, a middle-aged woman with bright orange lipstick, was pleasant and efficient. She didn't stare or question Hannah about her Amish clothing, and she seemed in no hurry to have them eat, pay the bill and leave the booth for the next customers. Hannah's iced tea was very good, and although she secretly thought her own crust was flakier, she found the pie delicious, too.

"How is Leah?" Albert asked between bites. Despite having already eaten something that morning, he'd ordered a full breakfast, complete with eggs, pancakes, sausage and a white, mealy looking mound of grits that

Hannah didn't think looked particularly appetizing. "Have you had a letter recently?"

Hannah nodded. "Just last week, I got two." She explained to Albert that mail delivery was erratic in and out of Leah and Daniel's mission. Daniel was a Mennonite missionary, and he, her daughter and baby grandchild made their home on the edge of the Brazilian rainforest. Albert's church, the same one that Daniel's aunt and uncle belonged to, were strong supporters of Daniel's work. Every year they held a fund-raiser to provide educational and medical supplies for the clinic and school.

"Daniel's been sick with fever again," Hannah said. "It's troublesome. His aunt was hoping he'd come home to be treated, but Leah says the need there is great. Their presence keeps the area from being overrun by farmers wanting free land and cutting down the jungle for pasture for beef cattle." Many of the people that her daughter and son-in-law served were only a generation away from a tribal existence. They were new Christians, and Daniel was afraid if he came back to the States, his congregation would slip away.

"It's selfless work they do, both of them," Albert said. "It can't be an easy life. And I know you miss Leah terribly."

"I do," Hannah admitted. "And I know she misses her home and family, but she feels strongly that God wants her to be there."

"How is Leah's health? And the baby?"

"Both well, thank the Lord. She remains healthy. But they are anxious to have another child." Hannah averted her eyes. How could she have admitted such a private thing to Albert? She, who was usually reserved about sharing family matters? But, if the remark made him uncomfortable, he didn't show it.

"You must be very proud of her," he said. "Of all your daughters."

She sighed. "I am, a fault I can't seem to shake." Their gazes met, and she could see instant understanding in his expression. Hannah rolled her eyes. "Pride is a sin I've prayed to overcome. It's not something a Plain woman should feel."

"But human." Albert reached across the table and covered her hand with his. "Very—"

A warm tingling shot up Hannah's wrist and forearm. She gasped and felt herself blush as she withdrew her hand with as much dignity as she possessed.

"I'm sorry," Albert said quickly. "I didn't mean…" He was turning red, as well.

"Ne," Hannah said. "It's nothing. You were just…" Just what? Like a guilty teenager, she tucked the offending hand under the table and concentrated on the remaining bites of pie.

Albert began to talk very fast about John's search for a pony for 'Kota, and gradually the tension in the air began to dissolve.

It was just a friendly touch, Hannah told herself. *It didn't mean anything. Albert didn't do anything wrong.* Stealthily, she glanced around the restaurant at the other customers to see if anyone had noticed. But everyone seemed to be concentrating on their own meals, eating, laughing and chatting. No one had seen the brief touch. There was no need for her or Albert to feel guilty.

But Hannah had never been good at deceiving herself. If Albert reaching for her hand had meant nothing, then why was her heart racing, and why were butterflies fluttering in her stomach? Had she mistakenly given Albert the idea that their friendship was something more? And more importantly, was it?

Chapter Nine

Rebecca's wedding day was as beautiful a day as any bride could ask for. It was warm and sunny with clear blue skies and a slight breeze that ruffled the maple leaves over Albert's head. He was seated on the ground in the alpaca pasture with his legs stretched out in front of him and his back against a tree trunk. Although Rebecca and Caleb's ceremony and worship service were being held at Samuel and Anna's house, they'd be joining immediate family and close friends at Hannah's for the midday meal. The dinner would be one long celebration that would stretch into the evening supper when even more family and friends, including non-Amish like Albert, were invited to join them.

Albert had intended to come by early that morning, tend to the alpacas and be well away before the wedding party arrived, but it hadn't turned out that way. He was called out early on an emergency and spent most of the morning in a barn with a client's valuable milk cow. He'd been able to help the animal and the farmer, but he'd been late arriving to feed the alpacas. Normally, Hannah or Irwin could have fed them, but with Rebecca and Caleb's wedding, they had more than enough to do without worrying about his livestock.

It had been two weeks since he'd brought the alpacas to Hannah and they seemed to be slowly settling in. One of the young females was friendly enough to allow him to pet her, but the rest—especially Estrella, the herd leader—still kept a wary distance. He'd thought that if he just sat still and gave her the chance to satisfy her curiosity about him, he might win her confidence. The previous owner had warned him that gaining Estrella's trust wouldn't be easy, because she was protective of her offspring, but once he did, the others would follow her example.

Since getting the animals home to Hannah's, his admiration for them had only grown. He loved watching them, as the llamalike animals interacted with one another. He liked the way their ears went up when something caught their attention, and the way that— if something displeased them, they clustered together amid a chorus of clicks and squeaks and swept away with all the grace of a flock of birds. The alpacas were intelligent. He could see that in their large, expressive eyes and the way they communicated with each other. He was particularly touched by the loving way that Estrella and the others behaved toward the little black cria. Wherever the baby alpaca wandered in the pasture, adults remained nearby, keeping an eye on him and answering his every cry with reassuring clicks.

"I'm not going to hurt your baby," he crooned to Estrella. He'd just sat down for a minute to see if he could coax the cria closer to him. "I wouldn't hurt any of you for all the world." Twice the adventurous little male had ventured almost within arm's reach, and both times, his mother had called him away with a sharp little snort of disapproval. Albert thought that if he could be patient and sit still just a little longer, he'd have the opportunity to stroke the soft fleece and scratch behind the baby alpaca's ears.

The little male thrust out his head and wrinkled his nose, moving closer to Albert, step by step. "That's it," Albert whispered. "Come on, just a little—"

The rattle of buggy wheels in the yard sent the cria racing back to the safety of his mother. Albert looked up in surprise as the whole herd of alpacas trotted to the far end of the pasture and formed a cluster around the baby.

Could it be that late? Hannah had assured him that the service would last until after one, and it was only… Albert checked his watch and grimaced. *No. It couldn't be.* He'd sat here in the pasture that long?

Feeling foolish, he got to his feet and brushed the grass off the back of his pants. He'd make his departure quickly and hope that Hannah wouldn't be put out with him. Things were already awkward enough between them. He didn't want to make matters worse. The Saturday that they'd retrieved the alpacas, they'd pretended that nothing had happened between them when he'd laid his hand on hers at the diner. But they had both been all too aware that it had, and the easy companionship between them had vanished, replaced with a polite tension and uncertainty. The friendship wasn't gone, but it had subtly changed, and he had no idea how to make things right again. He'd barely seen Hannah in the past two weeks. He told himself it was because he was busy with work and she with wedding plans, but he wasn't entirely sure that was true. Was she avoiding him?

He groaned. Would his intrusion on the wedding dinner add to the discomfort between him and Hannah? Why hadn't he paid closer attention to the time?

He hurried across the pasture and let himself out of the gate beside the stable, taking care to make certain the latch was closed behind him.

Several more buggies were coming up the lane behind the first one. There was no way that he could get out of the yard without being noticed.

He'd been such an idiot when he'd reached out and touched Hannah's hand in the restaurant. They'd been having such a good time. He couldn't remember a day when he'd enjoyed himself more. Taking her hand had felt so right, so natural, but it was *so* wrong. He could see that, looking back. A man didn't touch an Amish woman he wasn't closely related to. What must she have thought of him? He hadn't intended any disrespect. It had been a brief touch, but he couldn't get it out of his head and he couldn't stop remembering how warm and vibrant her hand had felt.

Albert didn't have all that much experience with the opposite sex, not as a young man, and certainly not in recent years, but he knew his own mind. He'd developed an affection for Hannah Yoder, a tender feeling that he'd never felt for another human being. He was afraid now that it was more than friendship, more than respect. After waiting his whole life for God to send him the right match—why had he opened his heart to a woman he couldn't have?

He strode purposefully across the yard toward his

truck and reached it with a sigh of relief, and put his hand on the door handle.

"Albert!"

He turned and forced a smile. "Hannah. How was the wedding?"

Her returning smile answered his question. "Good." She nodded. "Of all the men I could have chosen for my Rebecca, I believe Caleb will make her the happiest."

Hannah's gaze met his, and his heart leaped in his chest. He swallowed, wanting to congratulate her, afraid to break the first warm exchange they'd shared since he'd overstepped his bounds. "I... I'm glad," he mumbled. "I'm sorry. I was just leaving. I didn't expect to be here when..."

Hannah cut off his explanation with a gesture. "I'm so glad you are. I didn't want to bother you, but my friend Sara Yoder needs a vet." She motioned to a plump little woman in a lavender dress and black bonnet getting out of Charley's buggy. "Sara! Over here! This is Albert!"

As the woman walked toward them, Hannah went on to explain the problem. "Sara came for the wedding. Her van driver accidently stepped on her dog's foot. Molly won't put any weight on it, and Sara's afraid it might be broken."

"I'd be glad to take a look," Albert said.

"*Ya*. If you would."

Sara joined them, and Hannah quickly made the introductions.

Sara seemed a pleasant woman in a take-charge way, but Albert could barely take his eyes off Hannah. Maybe things would be all right between them, he thought hopefully. Maybe they could put that awkward moment behind them and go back to being friends. He didn't want to think about losing her.

"If you'd like to bring your pup out to the barn, I can have a look," Albert told Sara, glancing up as more buggies rolled into the barnyard.

"You'll have to excuse me, but I have to run," Hannah told Albert. "We have to have the food out before Rebecca and Caleb get here. "Don't worry, Sara," she reassured her friend. "Albert will take good care of Molly. He's the best."

"I'll see what I can do," he promised. "But if I suspect broken bones, I may have to take her to the clinic for an X-ray."

"Whatever it takes, Albert," Sara said. "I can pay. Molly is dear to me, even if she is just an animal."

"No need to talk about payment." Albert looked at the ground, knowing very well he couldn't just stand here and stare at Hannah. "You're Hannah's guest, and this is a special day for the family."

"Thank you, Albert," Hannah said with another smile. "I knew I could count on you." She started to walk away, then stopped and glanced back over her shoulder. "You are coming for supper with John and Grace and 'Kota tonight, aren't you?"

"I'm not sure if—"

"I won't take no for an answer," Hannah interrupted. "Spare ribs, beef brisket with sauerkraut and dumplings, leg of lamb, *hasenpfeffer,* and more shoofly pie than even you can eat."

Albert didn't know what to say. He'd been thinking of excuses, hadn't been certain that he would come with the family this evening. He didn't want to hurt Rebecca or Caleb's feelings, but he hadn't wanted to make Hannah uncomfortable by his presence.

A smile tilted the corner of Hannah's mouth. "Albert?"

"All right," he answered, knowing when he was beaten. How could anyone refuse Hannah when she was looking at him with those big, beautiful brown eyes? "I'll be here," he said. "Wouldn't miss it."

Twenty minutes later, Albert patted Molly's shaggy head and turned to Sara with a reassuring smile. "No serious damage done," he pronounced. Molly was a tricolored mixed breed, weighing about fifteen pounds, with a sweet nature. "She's more bruised than anything. She should be back to normal in a few days." He picked up the animal and handed her back to her owner.

Molly gave a small sound of pleasure, snuggled down in Sara's arms, and closed her eyes as Sara cradled the dog against her. "Thank you, Albert," she said. "It was kind of you to take the time to see her."

"You obviously take good care of her." The dog's muscle tone and weight were excellent, and he'd observed the thin scar that indicated that she'd been spayed. "Is she up to date on all her shots?"

"Ya," Sara replied. "She is."

"I wish all my clients showed as much care for their animals as you do," he said as they made their way out of the barn. "Well, I hope you enjoy your stay here in Delaware, and have a safe trip back to Wisconsin."

"Albert!" Charley called to him from the driveway. He was unloading two chairs from a wagon. "I've got to go back to Samuel's to pick up Miriam's *grossmama* and the twins. Would you mind carrying these around the house for me? Put them at the bridal table. They're gifts for Rebecca and Caleb."

"No problem," Albert said. The chairs were high-backed Windsors, fashioned of cherry. Ruth's husband, Eli Lapp, was a fine craftsman, so skilled that some of his furniture was sold in shops in Colonial Williamsburg. Albert had never thought much about buying good furniture, but these pieces, with care, would become heirlooms.

He carried the chairs, one in each arm carefully across the lawn to the shaded reception area. He'd never been invited to an Old Order Amish wedding celebration before, but Grace had explained the wedding dinner arrangements to him the previous night.

Just after dawn, volunteers had come to Hannah's to erect seven long tables under the trees on the lawn. If the weather hadn't cooperated, dinner would have had to be held inside, and the guests would have had to eat in shifts, but outside there was room for everyone to sit down at one time. One table, called the *eck,* was set at an angle under a spreading oak and decorated with an antique white-on-white hand-embroidered tablecloth, handmade candies and two fancy cakes. The bridal party, consisting of Rebecca, Caleb and two couples who served as their attendants would be seated there.

Teams of helpers had already set the tables with dishes, glassware and silverware. Now, those same helpers were busy carrying roasted chicken, duck and goose to the tables, along with bowls of mashed potatoes, turnips, green beans, peas and an assortment of yeast rolls and breads. Albert dodged one of the Beachy girls bearing a covered tureen of something that smelled delicious. He placed the two chairs next to four identical ones and looked around for Hannah. Then he wove past a bevy of young mothers with babies and started around the house to where he'd parked his truck.

As he came around the corner, Albert saw another table set with giant containers of lemonade, iced tea and sweet cider, and standing beside it was a smaller one holding empty pitchers. He stopped short, and his mouth gaped in surprise. It wasn't the liquid refreshments that caught his attention, but the young couple standing in front of it, lips locked together.

David King spotted Albert over Susanna's shoulder, gasped and stumbled backward, pulling her with him. The two of them fell against the drinks table, and as Albert darted toward them, one table leg collapsed and table, glass containers, tea, lemonade and cider all came crashing down. Susanna began to wail. David jumped up, looked frantically around and pulled her to her feet.

"Are you hurt?" Albert called, rushing to their sides.

Neither of them answered. Instead, David turned and fled, dragging a sobbing Susanna after him.

"Wait!" Albert looked from the fleeing pair to the wreckage in front of him. A gallon jug of iced tea had rolled, unbroken, across the grass to lodge against a maple tree trunk. An insulated drink cooler had fallen to the ground and was leaking what looked to be lemonade, but the rest of the drinks containers were a total loss.

"Was is do uff?" Hannah appeared at Albert's side. "What happened?" she cried, bringing her hands to her head. "Achh. What are we going to do? Rebecca and Caleb are about to be seated at the *eck*. I'll have nothing but water to offer our guests."

"It looks like a table leg gave way." Neither Susanna

nor David had appeared to have been hurt in the accident so he didn't think it necessary to tattle on them, at least not just yet. Not now in the midst of the celebration; it would ruin Hannah's day. "Let me handle this," he offered. "Go back to your guests. I'll find you more drinks."

"But how? We used all the tea and lemons in the house."

Albert was afraid Hannah was going to burst into tears. "It's not such a big thing," he soothed, resisting the urge to pat her arm. He'd made that kind of mistake once; he wouldn't do it again. "Go, and don't worry. I'll take care of it."

Hannah clasped her hands together. A wisp of reddish-brown hair had escaped from her *kapp* to fall across her forehead and he found himself wanting to touch it.

"Are you sure?" Despite her obvious capabilities and sensibility, she looked a little lost.

"I've got it under control," he assured her, thinking he would have done anything for her at this moment: fought a bull in a bullfighting ring, wrangled a herd of stampeding horses or walked to California to get more lemons for her lemonade.

She was still holding his gaze with hers.

He smiled and she smiled back and off she hurried.

Albert slipped his cell phone from his pocket. He punched in John's number and explained the emergency. "Ask one of the girls at the office to go for ice, juice, soda—root beer and grape, and a few cases of those fancy waters. I need everything ASAP. And lemons. And sugar—lots of everything."

"Grace is on her way home from class," John said. "I'll send her."

"Great. Thanks so much." Albert slid the phone back into his jeans pocket and set out to tackle the mess at his feet.

Fortunately, it took the dinner guests a little time to be seated, then Bishop Atlee's prayer was a long one. Grace arrived in less time than Albert would have thought possible, and he started squeezing lemons while she directed those women serving to carry trays of sodas and flavored water to the guests.

By three in the afternoon Grace was able to leave to pick up 'Kota from school, and shortly thereafter, Albert was on his way. Smiling to himself, he drove out of the yard. In a few hours, he'd be back to share another meal with Hannah, the bridal party, and their family, friends and neighbors. It wouldn't be soon enough to suit Albert, because in all the commotion, he'd missed his lunch again. Still, he felt good as he pulled onto the blacktop at the end of Hannah's lane.

The only thing that troubled him was wondering what to do about Susanna. Telling on her would mean upset for Hannah and for Susanna, but not telling might lead to bigger problems. The fact of the matter was, Hannah had a serious problem. Susanna wasn't like other girls her age. She was innocent in so many ways, but she was a grown woman in others. First Susanna was sneaking out in the middle of the night to be with a boy. Now she was kissing a boy. It was his duty to tell her mother what he'd seen, wasn't it?

Albert rubbed his chin and realized that it was bristly.

"First thing I have to do is shower and shave," he mur-

mured aloud. "That and have a good talk with the Lord."
Sometimes, life threw questions at a man he couldn't
answer. And then the best thing—the only thing—to
do was to take it to the Almighty in prayer.

Chapter Ten

At eight-fifteen the following morning Hannah walked out onto the back porch, saw Albert's truck parked by the stable door, and went to find him. She hadn't gotten to bed until late the previous night, but she'd slept in until six-thirty, which was a luxury. Usually, in spring and summer, she was up before the sun. The nice thing was that the house was absolutely quiet this morning, something she'd rarely experienced in all the years it had been her home.

Hannah's houseguest, Sara, had walked across the field to have breakfast with Lydia Byler. Susanna had left after the wedding supper with her sister Anna to sleep over, and Irwin was fishing today. As for the newlyweds, contrary to the usual custom of spending their wedding night at the bride's parents', they'd chosen to bundle Caleb's small, sleepy daughter into their buggy and return to their own home shortly after nine the previous night.

Tired but pleased by how well Rebecca's wedding had gone, Hannah couldn't help feeling a little guilty by how relieved she was that she'd found good husbands for all of her marriageable daughters. It had been her prayer for so many years. Now it had been fulfilled. But the niggling worry over Susanna was still there.

Hannah had kept an eye on her at the reception and later at the supper and the barn games that followed that the young people so enjoyed. Susanna had seemed to enjoy herself as much as anyone, but she and David King had barely glanced at one another. Was it too much to hope that they had grown bored with each other's company? So, life was good this morning, and she had much to be thankful for.

Albert Hartman was one of those blessings, and she wanted to thank him for his help the previous day. She didn't know why she'd panicked at so small a thing as an upset drink table, but at the time, it had seemed like a disaster. Mercifully, Albert had been there to take over. When she'd gone into the kitchen, she'd found him and Grace happily squeezing bags of lemons. Albert had heated the lemon juice and stirred in the sugar before pouring the mixture over blocks of ice, creating the best lemonade Hannah had ever tasted. And he'd brought bottles of fruit juice and the other drinks. There had been so much left over, even after supper, that she'd have plenty to take to church and share on the next worship Sunday. She had thanked him last night when he had left with his family, but she wanted to thank him again. He really had gone beyond what most would have done. Especially with him being male. Hannah didn't know a single man in her family who would have taken on the job so good-naturedly or with such success.

Hannah found Albert cleaning out the alpacas' water trough in the loafing shed. A circle of alpacas stood motionless a few yards away, ears perked and wide-eyed, watching his every movement. Every time Hannah looked at the animals, she wanted to laugh. They didn't look real; they were more like children's stuffed toys.

She had learned from Albert that alpacas were domesticated animals from the camel family, and originated in South America. They looked like llamas, but were smaller and cuter, in Hannah's opinion, with fluffy heads and bodies. They came in colors ranging from white to very dark brown and Albert's herd represented a variety of colors.

"Good morning!" Hannah called as she stepped through the doorway of the stable. At the sound of her voice, one of the alpaca females whirled around and trotted out into the pasture, followed by all the rest. "Sorry," Hannah said, watching them go. "Didn't mean to frighten them away."

Albert stood and wiped his wet hands on his pant legs. He looked especially nice this morning. He was freshly shaven and his hair, which had recently been cut, was neatly combed. He was wearing a new long-sleeved chambray shirt over tan twill trousers and leather boots. He had rolled up his sleeves, and Hannah couldn't help noticing how muscular his arms were.

Not proper thoughts for a respectable widow, she mentally chided herself. Unfortunately, although she could control her speech, there was little she could do about her sometimes wayward thoughts. She was approaching fifty, but she wasn't blind or in her grave.

"Don't worry about it." He smiled at her in a way that warmed her heart. "I think it's a game they play. I doubt they're nearly as frightened of us as they pretend to be."

"I think they can be brave if they need to be," Hannah agreed. "My friend said that her herd regularly chases coyotes away from the livestock. Some of her neighbors are buying alpacas instead of guard dogs."

"Maybe we should tell Tim Fisher. He lost two lambs to stray dogs last month." Albert opened the valve that would let water into the trough. The windmill pumped fresh water from the well to the house as well as to the barns. He folded his arms and leaned back against an upright post. "It was a nice wedding supper, Hannah. I ate so much, I don't think I'll eat again for a week." He patted his abdomen.

She chuckled. She liked the idea of providing Albert with good, home-cooked meals. Every man who worked as hard as he did deserved to be well fed. "I doubt that. I know what an appetite you have."

He grimaced in mock shame and glanced down at the ground. "Guilty as charged."

"I wanted to thank you for yesterday—for the drinks—the lemonade especially. You're a good friend."

He stepped away from the post and his posture stiffened. "I like to think so."

Albert's forehead creased and his expression grew serious, making Hannah think that there was something more he wanted to say and was finding it difficult.

"I mean it, Albert. I don't know what I would have done about replacing the drinks without delaying dinner and risking the food getting cold. I know it's prideful, but I'd have been embarrassed to serve nothing more than water."

He held up his hand. "Say no more about it. You would have made do, Hannah. I have every confidence that no one would have gone thirsty at your table."

She smiled, secretly pleased at his praise. "Thank you."

He glanced at the ground, then back up at her. "You may not be thanking me when I tell you what I saw yesterday. It's not my place to interfere in your family, but…" He hesitated.

She didn't like the look on his face. It was something awful. She could see that.

He closed the distance between them, his gaze meeting hers. "Hannah, the table with the drinks didn't just fall on its own," he said quietly. "I'm sure the one leg wasn't properly locked in place, as I mentioned before, but it fell because David and Susanna backed into it." He seemed to hold his breath. "They were kissing, Hannah. I came around the corner and surprised them. Kissing."

She caught the corner of her apron and clasped it tightly in her fist. "Kissing?" She thought for a moment, glancing at the ground, then back at him. There had been a minor kissing incident with Susanna and David before, but she thought she had nipped that in the bud. "Like, on the cheek?"

"No," he answered firmly. She saw his face redden. "More like kissing-kissing. A little awkward, but it definitely wasn't the first time for either of them."

"Oh, my." Hannah's knees felt weak. With a sharp inhale, she sank onto a bale of straw that stood by the shed door. "This is a bad thing, Albert." She shook her head. "A really bad thing."

"I'm sorry to be the bearer of bad news. I didn't want to trouble you with it yesterday. I wondered if it was my place to tell you, at all." He hesitated. "But, Hannah, if Susanna was my daughter and you had seen what I saw, I would have wanted you to tell me."

She looked up at him. "*Ne,* thank you. You were right to come to me with this." She shook her head again. "I'm such a fool. I thought maybe, *hoped* she had gotten over him." She lifted her hands and let them fall into her lap. "But obviously she hasn't."

"Is it such a terrible thing, Hannah?" He was standing close, his eyes clouded with compassion. "Kissing a boy?"

Hannah clasped her hands tightly. "There *is* a place for kissing, Albert. That place is in marriage. For Susanna and David to behave like a married couple is inappropriate." She pressed her hand to her forehead. "Not to mention dangerous." She glanced up at him. "You and I both know what other behavior it could lead to."

"She's a good girl."

"*Ya,* Susanna is a good girl, but her judgment isn't sound. Grace's 'Kota is a good boy, but you wouldn't hand him the keys to your truck and let him drive down Route 13. He's not ready for such responsibility any more than Susanna is ready to play flirting games with boys."

He was quiet for a minute, letting her think, which she appreciated. It didn't feel awkward, the silence between them. It was comforting to Hannah to have his opinion and offer hers. It had been a long time since she'd been able to talk to a man this way. Not since Jonas.

"What will you do about it?" Albert finally asked, taking a seat beside her on the bale. He was close, but not so close that his clothing or a knee or elbow touched hers.

"I don't know. I honestly don't know." She looked at her hands in her lap. "I'll speak to the two of them, of course. And David's parents must be told." Her throat felt scratchy as if she were about to burst into tears, but she wouldn't give in to emotion. "It can't happen again."

"Do you think this is happening because you've tried to keep them apart?" Albert asked hesitantly.

"I haven't been trying to keep them apart." She was quiet for a second. "Not really."

"Do *they* think you're trying to keep them apart?" He asked, then went on. "Have you considered that Susanna may know her own heart? What if she and David really are in love?"

Hannah frowned. "Susanna is too immature to understand that kind of love." She shook off his argument like stray raindrops. "I know my own child."

"Maybe," he answered, his voice gentle. "But what if Susanna isn't a child anymore?"

As she crossed the field to Anna and Samuel's farmhouse, the clouds overhead thickened and Hannah heard the rumble of thunder in the distance. She wondered if she should have taken the time to hitch the horse up to the buggy, but Anna's home was so close and David's parents not much farther in the opposite direction. It had seemed a waste. Besides, even if she did get wet, walking would ease some of her pent-up tension.

She couldn't get Albert's words out of her head. *What if Susanna isn't a child anymore?*

He was wrong, of course; he didn't know her well enough to understand. He only saw Susanna occasionally, in specific circumstances. Anyone who lived with her day in and day out would understand how unprepared she was for the responsibility of marriage, for running a household. Anyone who knew her as Hannah did would know she didn't understand the feelings that could exist between a man and a woman.

But doubt nudged at Hannah's conscience. What if her judgment was clouded by a mother's desire to protect her special-needs child? What if Albert was right and she was the one who wasn't seeing the situation clearly?

Hannah didn't know what to do with that notion, so for practicality's sake, she pushed it aside.

She would collect her wayward daughter, the daughter who'd been so well-behaved yesterday, at least when her mother was watching. And they would talk about what Albert had witnessed. Together, they would go to David's and speak with him and his parents. Somehow, they had to find a solution—a solution that didn't involve any more illicit kissing.

"Oh, Susanna," she fretted aloud.

Susanna and David knew better. Their parents had taught them better. Their community had rules and standards, and a member had to abide by those conventions or risk censuring, even shunning.

Hannah walked faster, pumping her arms, her bonnet strings flying behind her. The problem was that Susanna could be so obstinate. And something told her that her daughter had already made up her mind about David. So how in the name of decency was she going to stop Susanna's inappropriate behavior?

Late that afternoon, as rain pelted the windows and drummed on the porch roof, Hannah sat drinking herbal tea at her own kitchen table with her friend Sara. A chastened Susanna had come home, spent an hour in her library, and then hurried upstairs to her bedroom.

David, when Hannah had last seen him, had been shoveling out his mother's chicken house. He might still be at the task for all she knew.

"Sara, how could I have been so foolish?" Hannah asked. She felt as limp and powerless as a wet dishtowel when it was wrung out and hung up to dry. "To let it go on under my own nose—to not put two and two together?" She'd told Sara the whole unpleasant story, not about just the kissing, but the incident with the pony cart, and Susanna's recent rebellions and sullen stubbornness.

Although many miles separated them, Hannah had always considered Sara one of her dearest friends. They were close in age and both widowed. Through letters, phone calls and occasional visits, the two had remained close over the years. Sara was the kind of friend that, when they did come face-to-face, it was as if they had left off talking the day before. Sara was sensible and plain-spoken. Hannah didn't have to tiptoe around her, and she knew that any advice offered would be sound.

Sara nodded sympathetically and poured more tea from a pretty blue-and-white porcelain teapot. Sara preferred tea to coffee, and Hannah had made certain she had a good supply of her friend's favorites in the cupboard before her arrival.

"Did they try to deny what they'd been up to?" Sara asked, her plump, red-brown face shiny with concern. "Or did they own up to the mischief?" Her sloe-black eyes narrowed shrewdly.

Hannah grimaced. "Susanna tried to pretend she had no idea what I was talking about, but David turned red as a pickled beet and started to cry."

"What did his parents say?"

"They were shocked, naturally. Ebben, David's father, was angry. Apparently, David's never been a problem for them, not until my daughter came along, at least. Lately, there's been some misbehavior in their household, too. Apparently, David's been here without permission several times. Times when he led us to believe that his parents were aware of where he was. The two of them, Susanna and David, have been misleading us all."

"Young people," Sara said kindly. "It happens."

Hannah sighed audibly, her heart going out to Sadie and Ebben. "It can't be easy for them. They're new to our community, and trouble is the last thing they want." Hannah raised her cup to her lips and then put it back in the saucer untouched. She hesitated before speaking again. "Do you know what Sadie said?" Sara was listening intently; Hannah went on, "That we should consider letting them walk out together. Like any boy and girl. With proper courting rules."

"So," Sara pursed her lips. "What do you think of that?"

Hannah met her friend's penetrating gaze. "I didn't want to hurt their feelings, so I said I would think on the matter, but the idea is…it's impossible."

"Why impossible?" Sara broke off a piece of gingerbread and popped it into her mouth.

"To what end?" Hannah opened her arms and let her hands rest on the table again. "You know Susanna. And you've met David. There can be no real courting between them. Courting is done with the intention of marriage."

Sara slowly chewed her gingerbread and sipped her tea.

"You think I'm being overprotective." It was a statement, not a question. Hannah swallowed. The ginger-bread smelled delicious, but she couldn't eat a bite. Her stomach was still doing flip-flops. "I've always tried to treat Susanna the same as her sisters, but she *isn't* the same. There's so much about the world that she doesn't understand. That she'll never understand."

"It's a natural thing for young women to be attracted to men," Sara said. "And Susanna has watched every one of her sisters court and marry. Why wouldn't she think the same opportunity is available to her?"

"Because I've told her it isn't," Hannah said, firmly.

"And did that work?" Sara smiled and went on. "We can't help how we feel, Hannah. And God meant us to marry. Each and every one of us."

"You think marriage is the answer to everything." Their gazes met again, and Hannah realized how harsh that must have sounded to her friend. "I'm sorry, Sara. I didn't mean to snap at you." She pressed her lips tightly together, truly unsure as to what to do. It was times like this that she so missed the companionship of a husband. This had been so much easier when there had been two of them to make these kinds of decisions. "What do I do?" she asked softly. "I don't know how to protect Susanna, but still do what's right."

Sara didn't answer right away. Instead, she let Hannah's question hang in the air. She bit off another piece of gingerbread, chewed slowly and sipped more tea. "Maybe you should consider the Kings' suggestion," she said after several minutes passed. "Because, you know how stubborn Susanna can be. And frankly, short of locking her in the attic or sending her to Brazil, how *would* you keep them apart?"

Hannah shrugged. "Sadie thinks that might be the

root of all the sneaking around." Albert had said the same thing, but she didn't bring that up. "The more Sadie's tried to steer David away from Susanna, the more insistent he's become."

Hannah fiddled with her teaspoon. "It's all my fault. When David first came to Seven Poplars, I encouraged the friendship. I wanted Susanna to have a companion like her. I knew she was lonely, I—" She shook her head. "It never occurred to me that this could happen."

Sara sliced another sliver of gingerbread from the serving plate.

"Maybe Sadie's right. Maybe we've driven them to this." Hannah added more sugar to her tea. "But is letting them go to singings and young people's frolics really a solution?"

"I think it's an idea worth considering. If they were officially courting, the whole community would be chaperoning them. It's the way things are done for a reason, Hannah." Sara rose from the table and walked to the rocking chair where her Molly was curled up on an old blanket. Sara stroked the dog's head and rubbed her silky ears.

Hannah sighed. "Maybe you're right. I don't know. I just don't know."

"Then you must pray for an answer," Sara said. "I find that most problems are settled by prayer." She smiled. Her teeth were very white and even. Sara had a lovely smile. It was one of her best features. "He has a plan for each of us, although sometimes, it may seem to us that the path is rocky or muddy. We must have faith, Hannah."

"I try." Hannah took a sip of the tea and made a face. "But I have to admit, I find this tea bitter."

Sara laughed. "So, I'll make you some coffee. I'm not offended. To each her own. But I think we're a lot more alike than different. We are both accustomed to getting our way, and it's hard to give up control, even to a higher power."

"Or in this case, a wayward daughter." Hannah smiled back at Sara and reached for the gingerbread. She'd have a small piece. She hadn't eaten anything since breakfast. Maybe going without her midday meal was what had made her so jittery. "I'm so glad you're here," she said, purposely changing the subject. "Just thinking about the possibility of having you for a neighbor, it would be wonderful, Sara. Wisconsin is so far away."

"I have to say, I like your community and having you nearby would make settling in so much easier. The longer I'm in Seven Poplars, the more I think the Lord might be calling me here." She adjusted her white *kapp*, almost identical to Hannah's. "I've never gotten used to the Wisconsin winters. We had snow up to my shoulders in February and temperatures of thirty below."

"Brrr. I can't imagine." Hannah got up to make a pot of coffee. "You may want to have a look at the property next to Caleb and Rebecca's. The house is one story with modern appliances. It was an English house, so you'd need to have the electricity removed, but Caleb says the stove and water heater are propane. There's a pellet stove that heats most of the house, which would work for you."

"How much land?"

"Seven acres, maybe a little less, but there are some outbuildings. The garage might do for your horse and buggy. And there's another house on our road. It's about a half mile from here, on the right. It has less land, but the house is—" A knock at the kitchen door drew her attention. She crossed the room and glanced through the window. "Oh, it's Albert." She opened the door. "Albert, hello, come in."

He stepped into the kitchen, his dark green rain slicker dripping, saw Sara and stopped short. "Sorry, Hannah, I didn't mean to interrupt." He tugged off his ball cap. "Hello, Sara."

She nodded. "Albert."

"How's Molly doing?"

"Much better today," Sara said. "As you said, a few days of rest and she'll be her old self."

"I didn't mean to intrude." Albert looked to Hannah, his face reddening. "I was feeding... I was wondering how you... I knew that you were upset about Susanna," he continued as he backed out onto the porch. "I just wanted to see if you were..."

Hannah followed him onto the porch. Rain fell, making it seem later than five o'clock. Still, it was time she got an evening meal together. "Thank you, Albert. It's kind of you to be concerned for me and my family."

He retreated down the steps to the yard. "It'll be all right. With Susanna. You're a good mother, Hannah. The best. Susanna will be fine."

She thanked him again and returned to the kitchen. Sara had returned to her place at the table and had picked up her knitting bag. She was working on a small navy mitten.

"Albert is the one who caught Susanna and David kissing," Hannah explained.

Sara raised one dark eyebrow quizzically. "So you told me."

"He's a good friend," Hannah added.

"I can tell." She cut her dark eyes at Hannah. "Are you and Albert courting?"

"Courting?" Hannah's eyes widened with surprise. "*Courting?* Of course, not. I told you, he's a friend. He…he comes by so often because… Well, to look after the alpacas."

"Mmm-hmm." Sara studied her. "But I see the way he looks at you. Whatever you feel for this man, he considers you more than a friend."

"That can't be," Hannah protested, her thoughts immediately racing back to the restaurant, where Albert had taken her hand. And how she had felt when he touched her. She knew her face was turning red. She could feel the heat. "*Ne.* You're mistaken, Sara—" She was so flustered that she was having a hard time finding her tongue. She turned to the sink, embarrassed. "He…he's not Plain. It would never—"

"You were once Mennonite, weren't you?"

"*Ya,* but I could never…" She let her sentence trail off as she slowly turned to face her friend again.

"Maybe you could and maybe you couldn't," Sara replied, shrugging her broad shoulders, "but men and women, that's one thing I understand." She scrutinized Hannah with her dark eyes. "I'm glad you brought this up, because I wanted to talk to you about your situation. You've been alone too long. Whether it be Albert Hartman or someone else, it's high time you married."

Chapter Eleven

All Hannah could do for a moment was shake her head. *"Ne, ne,"* she stammered. "You must have misunderstood. Albert doesn't—"

"Mam!" Susanna pounded down the staircase. *"Mam,* there's a van." She skipped past Hannah and Sara to the window. "Look!" She pointed. "It a blue van."

Sara got to her feet. "It's about time. I expected them an hour ago."

Hannah joined Susanna at the window. Through the rain, she could see an English man come around the vehicle.

Hannah glanced back at Sara and nodded. *"Ya,* this must be your Ellie," she said as she went out onto the porch. Susanna and Sara followed.

"Is this the Yoder place?" the man called.

"Ya!" Sara answered. "You're at the right house."

They watched as he opened the sliding door of the van, removed a white plastic stool and set it on the driveway. The driver went around to the back of the van and lifted out a black suitcase, then hurried back to the sliding door where he opened a big black umbrella.

A small figure in a black Amish bonnet, white prayer *kapp* and black cape stepped down onto the stepstool and then onto the ground. She waved toward the house. "Sara! I'm here! I made it."

Sara laughed and waved Ellie in. "Don't be shy, girl. Come and get in out of the rain."

Ellie laughed and trudged across the muddy yard toward the porch steps, trying to stay under the umbrella the man carried.

"She's a *kinder,*" Susanna exclaimed, clapping her hands.

"Ne," Sara corrected gently. "Ellie is not a child. She's twenty-three, a year older than you."

"Ellie is a little person," Hannah explained. She gave Susanna a look and put her finger to her lips. "I expect you to be on your best behavior and make her welcome in our home."

"I will, *Mam,*" Susanna promised. A wide smile split her face. "She can sleep in my room."

At the steps, the man slid the suitcase onto the porch and handed Ellie the umbrella. They exchanged a few words, then he tipped his hat to the women on the porch and hurried back across the wet yard to his van.

"Wilkom, Ellie," Sara said. "We wondered when you'd get here. How was your trip?" She took the black suitcase. "And your mother?"

"Gut, gut," Ellie replied with a dimpled smile as she took the porch steps, one at a time. "We got a late start from the Shetlers' because the van wouldn't start. He called AAA and an Englisher garage man came, but he didn't have a new battery. Andy Shetler told him he should have had a mule because they don't need batteries." She chuckled as she folded her umbrella and

leaned it against the outside kitchen wall. "We got here to Kent County and then the driver had some trouble finding Leroy Hostetler's to drop off their cousins, but finding you was easy after that."

Hannah returned the smile. She liked the cheerful blue-eyed girl at once. "All that way you came. Sara said you live near her in Wisconsin."

"Ya," Ellie replied as they trooped into the kitchen. "But I came just from Pennsylvania today. The driver's already headed back to Wisconsin, picking up a family in Ohio on his way."

"We'll have supper in just a bit," Hannah said, after introductions and greetings were exchanged all around. "But first I think you'd best get into some dry things." She motioned to Susanna. "Can you take our guest to her room show her where to put her belongings?"

"Ya," Ellie agreed as she pushed a dripping lock of hair off her forehead. "I do need to *rett up* a bit before I'm fit for your kitchen."

Susanna nodded shyly.

"Will you be my first new friend in Delaware?" Ellie asked her.

"Ya." Susanna nodded. "I will be your friend. Come on!" Grinning, she led Ellie away toward the back of the house.

"She's lovely," Hannah said to Sara. "But are you certain that…"

"She'll find a good match, being so small?" Sara brushed a wrinkle out of her apron. "Just wait and see."

Albert had lured Nina over to the side of the stall with bits of carrot and was now stroking her back. She was turning out to be the friendliest of the herd, so far. Or at least the bravest. "Do you like that, girl?" he asked. The feel of the fleece, so soft and thick, never failed to amaze him. His love of animals had been a passion in his life since he was a young child, but the joy these alpacas gave him was a thrill of which he never tired. It was so peaceful here in Hannah's barn with the rain drumming on the roof. Albert suspected he should have felt guilty for leaving work early—something he rarely allowed himself, but he didn't. Here in the peace of the barn, he could feel the tension of the day's stress draining out of him.

Abruptly, Nina raised her head and stared past Albert. At almost the same instant, he became aware of the soft tread of footsteps. The alpaca flicked her ears, wrinkled her nose and retreated a few steps, just out of reach.

"Albert?" It was Hannah's friend, Sara.

"Yes," he answered, turning to face her. He couldn't imagine why she would seek him out. "Molly's okay, isn't she?"

Sara nodded. "*Ya,* all is well with her. I saw your truck was still here and I wanted to speak with you." Her tone was frank, not abrasive, but more direct than that of most Amish women with whom he came in contact.

He regarded her with curiosity.

"You and my cousin Hannah are friends, *ya?*" she asked.

Albert slid his thumbs into his pants pockets and nodded. "We are."

She took a step closer. She was plump and no taller

than five-one or five-two, but she had a way of commanding the space around her. This woman was a force to be reckoned with.

"Are you a man of faith, Albert Hartman?" she asked.

Albert blinked. *Faith?* He nodded again. "Yes, I think I am." Where was Sara going with this?

"Gut." She smiled at him with an expression of approval that lit her strong, plain face with an inner light. "And are you are a single man who is unmarried and has given no pledge to any woman?"

"Sara, I don't—"

She cut him off. *"Ne,* Albert. Hear me out." She slipped into the *Deitsch* dialect that he understood perfectly. "It is clear to me that you are very fond of our Hannah."

"Of course, I am." He glanced nervously away, and then back at her. "I have the greatest respect for Hannah."

Tiny lines crinkled at the corners of Sara's dark eyes. "How deep does this *fondness* go?"

"I... I'm not sure how to answer that question."

"Albert, do you know what I do?" Sara chuckled and rested her fists against ample hips. "How I make my living?"

"I don't. Hannah mentioned that you were widowed. I suppose I assumed—"

"That my husband left me well provided for?" She shrugged and made a gesture with both hands that could have been amusement or complete agreement.

Again, Albert found himself perplexed by this unusual visitor that seemed so similar to all the Amish women he'd known, and yet not, with her very non-

German features and her deep honey-brown skin. "I suppose I did," he answered.

"I am twice-widowed," she said. "And both my late husbands were blessed with substantial material possessions. But I have always been a woman who wanted to maintain a state of independence, and so I have my own trade." She chuckled and Albert saw that her teeth were white and even. "I am a matchmaker, Albert," she explained. "I specialize in arranging marriages among the Amish." Sara searched for the right way to continue. "For those women who, for whatever reason, have found it difficult to make their own matches."

"A marriage broker?" He could hardly believe it. An Amish matchmaker? He'd never heard of such a thing. It was true that most Old Order Amish women married, regardless of looks or disposition. But it had never occurred to him that such a service existed.

"*Ya,* it is what I do, and God has seen it to bless my efforts. No case is too difficult if my clients are willing to listen to reason. Naturally, you wouldn't know of my work or others like me. What I do is private, though well respected. It is a profession that stretches back centuries, to the Old World of Austria and Switzerland. But it isn't a tradition we care to share with the Englishers. Too often, they like to seize on every aspect of our private lives and call us quaint and old-fashioned."

Albert got the impression he was just supposed to listen, but not respond.

"You may know of one match I arranged. Aunt Jezzy, Hannah's mother-in-law's sister."

"Yes, I know Jezzy, but I thought—"

Again, Sara chuckled. "You think that a woman of Jezzy's age and shy nature would suddenly meet and be swept off her feet by an equally shy man who just happened to live nine miles away?" She folded her arms over her bosom. "A very good match, if I do say so myself."

He couldn't imagine where this was going. "You're telling me that you are paid to bring couples together, sort of like a horse-and-buggy dating service?"

Sara pursed her lips. "Not dating, Albert, *matchmaking*. I make marriages for people, solid marriages."

"But what does this have to do with me?" he blurted.

"Exactly what I was getting to. I need to know your intentions." Sara's dark, piercing eyes locked with his. "Speak up," she insisted, though she really hadn't given him the time to respond. "There can be no shyness between us if this is to work. Now, be honest with me. How deeply does this fondness for Hannah Yoder run? Could you see yourself as her husband?"

For a moment he was so astounded by what she said that he couldn't find his voice. "I—I'm Mennonite. She's Amish." He shook his head. "I assumed..." He met her gaze. "Surely, that would be impossible, wouldn't it?"

"Please answer the question," she said. "A simple *ya* or *ne* will do. Could you see the two of you as man and wife?"

He took a step backward. Wiped his mouth with his hand. "Maybe." He looked at his boots, suddenly as uncomfortable as he had ever been in his life. He knew his face had to be bright red. "I... I'm not sure," he mumbled. "I... I care for Hannah, but the differences in our faiths make it—"

"Albert Hartman. No wonder you've never married. You look for the negative rather than the positive. It is rare for people to meet someone who touches their heart. You and Hannah obviously have."

He lifted his gaze from his boots to Sara's face. His heart was now pounding. "Hannah would never—"

"Tish!" Sara gave a sound of impatience. "Didn't you just tell me that you were a man of faith?"

"Yes, but…" He grimaced. "Why are we having this conversation? I don't even know if she likes me *that* way. She and I have never discussed courting."

"Exactly my point. You haven't considered the possibility. So you sit there like a stump, enduring your loneliness, living a life that's only half-full when someone like Hannah—who is as lonely as you—longs for the love and companionship that you both deserve." She threw up her arms. "Show that faith you profess. Take a chance on being rejected. What do you have to lose?"

"What are you saying?" he asked, knowing what he thought she meant, but certain he had misunderstood somewhere along the way.

She blinked, shaking her head. "I'm saying, Albert, that you should court Hannah so you can get to know each other. Although from what I gather, you've already been seeing a good deal of each other."

"But how could we ever— I'm a veterinarian. Amish men don't become veterinarians."

"There you go trying to put the cart before the horse again. First see if this is something you both want. If it is, drop to your knees and pray to the Almighty to show you how to accomplish it. You can't surrender without even trying, or can you?"

He stared at the loose straw at his feet. "I have prayed for someone," he admitted. The warmth in his cheeks now seemed to be spreading through his whole body.

"I've wondered why it is that other people find someone, but never me."

"Do you believe that the Lord should drag you to the right woman by the scruff of your neck? Don't you think that He expects you to make an effort?" She made a dismissive sniff. "Make a start here and now. Come to the house and join us at the table. Show Hannah that you are interested in her in an honorable way and see where God's mercy leads you." Sara folded her plump arms. "Of course, she may reject you as she has rejected other suitors, but you'll never know unless you try."

"What if *I'm* not certain?"

"Then standing here will never help you to make up your mind. Fear, Albert. You've let fear and doubt rule your mind. You and Hannah must take a good look at each other."

"I can't just invite myself to her table," he protested weakly. Even as he spoke the words, he knew he would come. He couldn't not come if there was a chance that Sara was right—that there might be a way that he and Hannah could be together, if she cared for him as much as he cared for her.

Sara tilted her head and arched one dark eyebrow. "Oh, you won't be." A smile teased the corners of her mouth. "She sent me out here to ask you to share our meal."

Somehow, Hannah got through supper, although if her life had depended on it, she couldn't have said what she served or ate. Through the entire meal, she kept thinking of how foolish it was that she'd allowed Sara to talk her into inviting Albert. Where was her head? It had been one thing to invite him to eat with them when he was just a friend of the family, but now that Sara had come straight out and asked if they were courting, it seemed entirely different. It *felt* different. Hannah knew she was in over her head. She was a good swimmer, but she'd never gone into the ocean during a riptide, and that's what this felt like.

From grace to dessert she was giddy and *doplich*. Clumsy. She tried to pour sweet tea for Albert, missed and soaked his hand and the ivory-colored tablecloth. Then, carrying a blue-willow dish of flower-shaped butter pats that had been leftover from the wedding meal, she'd let the plate slip though her fingers and crash onto the floor.

Albert, true to form, had helped clean up the broken china and ruined butter, but she had been mortified. What must Sara's friend Ellie think of her? Hannah knew she was behaving as foolish as a teenager at her first singing with a boy. And she felt like it inside: excited and scared at the same time and trying hard not to show it.

As everyone talked and ate, Hannah told herself over and over that she would not, *could not,* seriously consider Albert as a suitor. So why did the forbidden thought keep bubbling up? There was no getting around it. She, practical Hannah, mother of eight, nine if you counted Irwin, was suddenly an emotional mess over a man.

Somehow, they all got through supper. Dessert and coffee were served and neither Ellie nor Susanna seemed to notice that anything was amiss. As for Irwin, so long as his plate was full, he wouldn't have noticed if the bishop had ridden a cow into the kitchen with a colander on his head and delivered a sermon. Whatever Albert thought of her capricious behavior, he was too much of a gentleman to let it show.

"Well, I guess I'd best be getting home." Albert got up and carried his plate and silverware to the sink where Hannah was standing. "It was a pleasure meeting you, Ellie. I hope you like Seven Poplars."

"I think I will," she replied. Ellie had already begun to help clear the table as if she were part of the family, further endearing her to Hannah. "Everyone here seems so nice," she added.

Albert slowly turned his gaze to Hannah.

Hannah glanced at the floor, then at the dishcloth in her hand and then at Sara. She wanted to look anywhere but at Albert. She could feel her cheeks growing warm again. *What's wrong with me?* Maybe what she needed was a good dose of peppermint tea. Peppermint was good for calming both a queasy stomach and an agitated mind.

"Hannah."

She started. Albert's voice was unusually firm. "Yes?" she said.

"Could I speak with you? Alone." He glanced at Sara and the others. "It was good seeing everyone. If you'll excuse us."

Hannah didn't know what to say. Her tongue stuck to the roof of her mouth. Her feet were anchored to the floor. She clenched the dishcloth so tightly that water dripped on her apron. He must have noticed there was something wrong at supper. Now he was going to ask. She couldn't very well tell him the truth, and embarrass herself further. Risk embarrassing him. What was she going to say? She slowly let the dishrag fall from her fingertips to land in the sink.

"Hannah, will you walk outside with me?" Albert asked. It was a question, but his tone surprised her. He wasn't really asking so much as telling her.

She left the comfort of the sink and followed him across the kitchen. She allowed him to open the screen door for her and to steady her arm as they went down the porch steps. The rain had stopped, but it was very humid.

"Albert, I..." She... What? What was she going to say to him? How could she explain her flustered behavior? Did she come right out and tell him what Sara had asked? Maybe then they would both laugh together over it and she'd stop feeling so foolish. "Albert, I should..."

"Hannah, don't talk." He seemed to tower over her. Had she noticed how much taller he was than her before this? "Please," he said, "I need you to listen to what I have to say before I lose my nerve."

His words immediately caught her attention. And something about the tone of his voice. She was getting that giddy feeling again.

They were standing by the gatepost, within arm's reach but not touching. She raised her head and looked into his eyes. For an instant, there in the fading twilight, she felt the jolt of his intense gaze. And then, before she could react, she got a face full of raindrops as another shower swept over them in a drenching wave.

Albert grabbed her hand. "Quick!" he said. "Into the truck!" He dashed across the yard, pulling her with him.

Hannah's heart was suddenly pounding. He was holding her hand! She knew that it was wrong, but it was impossible to break free. The wicked truth was, she didn't want to be free. Suddenly having Albert's big hand wrapped firmly around hers was as sweet as the smell of newly baked bread. Laughing, she threw caution to the wind and ran after him. She didn't care about the rain, didn't care if her children and guests were watching, didn't care if she was breaking every rule she'd lived by for more than thirty years.

He was laughing, too, as he flung open the vehicle door, caught her by the waist, and lifted her inside. She scooted over on the seat, and he scrambled up, slamming the door behind him. Rain beat at the windows, shutting them away from the world in a private place.

Hannah's *kapp* was soaked. Her hair dripped onto her wet skin and wetter clothing, but it was a warm summer rain and she was too happy to care. She felt the strength in Albert's broad hand and glanced down to see that his fingers were locked around hers. A strong hand, firm and warm. But a lifetime of modest behavior intervened. "Albert, you shouldn't be... We can't..." She knew she should untangle his grasp, but it felt so good, so safe that she didn't know if she had the strength. "Albert," she began softly, "this isn't proper."

He nodded, both his mouth and eyes smiling. He cleared his throat and his expression turned serious. "We aren't kids."

"*Ne,* we aren't." He hadn't let go. Her heart was still racing, her breath coming in short gasps. Could he feel her trembling? Thunder rumbled nearby, and it grew darker outside the cab. The rain came harder, and their breath was beginning to fog the windows. Hannah was aware of Albert's clean, manly scent, of wet leather boots, the faint smell of shaving cream, and the sweet odors of alpaca feed and timothy hay. She blinked back raindrops in an attempt to clear her vision. Albert filled it.

"I hope you won't be offended, but I… I have to say this," he said. "It's obvious to me that the two of us are attracted to each other." He took a deep breath. Exhaled. "Am I right?"

Hannah was surprised by Albert's forwardness. But maybe a little relieved. This was the chance for her to deny everything, to tell him that he was mistaken, that theirs was a friendship only. But she couldn't. She couldn't lie to Albert and she couldn't lie to herself. It was her turn to take a breath and find her courage. "*Ya,* Albert. I think so."

"You *think* or you *know?*" His eyes narrowed—large, brown, beautiful eyes, eyes that held her and took her breath away. "I don't think I'm imagining things. You care for me, Hannah."

She nodded, pressing her lips together. "I do."

"Good," he pronounced. "Because I care for you, too. A great deal." He hesitated, then went on. "So the question is, what are we going to do about it?"

She tore her gaze from his and murmured, "There's nothing we *can* do."

"We can't jump to that conclusion right away." He squeezed her hand harder, and a sensation of tingling warmth ran up her arm. "I've waited my whole life for someone like you," he said. "And I realized today that now that I've found you, I can't give you up easily. I… I won't."

"I don't know what you're saying."

He rubbed her hand in his with his other hand. "I…

I'm not sure, either. I guess what I'm saying is, Han-nah Yoder, I'd like permission to walk out with you."

There was a long moment of silence. "I don't know how to answer you," she whispered finally. "I… We don't take courting lightly." Tears suddenly welled in her eyes and she pulled her hand from his. She glanced away, blinking. "Albert, Amish don't date. The purpose of a boy walking out with a girl is to see if they're com-patible." A lump rose in her throat. She had to say it. She had to be honest with him. "For marriage."

"I understand that."

Even though they were not holding hands any lon-ger, they were still sitting very closely. Too closely. "You do?"

"What I'm asking is if I can court you with the inten-tion of asking you to be my wife. If we find ourselves compatible," he added. "Which, honestly, I think we already do, but—"

"No," Hannah heard herself say. "No, Albert. I'm sorry if I gave you the wrong impression." She tried to look out the windshield of his truck, but it was rain-ing too hard for her to see anything. The rain sounded loudly on the roof and the hood of the vehicle. She felt as if it was pounding in her head. "I won't leave my faith, Albert. Not even—" Her voice caught in her throat and she was afraid she was going to embarrass herself by crying outright. She made herself look at him. At his handsome face. "I cannot leave my Amish faith, even for you, Albert. Even though I do…care for you. A great deal."

He slid his hand across the seat toward hers, but stopped an inch from her fingertips. "I thought about that. After Sara came to speak to me about you."

"Sara spoke to you? About me?" she asked, eyes widening with shock. "About *you* and me?"

"She *is* a matchmaker after all," he answered with a little smile. "But anyway, what I was thinking was that I know that you were once Mennonite and became Old Order Amish to marry Jonas. And I know that you can't go back. That you wouldn't. Which means…" He went on faster. "Which means that if you and I decide to get married, I'll have to become Amish. I mean, I want to become Amish. To be with you. To marry you."

Hannah couldn't speak. She was touched, beyond words. And for a moment, she imagined sitting at the supper table with Albert, with her husband, talking about their day. She imagined walking down the hall together toward their bedroom, to sleep in each other's arms. But then reality came back to her. The reality of her life. The Old Order Amish life.

The rain was beginning to let up and she could make out the outline of the barn in the distance. "It's a long process," she argued. "A difficult one. You have to get permission from the bishop. It would have to be discussed by the preachers, the deacon. You have to live as if you were Amish for at least a year." Her thoughts raced. "I don't know what they would think about you being a vet."

"Would they ask me to give up my practice?"

"I don't know," she answered, feeling flustered now. "I suppose accommodations could be made. You could use a driver, maybe. Limit the use of your phone for business only…" Her voice trailed off.

"Faith," he said.

"What?" She looked at him again.

"Faith," he repeated. "I have to have faith. If we're

meant to be together, it will happen. That's what Sara told me. And…" He squeezed her hand. "I think you have to have faith as well, Hannah." He held her gaze with his warm brown eyes. "In me and in God."

"Albert," she whispered, sliding her hand just close enough to his so that their fingertips now touched.

"Hannah," he answered. "Let me see what the bishop has to say. Will you give me that?"

How could she say no? How could she give in without even letting him try? At least then, if Bishop Atlee denied his request, then Hannah would know they had tried. She would know she had given Albert—no, her and Albert—a chance.

"Say yes, Hannah."

"I…"

He smiled. "I'll take that as a yes." Then he took her hand, lifted it to his lips and kissed it.

Before she could protest, he released her hand, opened the door of the truck and stepped down. "The rain's stopped for the moment. You should make a run for the house now, while you have the chance."

Numbly, she slid down out of the vehicle. Her skin tingled where Albert had pressed his lips against it. She took one step and then another, away from the truck, away from the man who'd just turned her world upside down. She was giddy, so lighthearted that she wasn't sure she could keep her feet on the ground.

"Have faith," Albert called after her. "I'll find a way. I promise you I will."

She didn't dare look back. If she glanced back, she might wake and find that it was all a dream, that Albert hadn't just offered to become Amish for her, for them. She stopped and took a deep breath.

Faith. He was right. She had to have faith.

A small sound of joy escaped from her throat. If this was God's plan for her, if it truly was… Goose bumps rose on her arms and she hugged herself as she continued on toward the house, suddenly feeling younger than she had in years.

Chapter Twelve

The following morning, Albert was waiting for John in the employees' parking area at the office. Their other vet hadn't yet arrived, and the only other vehicle there was one of the technicians'. When John pulled in, Albert got out of his truck and walked over to John's window.

"Morning, Uncle Albert," John said with a big smile as he lowered the window. "You're here early. Alpacas all doing well?"

"They're all fine. Just got back from Hannah's. Sit there a moment. I'd like to talk to you." Albert walked around John's truck and slid into the front seat beside him. "I need some advice from you, for a change."

"Sounds serious." John's expression became somber.

"It is. I'm moving toward a decision." Albert took a deep breath. "And it could affect you and the clinic."

"You aren't sick, are you?"

"Oh, no," Albert assured him. "Nothing like that. Fit as a fiddle." He put a hand on his nephew's shoulder. "I know you think that I haven't been myself since Dad died and you've been worried about me."

"We all miss Gramps."

"He was the best father any man could have, even more remarkable when you think that his own dad died when he was ten." He wanted to talk to John about Hannah. About everything. He just didn't know how he was going to get there. "Did you know that my grandparents on both sides were Amish? My father left the Amish and later married your grandmother, who'd also left her order. They then became Mennonite."

"I had heard that we had Amish in our family. Gramps didn't talk a lot about his childhood." John rested his hand on the steering wheel. Waited.

"I've been thinking for a long time about my spiritual roots, John. Reading my Bible, praying." Albert gazed out the windshield, then returned his attention to John. "I'm going to ask to join the Amish church."

John's eyes widened. "Because of Hannah?"

It was Albert's turn to be surprised. "Have we... Have I been that obvious?"

John shook his head and smiled. "No, of course not. But Grace and I were talking about this just last night. I'd have to be blind not to see that you're attracted to her, but to change your faith." He glanced out the window, then back at Albert. "Are you sure that this is what you want?"

"If there's any future for me with Hannah, it would have to be that. She could never give up her church."

"But you would yours?" John asked.

Albert thought for a moment before answering. It was good that he was talking to John about this. He knew he could count on his nephew, to be sure Albert was asking himself the right questions. "The way I look at it," he said slowly, "I wouldn't be leaving my faith so much as going back to my grandparents' faith."

John nodded. "And it's what you want? You're willing to give up driving? Electricity?" He hesitated. "What if they wouldn't want you to continue to be a vet?"

"Hannah and I talked about that and I understand that it's a possibility," he said slowly. "And that's why I wanted to talk to you. Because obviously, this could affect you and our practice. I think we could work something out, but if not…" He stopped and started again. "The thing is, I'm willing to take that chance because none of what the world has to offer seems as important as what I've found on Hannah's farm. Family, peace, a feeling of living close to the land and close to God." His voice grew husky. "Finally finding the one woman I want to spend the rest of my life with."

"And she feels the same way?"

He thought before he spoke. "I believe she does, or at least, she could. Do you have any objections to me marrying Hannah? Because if you do, I need to hear them now."

John shook his head. "No, of course not. She's Grace's mother, or as good as. I can't think of any woman I have more respect for, other than my wife." He paused for a moment, then went on. "But, aren't you rushing into things? The two of you have never been out on a date and now you're talking about marrying?

"Your impulsiveness concerns me. It isn't like you. As long as I can remember, you're the one who has been advising me to take my time to make important decisions."

Albert smiled, folded his arms and settled back against the door. "Ordinarily, I'd agree with you. You're right. A man shouldn't rush into a life-changing decision, but you have to remember that I've known Hannah for years, first as a client and the wife of my friend, and then as a widow struggling to run her farm and raise her girls. I've eaten at Hannah's table more times than I can remember. I've gone to family weddings, community frolics and funerals. I never tire of talking to her, and just seeing her always brings a smile to my face." He was quiet for a moment. "Actually, I believe Hannah is the reason that I haven't married anyone else. I've gone out with some nice women, but in my mind, they never quite measured up to Hannah. So it's more than compatibility, John. To be honest, I think I'm in love with her."

"You think you love her?" he repeated.

"I've never felt this way about anyone before. Being with Hannah…well, it makes me feel complete. And if we walk out with each other for a few months, or longer, we can both be certain before we make lifetime vows."

"It sounds as if you're pretty certain that this is what you want," John admitted. "But what you're suggesting, to turn Amish, it won't be easy."

"I know that. It's why I've come to ask for your help." He glanced sheepishly at his nephew. "I was hoping you'd go talk to Samuel with me. I know he's just a deacon, but I think he's a good place to start. We know him a lot better than Bishop Atlee or the new preacher. Hannah's brother-in-law, Reuben Coblentz, him I know well enough, but I'm not sure he'll be all that keen on letting me into the church."

"Not if his wife, Martha, has anything to say about it," John agreed. "When do you want to talk to Samuel?"

"Soon. Hannah and I have already discussed the matter. I want to start spending time with her, and we aren't going to sneak around like teenagers. I'm willing to follow the rules, but I want to get started. Or know it's not a possibility."

"So you and Hannah just discussed this? Recently?"

"Yesterday," Albert answered.

"Well, my advice would be to think on it a few days. Let's make plans to go see Samuel at the end of the week."

"All right." Albert tapped the dashboard. "I'm not going to change my mind, but I can see why you'd say that." He grinned. "I'd likely tell you the same thing."

John ran his hand along the top of the steering wheel. "A year is what I've heard, a year living like one of them, attending church, adopting the clothing. It's to give you the opportunity to see if it's the right path for you and for them."

"Seems fair and reasonable," Albert mused.

Both men were quiet for a moment, lost in their own thoughts. Then Albert smiled wryly at John. "My chances aren't good that things will turn out the way I want them to, are they?"

"Maybe not," John agreed. "But remember what advice you gave me when I came to you about Grace. You told me to have faith. So, I'll tell you the same thing. Put your trust in God and plunge ahead. 'Faint heart never won fair *frau*.'"

Carrying a split-oak basket, Hannah walked barefoot across the thick, green grass to the garden gate. It was the kind of day that made her want to be outdoors. It was quiet in the garden, with no sound but the chatter of a Carolina wren and the buzz of honey bees. Johanna had taken most of her beehives to her new home on Roland's farm, but she'd left two colonies behind. The bees insured good pollination both in the garden and in the fields, and Hannah loved to see them flitting from blossom to blossom gathering pollen. There was something about bees that just felt right and good to her.

Susanna was busy polishing the stairway banister and woodwork in the parlor. Sara and Ellie had borrowed her horse Blackie and a buggy to meet a prospective bridegroom, and Irwin was working at the chair shop today. Here in her beloved garden, Hannah could find plenty to do, and she would have the peace and solitude to think about all that had happened in the past few days: Rebecca's wedding, her friend Sara's prospective move to Seven Poplars and, most of all, Albert.

Hannah entered the garden and latched the gate behind her, shutting out any stray sheep or wandering chickens. She suspected that her late strawberries were ripening, and she had a notion to bake a shortcake for the midday meal. Here and there, a few weeds sprouted between the rows of corn, string beans, tomatoes and peppers. Once she'd picked her berries, she'd have to fetch the hoe and see to those intruders. Since Johanna, Anna and Rebecca had left, it was harder to keep the kitchen garden free of weeds, but she had to be vigilant. Left to run wild, they'd choke out her vegetables and leave them without enough food to can for winter.

The warm earth felt good under her bare feet. It never bothered Hannah to drop to her knees when she was picking beans, or in this case, strawberries. Just as she'd thought, there were dozens and dozens at the perfect point of ripeness. She lowered her basket to the ground beside her and began to pluck the scarlet berries. The best thing about working in the garden was that once she'd decided what needed doing, her hands knew the chore, and her mind was free to wander where it would.

Who was she kidding? There would be no wandering.

Albert. He was what she wanted to think about! Hannah couldn't help giggling at her own foolishness. She had lain awake until the clock struck two last night, then slept late and had been disappointed to discover, when she got to the barn, that Albert had already been there to take care of the alpacas and gone. She'd so badly wanted to see him this morning, just to be sure their conversation in the truck the previous day had been real. It was, of course. She knew that. She just... had wanted to see him.

Hannah broke into a wide grin; she couldn't help herself. Albert wanted to court her. He'd offered to join the faith to be with her. It was impossible. She couldn't let herself hope, let herself think what it might be like to cook for Albert, to walk to church with him and to sit with him on snowy winter nights and talk over the day's happenings. But she couldn't help where her mind took her. She imagined him sitting at the head of the table, waiting as she carried a freshly baked sweet potato pie to him. One slice wouldn't do. On second thought, she'd best cut the pie on the counter and bring the plates to the table to keep him from eating the entire thing. The way that man liked to eat, it was a wonder that—

"Han-nah."

She was so surprised by a voice in the garden that she dropped the handful of strawberries she'd just picked. Berries rolled into the plants and spilled between the rows. Hannah let the last two fall and twisted around to see David King standing a dozen feet away in his

Sunday church clothes. "David!" She pressed her strawberry stained fingertips to her beating heart. "You startled me."

David's face froze, mouth open, eyes wide beneath the brim of his straw hat. And just beneath the hat, she could make out a tattered cardboard king's crown. Now that the community knew David liked them, everyone brought them to him whenever they frequented Burger King.

"S...sor-ry." He looked as if he was about to burst into tears.

Hannah rose to her feet, adjusted her apron and brushed the dirt off. "It's all right, David. You didn't do anything wrong. I just didn't know anyone else was in the garden."

"Me. K... King David." He rubbed his hands on his pant legs. Obviously, he had something to say, but she could see that he was nervous.

"What is it, David? Did you come to see Susanna?" Hannah prayed for patience. Had he forgotten that they weren't supposed to see each other until church tomorrow?

"Ne." David shook his head. He looked down at his feet and scuffed the toe of one black leather shoe in the dirt. "You. See y...you." Each word was painful. Hannah had to strain to understand him.

"Tell her why!" A new voice, a very familiar voice, came from behind the big lilac bush on the other side of the garden fence. "Say it!"

David's face turned red. He looked over his shoulder toward the "mysterious" voice coming from the lilac bush, then back at Hannah. "To a...ask you..."

He hesitated and chewed at his bottom lip. "Ask you," he repeated.

"Say 'if you can court Susanna!'" Susanna prompted.

David breathed a sigh of relief. "IfyoucancourtSusanna," he repeated in a rush. Then, he looked over his shoulder. "I… I told her."

"Shh," Susanna yelled back.

Hannah stared hard at the lilac bush as branches moved on one side, and she caught a glimpse of a navy blue headscarf and a maroon dress. "Susanna?" she called. "Come out here. There's no need for you to hide. I know you're there." It was all she could do not to laugh. This was obviously a joint mission, and there was no doubt who was in charge.

"Not Susanna," came the answer. "Susanna's polishing chairs in the house."

David laughed. "*Ne,* Susanna. You… You're not in the h…house. That's you. I s…see you."

"Susanna," Hannah called. "You may as well come and join us in the garden."

Susanna appeared from behind the bush and reluctantly trudged around the fence to the gate.

"See." David grinned and pointed. His speech was very difficult to comprehend, but Hannah was beginning to be able to understand him. "It is Susanna. She was hiding. Playing a joke on me."

Hannah folded her arms and waited as her daughter came to stand beside David. Susanna's expression was determined, her lips set in a tight line that reminded Hannah of Ruth's mouth when she was displeased. Hannah forced herself to appear serious. "I'm waiting for an explanation," she said to Susanna. Hannah expected

Susanna to be contrite, even tearful, as she usually was when caught in mischief, but Hannah was mistaken.

Instead, Susanna boldly reached out and took hold of David's hand. "We're old enough," she declared. "I am not a baby. We want to court like Rebecca. And..." Her blue eyes fixed on David. "Tell her," she urged.

David's mouth opened and closed.

"Tell her we want to get married," Susanna insisted in a loud whisper.

"Ya," he agreed. "To g...get married."

"King David is smart," Susanna said, looking not at Hannah, but at David with shining eyes. "He can read McGuffey fourth reader. By himself."

David shook his head. "Five. I c...can read five."

"And he works hard, don't you?"

"Hard." David grinned and nodded.

Susanna glanced back at her. "And we want...we want to be together. All the time! Him and me. Together."

Hannah's heart sank. They were so young and so determined. And they didn't have the faintest idea how hard marriage was or the challenges they would have to overcome. The idea of allowing Susanna to become a wife was ridiculous...impossible. Yet, Hannah mused, was it any more impossible than what she and Albert were attempting? That Albert become Amish at his age? That the two of them find happiness together? "What does your mother say, David?" Hannah asked.

"She says we should court first," Susanna answered for him. "And we want..." She stared hard at David. When he didn't speak, she tilted her head and looked directly into his face. "The frolic," she hinted. "Wednesday."

It took Hannah only seconds to realize that Susanna was talking about the young people's singing and haystack supper that Lydia and her husband were hosting Friday evening. Any date in the future was always Wednesday in Susanna's mind.

"Tell her!" Susanna insisted.

"We w...want to go," David said in a loud voice. "Her and me. T...together."

Hannah looked from one eager face to the other. And felt herself soften. Maybe she had been wrong. Was Albert right? In her desire to protect Susanna, was she preventing her from living a full life? Didn't Susanna deserve the same chance at happiness that she wanted for all her daughters? That she wanted for herself? "All right," she agreed. "You and David may go to the Beachys' singing, but you will go with Charley and Miriam, and you will behave yourself. Do you understand?"

"Ya, Mam," Susanna said.

"We w...will." David nodded.

"And there will be no kissing. Not when people are looking, and not when they aren't."

"Ne," Susanna promised. She raised a warning finger and shook it in David's face. "No kissing. You understand?"

He nodded even more vigorously.

Hannah put her hands on her hips. "Friday night." She glanced at Susanna. "As for you, so long as you're here, I presume you've finished polishing the furniture. You may help me pick the rest of these strawberries."

Susanna sighed. "Go home, King David," she ordered. "But come talk to me tomorrow at church. It's church Sunday. And come back Friday."

Obediently, David strode away.

"Bye," Susanna called after him. "Bye."

David waved back. He was grinning from ear to ear.

"Strawberries," Hannah reminded her daughter.

Susanna knelt and began to pick the fat berries, but she was humming an off-key tune under her breath, and Hannah could just make out the repeated words. "First courting, then married, first courting, then..."

Hannah rolled her eyes and gazed skyward. *What have I just agreed to? Pray God I won't live to regret it.*

Chapter Thirteen

On Friday evening, nearly a week later, Albert and Hannah rode with John in his truck to Samuel's home. The days since he and Hannah had run through the rain together had passed quickly. Each evening and three of the mornings, he'd come to the farm to care for the alpacas, and he and Hannah had talked, not of serious matters but of everyday occurrences—the difficult delivery of twin calves, his great nephew 'Kota's progress at school, a much-looked-for letter Hannah had received from her daughter in Brazil.

He and Hannah had not held hands again or touched, but Albert had savored the intimacy of having someone who listened to him and cared about him. Hannah had invited him for breakfasts and suppers, always surrounded by family and friends, always careful not to do anything that would compromise the fragile relationship that was rapidly growing between them.

They'd not discussed the proposal he was about to make to her church, but it remained central in his thoughts, as he suspected it did in Hannah's. And even with his hopes and future in turmoil, Albert had closed his eyes each night at peace with himself and utterly happy. He'd always found fulfillment in his work and in the love he felt from John, Grace and little 'Kota, but this feeling for Hannah was something he'd never known before and it was precious.

On Sunday last, Albert had attended the morning Mennonite worship service with John and his family as he did every Sunday, but he'd refrained from speaking to his pastor or neighbors about his desire to court Hannah Yoder. He hadn't done so to hide his intentions, but because, at least for the present, it was a private matter between him, Hannah and God. Afterward, Ted, one of Albert's acquaintances from church, invited him to join them for dinner. Ted's sister, an attractive, forty-year-old RN who Albert had met several years ago, would be there. Ted hinted that she and Albert might be compatible. Albert gently refused the invitation. Courtship with a suitable Mennonite woman would be simpler, but she wouldn't be Hannah, and the more he thought about it, the surer he was that his future lay with her and the Amish.

When Hannah had insisted midweek that she wanted to come with him and John to speak to Samuel, Albert hadn't been able to hide his surprise. *Of course,* he'd replied, *whatever you want. I didn't think that you...* He'd felt his throat and face grow warm. *That you'd...*

His Hannah had laughed. *Albert. I'm not a shy, young* maedle. *And if there's a case to be made for you, I need to be there with you to speak to our deacon.*

Funny how Samuel Mast, Hannah's son-in-law, neighbor and longtime friend, had become someone to be approached with trepidation. Among the Seven Poplar Amish, the position of deacon was one of great authority. He was the enforcer of rules and the first member of the elders to contact a church member about possible wayward behavior. Bishop Atlee would make the final decision as to whether or not Albert and Hannah would be able to court, and his judgment would be final. But before that, the bishop would likely talk over the matter with Samuel and the two preachers, Caleb Wittner and Reuben Coblentz.

Albert and John had waited until 7:00 p.m. to pick up Hannah so that Samuel and Anna would be finished with the evening meal and chores. Wondering if Hannah was as nervous as he was, Albert glanced at her as John pulled into the Mast lane. None of them had spoken in the short ride around the corner from Hannah's to Samuel's place. Hannah sat on the truck seat between them, tall and serene, her hands folded in her lap. She wore a blue dress, a black apron and a black bonnet over her starched white *kapp.* Albert was glad that he'd taken the trouble to change into his Sunday clothes, a black suit, a tie and a white shirt.

John parked the truck in the yard, and the three got out. "You look nice," Albert whispered to Hannah, and was rewarded by a warm smile.

"You, too," she teased. "You *redd* up nicely."

They stood together in the driveway. "You're with me on this?" he asked.

A pink flush tinted her cheeks. "*Ya,* Albert," she answered softly. "On this, we are together." Her expression grew serious. "But remember, I am agreeing only to walk out with you, to see if our feelings are real, if this is the right thing for us. And only if there's hope for a future for us here in Seven Poplars."

"I understand. I already think it is the right thing for

us—I'm sure it is. But being together—courting—will make certain that we aren't being hasty."

"One step at a time," she insisted. She was standing close to him, and for an instant, Albert thought that she might take his arm, but she didn't. "If the Lord wills it," she whispered. "Last night, I prayed for guidance."

"Me, too." He smiled at her. "On my knees, and that isn't as easy as it once was."

She chuckled. "I've seen you lift fifty-pound bags of alpaca feed, and I've watched you pitch in to help with the haying. Any man who can throw bales of hay all afternoon onto a wagon isn't ready for a rocking chair."

"Are you two coming?" John called from the porch. "Or are you going to make me do this by myself?"

"We're coming." Albert's hands felt damp and he rubbed them nervously against his trouser legs. He could feel his pulse racing. Hannah had put it right, as always. This was the first step. They would take the journey together, one step at a time. And if things worked out, he would know that he was doing the right thing for both of them…and following the path that God had mapped out for him from the start.

"John!" Hannah's daughter Anna opened the door. "Come in!" She caught sight of Albert and her mother. "Albert! *Mam!* What a nice surprise!" She ushered them in with a wide smile and a genuine hug for her mother.

Usually the Amish that Albert knew were shy about showing affection in public, but Hannah's family was different. She, her daughters and her grandchildren were open about their love for each other. He liked that, and, next to John's Grace—Anna was his favorite among Hannah's children. Anna had a way of making everyone feel so welcome.

"Samuel!" Anna called. "We have company." She noticed Albert's suit and exchanged a glance with her mother. "And I think maybe they've come to talk with you."

Propane lamps cast light around the huge, spotless kitchen. Samuel, shoes off, had been sitting in his chair with a toddler on his lap. There were children of various ages sprawled on the floor playing Dutch Blitz; a girl was curled up in a window seat with a book. Albert didn't see Hannah's mother-in-law, who lived here with them.

As if reading his thoughts, Hannah asked, "Where's Lovina? She's not under the weather, is she?"

Anna chuckled and shook her head. "*Ne, Grossmama* is *gut*. Tonight is an open house at the Englisher senior center where she teaches her rug making. They wanted her to give a demonstration. The center's van came for her and will bring her home."

Albert remembered that Hannah had told him that it was Anna who'd gone over Samuel's head to the bishop to ask permission for her grandmother to attend the senior center. Clearly, it had been a good thing for the aging woman because Hannah insisted that Lovina's memory seemed stable, and her periods of dementia troubled her less often since she'd started going there. Albert took heart from that. Maybe seeing how the elderly Lovina had benefited from bending the community rules and allowing her to associate with the English community would make Samuel more inclined to support his courtship of Hannah. If Samuel was in favor, it would help their cause.

"Actually, we did come to speak with Samuel," John said after the usual greetings were exchanged, as well as inquiries about everyone's health and a discussion of the weather and other general topics. Albert was well aware that no business could be conducted with the Amish until courtesies were observed.

"Of course," Anna said. "Children!" She motioned to them. "Your father has—"

"No need for them to put away their games," Samuel said. "There's yet an hour or so before bedtime. We'll go into the parlor."

"I'll bring coffee," Anna offered. "And rhubarb pie." John started to decline, but Anna wouldn't allow it. "Nonsense," she said. "I've never known you or your uncle to turn down a slice of pie."

Samuel led the way to the formal parlor, a room at the front of the house with double doors that opened to provide a large space for religious services.

"Uncle Albert wants to make a request," John said. "And he'd like you to take it to the church elders."

"Sit, please, everyone." Samuel sat in a recliner and placed the reading glasses in his hand on a table beside an old German Bible. "Now tell me, Albert," he said when the three of them had sat on the couch across from him. "What important matter has brought you three to my door tonight?"

Hesitantly, at first, and then with more confidence, Albert began to explain how he and Hannah wanted permission to court and how he wanted to be considered for membership in the Amish church. "I realize that my veterinary practice could be an issue," he said. "It's something that I've given a lot of thought to, and I would be willing to do whatever is necessary to become a part of the community."

Samuel's brow furrowed, and he stroked his whiskered chin thoughtfully. "You want to court Hannah?" he repeated. "And you want to become Amish?"

"I do," Albert answered. "My family roots lie with the faith."

There was a knock at the parlor door and Anna called softly, "Samuel? I've brought the coffee and pie."

Samuel got up and went to take the heavy tray from her. "Best make another pot, wife," he said, glancing in his guests' direction. "I think we're going to be here awhile."

The following morning, Hannah, Sara, Susanna and Ellie left early to go to Ruth and Miriam's house to put up some early string beans. Together they snapped the beans, packed them into canning jars and processed them in a pressure cooker. It was time-consuming work but satisfying, because the results were lovely quarts of vegetables that would keep all winter. Hannah was glad for the opportunity to be with her daughters and friends and happier still to be busy.

Miriam's husband Charley came into the house mid-morning and said that Irwin had made a minor repair to the alpacas' fence as instructed. He'd also mentioned that Albert had come by earlier to feed and care for the animals.

Hannah was sorry that she hadn't been home and had the chance to speak to Albert that morning. Even if they couldn't spend private time together while Samuel was considering their case, she looked forward to seeing Albert when he came to tend to the alpacas. Sometimes just catching a glimpse of him pulling into the yard made her smile.

Samuel hadn't given them an answer the previous

night, but Hannah really hadn't expected one. He took his position of deacon seriously and wasn't a man to make snap decisions. She'd explained to Albert that Samuel would want to consider their proposal seriously and pray on it before responding. And she'd warned Albert that a final answer from the bishop might take weeks or even months. Old Order Amish didn't stray from the accustomed way of doing things easily or often. And if she were to make a guess, she would think that the bishop would refuse to allow the two of them to walk out together. But Albert had seemed so hopeful that she didn't want to say so. Still, she couldn't help being just a little sorry that she didn't have a cell phone. It would have been nice to hear Albert's voice, even if they couldn't see each other in person.

The following day was a visiting Sunday rather than a day of worship, and Johanna and Roland had invited the whole family, including Sara and Ellie, and Aunt Jezzy and her husband, to their house for a potluck picnic lunch. Roland, Charley and Eli set up tables outside, and Johanna had prepared ham and chicken salad sandwiches and gallons of lemonade and iced tea. Rebecca had baked three sheet cakes, and Miriam and Ruth had brought potato salad, coleslaw and green bean salad. Grace, John and 'Kota had been invited, and 'Kota was eager to play with all his cousins, especially Johanna's boys, J.J. and Jonah, who were close in age. Roland had built a child-size sulky cart with a wide bench seat so that the kids could take turns pulling each other around the farm.

Soon babies were playing on blankets, toddlers trailing after older children and the men were sitting under the trees with glasses of cool drinks. Hannah's girls, all but Anna, were busy going in and out of the house carrying food. "I wonder where Anna can be," Johanna said to Grace. "I told her that we'd be eating early. We'll have no peace until the children and husbands are fed." She smiled at her mother. "Honestly, I don't know how you managed all those years. Sometimes, I think Roland is worse than the kids about eating. He's hungry all the time."

"He works hard," Hannah said.

"He does," Johanna agreed. "He's a good man, *Mam.* Maybe better than I deserve."

"Never say that." Hannah hugged her. "You've had your share of troubles. It's so good to see you happy. And you are, aren't you? Truly happy in your marriage?"

Johanna nodded and hugged her back. "Truly, *Mam.* I'm just sorry it took so long for me to realize what a treasure he is."

"For everything there is a time," Hannah said. "You've wept bitter tears, now this is your time to find laughter." She glanced at Rebecca who was whispering to Miriam and giggling. Hannah didn't need to ask Rebecca if she was pleased with her new bridegroom. The joy in her eyes said it all.

"Anna and Samuel are finally here!" Grace called. "They've brought two buggies, so *Grossmama* must be with them."

Hannah hurried outside after her daughter to meet Anna, Lovina and all the grandchildren. Anna handed Rose to her and then helped *Grossmama* to climb down out of the buggy. Behind them, Rudy reined the other horse and buggy to a walk. As the vehicle rolled past,

Hannah gasped in surprise. Albert was seated on the front seat beside a grinning Rudy.

"Samuel invited him," Anna murmured to Hannah.

"Samuel did?" *Did this mean that Samuel approved of them?* She bounced Rose against her shoulder, nuzzling her neck, glad to have the little girl to hide behind.

"It's a picnic, *Mam*," Anna said. Her large, blue eyes twinkled with mischief. "Grace and John and 'Kota are here. Why not Albert?"

"Ya." Hannah nodded. "Why not Albert?"

Peter opened the door at the back of the buggy and lifted out a tall stack of pizza boxes. "Albert brought pizza," he announced.

Johanna's Jonah shrieked with excitement. "Pizza!" he cried. "J.J.! 'Kota! We're having pizza!"

Albert approached Hannah. "I hope it's all right that I came."

"And why wouldn't it be? How many times have you shared our meals?" Anna asked as she assisted her grandmother to a comfortable chair. Almost before Lovina was seated, one of Anna's girls came with a tall glass of lemonade for her.

"Pizza pie," Lovina grumbled. "Store-bought Englisher food. My father would never have permitted his children to eat it. But nobody stays by the old ways anymore. And nobody listens to me." She scowled. "This lemonade needs more sugar, Hannah. Did Hannah make it? She makes lemonade so sour it puckers your mouth like green persimmons."

"I'll sweeten it for you, *schweschter*." Aunt Jezzy reached for the glass.

"Ne, no need to make a fuss over me. I'll drink it like it is," the old lady conceded with a sigh.

Hannah looked up at Albert. "There are some chairs in the kitchen that need to come outside. Would you mind helping me?"

"Anything I can do to help."

She went into the house followed closely by Albert. "It was good of you to think of pizza," she said. "The children will love it."

"Your mother-in-law doesn't seem too happy that I brought it," he said.

Hannah glanced back over her shoulder at him and chuckled. "Lovina loves pizza. Wait until you see how many pieces she eats." When they got inside, the kitchen was deserted. "Do you think it's a good sign that Samuel invited you?" she asked in a low voice as she turned to him. "I'm so glad you accepted. I'm sorry we missed each other yesterday."

"Me, too," he said. "Samuel called me on my cell phone. I suppose he must have used the phone at the chair shop. He said that I was a good friend and part of the family, no matter what the bishop decided."

"He couldn't have spoken to Bishop Atlee yet."

Albert shrugged. "I think he did. One of the twins said their father went out early this morning. He didn't say where he was going, but he put on his black coat and good hat before he left."

An emptiness settled in the pit of Hannah's stomach. "*Ach,* I didn't think he would say anything so soon. He'd want to talk with Reuben and Caleb, too." Goose bumps rose on her arms and she rubbed at them.

"Don't worry. Your bishop is a reasonable man. We've always gotten along well."

"*Ya,* I suppose." Hannah's gaze met his and they stood there for what seemed like hours, although it could only have been seconds. Hannah's heart was beating fast, and she could feel the heat on her face and throat.

Was it possible? Would Bishop Atlee approve? Would this wonderful man give up everything he'd ever known to be her husband and join her church?

"This will all work out. I'm sure of it." Albert took her hand. "Because I... I love you, Hannah. And I want you to be my wife."

"Do you understand what that would mean?" she murmured. His grip tightened on her fingers and she went on. "If you marry me, Albert, you marry my whole family, my children and my grandchildren. Do you think you can love them, too?"

"I'd consider it an honor," he answered. "I'd never try to take Jonas's place, but maybe they could find a place in their hearts for me, as well."

Hannah felt light enough to float off the floor. She opened her mouth to tell him that she loved him, too, but before she could, the moment was broken as Susanna charged into the kitchen. Hannah snatched her hand from Albert's, hoping the daughter she'd been admonishing for improper behavior hadn't caught her.

"*Mam! Mam!* King David is here. He came." Susanna's face glowed and she clapped her hands. "He said he would sit with me. To eat."

"I told you they were coming. Lydia told me that you two were very well behaved at the singing. That shows me that you listened. So, I thought you might enjoy having David eat with us today."

"*Ya!*" Susanna hopped from one foot to the other with excitement. "I was *gut*. I remembered what you said. Courting. Not kissing. *No* kissing." She shook her index finger for emphasis. "And no hand holding." She spun around and raced out the door.

Albert chuckled, watching Susanna go. "That sounds like good advice." He glanced at Hannah and winked. "For more people than Susanna and David."

Hannah tried not to let her amusement show as she raised a finger to her lips. "Shh." Albert grinned, and Hannah couldn't help thinking what a good-looking man he was. Not flashy handsome, but solid and dependable-looking with a strong chin and kind eyes.

It was worldly to judge people by their outward appearance, but Hannah had always liked men with strong chins. It was difficult to take a man seriously if he had weak features. It was obvious that Albert had shaved this morning, but he already had the faint shadow of a beard. She was sure that Albert could grow a good, thick beard, and he would need to if they married. All Amish married men had beards, even if some were a little thin and straggly.

"Let's eat," Johanna called through the door. "*Mam!* Are you getting the chairs?"

"I think we'd better get outside," Albert said as he picked up the chairs Hannah pointed to. "Before we cause a scandal."

Hannah smiled. "I'm afraid it's too late for that, Albert."

Chapter Fourteen

The afternoon picnic was everything Hannah could have wished for. Dinner went off smoothly. Babies slept, children laughed and played, dogs barked and chased rabbits, led by Albert's hound, old Blue, who had come in the carriage with him. The women talked and soothed kids' scraped knees and hurt feelings. After the last dessert had been admired and eaten, the men offered to clear away and wash the dishes, a task the wives, daughters and neighbor women were happy to delegate. After the chores were done, Charley and Eli challenged all comers to a horseshoe throwing match, and all the men, including Albert, enthusiastically headed to the horseshoe pits, leaving Sara, Aunt Jezzy, Sadie, Hannah and her daughters and their new friend Ellie to sit under the trees with their shoes off and sip iced tea. Even Lovina had stopped grumbling and drifted off into a deep sleep, causing not a few smiles by her loud snoring.

"Mam," Johanna said. "I think we need more lemonade. Do you mind coming in and helping make some?"

Hannah looked at her quizzically. She was sure that

she'd seen another two gallons of lemonade standing ready on the kitchen counter.

"I'll help," Miriam offered, rising quickly to her feet. She cut her eyes meaningfully toward the kitchen door, and Hannah realized that the girls were trying to get her alone. Nodding, Hannah rose and went inside.

Rebecca and Anna were already waiting for them. "What did Samuel say?" Rebecca demanded eagerly. "Anna said he went to the bishop this morning."

Hannah looked from one daughter to the other as Ruth entered the room.

"Come clean, *Mam*," Miriam said. "We've all been wondering what's been going on between you and Albert. We couldn't imagine what you were thinking. But then Anna said that Albert has offered to become Amish. That's wonderful. I can't believe it." She clasped her hands. "He's perfect for us."

Suddenly weak-kneed, Hannah dropped to a high kitchen stool and looked at Anna. "You told them?"

A smile spread over Anna's round face. "Better I tell them what's really happening than they think the worst—that you were going to abandon us and turn Mennonite."

"And would that be the worst?" Hannah said. "If I went back to being Mennonite?" She looked from one daughter to the next.

"You've been baptized, *Mam*. You know what that would mean," Rebecca said gently. "It's not the same thing as Grace or Leah becoming Mennonite."

They were right, of course. "Be at ease, daughters. I've given my promise, to all of you and to God. Amish I am, and Amish I will remain."

"So Albert's courting you?" Miriam said. "Were you trying to keep that a secret from us?"

Ruth snickered. "Look who's talking about keeping secrets, sister."

"I was going to tell her today," Miriam said.

Hannah stared at her. "Tell me what?"

Miriam could hardly contain her giggles. "I'm sorry, *Mam*. It's just that after the last time that we thought I was, it turned out to be a false alarm."

"Will you just tell her and get it over with," Rebecca urged excitedly.

Miriam let out a dramatic sigh. "Charley didn't want to disappoint anyone again, so that's why we waited. But this time it's for sure." She threw up her hands. "We're going to be parents."

"You're having a baby!" Hannah got up and enveloped Miriam in a bear hug. "That's wonderful!"

Miriam laughed and hugged her mother. "It is, isn't it? I've seen the midwife three times and she heard a strong heartbeat. Just one baby, though." She cut her eyes at her sister. "I was afraid I'd have twins like Ruth." She laughed again. "Charley was hoping for twins, but one at a time is plenty for me."

Hannah looked suspiciously at her daughters. "And who else knows?"

"Just us," Anna replied. She'd found a dishcloth and was wiping down the counter. "And Charley and Eli. And Samuel. And Grace, of course. Not Leah, because it takes so long for letters to get back and forth. And we didn't tell Susanna because you know she can't keep a secret for two minutes. The whole church would know. Oh, and our Naomi. There isn't much that goes on that she misses."

"The whole community will know soon enough." Miriam patted her midsection, which Hannah realized *did* look thicker than usual. "We're ready, *Mam.* Charley and I are."

"I'm so happy for you," Hannah said.

"So let's get back to Albert." Miriam glanced toward the door. "It makes me happy to hear that you're ready. To think of marrying again."

Hannah sat down on the stool again and folded her arms, not wanting her girls to see how vulnerable she felt right now about her and Albert, or how much she wanted their approval. "I think I am ready to have someone again, to be with Albert." She glanced into their faces, afraid of what she might see there. "Do you mind terribly? It's not that I've forgotten your father. I could never do that."

"We know," Ruth assured her, looking around at her sisters. "We all agree it's been a long time. We've been holding our breath, afraid that you'd choose someone we didn't like or some man from another state and you'd have to leave us. But Albert, he'll make a good stepfather—provided he joins the church."

"So long as the bishop permits it," Miriam added. "Samuel didn't say he wouldn't, did he?"

"Samuel was shocked at first," Anna admitted. "You know how Samuel can be, but he thinks it should be considered, otherwise he wouldn't have gone to Bishop Atlee. Of course you know Uncle Reuben will be against it. Aunt Martha leads him around by the nose." She grimaced. "She makes *Grossmama* seem like a spring lamb for contrariness, at least where any of us are concerned."

"But Caleb will have a say." Ruth paused, broom in

hand, and glanced at Rebecca. "What do you suppose he'll think of all this?"

Rebecca shook her head. "I don't know. He hasn't been a preacher that long. I imagine he'll pray on it, give his counsel and then go along with whatever Bishop Atlee decides to do."

"Could he do it?" Miriam asked between sips of water. "Albert? Could he give up his Englisher life? His truck? Electricity? And what about his job?" She shook her head. "It won't be easy." She hesitated. "Will Albert want to take over the farm?"

"We haven't talked about any of that. Not yet. We only agreed we'd like to court to see if marriage would suit us. But if Albert does want to farm, he has his own land. Don't worry. Our farm will always be your home."

Miriam nodded. "That's good to know, because Charley has his heart in that land." She smiled. "And so do I." She went to the refrigerator. "Are there any sweet pickles left, Johanna? Oh, there they are, stuck behind the relish."

"She's eating pickles all the time," Ruth put in. "It's going to be a boy."

"It would mean so much to me if I know that you girls support me in this," Hannah said. "That you approve of Albert."

"Of course, we do, *Mam,*" Anna assured her. "He's a good man, even if he is a Mennonite." She laughed again, and her sisters chuckled with her. "You know I don't mean that in a bad way. We can see that he makes you happy, and that's what's important to us."

"Besides," Miriam added. "He'll be handy to have around when our livestock has an injury."

"Well, we shall see." Hannah rose from the stool.

"We'd better get back to the others. See if the twins are up from their nap. Maybe check out that horseshoe game?" As she started for the door, she heard a baby wail. "Told you," she said.

When all the babies had been changed and fed, the younger boys told to take their ball game farther from the house and the little girls entranced by a story that Ellie was telling them, Hannah, Rebecca, Sara and Lovina walked toward the area where the men were pitching horseshoes. They were halfway across the barnyard when a horse and carriage came up the lane.

"I wonder who that can be." Hannah turned to get a better look. "I don't recognize the sorrel."

"It's Bishop Atlee's buggy," Rebecca said. "Caleb mentioned he just bought a new sorrel pacer."

"The bishop?" Lovina's hand flew to her *kapp*. She patted it to make certain it was on straight and then tied her strings tightly under her chin. "He's come to help Jonas milk the cows," she said. "Such a nice young man, Bishop Mordecai. He wanted to court me, you know. But I'd set my *kapp* for Jonas's father."

"That's our bishop, Bishop Atlee, *Grossmama*," Rebecca reminded her gently. "Bishop Mordecai passed away when *Dat* was a baby."

Hannah watched as the bishop came toward them in the driveway. Tentatively, she raised her hand to wave. He nodded, reined the sorrel to a walk, and drove past them. Had his expression been stern?

"I'm sure you're wrong," Lovina said. "I think I know Bishop Mordecai when I see him."

Hannah quickened her step. As she approached the gathering of men at the horseshoe pits, she saw that Albert was showing David how to improve his pitch.

David flung the first shoe far to the left of the peg. But his second horseshoe flew gracefully in an arc and dropped around the peg. It spun several times and came to rest firmly on the peg. David let out a yelp of pure joy and began to jump up and down.

Susanna ran out to the peg, grabbed the horseshoe and waved it in the air. "He scored!" she yelled. "My David made a home run!"

David beamed with pride as his father, Albert and Hannah's sons-in-law praised him and patted him on the back. "Did you see?" David shouted to Susanna. "Did you see me, Susanna?"

"*Ya!* I did see!" Susanna replied. She glanced around, realized that she was standing in the center of the horseshoe pits and hurried toward Hannah, still holding the horseshoe. "David won," she declared. "My David won."

Hannah nodded, but her gaze followed Albert as he walked away from the others toward Bishop Atlee, who had gotten out of his buggy. Apparently, the bishop had known Albert would be there today and had come to talk to him. Hannah's heart sank. No positive decision could have been made so quickly. He must have come to forbid Albert from seeing her. She felt sick.

"It doesn't have to be bad news," Sara said softly in Hannah's ear.

"I know," Hannah replied, "but tell my stomach that." She wished she hadn't eaten so much at lunch. Her chest felt as though it was full of butterflies.

The waiting was awful. Sara kept trying to keep her from thinking the worst, but Hannah felt as though everyone was looking at her. Why hadn't Bishop Atlee asked to speak with them both? It wasn't as if this decision didn't affect her as much as it did Albert. She wanted to explain her position to the bishop, but it would be impolite to intrude on his conversation with Albert, and she didn't want either of them to think badly of her.

"This sun is really warm today, isn't it?" Sara remarked. "Wisconsin summers can be brutal, but it doesn't get this hot in June. Let's go back and sit under the trees."

Hannah glanced at Albert and the bishop speaking privately. "Am I being a fool, Sara?" she asked.

"*Ne,* my friend," Sara answered, patting Hannah's arm. "We have to keep hoping for the best. As I do with Ellie."

Hannah realized that she hadn't asked Sara how the interview went with Ellie's prospective husband. Sara was careful not to divulge personal information about her clients, and Hannah didn't want to pry, but she felt as though she'd been so wrapped up in her own life that she hadn't considered Sara's. Ellie hadn't said anything, but she had seemed happy today. "Your match, for Ellie," Hannah said. "Is it going well?"

Sara grimaced. "Actually, it isn't going at all. The family was pleased with her and the boy seemed willing, but Ellie refused him. She said she didn't think they were *compatible*." Sara arched her dark eyebrows. "Ellie's father and mother will be disappointed, but eventually I'll find her a husband. I always do." She lifted her chin. "Look, I think your Albert is coming this way."

Hannah looked up, and saw Albert and his dog walking in her direction. Sara discreetly moved away to speak to Lovina. Bishop Atlee joined the men, and someone handed him a glass of iced tea. Hannah could hear the bishop's voice, but couldn't make out what he was saying.

Albert stopped in front of her. Old Blue, who'd been trailing behind him, dropped at his feet. "Do you feel all right, Hannah? You look as though you've seen a ghost."

"What did he say?" She tried desperately to maintain her composure.

"About what I expected. He wants to pray on it. And to talk to Samuel and his preachers some more. But he didn't say no. He listened to me, and he advised us to both think carefully about our decision." Albert breathed a sigh of relief. "In the meantime, he said that I was free to *walk out* with you until the council of elders reaches a conclusion." His smile became a grin. "So long as we maintain decent and proper behavior."

Hannah smiled, suddenly feeling shy. "And can we?"

Albert chuckled. "We can try, Hannah. We can try."

And try they did. Albert continued to come mornings and evenings to care for the alpacas, and Hannah was careful to be sure they remained outside in the yard when he was on the farm unless two other people were present. If Irwin and Susanna were there for breakfast and, or supper, she would invite Albert, and he would accept.

Sara and Ellie returned to Wisconsin the Tuesday following the family picnic. Sara hadn't signed a contract on property in Kent County, but she'd told Hannah that she would be moving to Delaware soon. Final arrangements would depend on negotiations with her late husband's sons and whether or not she had to sell the farm where she presently lived. Hannah was sorry to see both of them go. She'd grown quite fond of Ellie and had hoped that she would become a part of the Seven Poplars community, too. As for Sara, the sooner she returned, the better. As much as she valued her good friends, Lydia Beachy and Fannie Byler, Sara was special. When she left, Hannah assured her that she was welcome to come back and stay as long as she liked.

Wednesday was a workday at the schoolhouse. With school out for the summer, there was painting and general maintenance to do, and Charley had recruited the Gleaners, the local Amish youth group, to help. Hannah and the girls scrubbed windows, polished woodwork, desks and cleaned out the cast-iron wood stove. Hannah hadn't expected Albert to come, as she'd supposed that he would be busy with his veterinary practice, but he arrived, toolbox in hand, ready to do whatever he could to help. It turned out that Albert was handier than Hannah had suspected. He fixed the drawer that was sticking in her teacher's desk, and made some much-needed repairs to chair-and-desk combinations. Finally, he and Irwin had surprised her by installing, along the back wall of the schoolhouse, a six-by-ten-foot old-fashioned blackboard that he'd found free on the Internet.

"You never cease to amaze me," Hannah declared when the project was complete.

"You thought doctoring animals was my only skill?" Albert grinned, clearly pleased by her praise. "I wasn't always a vet," he reminded her. "And remember, I grew up on a farm. I can still swing a hammer."

Ten minutes later, a pizza delivery boy drove into the school driveway with a stack of hot pizzas. The treat was much appreciated by Charley and the Gleaners, who washed their lunch down with cold well water.

"You'll spoil them," Hannah warned Albert. "They'll start expecting pizza every time you attend an event."

Albert grinned and shrugged. "Better that than if I'd baked them cupcakes. My father and I used to argue over which of us was the worst cook. The truth is, I'm pretty sad."

"Is that why you want to marry me?" she teased as she reached for another slice of mushroom-and-sausage pizza. "For my cooking?"

He smiled. "Marriages have been made for worse things."

On Saturday, Albert rented a fifteen-passenger van and took Hannah, Grace, Susanna and David, Johanna and her three children, 'Kota, Anna's twins, and Rebecca and Amelia to the Salisbury Zoo. It was next to a small park with lots of trees, a large playground and a picnic area where they could eat the big lunch that the women had packed. The zoo was a small one, featuring South American animals, and the children were fascinated by the monkeys, alligators and lizards, which were like those their Aunt Leah described in her letters.

But as much as the children enjoyed the exotic animals, the otters were hands down their favorites. Hannah couldn't even find it in her heart to admonish Susanna when she and David stood side by side, holding hands, fascinated by the antics of the playful mammals. Parts of the otter habitat had been fashioned to replicate a fast-running stream, complete with water slide, and the excited giggles and squeals of her grandchildren delighted Hannah.

"Are you having a good time?" Hannah asked Albert. "I am. It was so thoughtful of you to arrange this trip for us."

'Kota tugged at his hand. "Uncle Albert, look! The sign says there are llamas. Can we go see the llamas? They're like alpacas, but different. Mom says they're bigger."

"We'll see everything. I promise you," Grace assured her son. "You'll wear Uncle Albert out. A few more minutes, and then we'll go on to the bison."

"J.J. and I want to see the llamas," 'Kota pestered.

"You'll wait for the rest of us," Grace warned him quietly. "Why don't you two go on," she urged Hannah and Albert. "We can manage the children. Take some time for yourselves. We're in a public park. It's perfectly permissible."

Hannah glanced at Susanna and David.

"And I'll look after those two," Rebecca promised. "Go while you have the chance. We'll catch up with you in the picnic area."

Hannah looked at Albert for confirmation. "We'll take you up on that offer. I'm sure Albert's ready for a few moments of peace."

"Whatever you want," Albert said. "I'm good."

Hannah nodded. "But you'd be better with a little quiet." He didn't protest when she walked away.

They walked for a while, side by side, until they came to a bench, surrounded by flowering trees and bushes. They sat there in comfortable silence for nearly half an hour, not talking, just looking at the birds in the trees, and watching the other visitors wander past. It was a good feeling. Hannah liked this about Albert. He didn't always have to be talking. There was something intimate about being near one another, experiencing new sights and sounds, learning more about each other.

"I'll make you happy, Hannah," he said finally, turning to look at her. "At least, I'll do my best."

She met his gaze. "And you don't mind giving up your life for us to be together?"

"When I'm with you, Hannah, I don't feel as though I'd be giving up anything. Having peace, family, not being alone—it's what I've always wanted."

"And the Amish faith? Do you think you could accept it? Accept the *Ordnung?* Obey the wishes of the elders and the community?"

"I think it feels right," he admitted. "No matter what, I think it's what I need to do. And being part of your family, it's almost too much to ask."

She sighed. "You realize the bishop could refuse us. And then, I'd have no choice. I'd go on loving you, Albert, but it would mean we couldn't be together."

"I understand." He nodded. "It's a chance I have to take."

She cradled her hands in her lap and looked up into his face. "I'm afraid," she admitted. "I want to have faith, but I'm afraid we're asking too much." She swallowed the lump rising in her throat. "You know that even if the elders agree, we would have to wait at least a year."

"It would be hard, because I want to marry you now," he said. "I'd marry you today if I could. But it will be worth every moment, because I know that at the end of the time, we'll be husband and wife."

"Then we'll keep praying," she agreed, trying to find the confidence he seemed to feel. "And hope that whatever happens, we'll have the faith to accept the answer and live with it."

"We'll keep praying," he agreed. "And in the—"

"Hannah! Come quick!" Anna's Rudy came running toward them. His face was as red as his hair, and he'd lost his straw hat. "It's Susanna!" he shouted. "She fell down the steps! Johanna thinks her arm is broken!"

Chapter Fifteen

Albert heard Susanna shrieking before they reached her. Grace and Johanna had her seated on the ground, her injured arm in her lap. They were attempting to soothe her, but Susanna was either suffering intense pain or she was hysterical. The younger children sat solemnly on the steps with Rebecca, staring at Susanna.

"Thank goodness you're here." Grace stood up. "I'm pretty sure that her arm is broken."

Hannah crouched beside her youngest daughter. "Hush now, Susanna. It will be all right. No need to carry on so. You'll upset all the animals. You don't want to do that, do you?" She rested a hand on the back of Susanna's shoulder. "Show me where it hurts."

"My…my arm!" Susanna wailed.

Hannah's eyes showed her concern, but she remained calm and kept her voice low. "Tell me what happened, Susanna." She took her chin and lifted it so that she could command all of her attention.

"I fell." Susanna was sobbing now, her face red, great tears streaming down her cheeks. "It hurts!"

Hannah glanced around. "Where's David?"

"He got upset and felt sick to his stomach," Johanna said. "Peter took him to the restroom."

"Could you look at her arm, Albert?" Hannah asked. "I don't see anything definite other than bruising, but you would know better."

"He's an animal doctor, not a people doctor," 'Kota remarked loudly.

Grace raised a finger in warning. "Hush, now. Uncle Albert knows about bones."

Albert moved toward Susanna to inspect her arm. "And bones are bones." He lowered himself to his knees, looking directly into her eyes. "Now, I'm going to touch your arm," he quietly told her. "But I promise, I'll be very gentle."

Susanna shook her head and shrank back against her mother. "*Ne! Ne!* I want David. My David," she sobbed.

Albert exchanged glances with Hannah. "All right, Susanna," he said. "I won't touch it if you don't want me to." He didn't really need to. The slight misalignment of her forearm spoke for itself. Fortunately, there was no break in the skin, so it was a simple fracture rather than a compound one. "She needs to go to an E.R. or an urgent-care facility."

"Should we call an ambulance?" Grace asked. "I have my cell phone."

"I don't think that's necessary." Albert stood up. He knew that Hannah, like the majority of the Old Order Amish, carried no health insurance. Even a short ambulance ride would cost her hundreds of dollars. "There's an excellent hospital within a half a mile of here. We can drive her there." He looked at Johanna. "It might be better if the rest of you remained here."

"Absolutely," Hannah agreed. "No need to overwhelm the hospital staff. Besides, these children are hungry. They need their lunch, and they may as well enjoy the playground, as we promised. If Susanna's arm is broken, it will take time to have it x-rayed and cast. The family may as well spend the rest of the afternoon here at the zoo."

"If you're sure you don't need me, *Mam,*" Johanna said. "I agree that the hospital waiting room isn't the best place for all of us. We can all say a prayer for Susanna before lunch."

"It's settled, then." Albert put his hands together. "Susanna, do you think you can walk?"

"It hurts!" Susanna cried and again began to sob.

"Susanna, listen to me." Hannah planted a kiss on the top of her head. "Big girls grit their teeth, stand up and walk to the van. Otherwise, Albert will have to carry you. You don't want that, do you?"

"Don't want to go to hospital. Want to go home."

"I don't want to go to the hospital, either," Hannah agreed, "but we have to. The doctors need to look at your arm."

"Want King David," Susanna whimpered as she allowed her mother to help her to her feet. "I want David. Now!"

"*Ne,* daughter," Hannah said. "David has to stay here. His belly doesn't feel good."

"Rudy, you wait here for your brother and David," Rebecca instructed. "Bring them to the picnic area and make sure that David isn't separated from the rest of you."

Quickly, the group moved down the walkway to the parking lot where Albert helped Susanna into the backseat of the van and Hannah got in beside her. Grace, Johanna and the children unloaded the lunch baskets while Hannah fastened Susanna's seat belt. Susanna was still crying, but not so frantically.

After making certain that all the children and adults were accounted for and out of the way, Albert drove the short distance to the hospital emergency room.

Once they got Susanna inside, Albert was aware that they attracted a lot of curious stares, but whether it was because of Susanna and Hannah's Amish clothing or Susanna's renewed wailing, he wasn't sure. Susanna's injury was quickly assessed, and they took seats in the waiting room. Albert had assumed that Susanna would calm down, but she continued to cry and to ask for David.

"I'm so sorry, Albert," Hannah said between Susanna's wails. "You planned a fun day for us, and then this had to happen."

He shrugged. "I'm just glad I'm here to help."

"Please stop, Susanna," Hannah coaxed, turning back to her daughter. "There's a soda machine. I'll buy you a soda if you stop crying."

"Want my David!" Fresh tears commenced.

Hannah sighed and glanced away, obviously unsure what to do.

"Maybe I should go back and get him," Albert suggested. "I can always take him back to the park if it doesn't help."

Hannah hesitated, and then nodded. "Maybe you should." She turned to Susanna. "Do you hear that? Albert's going to go get David and bring him here. But if you keep crying, you'll make him cry. And you know his belly hurts when he's upset."

Susanna clamped her lips and her eyelids tightly shut, but tears kept seeping down her face, and she was trembling all over. Hannah looked at Albert. "She's always like this when she hurts herself, even a stubbed toe. She has a difficult time adjusting to pain."

"Want my David," Susanna repeated, eyes still shut. "Want David."

They were still in the waiting room when Albert returned to the emergency room half an hour later with David. The young man seemed nervous, but also eager to be with Susanna. Albert found much of David's speech hard to understand, but the one word he did get, repeated over and over, was Susanna's name.

People twisted their necks to stare as David lumbered across the waiting room to where Susanna sat, but he didn't see them. His gaze was locked on her. Hannah got up and waved him to the seat beside Susanna.

Albert waited to see what David would do. If he'd made an error in judgment, they might have two frightened, adult-size kids to deal with. But just the opposite happened. David took a hold of Susanna's hand and spoke to her, and she opened her eyes. A quavering half smile lit her face as she pointed to her arm. "It hurts," she said and sniffed.

David pulled a large blue paisley handkerchief out of his pocket and held it out to Susanna. "Blow," he ordered. She did. "Don't cry, Susanna. The d…doctor will make it all better."

"He will?" Susanna handed back the handkerchief.

David nodded, found a clean corner and wiped her wet cheek. "I'm s…sorry you hurt bad."

She nodded, sniffed and gave a small sound of agreement.

"My *dat* said 'No…no crying.' And he bought m… me ice cream." David held up his thumb to show a faint white scar. "Th…three stitches. Three." He held up three fingers to emphasize his point.

"Ya." Susanna nodded again. "He sewed it up." Her lower lip quivered. "I don't want the doctor to sew my arm."

"He won't," Hannah assured her. "First they will take a picture of it, and then they'll fix it so it can't move until it's all healed."

David leaned close to wipe a dirty spot on Susanna's chin. "I g…got your feather," he said, pulling a much-the-worse-for-wear green feather out of his other pocket. "F…found it on the ground."

Susanna clutched at the bent and wrinkled parrot feather and smiled. "You found it."

Hannah came to stand by Albert, watching David and Susanna. "The wind blew it out of her hand and she was running after it when she tripped and fell down the steps," she explained.

David and Susanna had their heads together whispering. Susanna's tears had subsided. "They seem very fond of one another," Albert mused aloud. "And David is good for her."

"Ya," Hannah agreed with a sigh. "He is. And I think that they care for each other very much."

Albert nodded. "So maybe…"

"Maybe I've been wrong," she said, softly. "Very

wrong. Maybe David is what God planned for Susanna all along."

Albert looked down at Hannah. "You think you're ready to let her marry?"

"Well, I didn't say that." She grimaced. "I still think I'll need a little time." She looked up at him, her eyes moist. "Would that be so terrible? To let them be husband and wife? They couldn't live alone, but they could live with me. With us," she dared.

"I think that might be the perfect solution." He smiled, feeling a tenderness in his heart he'd never felt before. "Maybe the answer to your prayers."

"Have you lost what little sense you ever had?" Martha crossed her arms, jutted one angular hip and scowled at Hannah.

It was Friday morning, nearly a week after Susanna had broken her arm at the zoo. Hannah had seen her sister-in-law at church the day after Susanna's accident, but they'd had no opportunity to have a private conversation. Hannah had been inspecting her peach trees for signs of insect infestation when Martha marched down the lane that led from her home to Hannah's farm.

"Good morning, Martha."

"I shudder to think what my brother would make of this. If you ever gave a minute's consideration to what he would want," Martha shook an admonishing finger. "Poor Jonas. You should be ashamed of yourself, Hannah. I saw Fannie at Fifer's Orchard and she told me that you and that Mennonite are courting. A Mennonite!"

Hannah stiffened. "*Ya,* Martha, we are." And then, instantly, the realization hit her that Reuben must not have discussed any of this with her. That was a shock. She didn't think Reuben kept anything from his wife.

"You're going to leave the church, aren't you? I knew it," she insisted, before Hannah could get in a word. "First Leah and now you. But she was never baptized into the faith. You were, Hannah. You'll be shunned if you turn Mennonite." Her face was getting redder by the second. "You know what this means. Your own daughters and grandchildren won't be able to eat at the same table with you. All of your friends, your neighbors will have to—"

"Albert has petitioned to convert," Hannah cut in.

It only took Martha a moment to pick up steam again. "That's the silliest thing I've ever heard. Albert can't be Amish. What makes him think he can be Amish? He wasn't raised Amish, he was raised Mennonite."

As Martha went on, blood pulsed at Hannah's temples. She wanted to say awful things to Martha—to ask her why she always felt compelled to interfere in other people's private lives, why she had to approach every conversation with such criticism. But she took a deep breath and interrupted again, "Albert wants to become Amish. It's what I want, too."

"I know you think I'm a busybody, that I constantly look for fault in others, but I do care for you, Hannah. Believe it or not, I do. And I care very much what happens to you and your family." Martha's face took on a pinched expression and her lips paled. "I'll admit that I'm too outspoken and that I've harbored jealousy against you in the past. It's not something I'm proud of, but it's true." Tears suddenly filled Martha's eyes. "You don't know how difficult it's been to watch each of your girls make wonderful marriages while my Dorcas sits at home growing older and older."

Hannah stared at her sister-in-law for a moment. She was speechless. Had Martha truly just admitted such a thing? And suddenly Hannah's heart ached for her bristly sister-in-law. She crossed the short distance between them and wrapped her arms around Martha. For a moment, Martha stood stick-straight, and then Hannah felt a tremor pass through her and she sagged against her, awkwardly returning the hug.

"I'm sorry for the discord I've sowed. It's always been my biggest fault, one I've struggled with since I was a child, but you don't understand how it was for me growing up," Martha said. "My mother was never the kind of mother you've been. Jonas was always her favorite. Jezzy, me, my sisters, we were only girls when my parents needed sons to work the farm."

"*Actch,* Martha, hush now." Hannah rubbed Martha's back. "I'm sure that's not true."

"None of us were ever pretty, but Jonas didn't seem to notice or care. He loved us anyway. Then he met you. Pretty, smart, capable Hannah. Then he was too busy to come by and share jokes or spend time with me."

"Jonas loved you very much," Hannah said. "I never heard him say an unkind word about you or his mother."

"He was like that. He always saw the good in people." Martha disengaged herself and smoothed her faded dress. "But I was born more like Mother. And for better or worse, I speak my mind."

"I've not always been as good a sister by marriage as I should have," Hannah said. "And I admit that if we've clashed at times, I was probably at fault as much as you."

"I'd like to tell myself that, but I doubt it's true," Martha scoffed. "I didn't like the freedom you gave your girls, letting them sashay around the countryside with young men. It wasn't the way I was raised. But it doesn't seem to have hurt any of them. They've all made decent marriages and live according to the *Ordnung*. Maybe if I'd given Dorcas more leeway," she fretted, "she'd have found a fellow when she was eighteen, rosy-cheeked, and sweeter-natured."

"It isn't too late for Dorcas. She's a good girl, a hard worker."

"And where are the young men beating a trail to our door? There's none in Kent County who've shown her more than a passing glance."

"Then maybe you should look farther afield. There are other conservative communities with lots of respectable candidates." Hannah thought for a moment. "You know, your cousin Sara has been very successful in making good matches. If you're concerned about Dorcas, maybe you should talk to Sara."

"And where's her fee to come from? My Reuben was laid up with his broken leg. We had medical bills. We've no extra money to spend on matchmakers." Martha's tone was brittle, but Hannah knew that finances were often a real problem for Reuben and Martha.

"Not all the families of the girls provide the fee. Sara said that just as often, it's the boy's family, and with a widower, it's usually the case. As he's more established and getting a younger wife, he's expected to assume the expense."

"So I'm to put my daughter up for some old man to bid on?"

Hannah allowed herself a smile. "Dorcas would have

the right to refuse any match she didn't want. Sara's client Ellie did just that with the young man they came to consider. He was willing, but she didn't think he was right for her."

Martha eyed her. "Ellie, the...*short* girl?"

"Ya." Hannah smiled to herself. "It's just a suggestion, Martha. Could it hurt to discuss it with Dorcas?"

"I suppose not, but what would Reuben say? He's a proud man. Not right to say about a preacher, but they're only human, too. He sets some store by our Dorcas. I think it would suit him if she never married and stayed home to care for us in our old age."

"Easier for Reuben perhaps, but would it be right for Dorcas? I've struggled with much the same thought with Susanna. And I think I've been holding on to her too tightly. She and David King, they care for each other deeply."

"You think I don't know that? Saw it months ago. Those two are smitten, all right." Martha set her hands on her hips. "He's a good match for Susanna. David is a decent boy. He was born with troubles, but so was our Susanna. Together, they make up for some of what they lack. And in God's eyes, they're His creations, not ours."

Hannah blinked in surprise. "You would approve of me letting Susanna walk out with David?"

"Why not? Isn't that what the Bible tells us? It's the natural order of things. They should court and then marry. And the sooner the better, I say." Martha drew herself up like a banty hen. "You surprise me Hannah, for all your modern ways. Why doesn't Susanna have as much right to marry as Rebecca did? Of course if they have children, then you and David's mother would have to help—"

"No babies," Hannah said quietly. "David can't father children. Sadie assured me of that."

Martha opened her arms. "There you go, then. I'd say the decision's been made. You should have the banns read as soon as possible. The two of them are innocents now, but they're better married than not. Safer for them both."

"You're right," Hannah agreed, still completely surprised by Martha's view. "It took me a long time to realize that." She looked up. "But after a decent time of courting, I should allow her to marry him if she still wants to."

"*Gut*. That's sensible." Martha looked into her eyes with eyes that had once been as blue as Jonas'. "So why can't you show the same good sense where Albert is concerned?"

Hannah took a step back. "We're not going to argue again, are we?"

"It took a lot for me to come here and bare my faults to you," Martha said. "You owe me the decency of considering what I have to say. It's meant in the best way. Honestly, Hannah. If the congregation did accept Albert, if he did become one of us—and I say *if,* because I doubt the elders would ever approve—how long would your marriage last before he began to regret his decision? Albert would have to turn his back on worldly things—his motor vehicle, his television, his cell phone. You're kidding yourself if you think that such a marriage could ever work."

"I converted for Jonas. I gave up my family and my life for his, and I've never regretted it, not for a single day."

"But you were just a young girl. It's not the same for

a man. Not a man his age, set in his ways. You're making a mistake, and that mistake will threaten the stability of our community and your family. He may be a good man, Hannah, but he isn't Amish and he can never be. And for you to ask him to do this for you, why it's just plain selfish."

Chapter Sixteen

"*Selfish...just plain selfish...*" Martha's words echoed again and again in Hannah's head as she moved through her day. She tried to keep busy. She cleaned off the back porch. She washed strawberries, and then made a short-cake. She tried not to second-guess herself.

But the seeds of doubt, once sown, found fertile ground to grow. Was Martha right? Was she being selfish? Had she run roughshod over what should have been common sense? Was she allowing Albert to make sacrifices that he would later regret? And worst of all, would a marriage with Albert end in unhappiness for both of them?

She never expected to hear good advice from Martha, but she'd never thought to hear her sister-in-law admit jealousy or interfering in other people's lives, either. Could there be threads of truth in what Martha had said about Albert?

From there, the "whys" set in. Why had she allowed her friendship with Albert to become love? Once she'd realized that his feelings for her were growing, why hadn't she rejected further advances? Instead, she'd welcomed them, lain awake thinking of Albert like a love-sick girl. And now they'd taken their case to the elders. It was all in motion. What if Bishop Atlee approved? It was a possibility. Then what? Did Albert truly understand how different his life with her would be?

There was no divorce among the Amish. The sacred bonds of marriage were for life. What if she married Albert and then they found that they had made a terrible mistake? The fault would be hers because she knew all too well the vast divide between the English world and those who practiced the conservative faith of the Amish. Was Martha right? Was she allowing her own selfishness to threaten Albert's future happiness?

Her doubts troubled her so badly that she didn't go outside to meet Albert that evening when he came to tend the alpacas. She barely spoke to Susanna during supper, and went to bed early, but hardly slept a wink. The next morning, she awoke as confused as she'd been when she'd finished her nightly prayers. She found an excuse to go to Miriam's and Ruth's house just as Albert's truck pulled off the blacktop into her lane.

Grace stopped by at midday to invite her and Susanna to share the evening meal. "John's already invited Uncle Albert. I'm making my famous spaghetti sauce." But Hannah begged off, giving the excuse that she had a headache, which was true. And Susanna couldn't go because she'd already accepted an invitation to eat with the Kings.

Sunday morning, Irwin did the feeding, and since Sundays were always busy, it was easy for her to be absent when Albert came that night. Hannah had never considered herself a coward, but she felt like one now. Did she just need to go to Albert and tell him her fears?

She prayed for guidance, but the answer eluded her.

Was she making a terrible mistake? Would she hurt Albert less if she put an end to this entire courtship now, before worse happened? Had she put her happiness ahead of what was right for Albert, her family, her community? How was she going to talk to Albert about this? What was she going to say to him?

Monday morning she was still fretting over how to tell Albert her fears when he drove into the yard, pulled his truck up to her back porch and knocked on her door. "Hannah," he called. "Come out, or I'm coming in."

She stood in the kitchen, her heart racing in her chest. She glanced at Susanna. "Please go upstairs and change the sheets on the beds."

"Albert's knocking," Susanna said.

Hannah touched her head nervously, making certain that her *kapp* was in place. Her knees felt weak. "Please, Susanna, the beds. We need to put the sheets into the wash."

Susanna trudged off, but not before Albert pushed open the screen door. "Are you coming out or—"

"I'm coming, Albert."

He held the door for Hannah and she stepped out onto the porch. Two red hens had escaped from the chicken yard and found their way inside the picket fence that enclosed the back of the house. Clouds of dust flew up as they scratched at her marigolds in search of bugs. Ordinarily, she would have chased the chickens, but now she couldn't summon the energy.

Albert took her arm as they descended the steps. "You've been avoiding me. Are you going to tell me why?"

He sounded hurt, and she inwardly winced. The last

thing she wanted to do was to hurt him. "I wasn't avoiding you," she hedged. "I've been busy. We've both been busy."

"Hannah." He stepped in front of her. "We've always been honest with one another. I haven't seen you or talked to you since Friday morning. What's wrong? Have I done something? Have I said something that's upset you?"

Shame flooded her. *"Ya,"* she admitted. "I have been avoiding you." She rested her hand on the gate. It wasn't white like the pickets, but a soft, robin's-egg-blue, a foolish color for a gate, but Susanna had wanted it. And Hannah had to admit that she found herself smiling whenever it caught her eye. Now, her fingers brushed the top rail. "I have been struggling, Albert." She closed her eyes for just an instant before opening them and looking up into that kind, gentle face. Again it struck her how handsome his eyes were, how full of life and compassion. *You're a good man,* she thought. *It wouldn't be fair of me to—*

Albert took hold of her shoulders. "Tell me. What's happened to make you so sad? You can tell me anything. Have you received an answer from the bishop? Has he turned down my request to join the church?"

She shook her head as moisture clouded her vision. "I can't marry you," she blurted.

She heard him catch his breath.

"It's not fair to you," she told him.

"What do you mean, not fair to me?" He dropped his hands to take hers and held them as he gazed deeply into her eyes. "I love you, Hannah. Can you tell me that you don't return that love?"

Her throat constricted so that it became impossible to speak.

"Say it," he insisted. "If that's it, say that you don't love me, and I'll walk away."

She couldn't, because she *did* love him. It didn't matter that their lives were half over or that she was a mother and a grandmother. She loved Albert, and she wanted to spend the rest of her life with him…but she couldn't ask him to make the sacrifice for her. "It's because I *do* love you," she murmured. "That's why I can't marry you. It would be wrong of me to force you to join my church, to give up everything for me. I've been selfish to think that—"

"Oh, Hannah, is that what all this is about? That you think you're asking too much of me?" A genuine smile of relief and joy spread across his face. "You love me? You really do?"

She nodded, looking down at their feet. "*Ya,* Albert. I'm afraid I do, but—"

"No buts. Listen to me. You don't get to decide what's best for me. I'm not one of your children. We're both adults, here, Hannah. Marrying you, becoming Amish, it's what I want, what will bring me peace of mind. Happiness. It's like coming home, Hannah. And that's what I want to do, come home to you, every day."

"But, what if they say you have to give up being a veterinarian? It's all you've ever wanted."

"It's not all I've *ever* wanted. I've wanted someone like you. You're a gift from God to me, and maybe, just maybe, I'm a gift to you from God. That's more important than how I live or what I do for a living."

A gift from God. Albert's words cut through her despair like sunshine through dark clouds. Without thinking, she stepped closer to Albert, slipped her arms around his neck, and rose on tiptoes to kiss him full on the mouth. And then, as if it were the most natural thing in the world, Albert's arms were around her, and he was kissing her back, a tender, sweet kiss full of promise and the thrill of two hearts beating to a single note.

Albert's lips were firm and warm, and they fit hers perfectly. They kept kissing, standing there, wrapped in each other's arms in the full light of day.

Which is exactly where Samuel, her son-in-law, the deacon of her church and enforcer of proper behavior found them. "Hannah! Albert!"

They broke apart, shocked at being caught, laughing, and as silly as any two kids caught in a similar situation.

"Kissing?" Samuel attempted his sternest deacon tone, but Hannah detected a hint of disguised humor.

"I'm afraid so," she admitted. "You see, Samuel. We love each other, and it would be better for the family and our community if you would allow us to be together in holy matrimony."

"Better than continuing to cause a scandal," Albert supplied. She glanced at him. He winked, and she had to stifle a giggle. She had lost her mind. Truly. But it was all she could do to keep both feet on the ground and give her son-in-law the respect he deserved while her lips were still deliciously tingling from Albert's kiss.

"Hmmph." Samuel's expression grew serious. "That's exactly why I'm here. To talk to you. Bishop Atlee and the elders have come to a decision." He hesitated. "Are you prepared to abide by it?"

Albert reached for her hand, captured it and held it tightly. "We are."

"Ya," Hannah agreed. "We are."

"*Gut*. Then we start at the same place." Samuel clasped his hands. "Bishop Atlee has prayed for guidance, as have Reuben and Caleb and I. Yours is a very unusual request, but then we think you two are unusual people." He broke into a smile. "You know of course that it's our tradition that a man or woman may ask to join our congregation only once he or she lives as Amish for one year."

Hannah's rush of happiness smacked into the solid wall of the realization that they would have to wait an entire year to be together. A year? She wanted to have the banns read tomorrow. But the *Ordnung* was the *Ordnung*. The elders' word was law. She glanced up at Albert, reading both the joy and the disappointment of having to wait lingering there.

"I understand," Albert said.

"But we believe your case is special," Samuel went on. "You are not English, and Anna has told me that your grandparents were born Amish, and that you share our history and traditions."

Albert nodded. "My father's people."

"Bishop Atlee and I discussed these special conditions, and he believes that you would know your heart and God's will in six months' time."

"Six months!" Hannah was unable to cover her excitement.

"Now, it's customary for a convert to live among us and as one of us for that time," Samuel continued. "So Anna and I would like to offer our home as that haven."

"Thank you," Albert said. "I'd consider it an honor."

Hannah was too full of joy to speak. Albert would be there, just across the pasture. If he lived with Samuel and Anna, no one would question that he fulfilled his promise. The tears that had threatened overflowed and wet her cheeks.

"Now, we expect you to give Hannah a proper courtship under the eyes of her family and community. You will come to our worship services and share in our work frolics and holidays. You will be part of my family, Albert." Mischief twinkled in Samuel's eyes. "And you will have to dress Amish. Plain."

"I can do that," Albert said.

"Remember, marrying Hannah may be your goal, but it isn't a reason to convert to our faith. Conversion must be heartfelt. It must be genuine. And if you feel that it isn't right for you, you must be brave enough to admit it," Samuel continued.

Again, Albert nodded. "I understand."

"Good." Samuel folded his arms over his broad chest and grinned. "It's settled. But there will be no more kissing until after the marriage. Is that clear?"

"*Ya,* Samuel," Hannah said. "No more kissing."

"We'll try," Albert promised. "But it won't be easy."

"There is one more stipulation that is most unusual, but I think you'll find a way to make it work," Samuel said. "Bishop Atlee doesn't want you to waste your veterinary skills. Our community depends on you too much. You can continue to use your motor vehicle to care for your animal patients, but you'll have to hire a driver to take you to and from the office. Or have your nephew transport you. When you're not working we'll expect you to use a horse and buggy. Is that clear?"

"He can still practice?" Hannah asked. "That's wonderful."

"And why not? We follow tradition, but we are not

inflexible. As Bishop Atlee says, 'It would be a sin to waste the skills that the Lord has given him.'"

Hannah turned to face Albert and for a moment, it was as if Samuel wasn't standing there. "Albert, we're getting married," she murmured.

His smile filled her heart with joy. "We're getting married, Hannah."

Epilogue

Six months to the day that Albert first dressed in traditional Old Order clothing, Bishop Atlee baptized him into the faith. The community welcomed Albert with open arms, and two weeks later, Samuel announced the intent of couples Albert Hartman and Hannah Yoder, and David King and Susanna Yoder to join in holy matrimony on the second Tuesday of February. The publishing of their banns launched Hannah into a frenzy of preparation: sewing, house cleaning, compiling a guest list and handwriting invitations.

The weeks between the announcement and the ceremony flew by, and almost before Hannah could catch her breath, she found herself standing beside Albert in front of the bishop, surrounded by family, neighbors and friends in Samuel and Anna's parlor. "Are the two of you prepared to enter marriage according to God's word?" Bishop Atlee asked.

"*Ya*, I am," Hannah said, her response nearly drowned out by Albert's deep and heartfelt assent. Her heart raced; she felt giddy with excitement. All the troubling doubts had evaporated, leaving her with a feeling of peace and anticipation.

"Albert, are you certain that this is the woman that God has chosen to be your wife?"

He squeezed her hand. "I am."

"And you, Hannah," the bishop continued. "Are you certain in the deepest part of your heart and mind that Albert is the man that God has chosen for you?"

"I am."

Bishop Atlee's beard was as white as the snowflakes that softly fell against the tall windows, and his eyes sparkled with affection. He looked to Hannah like some prophet from the Old Testament as he spoke the familiar words. "And do you both promise to cherish and sustain each other in sickness and in health according to God's laws, and to remain as one so long as you both shall live?"

"I do," they said together. And with that, the bishop nodded and motioned them back to their seats on the bench.

"David and Susanna?" the bishop said.

Susanna looked at her mother and Hannah smiled, fighting tears. "Go on," she whispered.

Hand in hand David and Susanna made their way to the bishop and repeated the same words Hannah and Albert had just exchanged. Their speech might not have been as clear and they stumbled over some words, but no one present could have doubted the love that shone in David's and Susanna's eyes. And before Hannah knew it, the couple was seated beside her. Two hymns and a final prayer concluded the ceremony, and then everyone rose and helped to rearrange the chairs so that the men could carry in tables for the wedding feast.

Charley and Eli directed the creation of a special table for the bridal parties. Women quickly covered the surface with white tablecloths, added plates, glasses and silverware, and adorned the *eck* with a large pewter bowl of fruit. Hannah had eyes only for Albert, with a few motherly glances at Susanna. Her precious youngest daughter glowed with an inner light, seemingly so overcome with happiness at finally having her new bridegroom, David, that she refused to let go of his hand, and couldn't stop talking. David seemed equally ecstatic, but rather than bubble over with excitement, he simply grinned, nodded and stared at Susanna as if he was afraid that she might disappear at any moment.

At last, guests and bridal party were all in their places, Hannah and Albert to the left of the corner, Susanna and David to the right, both couples flanked by their attendants—Anna, Grace, Samuel and John on Hannah's side and Rebecca, Ruth, Eli and Caleb on Susanna's. Seated along the walls were the rest of the family and honored guests, including Sara and Ellie, who was moving to Seven Poplars.

"Finally," Albert whispered to Hannah as volunteers began to carry in platters of roast turkey, ham, fried chicken and sausage. "I'm starving."

"Aren't you always?" Hannah teased, thinking how handsome he looked in his plain black coat and trousers and starched white shirt. For just a second, she closed her eyes and savored the joy of God's love. How blessed she was to have this new beginning with this strong and caring man at her side.

"And why wouldn't I be?" Albert asked, reaching for her hand and squeezing it, pulling her out of her reverie. "This getting married stuff is hard work."

She nodded and smiled back at him. He was her husband and now the head of her house. It seemed right, and she was content, so content that she had resigned her position as schoolteacher and planned to stay home and take care of him, and Susanna and David. "No regrets?" she whispered to Albert.

"At leaving Samuel and Anna's house, and her pie, now that we're wed?" Mischief lurked in his dark eyes. "Well, maybe just a little. Her apple-cranberry—"

Hannah laughed.

"Ah, look what's coming now." Girls carried mountains of sweet potatoes, mashed potatoes, egg noodles, rice and vegetables of all kinds, followed by boys with woven baskets of yeast breads, hot rolls and biscuits.

Samuel rose from his place at the table and asked for a moment of silent grace before the meal began. Heads bowed, and peace descended on the house, a quiet broken only by the rustle of the wind through the eaves and the soft patter of snowflakes against the windowpanes. Albert didn't let go of Hannah's hand and she was secretly proud that he didn't care if people saw them. The prayer ended and everyone began to eat.

Hannah had just taken a slice of turkey on her plate when Albert's cell phone rang. Eyes widened. Heads turned. Neighbor's craned their necks to see who had brought a forbidden phone to the wedding supper.

Albert took the small flip phone from his pocket. "Sorry," he called. Whispers and amused glances rippled around the room. As a veterinarian, he had received special dispensation from the bishop to carry his cell phone with him. He stood up and pushed the button. "Hello." A nod, and then, to Hannah's surprise, he handed the phone to her. "It's for you."

"For me?" She stared in surprise. "Who would be calling me?"

Albert laughed. "It's my wedding gift to you. I'd hoped it would be here today, but it seems it's arriving tomorrow."

Nervously, Hannah rose, bringing the cell phone to her ear. "Hello?"

"Mam?" Leah! It was Leah, the only daughter not here with her today! *"Mam!* It's me," Leah said. "The baby and I are coming home for a long visit. Albert bought us a plane ticket."

Hannah's heart leaped. "You're coming home?" The phone slipped from numb fingers as she threw her arms around Albert's neck and kissed him full on the mouth.

Laughing, he caught her by the waist and lifted her up, kissing her so hard that her *kapp* slid halfway off her head. Hannah didn't care. All that mattered was the love that welled up inside her and the warm shouts of approval from those who mattered most in her life. "You wonderful, wonderful man!" she exclaimed. "I love you!"

"And I love you," Albert replied. And then he kissed her again, his strong embrace and tender caress making her feel like a young bride and filling her heart to overflowing with the sweet joy of God's abundant grace.

* * * * *

And when ye stand praying, forgive, if ye have ought against any: that your Father also which is in heaven may forgive you your trespasses.
—*Mark* 11:25

A MOTHER
FOR HIS CHILDREN

Jan Drexler

For my aunts, Martha, Waneta and Nancy.
You taught me what a joy it would be to have sisters!

And with special thanks to Dawn Field, DVM,
who was willing to discuss the details of calves
and cows over lunch.

Soli Deo Gloria

Chapter One

Shipshewana, Indiana
January, 1937

"She's old. *Dat* said so."

"*Ja.* Old and mean."

"Old and mean, and she has a big nose."

Levi Zook gave his four younger boys a meaningful glare before David could add to the list. "We don't know what she looks like, but she sounded nice enough in her letters."

The notes Levi had exchanged with his new housekeeper from Lancaster County had been all business, but the letter of recommendation he received from the bishop in Bird-in-Hand had held the description he hoped for. The bishop had used words like *competent, faithful* and *dedicated,* all qualities he welcomed in a housekeeper. He could picture her in his mind: slightly plump, eager to please, gray hair and a face lined with comfortable wrinkles. A grandmotherly type who could teach his daughters the way to keep house.

His youngest son, five-year-old Sam, bounced on

his toes in anticipation when he heard the train blow its whistle at the edge of town. Clouds of steam rose in the air above the stark, black tree limbs as the train slowed. All four boys pressed forward to be the first to see the engine as it rounded the last curve before arriving at the Shipshewana depot.

A good half foot taller than the crowd of people on the platform, Levi watched the train rumble over the crossing at Morton Street. Three passenger cars followed the tender. Behind them, freight car doors slid open as furtive figures jumped from the train to disappear between the grain elevator and Smith's machine shop. Hobos. Tramps. Even on such a frozen day as this. Levi hunched his shoulders at the thought of how cold those men must be as they searched for food and shelter for the night. He doubted if any of them would make it as far as his farm. In weather like this, the men looked for handouts or jobs closer to town.

The squeal of metal grinding on metal brought him back to the passenger cars. He ducked to see into the windows, but all he could see were *Englischer* faces. No Amish bonnet.

Jesse tugged at Levi's sleeve as he pointed a mittened hand toward the last of the passenger cars.

"Is that her, *Dat?*"

A tall Amish woman appeared in the doorway of the far train car. Levi watched as she scanned the crowded platform. Could this be her? *Ne,* she was much too young. She couldn't be very far into her twenties. Her blue eyes met his, then passed him by before she stepped off the train and onto the platform.

Levi continued watching each person alight from the train until no more appeared. There were no other

Amish women, certainly not the middle-aged spinster he was expecting.

"She's the only one left, *Dat.* Could she be the one?"

The lone Amish woman stood in the middle of the platform with a suitcase at her feet as the people around her made their way to waiting automobiles, trucks and wagons.

"I don't think so, Sam." Levi looked at the young woman again. She glanced their way once, her face uncertain. She looked a bit lost, as if she had been expecting someone to meet her. Meanwhile, Ruth Mummert, the housekeeper he was expecting, had never shown up. Had they miscommunicated? Did he have the date of her arrival wrong?

"That isn't her." James turned his back on the train and the lone figure on the platform. "She's too pretty."

"Well, boys, we can't stand here all day. We'll have to come back tomorrow."

David nodded his head at the young woman. "Should we give her a ride?"

"*Ja,* son." Levi herded the boys in the direction of the woman, now standing with her back to them, her eyes on his big family buggy with Champ tied to the rail. "We can't leave her here by herself."

The woman turned to watch him as they approached, her blue eyes deep within the shadows of her black bonnet flashing with hope before dismissing him by turning her head away again.

"Can we help you?" Levi's question brought those eyes back to his. "Can we give you a ride somewhere?"

"I was expecting someone to meet me at the train…." Her accent betrayed her eastern home.

"We were meeting someone, too," Sam said.

Levi laid his hand on the boy's shoulder to remind him to let his elders speak. "Who were you meeting? I probably know where they live and can take you there."

The young woman's cheeks were red with the cold. Levi wanted to hurry her into his buggy, where the foot warmer was waiting for them. "I was supposed to meet Levi Zook, but he hasn't shown up. Do you know him?"

"I should know him. I'm Levi Zook. You aren't Ruth Mummert, are you?" This young, beautiful woman couldn't be the spinster he had been writing to.

"*Ja,* Ruth Mummert." She nodded, eyeing him. "But you're not the Levi Zook who has hired me to be his housekeeper. He's a much older man than you."

The boys stifled giggles while Levi pulled his glove off and dug in his pocket for her latest letter.

"I am Levi Zook." He held the paper out to her. "Here's your letter accepting the job as my housekeeper and telling me which train you'd be on."

She took the letter from his hand and unfolded it, nodding quickly when she saw the handwriting.

"It looks like I assumed wrong, Levi Zook." She smiled at him as she folded the paper again and gave it to him. "But now that's cleared up and I'm sure we won't have any other misunderstandings."

Levi's return smile faded as she turned to greet the boys. What would she say when she met the rest of his children? In all their correspondence, he had never mentioned how many children he had, and she had never asked. He scratched his beard. He had never asked about her age or circumstances, either. Wasn't she too young for this job? She couldn't have the experience he had hoped for. They had both made assumptions, but she was here now, and he might as well give her a try.

"We should start for home. Our buggy is over here." Levi leaned down to take her bag and led the way, the boys following. Before giving her a hand into the seat, Levi felt the warming pan on the floor. He'd need to replenish it before starting the trip home.

"I'll just take this into the station and get some fresh coals. Make yourself comfortable and I'll be right back."

Ruth Mummert made a quick nod at his words, but the glance she gave him was unsure, as if she already regretted her decision to take the job. And then the uncertainty was gone, replaced by a quick smile. When she discovered the extent of the job he had hired her for, would she smile and call that a "misunderstanding," too?

Ruthy climbed into the front seat of the strange-looking black buggy. The ones at home had gray covers—just one of many differences she would have to adjust to, she decided. Gathering her shawl closely around her, she buried her chin in its folds. Indiana was colder than the winter weather she had left at home in Bird-in-Hand.

She peered out the front window of the buggy at the man walking into the train station with the warming pan. Levi Zook wasn't what she had been expecting. When he described himself as a widower and said his daughter had been caring for him since her mother died, she had assumed he would be nearly her father's age, but this man looked closer to thirty than sixty.

The boys were a surprise. Her mind skirted around the glaring omission in Levi Zook's letter. He had mentioned that he expected her to care for his children, but he never said how many children he had. What did it matter? How many could he have? Five, maybe six?

After growing up with three brothers, Ruthy knew how to handle boys. Washing muddy trousers and feeding hungry, growing young men was nothing new to her. And then there was his daughter, Waneta. So one girl to help out, at least.

The back door of the buggy opened and the biggest boy jumped into the middle seat, and then two of his brothers followed. They all wore identical dark coats and navy blue knit caps.

"I got here first, David. Let me sit by James."

"*Ne,* I want to sit in the middle."

"Sam, you sit up front with her."

"*Ne, ne,* I don't want to!" This last cry came from the smallest of the boys, still standing on the buggy step.

Ruthy turned her face toward the front of the buggy, trying to stay out of the squabble. They made the buggy sway as they pushed at each other, like a bunch of half-grown puppies.

So these were Levi Zook's children. *Mam* had urged her to learn more about her position before traveling all this distance, but staying another day in Bird-in-Hand was out of the question. How could she stay there after what Elam and Laurette had done?

"Boys, you know where to sit." Levi's deep voice broke through the noise. "Stop this arguing, now. Jesse, move over so David can sit in his own place."

Levi slid the warming pan across the floor of the buggy and Ruthy tucked her feet up to it. The January air had a bite to it, even in the shelter of the buggy, and she craved the heat that seeped through the leather shoes to her toes.

"But *Dat,* I don't want to sit by her." The littlest boy

still stood on the buggy step, his face glaring at Ruthy as she turned to smile at him.

"If you sit between your *daed* and me, you'll be able to share the warming pan."

Ruthy knew her words had struck gold when she heard the envious groan from one of the boys behind her. The young boy heard it, too, and his face lit up.

"Can I really?"

"*Ja,* for sure." Ruthy tucked her skirt in close as he scrambled onto the seat next to her. She glanced up to see Levi Zook giving her a grateful look. It seemed her job was starting out well so far.

As the buggy jolted over the railroad tracks, Ruthy smiled at the boy next to her.

"You know my name, but I don't know yours."

"I'm Sam. I'm five years old, and I like cows." The words burst out of him as if he had been holding them in all day. "And that's James. He's eleven and doesn't like girls. David is nine and likes school. And that's Jesse. He's seven." He nodded toward the backseat as he introduced his brothers. "And at home…"

"How was the train ride?" Levi Zook interrupted, his face red as he concentrated on driving the horse through the town traffic.

"It was long, but comfortable." Ruthy glanced out the window. The roads were smooth with packed snow. "How far is your farm from here?"

"We're about six miles from Shipshewana, down in Eden Township."

"It's the biggest farm around," Sam said, and then his pink cheeks reddened even more and he ducked his head into the collar of his coat. "I mean, it's plenty large for our family."

Levi cleared his throat, drawing Ruthy's attention away from Sam's boasting words. "I hope the arrangements I mentioned in the letter are to your liking."

"Ach, ja," Ruthy said. "There's a *Dawdi Haus* I'll be living in?"

"Ja. It's attached to the main house, and there's a passageway in between. It's handy to the kitchen and cellar."

Ruthy shivered as the horse trotted swiftly down the snow-covered road. The farm fields were January bare, with flat expanses of snow between the fence rows. As the buggy grew colder, she drew her shawl closer to her neck. Even the boys in the back fell into silence in the frigid air.

By the time Levi turned onto a farm lane, the coals in the warming pan had lost all their heat. Sam pressed against his *daed* to keep warm, but Ruthy looked up the lane, anxious to get the first glimpse of her new home. The house was large, with additions made over the years like train cars, and the little *Dawdi Haus* a tacked-on caboose following behind. Smoke poured from a chimney at the end of the house closest to the *Dawdi Haus,* a sign someone was home. Levi pulled up to the back door.

"Sam, take Ruth in to the kitchen while the boys and I take care of the chores." Levi looked over Sam's head at her, with an apologetic look in his brown eyes. "We'll be in for supper."

Ruthy nodded, looking forward to getting into the warm kitchen. The look in her employer's eyes mystified her, though. Why would he feel bad for leaving her alone with little Sam?

She climbed down from the buggy and took her suit-

case from the back, then followed Sam to the door.
The back porch was enclosed, with a wash bench along
the outer wall, hooks for coats on the wall next to the
kitchen door and planks to hold muddy boots off the
floor below. Warmth seeped into the porch through the
closed kitchen door and Ruthy unwrapped her winter
shawl as Sam hung his coat on a hook.

The door opened to welcome them in, and a young
girl smiled shyly at Ruthy.

"Nellie, close the door!"

Ruthy stepped into the kitchen quickly as the girl,
about eight years old, obeyed the voice of an older girl
who stood with her back to Ruthy as she removed a loaf
of bread from the oven. It must be Waneta, the oldest.
Four boys and two girls? So, Levi Zook had six children she was to care for? She should have asked more
about the children in her letters.

"Hallo," the older girl said as she closed the oven
door. "You must be Ruth. I'm Waneta."

"It's good to meet you," Ruthy said, smiling at her.
The heat of the oven had given Waneta's face a pretty
flush.

"You've had a long journey, and I'm sure you want to
get settled. Martha built a fire in the *Dawdi Haus* when
she went to make up your bed, so it should be warm in
there for you by now."

"Martha? I must have heard wrong. I thought I heard
you call your sister 'Nellie.'"

Waneta laughed and hugged the little girl. "This is
Nellie. Martha is the twelve-year-old sister."

Seven children? Ruthy grasped her satchel closer,
her lips pressed together. Seven children would be a
challenge, but she could do it. She had always enjoyed

large families. She followed Sam through the kitchen door leading to the chilly passageway between the two houses. Windows on both sides made it feel large and open, but sheltered from the weather.

She followed Sam into the house, where a girl sat in a chair, a book open in her lap. She looked up with startled eyes as Sam opened the door.

He looked up at Ruthy with disgust. "Martha's always reading when she's supposed to be working."

Ruthy smiled at Sam and glanced at Martha. "I like to read, too. It's hard to put a book down when there are chores to be done, isn't it?"

"*Ja,* for sure." Martha's sweet smile warmed the room. "*Dat* said we should leave you be so you can settle in today." The girl looked at Ruthy's suitcase. "Or I could help you unpack…"

"I'd love your company, but don't you think Waneta needs your help?"

Martha's face told her she had guessed right, and Sam tugged at his sister's hand. "Come on, Martha. 'Neta's going to be mad if you don't help her instead of mooning around."

"I'll see you later, all right?" Ruthy gave Martha a smile as the girl followed Sam back into the main house.

Ruthy closed the door behind them, looking around her new home. The front sitting room was cozy, with two chairs and a small side table. It would be a comfortable place to sit in the evenings while she worked on her sewing.

At this thought Ruthy sank into the rocking chair. Sewing for seven children? And their father? First thing tomorrow she would need to start in on taking inventory and planning for their summer clothes. Although

Sam's trousers seemed pretty short—she may need to make sure they had enough winter clothes first. Why hadn't Levi Zook told her how many children he had in his letter?

And why hadn't she followed *Mam's* advice and asked before making this trip?

She knew why. Even if he had told her the size of the job, she would have come anyway. Any excuse to get away from Lancaster County and the gossip. If she had to suffer the sight of her Elam with Laurette Mast one more time...

Ruthy bit her lip. *Ne,* not Laurette Mast. She was Laurette Nafziger now—Elam's Laurette.

Well, nothing would get done if she sat here wasting time. She went into the bedroom to put her clothes away. The bed had three quilts layered on it, with an extra one folded across the end of the bed. At least she would sleep warm.

Smoothing the quilt beneath her hand, Ruthy felt the empty silence of the little house. Her own quiet, empty house.

For sure this was the future God had waiting for her. Life as a *maidle,* forever unmarried, caring for other people's houses and families. It wouldn't be a bad life, giving herself in service to others.

Ruthy's eyes stung. *Ne,* not a bad life, but not at all what she had dreamed of during the eight years Elam had courted her. The life she had planned was at Elam's side, raising his children, building their future together. She rubbed her hands together, working some warmth into them. Her bony hands, too large for a woman. No wonder Elam had turned from her to pretty, petite Laurette.

Ruthy knew what she looked like in Elam's eyes. She was too tall, too thin, her mouth too wide. Even though she tried to shrink down when she was near him, he must have felt small next to her. No man wanted a wife who towered over her.

Ja, a *maidle.* That's what she would always be.

And if she wasn't careful, she'd sink into that trap of self-pity she had tried to leave behind.

Work—hard work—was what she needed, and it looked like she had found it. Well, first things first. Unpack and then out to the main house to help Waneta with the afternoon chores. There were nine mouths to feed, and that meant there was no time for lazing around, even as exhausted as she felt.

At the sound of a knock on her door, Ruthy opened it to find a little girl on the other side.

"*Hallo.* Nellie, right?"

The girl giggled. "*Ne,* I'm Nancy. Nellie is my twin sister."

Eight children? This was really too much. Levi Zook should have told her.

Nancy's cheeks were rosy and chapped.

"Have you been outside in this cold?"

"*Ja,* I was helping Elias with the chickens, but when *Dat* and the boys came home he didn't need me anymore."

A cold knot tightened in Ruthy's stomach.

"Nancy, who is Elias?"

"My oldest brother. He and Waneta are twins just like Nellie and I are twins."

Ruthy gripped the door, watching the eight-year-old bounce on her toes as she spoke. She counted up in her head. Nine. Nine children. She smiled at Nancy, the innocent bearer of this shocking news.

"Where is your *daed* now?"

"In the buggy shed. Do you want me to get him for you?"

"*Ne, denki.* I think I'll go out and see the buggy shed myself."

Ruthy closed the door of the *Dawdi Haus* and headed through the short breezeway to the kitchen, with Nancy following. Waneta nodded a hello to her as she peeled potatoes, the noise of the children's voices making it impossible to say anything more. As Ruthy opened the door to the back porch, she kept Nancy from coming with her.

"I want to speak to your *daed* alone."

Nancy nodded as she closed the door, and then she twitched her winter shawl from the hook and threw it around her shoulders as she barreled out the door. Five boys were throwing snowballs at each other in the yard as she passed. Would she ever remember their names? As she reached the door of the buggy shed at the side of the barn she stopped with her hand on the latch, trembling. Five boys? Sam was inside the house. She turned to the boys in the yard again, counting. There was James, David and Jesse, the three she had met in town, and two older boys with them. One of them had to be Elias, the oldest brother, but who was the other big one?

Just then one of the boys shouted to him, "Hah, Nathan, you missed me again!"

Biting back her anger, she swung open the door of the shed and stepped in, face-to-face with Levi Zook as he rose from wiping the buggy wheels with a rag. He loomed over her in the confines of the room, suddenly dark as she shut the door on the bright midafternoon sunshine. But for all his size, his eyes were the gentlest she had ever seen, with lines that crinkled when he smiled at her.

A snowball hit the outside of the shed with a thud, bringing Ruthy back to the anger that had propelled her in here. She opened her mouth to speak, but Levi Zook only bent down to wipe the wheel hub again.

"Levi Zook, just how many children do you have?"

Levi gave the freshly greased wheel hub a final wipe with his rag before he looked into the face of the furious young woman. He knew this confrontation was coming—he had been dreading it ever since before Christmas, when she had agreed to take the job. He should have told her, but he hadn't wanted to risk her turning down the job. If Ruth weren't here, Eliza would be sure to take the younger girls to live with her as she had insisted she'd do ever since Salome died a year ago.

"Only ten." He stumbled over his words as her face paled and she reached out to the wall for support. "But they're *gut* children and they won't be a bother to you."

"Only ten? You didn't think you should tell me this before I accepted your job?"

Levi rubbed his hand across his face and through his beard, sighing. "*Ja.* I should have told you."

She stared at him, her mouth twitching. Was she going to break out into tears? He wouldn't blame her if she insisted on going back to Lancaster County, but then what would he do? Finding a wife who would take on ten children wasn't as easy as he thought it might be when he first started looking. He pushed up the front of his broad-brimmed hat and rubbed his forehead. Tension made his head ache.

All the single women he knew were either much too young or they had better offers than he could give them. Hiring a housekeeper was the only alternative he could think of to keep his family together. This situation had to work, but how could he make her stay?

Ruth covered her mouth with her hand, turning away from him. When she glanced back he could see she was laughing. Laughing at him?

"I'm sorry," she said, her laughter bubbling up so that she could hardly breathe. "*Ach,* Levi Zook, you should see yourself. You just wiped grease all over your face."

Levi pulled his hand away from his face. She was right. It was covered with black grease. He wiped at his face with his rag, but Ruth stopped him.

"There must be a clean cloth here somewhere," she said between gasps. She sorted through the rags on the workbench and found a folded scrap at the bottom of the pile.

"Denki." Levi took the rag and wiped his nose and forehead. His beard would have to wait. What must she think of him? He must have looked like some schoolboy the way he kept spreading the grease around. He tried to wipe his hands clean and waited for her to stop laughing. Could he live with a woman who laughed at him, no matter how her eyes danced in the dim light of the shed?

"I'm sorry I didn't tell you about the children earlier. I meant to, but I just didn't know how to do it in a letter."

"So you thought you'd let me figure it out as I met them."

"For sure, I didn't plan it that way."

cake waited to be frosted. Waneta struggled to pull a roasting pan from the oven, her hair falling around her face and her *kapp* limp and nearly falling off.

Seizing a towel from the counter, Ruthy grabbed one end of the roaster.

"Waneta, this ham smells *wonderful-gut.*" Together, they lifted the roaster onto the counter next to the stove and Waneta closed the oven door with a bang.

"*Denki,* but you're supposed to be resting. *Dat* said you'd be tired from your long trip."

"I've rested enough, and you look like you could use some help."

"*Ja,* for sure I can, but you shouldn't have to help with your own welcome supper."

"Never mind that. Just let me help."

Waneta's brown eyes startled wide and she dashed around Ruthy. "Sam! You know better than that! Look what you've done to the cake!"

Ruthy turned to see Sam holding a chunk of unfrosted cake in his hand. Her smile froze on her face. If this was the way Levi Zook raised his children, he needed her more than he thought. It was time for her to start earning her money.

A vision of her elementary school teacher, Mrs. Studer, flashed into her mind. The *Englisch* woman had ruled a classroom full of forty-five children from first through eighth grades with a calm voice and a no-nonsense approach to rules. Ruthy had loved her. What would Mrs. Studer do with this mess if she were here?

Stepping to the table, Ruthy caught each of the eight-year-old twins by the arm as they ran past her. "What are the two of you supposed to be doing?"

Their flushed faces looked into hers, and then they both glanced at Waneta.

"We're setting the table," one of them said, grinning at Ruthy. When Ruthy kept her face stern, the grin vanished.

"Then you should be setting the table, shouldn't you? Games like this should be saved for outdoors."

The girl who had spoken nodded her head. Ruthy turned to her twin sister, ready to scold both of them, but the tears in the girl's eyes stopped her words. She was so much more sensitive than her sister. How different could twins be?

"You will need to help me with your names for a while. I know one of you is Nellie, right?" The silent twin nodded her head and she turned back to the more daring girl. "So you're Nancy."

"You're right." The girl grinned again, her blue eyes sparkling.

"Nancy, you go ahead and finish putting the flatware on the table and Nellie can get the plates."

Nellie went to a cupboard near the sink and opened it, revealing a generous stack of white plates. Such a tender child in this boisterous family seemed out of place. Ruthy turned her attention back to Sam, who was sitting on the chair next to the decimated cake, calmly eating the piece he had stolen. Waneta glanced at Ruthy as she opened a jar of pickled beets and gave her a quick smile. At least one person approved of the way she was handling things so far.

Ruthy knelt next to the little boy.

"Are you enjoying that cake?"

Sam nodded and grinned at her. His blue eyes were

full of mischief, but his sweet smile made her long to give him a hug.

She couldn't give in to that! This boy was a little thief who needed to be taught a lesson.

"It would taste better with frosting on it, wouldn't it?"

"Ja," Sam said between bites. "'Neta makes the best frosting."

"It's too bad you won't get any, then."

Sam stopped, the cake halfway to his mouth for another bite. "Why won't I get any?"

Ruthy rose and took a spoonful of frosting from the nearby bowl. "You're eating your cake now instead of after supper. So when the rest of us have our pieces with frosting, you won't be able to have any." She started frosting the untouched layer of cake and exchanged a glance with Waneta. The girl gave her a grateful smile.

"If I give it back, will you put frosting on it?" Sam held out his remaining chunk of cake.

"Will you promise to leave desserts alone until after the meals from now on?"

Sam stared at the cake, considering. Then he nodded. "I'll try."

"All right then." Ruthy got a plate from the cupboard and Sam deposited his cake on it. "I'll frost this piece just for you." Sam slid down from the chair and headed into the front room.

"Denki," Waneta whispered. *"Dat* always complains about pieces missing from the cakes, but I don't know how to stop him."

"I have a brother who tried the same thing when he was Sam's age. *Mam* made him give up his desserts for a month when he didn't stop."

Waneta giggled. "You'll have to threaten Sam with that. Nothing I say will make him behave."

Ruthy set the broken cake layer on top of the first one and spread it with another dollop of frosting. Dessert wouldn't be pretty, but from the way Sam liked his sister's cake, she could tell it would still taste good.

"Do you always make the meals by yourself?"

Waneta drained a pot full of cooked potatoes. "Usually. Martha is supposed to help me, but she always disappears just when I need her."

Ruthy tried to remember who Martha was, then placed her. The girl with her nose in a book in the *Dawdi Haus* earlier. Levi Zook needed more than a housekeeper—that man needed someone to take his younger girls in hand. He had been right when he said this task was too big for Waneta.

While Waneta piled slices of ham on a platter and filled the table with green beans, carrots, bread and pickles, Ruthy mashed the potatoes. Waneta sent Nancy to the back porch to ring the dinner bell, and soon the kitchen was full of children finding their places on the long benches that sat along the sides of the big table. Levi Zook came into the kitchen last, combing his fingers through his beard. Once he took his seat at the head of the table, Ruthy took the only place left, on the end opposite Levi Zook.

Every eye at the table was focused on her and she felt her face grow hot. Had she done something wrong? Were they waiting for her to do something?

"She's sitting in *Mam's* chair," said one of the older boys.

Ruthy started to rise. She wasn't here to take their *mam's* place.

"It's all right Nathan," Levi said. "Ruth, that is your place at the table for now." Levi looked at the boy who had spoken and the older brother sitting next to him. "Your *mam* is gone. We will not make her place at the table a shrine."

Both boys lowered their eyes, their necks red. *Ach, ja,* they missed their *mam.* It would take some time for them to get used to Ruthy being here.

Levi cleared his throat. "Let's pray."

Ruthy bowed her head and silently began reciting her mealtime prayer in her head. Before she was done she heard the distinct clink of Levi's fork against his plate. Was that his signal the prayer was over? She raised her eyes to see him staring at her, an unreadable expression on his face.

How did he feel about her sitting in his dead wife's chair? However he felt, Levi Zook needed her.

As soon as Levi had come into the kitchen for supper he could feel the change. The bustling kitchen, normally noisy and chaotic, had an undergirding of order Levi hadn't seen since before Sam was born.

And now the reason for that difference was sitting at the opposite end of the long table from him. Ruth sat at the foot of his table as if she had always done so, accepting the dishes of food passed to her and helping Sam cut the meat on his plate. She smiled at each of the children as she spoke to them, introducing herself to Nathan and Elias, who had been outside since she arrived, and asking about each of the children's favorite foods.

The sound of her voice was a balm that soothed a festering need. When Salome died a year ago, a light had gone out in his home, but now the small flame of a woman's influence was sputtering to life again.

Levi speared a chunk of ham and swirled it in his mashed potatoes before bringing it to his mouth with a satisfied sigh. He had done a good thing when he put that notice in *The Budget,* no matter what his sister, Eliza, said. His children needed a woman's touch, that's all, and they belonged at home. Farming them out to relatives wouldn't be good for them at all.

He took another bite of ham and potatoes, and then reached for his glass of milk. Eleven pairs of eyes followed every movement, and he became aware that silence had descended on the table. He glanced at Ruth, and found her staring at him.

Levi finished chewing, and then took a swallow from his glass. His children looked expectant, except Sam, who looked down at his plate when Levi's gaze reached the far end of the table. Ruth's expression hadn't changed.

"Did you hear me, Levi Zook?"

Her hair glowed like gold in the light from the kerosene lamp above the table. Had she said something to him?

"*Ne,* Ruth, I didn't hear you."

"I said Sam seems to be at loose ends here in the house all day. I asked when you will take him out to do barn chores with you."

His face grew hot as Ruth kept her gaze on him. She hadn't been here more than a few hours, and already she was telling him how to raise his son?

Ja, well, she was right, it was time for Sam to join him in the barn. It was another thing he had neglected in the last year. Shame threatened, but irritation quickly squelched it. He should have taken this action sooner, but no woman was going to dictate how he raised his children.

"Sam will join me in the barn when I'm ready for him to, and not a moment sooner."

Ruth's face reddened as her eyes narrowed. She opened her mouth to speak, but Sam's voice piped up. "I'm ready now, *Dat*. Jesse has been helping you since he was little, and I'm almost as big as him."

Levi glanced at Jesse. At seven years old, he still wasn't much bigger than his little brother. He hunched his shoulders around his slight frame as if he wanted to slink away from the table. He hated being the center of attention.

Jesse had been helping in the barn for a couple of years already, but he still needed a lot of help and training with his chores, which took time. With Sam there, it would take even more time away from his own work, but on the other hand, the two smaller boys could help each other.

She was right.

But he would take himself behind the woodshed for a thrashing before he gave in to this woman now. This was his family and he would have the final say in how his children were raised.

He stood up, his chair scraping against the wooden floor. "I'm going out to finish the chores."

He grabbed his hat from the hook by the back door and stormed through the porch, snagging his coat from the wall as he went.

The meal had started out so well, before she interfered. Levi stopped beside the chicken coop, taking a deep breath of the frigid January air. Before she made a simple suggestion.

He reached into the pockets of his coat for his gloves and pulled them on, turning to face the house. Light from the kitchen windows gave a warm glow to the snow of the barnyard, pulling his gaze back to the table he had just left. He could see the shadowy forms of his children through the white curtains and their voices drifted to him in the still night. Elias's deep bass chuckle rumbled through the higher pitches of the other children's laughter.

Pride had forced him out here into the dark, but he was right, wasn't he? He was the man in this house, not some upstart woman who comes in and tries to take over.

A woman he had invited. A woman he was paying to run his house for him.

What bothered him most was that she was right. It was past time for him to bring Sam along as he worked. Next year his youngest son would start school, and he would have missed his opportunity to start him out right.

Cold forced him away from the golden glow of the kitchen window and into the cowshed. He lit the lantern and checked on Moolah, the tall, bony Holstein. She was his best milker and due to drop a calf in a few weeks. She blinked an eye at him and chewed her cud. She was nice and comfortable tonight.

Levi went through the cowshed and into the main barn. The constant rustling in the vast haymow above him was interrupted by a thump and a squeak as one of the barn cats ended a successful hunt. A moment of silence, and then the rustling started again as the mice resumed their endless quest for food. He opened the door of the workshop and hung the lantern on its hook. He had been sharpening knives before the supper bell rang, and he might as well finish the job now.

He picked up one of the kitchen knives and tested its blade with his thumb. Taking the whetstone, he started the circular motion that would bring back the fine, sharp edge. From the workbench he could see the kitchen window. Movement behind the curtains told him the girls were clearing the table. Before long the children would bring out the projects they were working on during their Christmas vacation from school. This was the time of the evening when he enjoyed sitting close by, reading *The Budget* or a farm magazine, ready to answer any questions they had.

In the days before he lost Salome, she would sit in the rocking chair he had placed in the kitchen for her, knitting or mending, and enjoying their family. He could see her now, if he closed his eyes to the tools and workbench surrounding him. His Salome, rocking softly in her chair, and the gentle smile she kept on her face in spite of the pain.

The pain that had been her constant burden during those last months. Pain so horrible, that when she died, he had wept as much from thankfulness that she had been released, as from grief that he had lost her.

Levi pulled his mind away from the memories. Salome was free of pain now, safe and secure in the Blessed Land.

The knife lay loose in his hand, forgotten. He turned the blade over, working the other side.

He had taken her presence for granted, he knew that. From the time he first met her when they were children, he had thought Salome would always be with him. His partner in life, and together in their old age. But it wasn't to be. God saw fit to let him carry on alone.

And alone he would stay, it seemed. He had exhausted the eligible women in the district and beyond, and not one of them would agree to be his wife. He had settled for the next best thing—a housekeeper.

And God provided Ruth. He had expected an older woman, but Ruth seemed capable and she was already making friends with the children. And at least now his family was safe from his interfering sister.

As the door slammed behind Levi Zook, Ruthy's stomach turned. *Ach,* she had spoken before thinking again! As the father, he was the only one who had the say in how Sam was raised, not her. He certainly wouldn't want her meddling, especially her first day here.

The children's laughter broke into her thoughts as Elias told a joke and Ruthy smiled along with them. Surely they would have noticed their *daed's* mood when he left the house? But it didn't seem like they thought anything unusual had happened. Perhaps Levi acted like this quite often.

She bit her lip at the sudden thought that perhaps his mood had nothing to do with her. He had recently lost his wife, and he was probably still in mourning for her.

That must be the problem. She must be more understanding of the poor man.

After supper and dishes were done, the children brought books, sewing projects and knitting needles and gathered back at the table under the bright light.

"What do you have planned for tomorrow?" Ruthy

gave the dishrag a final rinse as Waneta set the last plates in the cupboard.

"Whatever has to be done." Waneta leaned against the counter with a sigh. "There's always work waiting, isn't there?"

"Do you follow a schedule?"

"*Mam* did, but I don't know how she did it. I try to do laundry on Monday, the way she did, but then everyone runs out of clothes after only a few days, and I have to do laundry again. Then there aren't enough dirty clothes to wash on the next Monday...." Waneta's words faltered and she sent a pleading look at Ruthy.

"It sounds like all you need is some organization." Ruthy silently thanked her mother for teaching her to run an orderly home. She would certainly need all those skills now. "Let's sit down and make a list of what needs to be done."

As she and Waneta planned their week, Ruthy worked to keep her rising impatience out of her voice. Levi Zook's wife had only been gone a year, but from what Waneta told her, she had been bearing the heaviest load of the housekeeping for several years. Her father had expected entirely too much from this young girl.

When Levi and Elias came into the back porch just as the clock was striking eight o'clock, stomping the snow off their boots on the wood floor, Ruthy rose to make her way to the *Dawdi Haus*.

"We'll start on the mending tomorrow, right after we *redd* up the house in the morning."

Waneta gave her a grateful smile. "That sounds *wonderful-gut*. It's so much better to have everything planned out, isn't it?"

"We'll tackle things one day at a time for now, and

then on Monday we'll put together a schedule for the week." Ruthy patted the girl's arm. "And don't be in any hurry to get up in the morning. I'll get breakfast started, and you can come down to help when the others do."

Waneta's smile broke into a big grin at that, and Ruthy slipped through the door into the passageway just as the door from the porch burst open. She had intruded on this family enough for one day.

Closing the door of her *Dawdi Haus,* Ruthy lit the lamp on the table in her front room. After building up the fire in the small stove, she hunted out the yarn and knitting needles she had brought with her. Keeping this family in stockings would keep her needles busy every evening.

The rocking chair creaked in the quiet room as she cast on the stitches she needed to make the first of a pair of men's stockings. Her mind drifted back to Lancaster County, to the home she had left behind. *Mam* would be knitting tonight, while *Daed* read aloud from *The Budget.* The thought brought tears to her eyes and she laid her needles down. Why had God called her to leave her home and come here? Soon *Daed* and *Mam* would be saying their evening prayer before they went up to bed, and she wouldn't be in the family circle.

She brushed away the tears and resumed working on the stocking. As she rocked and knitted, she recited the prayer she had heard every night of her life, hearing *Daed's* voice in her memory.

When she finished, Ruthy let the stocking drop in her lap again and gazed at the empty room around her. Of all the things she had considered about choosing to follow God's call to be a *maidle* and to serve Him by working in strangers' homes, she had never considered this solitude. The clock ticking on the wall struck the half hour, the single chime echoing in the silent room. Years of empty, silent evenings stretched before her.

Without a family of her own, she would always be only that single note.

"She isn't *Mam*," Nellie said as she snuggled next to Levi on the sofa.

"*Ne,* she isn't *Mam*." Levi held his daughter tightly as he kissed the top of her head.

"I like her," Waneta said. "She was a big help with supper and afterwards."

Levi took in the faces of the other children as they gathered in the front room for their usual before-bed-time talk. When Salome was alive, this had been the time when he had led his family in evening prayers, but he hadn't had the heart to resume them since she had left him with their children to raise alone.

"What do you think, Elias?" Levi turned to his oldest son, only sixteen and already finding ways to spend time away from the family. He was serious about some girl and spent every Saturday evening out with his courting buggy.

Elias rubbed the back of his neck, his chin rough with young whiskers. "She's all right. She's just keeping house, right? You haven't brought her here to marry her or anything, have you?"

"*Ne.* I only hired her to be our housekeeper and help with the girls."

"Well, then," said Nathan, "she can stay. Anything so we don't have to eat Waneta's cooking anymore." He grinned and ducked away as Waneta aimed a playful slap at his head.

"She can't stay. She's mean." Sam shifted on Levi's lap, where Levi thought he had been sleeping.

"You only think she's mean because she wouldn't let you eat cake before supper." Nancy was snuggled against one side of him the way her twin, Nellie, was snuggled against the other.

"You shouldn't eat cake before supper anyway." Martha was lying on the floor, staring at the ceiling, always the dreamer.

Levi stood up, lifting Sam in his arms. "Come now, it's time for bed."

James and David finished their game of checkers while the others filed up the stairway. Jesse didn't move from the corner of the sofa, where his head leaned against the padded arm as he snored softly. Levi smiled. He'd carry Sam up to the bed the two little ones shared and then come back down for Jesse. At least both boys were still small enough for him to carry.

After tucking the two boys into their bed and saying good-night to each of the others, Levi steeled himself for the late-night visit to check the barn. Braving the bitter cold one more time was necessary if he was going to be able to rest peacefully tonight.

He crossed the big front room to the kitchen door in his stocking feet, following a path of light across the dark floor. Someone had left the lamp burning in the kitchen. It was a waste of good lamp oil when he was scraping for cash to pay his new housekeeper.

At the doorway, he stopped. She was in the kitchen, her back to him, wearing a white flannel nightgown. The lamp from the *Dawdi Haus* burned on the counter next to her, its gentle flicker mingling with the sound of her voice humming a tune in the quiet room. Her golden hair trailed down her back in a thick braid as she worked with the dough trough, setting the sponge for tomorrow's bread.

Levi's mouth went dry as he stared at the lustrous rope. Salome's hair had been beautiful, brown and fine, falling down her back like silky water when she brushed it out, but that had been before her illness caused her hair to become dry and brittle. It had been a long time—too long—since he had run his hands through a woman's hair.

Lamplight glowed around Ruth's white gown with an ethereal light. When she reached up into the cupboard, that golden braid swung across her back, pulling a moan from him that he strangled with a cough. At the noise she turned around.

"Levi Zook! I thought you had all gone to bed." She backed away, even though the entire kitchen stretched between them. "I forgot to set the sponge for tomorrow's bread…." Then her eyes narrowed as she focused on his feet. "Why are you walking around in just your stockings?"

She sounded like his mother. "I'm going out to check the barn before I go to bed like I always do. Don't worry, I'll put my boots on before I go outdoors."

Ruth put one hand on her hip and pointed a wooden spoon at his feet with the other. "You'll put holes in your stockings if you don't wear something over them."

Levi gritted his teeth, but he fought to keep his words even. "I won't wear my boots in the house."

"Don't you have slippers?" She cocked her head to one side, facing him down the way he did his Percheron gelding.

"*Ne,* I don't. But at least I'm not walking around barefoot on a freezing night."

Her face blanched as she looked down at her bare toes below the hem of her nightgown. She reached her hand up to where her *kapp* should be and blood rushed to her cheeks. "*Ach,* I forgot… You must think… I'm so sorry…" She dropped the spoon on the counter and fled through the door to the *Dawdi Haus.*

Levi stared at the door she slammed behind her, his mind filled with the image of her flowing white gown and that trailing braid. Taking a deep breath, he rubbed his hands over his eyes then smoothed his beard. This wasn't what he had bargained for when he set out to hire a housekeeper.

Chapter Three

Levi reached out with one hand to turn off the alarm before it could ring. Four o'clock and time to get up.

He pushed himself to the edge of the half-empty bed with a groan. Nights were short enough when he slept through them, but he had fought to get even a few hours' sleep last night. Every time he closed his eyes, the sight of that tall, willowy form with the golden braid taunted him. He rubbed his face with both hands and paused with his eyes covered, capturing the vision again before the day's work stole it from him.

Would it be wrong to think she might welcome his attention?

Levi combed his fingers through his beard. The last time he approached a woman… His face grew hot when he remembered how Ellie Miller, in front of everyone at the barn raising last summer, had refused his request to court her. He should never have mentioned it in the middle of a crowd of onlookers, but Eliza had cornered him that very morning and insisted he either marry or send Nellie and Nancy to live with her in Middlebury. He had been desperate.

He still was. But desperate enough to risk a rejection from his housekeeper?

Making a marriage wasn't what he had intended when he set out to hire a housekeeper, but then, he also hadn't intended to hire someone so eligible. He was crazy to think she'd even look at an old man like him.

Or maybe it wasn't so crazy. A lot of men married girls younger than they were, and made good marriages, too. His own *grossdawdi* had two wives, marrying his *grossmutti* only months after his first wife had died in childbirth.

And then he had gone on to have twelve more children with his second wife.

At this thought Levi pushed himself out of bed. He paused to check the weather, pulling up the shade to look through the window at the bright stars and white fields, ghostly gray in the moonlight. His farm, his *dat's* farm, his *grossdawdi's* farm. The cabin his *grossdawdi* built in 1845 was just out of sight in the woodlot. But this farm meant nothing compared to his family. He'd do anything to keep them together.

Anything, including keeping Ruth Mummert on as his housekeeper. Would Eliza think her too young and inexperienced to take over the housekeeping? From the way supper went last night, she seemed competent enough.

But could he keep her around, having her become part of the family and a substitute mother for the younger ones? What would the other church members think of such a young woman in his home?

He should send her back to Lancaster County. He could spend ten minutes listing all the reasons why she wasn't right for the job. She was too young, too outspoken, too bossy....

He let the shade fall back in place and turned to his dresser. Ruth Mummert...what was he going to do with her? He couldn't let her go home. Not now. He had to make her fit in, become part of the family. A hired hand, a helper. Eliza and everyone else would see how *wonderful-gut* she was with the children and how well she handled herself in the kitchen.

And when it came right down to it, he didn't *want* to send her away.

Picking up his razor, he paused, and then turned to the small chest at the foot of his bed. Salome's chest. What would she think of Ruth Mummert? They'd get along fine, wouldn't they? Salome would welcome her as a sister, a helper. He turned back to the mirror, ready to shave his upper lip, when he saw the scowl on his face. Why did he think of Salome at a time like this?

Ach, when didn't he think of her?

He gave his upper lip a quick shave, the tiny shaving mirror reflecting his tired eyes. Old eyes. Levi swished the razor in the cold water and wiped it on the towel. Turning away from the mirror, he pulled on his work clothes, stretching his suspenders up over his shoulders and padding out of his bedroom.

The big house had been built before *Dat* was born, and the upper floor had been added to the house several years later to accommodate the growing family. Levi often thought of *Grossdawdi* in these quiet mornings as he climbed the worn treads of the stairway. His only memory of him was a blurred image, and he was surprised he remembered that much since *Dawdi* had died while Levi was still in dresses.

He stopped at the first bedroom and knocked on the door frame. "Elias, Nathan, it's time to get up." Then crossing the hall, he knocked on the opposite room. "James, David, it's morning." He waited until he heard them stirring before heading back down the stairs.

The kitchen was warm even though the fire lay quiet and dormant in the stove. He shook down the ashes and laid kindling on the glowing coals, each movement automatic. He blew the fire to life, fed it with more kindling and then set two split logs on top to keep it going. Waneta would be down soon. She always woke when she heard him in the kitchen.

What would he have done without Waneta when Salome died? Even though she was only fifteen at the time, his oldest daughter had stepped into her mother's role without hesitation.

There were a few burned biscuits at first, for sure, but she learned quickly. Too quickly. She acted too much like an old married woman at times. He rarely saw her smile as she went about her work, and she was often short-tempered with her brothers and sisters.

Well, with Ruth Mummert here now, Waneta would be able to join the other youth at the Singings and enjoy herself for once. Maybe she'd even notice Reuben Stoltzfus trying to catch her eye at Sunday meetings.

"Mornin', *Dat*." Elias mumbled the greeting, but the other boys were silent as they jostled their sleepy way out to the back porch for their boots and coats. As crisp and clear as the stars were this morning, they'd all be wide-awake and half-frozen by the time they reached the barn.

Levi glanced at the *Dawdi Haus* door as he followed the boys. It was just an accident that he had seen Ruth in her night clothes. It was a mistake, nothing more, and he'd make sure it was never repeated.

Ruthy stood at the door of the *Dawdi Haus*.

"It was just a mistake. A terrible, horrible mistake." For the third time since she had woken up, she repeated the words to herself, but she still didn't want to touch the doorknob.

The look on Levi Zook's face the night before made her cheeks burn. He had been amused by her shameful appearance, without her *kapp* or even stockings. Every time she looked at him she would remember those brown eyes and the laughing crinkles around them. She could kick herself for being so careless.

But how could she face him—how could she face the children after this?

She must. Somehow she must go back into the kitchen. She had heard Levi go out to do chores, so this was her chance to do her work without him around. By the time he got back from choring, the rest of the children would be awake and she wouldn't have to face him alone.

Checking her *kapp* and smoothing her apron, she took a deep breath and then forced herself to open the door, pass through the short hall between the houses and walk into the kitchen. As she lit the kerosene lamp, she looked for the mess she had left behind when she fled the kitchen last night, but there was no sign of it. The sourdough sponge rested in its bowl under a clean towel, the counter was wiped clean and even the wooden spoon she had used was washed and put away.

She leaned her hands on the counter, ashamed and mortified. Levi had to have been the one to clean up after her. What must he think of her? Not only had she paraded in front of him dressed only in her nightgown, but she had also left her work for him to finish. She wouldn't be surprised if he sent her back to Lancaster County that morning.

Never mind. Even if her first day was her last one, she had work to do. It was four-thirty already and the men would be hungry when they came in from choring.

Putting more wood in the stove, Ruthy turned the sourdough onto the bread board and started kneading it, adding flour as she worked. She went through the breakfast menu in her mind. What did this family eat? Eggs, potatoes and biscuits were what *Mam* would be fixing this morning, and Waneta had mentioned sausage last night. She'd make just that.

As she started the sausage frying, the children started showing up one by one and the predawn quiet was broken. Waneta and Martha said soft "good mornings" as they tied on their aprons, Martha throwing on a shawl to go out to the chickens.

"*Dat* likes oatmeal with breakfast. Did you start any?" Waneta asked as she started peeling potatoes with quick efficiency.

"*Ach, ne,* I didn't, but it's too late now. I should have started it last night."

"Don't worry. *Dat* bought this quick-cooking kind. It only takes one minute."

Ruthy took the round box of instant oatmeal from the shelf and read the cooking directions. Only one minute? It would probably end up tasting like wallpaper paste. Real oats were going on her shopping list. She measured the oat flakes and water into a pan and set it on the hot stove.

When Martha returned with a pail full of eggs, Waneta started breaking them into a large bowl to scramble. Ruthy put the sausage patties on a plate in the oven to keep them warm and turned the peeled and sliced potatoes into the frying pan. Her stomach growled as the wet potatoes hit the hot grease with a burst of hearty fragrance.

"When *Mam* was here, we'd have pie for breakfast," Martha said as she leaned toward the stove and inhaled the scent of the frying potatoes.

"Well, *Mam* isn't here, is she?" Waneta grunted as she beat the eggs. She must have broken three dozen into the bowl. "I have enough to do without making pies, too."

"I'd make them if I knew how," Martha said as she got a dozen plates from the cupboard.

"I'll teach you," Ruthy said as she mixed biscuit dough. "What kind of pie is your favorite?"

"Anything. Apple, sugar cream, peach…"

"Do you like shoofly?"

Martha gave Ruthy a puzzled look. "Shoofly? I've never heard of it."

"I have," Waneta said as she poured the beaten eggs into another pan. "*Grossmutti* said she ate it when she was a girl in Lancaster County, but she never had the recipe."

"I have a recipe for it. It's my *mam's* favorite. We can make one this afternoon and have it for supper." Ruthy slid the pan of biscuits into the hot oven and then turned the potatoes one more time. She moved the pan to the back of the stove. They were done perfectly.

"Martha," Waneta said, "make sure the little ones are up. Breakfast is almost ready." She stirred the eggs one more time, and then moved the pan of oatmeal away from the heat.

"Let's see," Ruthy said, "we have sausage, eggs, potatoes, oatmeal, biscuits, canned peaches... Is that everything?"

"You made the coffee, didn't you?" Waneta looked up from stirring the eggs, her eyes wide.

"Coffee! How could I forget?"

Waneta shook her head and reached past her for the coffeepot. "*Dat's* a bear without his coffee in the morning."

Just what she needed, a bear.

The girls came into the kitchen, sleepy-eyed but dressed. Ruthy had them finish setting the table, then she glanced out the window and saw Levi and the older boys heading toward the house from the barn.

Waneta saw them, too. "Martha! *Dat's* coming!" She directed her voice toward the stovepipe, and then saw Ruthy staring at her. "The stovepipe goes right up through the little boys' room. She's there getting them out of bed."

Somehow, with Waneta and Martha's help, breakfast was on the table before Levi Zook and the older boys finished taking off their boots and washing up on the back porch. The younger children slid into their seats, and the family took their places around the table. Ruthy didn't look at Levi, but kept busy helping Sam sit straight on his end of the bench.

Silence fell, compelling Ruthy to risk looking at the stony face at the other end of the table. Waneta was right, he could be a bear in the morning. Last night forgotten, she stared back at him.

"Is there something you need, Levi Zook?"

"What happened to the coffee?"

Ruthy's knees shook beneath the table. How dare he! Her first morning in a new kitchen, breakfast on the table on time, the children all awake and dressed and he questions her about coffee?

The coffeepot gurgling on the stove was the only sound as she kept her eyes locked on his.

"Your coffee will be ready after we thank the Father in heaven for our food."

Out of the corner of her eye, Ruthy saw Nellie look from her to her father, and back again. Jesse stared at her with an open mouth, and Nancy giggled.

David broke the stony silence. "*Dat,* can we eat now?"

Levi Zook didn't answer, but lowered his head as a signal for the silent prayer. Ruthy closed her eyes, but her mind wasn't on the food before them.

"Dear God, help me survive this day."

Levi cast about in his mind for words to pray. Any words would do, but they were nowhere to be found. Making do with a quick *Denki for this food,* Levi raised his head and lifted his spoon. Every morning since his marriage the clink of his spoon in his coffee cup was the signal for his family to begin eating, but without a coffee cup he made do with a sharp rap against the edge of his plate.

Taking the platter of sausage, he shoveled four or five patties onto his plate, and then passed them to Waneta at the same time Elias passed the bowl of scrambled eggs to him. When Elias handed him an empty bowl with oatmeal clinging to the sides he looked at Waneta.

"*Ja,* for sure, *Dat,* there's more on the stove to take up."

She turned to get it, but Ruth took the empty bowl from Levi's hands.

"You sit and eat. I'll fill the bowl and get the coffee at the same time."

Under the tantalizing breakfast smells of sausage and potatoes, Levi caught the scent of clean laundry as she turned from him to the stove. The slight nudge sent his memory whirling back to the night before, when this same woman stood in the shadowy kitchen in her long white nightgown.

"*Dat,*" Elias said, bumping his arm with the bowl, "take the potatoes."

Levi took the bowl and passed it on to Waneta, his appetite gone. He picked up his fork, hesitating, watching both benches full of children's heads down, focused on their meal.

"Here you are, Levi Zook." She was at his left elbow, setting his coffee cup by his plate and handing him the dish of oatmeal.

He took it without a glance at her and spooned some into his waiting bowl. Perhaps if he didn't look at her, didn't speak to her, she would take her place as a welcome employee. Think of her as someone helping out on the farm. Think of her as a sister.

She sat at the end of the table again and leaned over to help Jesse cut his sausage patties, her golden hair, framed by her heart-shaped *kapp,* shone in the lamplight. He focused on his plate, shoveling tasteless food into his mouth. Even if he wasn't hungry now, it was many hours before dinnertime.

His plate finally empty, he downed his coffee in three swallows, shuddering as the bitter drink poured down his throat. He had forgotten the cream and sugar, but it was too late to add it now. He wiped his beard with his napkin as he stood.

"Elias, I'm going to get started on the repairs for the plow. You come out when you're done."

"Ja, Dat," Elias answered, "I'll be out soon."

"Dat," Waneta asked, "what about your second cup of coffee?"

Levi kept his eyes on his shirt front as he brushed off crumbs that weren't there. Anything to keep his eyes from straying to the other end of the table.

"I'll have it later. Maybe you can bring it out to the barn, *ja?*" He patted her cheek and escaped to the back porch.

He sat on the bench, lacing his boots, the cold pressing him even in the sheltered area. Voices came to him through the door as the children finished their breakfasts. He leaned back against the wall, one boot in his hand, forgotten, as he listened. The words were indistinct, but one voice floated above the others in calm, even tones. Even as old as Waneta was, she didn't have the gentle, womanly influence Ruth had brought into their home.

Levi thrust his foot into the well-worn leather of his second boot. It looked like bringing Ruth Mummert here was going to turn out to be just what his family needed.

The next Monday brought the beginning of the new school term. Once breakfast was finished, the children raced to get ready on time. Ruthy started clearing the table, but Waneta stopped her.

"Would you mind braiding the girls? I hate doing it, and they never look good for school."

"*Ja,* sure I will."

Braid the girls? As she went up the stairs to find the twins' room, Ruthy's mind flew back to when she and Laurette would braid each other's hair after playing too wildly in the school yard. Laurette's hair was so dark it was almost black, while Ruthy's was blond with a stubborn curl to it. She had loved to twist and braid Laurette's smooth hair.

But she didn't have any time to brood over memories as she quickly tamed Nancy's and Nellie's tousled brown hair and braided them with deft hands ready to fit their *kapps* on. When she was done, Nellie and Nancy looked at each other, then to Ruthy, Nellie almost in tears.

"You didn't do it right," Nancy said.

Ruthy looked at the two girls, their silken hair twisted neatly away from their faces and two braids falling down their backs. "What do you mean?"

Nancy pointed to the side of Nellie's face. "You twisted it. The girls will say that's fancy. You have to do it right."

Martha looked in the door. "Come, girls. It's time to go." She stepped into the room, staring at them. "What have you done to your hair?"

"I braided it the way I would have done at home," Ruthy said. "I guess the style is different here."

"*Ja,* if they went to school like this they'd be teased to no end." Martha sat down on the bed and started undoing Nancy's braid. "Here, you watch me, and then you'll know how we do it."

Ruthy watched as Martha's fingers sped through

Nancy's hair. It wasn't hard at all, just one more difference between home and this strange place. She finished braiding Nellie in time for them all to meet the school bus at the end of the lane.

After the scholars had left, Ruthy picked up a towel as Waneta shaved soap flakes into the dish pan.

"After we do our morning work, we need to get started on the laundry." Ruthy filled a second dishpan with hot water from the stove's reservoir. "You'll have to show me how you do it."

"It's going to take all day." Waneta's voice was resigned.

Irritation at Levi Zook rose before Ruthy squelched it down. This girl had been carrying the full burden of running this house far too long, but now she could have some help.

"It will go twice as fast with two of us working, *ja?*"

"Ja." Waneta's voice sounded a little brighter with that thought. "And then what job gets done tomorrow?"

"My *mam* has a job for each day of the week, and all the work gets done in its own time. Tomorrow we'll iron the clothes, Wednesday will be for mending. Thursday we'll do the baking, Friday the marketing if we go to town, and Saturday, when all the scholars are at home, we'll do the cleaning."

"That sounds like what my *mam* did before she got sick. I remember cleaning the house every Saturday."

"Was your *mam* ill for a long time before she passed on?" Ruthy hated to ask, but she was curious about this woman who had been Levi Zook's wife and the mother to all these children.

"Ja, the illness started even before Sam came." Wa-

neta stared at the cooling dishwater, her hands resting on the edge of the pan. "There were lots of days she never got out of bed. After the baby came she just stayed there until she…"

"How old were you when Sam was born? Eleven?"

Waneta nodded, and then reached for the next stack of dishes. "I tried, but I could never keep house as well as *Mam* had before she got sick."

"And your *dat* has never remarried?"

Waneta gave Ruthy a shaky smile. "Would you marry a man with ten children?"

"Why not? Children are a blessing."

"Not everyone thinks so. *Dat* thought Ellie Miller would make a good *mam* for us, since she was a widow herself and her little ones needed a *dat,* but she married Bram Lapp last fall."

"Maybe she just didn't think it was God's will."

Waneta shook her head. "I've watched her with Bram, and I can tell they really love each other. She didn't love *Dat,* that's why she didn't marry him. I've always wondered if she would have learned to love him if it hadn't been for us children."

Ruthy dried the next plate and stacked it with the others. Did love make any difference when it came to marriage? She had loved Elam, hadn't she? But now that marriage would never happen.

Ne, love had nothing to do with it. Marriage was all about making promises and believing both you and your husband could keep them.

Ruthy picked a handful of spoons out of the rinse water and dried them one by one, dropping each one into the silverware drawer.

She had thought she could trust Elam, but his word

hadn't meant anything. She dropped the last spoon and closed the drawer with a shove.

Perhaps being a *maidle* wasn't such a bad thing after all.

Chapter Four

Levi's fork sliced through the crumbly topping and the gooey layer of molasses pudding. He hesitated before he put the bite of pie into his mouth, teasing Martha with his delay. The girl wiggled in her seat, her eyes glowing as she watched him. He took the triangle off his fork and chewed slowly, tasting the blend of molasses and the crumb topping.

"Mmm." He closed his eyes and nodded. "Mmm, *ja* this is perfect. Even better than last week." He opened his eyes to see Martha's face blushing.

"*Dat,* it's really good?"

"Martha, this is the best shoofly pie I've ever had."

Martha turned to Ruth Mummert with a grin. "Then I guess we can serve everyone else, if *Dat* likes it."

David reached for the pie plate. "I won't complain if Martha turns out to be a pie baker. I could eat pie for every meal."

"It was Ruthy's recipe," Martha said, her ears turning red at the praise. "She's the one who taught me."

"And Martha is an excellent student." Ruth started

clearing the supper dishes as the pie was passed. "She will be a *wonderful-gut* baker."

Levi took another bite and savored the sweetness. Pie was the best end to a meal. Pie and coffee, he amended as he sipped the fresh cup Ruth put in front of him. He took his time to finish his dessert, listening to the conversations between the children. The girls discussed which kind of pie Martha should try next, while the big boys argued about who had won the game that afternoon. He couldn't hear what the little boys at the end of the table were talking about, but they were deep in conversation.

He took the last bite of pie as the girls rose to wash the dishes. *Ja,* with pie for supper life was *gut.* He had done a *wonderful-gut* thing when he brought Ruth Mummert here. If she could teach Martha to make pie, she could teach his girls everything else they needed to know. There would never be a reason to send any of his children away.

"Do you want some more coffee?" Ruth asked, appearing at his elbow with the coffeepot in hand.

"*Ne,* it will only keep me awake."

"It would me, too."

Levi let her take his empty plate and swallowed the last of his coffee. "Boys, you can start on your studying. Martha and the twins will join you when the dishes are done."

"*Dat,*" said Jesse, "I need help with my arithmetic. I got all the problems wrong today."

"I'll help you. Bring your book in here."

When Jesse brought his book, he opened the page and showed Levi where he was having difficulty. "It's here, *Dat.* I added one plus one, but Miss Shrock said the answer was eleven, not two."

Levi smiled. *Ja,* it was the same with all his children when they encountered adding ten and one for the first time. "Go in my bedroom and get a dime and the pennies off my dresser."

Jesse brought them and Levi showed him how ten pennies turn into a dime. "Now, if I add one penny and one dime, what do I get?"

"Eleven cents."

"*Ja, gut.* Now look at your arithmetic. If you add ten and one, what do you get?"

"Eleven?"

"*Ja,* that's it. Now try the next one."

While Jesse worked on his arithmetic problems, the girls joined them at the table, and Levi's eyes strayed to Ruth. She was setting the sponge for tomorrow's bread, her movements quick and practiced.

As he watched her, the memory of her tall, graceful form in the flowing white gown hit him with full force. How could he put it out of his mind? Or did he even want to? Her golden hair gleaming under her heart-shaped kapp, her efficient hands, his children content and well-fed, the worry lines disappearing from Waneta's face… *Ja,* he had done right when he brought Ruth Mummert here.

"*Dat,* is this right?"

Jesse's question brought him back to the present. As he looked over Jesse's arithmetic paper, the reality of what he had been thinking hit him square in the jaw. Ruth Mummert wasn't much older than his Waneta. A grown woman, *ja,* but still a young woman. A beautiful young woman. How long would she be working for him? The first Singing she attended, she'd have a flock of young men buzzing around her.

He glanced back at Ruth, noting how quickly she had brought the kitchen to order after feeding all twelve of them. After less than a week, she had settled into the role of housekeeper very easily. Not just housekeeper, he amended as he surveyed the row of heads around the table, his scholars busy with their evening studies. She was taking his daughters under her wing like an older sister.

Ruth took off her apron, and after hanging it on the hook next to the sink, came over to look at Nellie's homework. Levi watched Nellie's face light up when Ruth whispered in her ear and gave her shoulders a hug. He swallowed the lump rising in his throat.

Ne, not an older sister. More like an aunt or...

Ruth turned to Nancy and laid her hand on the girl's shoulder as she leaned down to catch Nancy's explanation of her homework.

Ne, not even an aunt. A mother. The mother he had been hoping to find for his children.

But wasn't she too young to take on such a responsibility?

Levi turned back to Jesse's paper as Ruth left the girls and walked toward him.

"I'll say good-night now, Levi Zook, unless you have anything else you need me to do before morning."

Levi glanced up at her, his mouth dry. Would his thoughts show on his face?

"Ne, denki." He cleared his throat to stop the adolescent squeak that threatened to escape. "That was a fine meal."

She blushed and lowered her eyes at his praise. "Your daughters were a *wonderful-gut* help. Good night."

The kitchen table filled with children was silent as she closed the door to the *Dawdi Haus*.

"Dat," Sam said, standing in the door of the front room with a drawing tablet in his hand, "why didn't she stay with us?"

"Ruth works hard. She probably wanted to rest or write letters before she went to bed."

Nellie, his quiet Nellie, said, "She could have stayed and written her letters here."

"Tomorrow we'll ask her to stay."

But would she? Levi had the sudden urge to follow her, to ask her to stay tonight. But he sat, the final snick of the *Dawdi Haus* door latch echoing above the children's voices.

Ruthy leaned back against the kitchen door before heading down the short hall to the *Dawdi Haus*. The kitchen had been cozy and warm, and the lantern hung over the table had enclosed them all within its light. The scholars bent to their studies, Waneta copying recipes, Elias and Nathan sharing sections of *The Budget*—they were a family, but not her family. From the table-flat farmland outside the window, to the stark stiffness of the girls' *kapps,* to the flat tones of their words, every moment she spent with Levi Zook's family showed her just how far from home she really was.

But this is where God wanted her to be, wasn't it? And she was needed here. Even after this short time, she could see how much this family needed her help, especially the girls and little, lonely Sam. Several times during the day he would come to her and she would take quick breaks from her work to sit down and hold him on her lap while he chatted with her or showed her his drawings. His little-boy body had molded into hers, showing her how he missed the comfort of a mother's arms.

They all missed their mother, even Elias and Waneta. *Ach,* and she missed her own mother, even though they had only been parted a short time. But she could still write, and she knew she could visit whenever it was convenient. Her *mam* was only a train ride away.

With that thought she hurried into the *Dawdi Haus* and relit the fire in the stove. She retrieved her writing desk from the bedroom and sat at the little kitchen table, as close to the fire as she could get.

Putting the ink bottle on the side of the stove to warm it, Ruthy took out a sheet of paper and her pen, composing a letter to *Mam* in her head as she waited.

Her first week had gone well, she would write. Waneta was a sweet girl and a joy to work with. Martha had loved learning to make pies. Nellie had come to her wanting to learn to purl so she could knit a pair of stockings for her *dat,* but Ruthy had convinced her to start out with a blanket for her doll to practice the stitches. Nancy had come home from school yesterday with snow inside her boots, complaining that David had pushed her into the ditch on the way home. The boys... She didn't know any of them very well yet, except Sam.

And then there was Levi. What would she tell *Mam* about Levi Zook?

Ruthy picked up the bottle of ink and shook it as she considered this problem. The ink was almost warm enough to use.

Levi hadn't lied to her, but *Mam* and *Dat* would say he misled her by not telling her how many children he had. They would ask if she wanted to stay on, knowing he had kept that important information to himself.

She smiled to herself. Of course she was going to stay. Ten children seemed like such a large number... until she started getting to know them. Now that she had met them, had seen how much they all longed for a mother in their lives, she couldn't bear to think of leaving them.

But... Ruthy shook the ink bottle again, and then brought it to the table and uncorked it. She filled her pen as she considered something that had been hovering at the back of her mind. What if there was something else Levi had forgotten to tell her?

What if he already had a new mother chosen for his children and he had only hired her so the house would be orderly and running well before his new wife came to live here? She wouldn't be surprised. Just because he hadn't been successful in courting that other woman Waneta had told her about didn't mean he didn't have his eye on someone else. A man like him wouldn't stay single very long.

And if she got along well with the new wife, perhaps she would be asked to stay on. A new wife would need a helper, *ja?*

The clock's ticking echoed in the silent room. It was a pipe dream at best. When Levi married again, she would have to move on. Find another position as a housekeeper, or a mother's helper...

A tear fell, raising a spot on her paper. Ruthy quickly crumpled the sheet and threw it into the stove. She couldn't send a letter home with a tearstain on it, could she?

Home. Would she ever know the sweetness of her own home again?

Chapter Five

Levi recognized Eliza's sleigh as soon as she turned the corner half a mile away. Her feisty horse, Ginger, had a flashy step that matched Eliza's own personality. She never did anything partway.

He poured the bucket of slop he was carrying into the pig's trough and then went back out to the yard to wait for her. She slowed Ginger for the turn into the farm lane, but then the horse picked up speed again before he reached the barn. Levi caught the reins as the horse neared the buggy shed. How could he convince Eliza this horse was too much for her? Levi struggled to hold the horse still. He had never been able to convince his older sister of anything.

Eliza climbed down from the sleigh and looked him up and down. "Well, Levi, I guess you aren't starving yet. Waneta must be doing a good job feeding you."

"*Ja*, Waneta's doing a fine job."

His sister sniffed, looking from the barn to the house. "You're all well? The whole family?"

"*Ja*, Eliza. We're all well. And you?" Levi stroked Ginger's neck. What was Eliza doing here? It was an eight-mile drive from her home near Middlebury, and it wasn't like her to drive that far on a Thursday just to see if all the children were healthy.

"I'm well enough, considering. It isn't easy living alone, you know."

He didn't know. He had never lived alone.

"I'll take care of Ginger if you want to go on in the house. I'm sure there's still coffee on the stove."

Eliza moved closer to him, stepping around a clump of snow. "I heard you picked up a woman at the Shipshewana station last week."

Levi sighed. Here it was. He had been wondering how to tell Eliza about his new housekeeper, but he should have known word would get to her.

"*Ja,* her name is Ruth Mummert. She's our housekeeper."

"A housekeeper? You're spending good money on a housekeeper when you know very well I had everything arranged for you?"

That was just the problem. She had everything arranged, whether he liked it or not.

"Eliza, I want to keep my family together."

"Humph."

Ginger moved restlessly, reminding Levi the horse needed attending to after the long drive.

"Why don't you go on in the house and meet Ruth? She's been a *wonderful-gut* help to us already, and I think you'll like her."

Eliza turned her bulk toward the house, but then looked at Levi. "I'll meet her, but I can't promise I'll like her. It seems like backward thinking to bring an outsider into your home while I'm here."

Levi watched Eliza pick her way across the snowy

barnyard to the house. At least Waneta was there to provide a buffer between Ruth and his sister. He started unhitching Ginger.

He'd better get inside as soon as he could.

"How many jars of chowchow?"

Waneta counted, bending down to see into the back recesses of the cellar shelves. "Twenty-four, and then there are ten jars of pickled cauliflower."

Ruthy wrote the numbers down and glanced over the list. Green beans, navy beans, tomatoes, vegetable soup, plenty of pickled vegetables... "Is there any corn?"

Waneta searched through the jars. "*Ne,* no corn left."

"What about fruit?"

Waneta moved to the next shelf. "Lots of prune plums."

As she started counting, Sam clattered down the wooden steps.

"'Neta! Aunt Eliza's here."

"*Ach, ne,* not today!" Waneta stood so quickly her head bumped against the shelf above her. "Ruthy, is my *kapp* straight?" She dusted off her skirt and retied her apron.

"You look fine. Why don't I finish counting the fruit while you go up to greet your auntie."

Waneta laid her hand on Ruthy's arm, her voice an urgent whisper. "Don't make me face her alone!"

"You aren't afraid of her, are you?"

Waneta's gaze went to the ceiling as they both heard heavy footsteps in the kitchen above them. "I can never do anything right for her. I know she doesn't like me."

"I understand. I have an auntie like that, too." Ruthy smiled at Waneta. "Come, we'll face her together."

Waneta led the way up the bare wooden steps, glancing back once to make sure Ruthy was following her.

"Go on, I'm right behind you."

Ruthy smiled at Waneta's back. She remembered hating to face her overbearing Aunt Trudy when she was a young teenager, so Waneta's reaction didn't surprise her. Aunts could be very particular about a girl's behavior.

The woman waiting for them in the kitchen didn't look anything like thin, pinched Aunt Trudy. Eliza stood in the middle of the floor, still wearing her woolen shawl and black bonnet, leaning heavily on a gnarled cane. Her expression was the same as Aunt Trudy's, though, as she surveyed the spotless kitchen shelf. If she were looking for a fault with Ruthy's housekeeping, she certainly wouldn't find it in the kitchen.

"Aunt Eliza, you should sit down. Would you like some coffee?" Waneta hurried to the stove and moved the coffeepot to the front.

Eliza's cane thumped as the woman turned to inspect Ruthy.

"So you're the housekeeper my brother hired." Eliza's gaze took in everything from Ruthy's heart-shaped *kapp* to her shoes, dusty from the cellar.

"*Ja,* I'm Ruth Mummert."

"You're from Lancaster County?"

"*Ja.*" Ruthy smiled. Eliza was gruff, but didn't seem to be as scary as Waneta acted. Sam had disappeared into the front room.

"I once met a Mummert from Lancaster County." Eliza let Ruthy take her shawl and untied her bonnet.

"You did? I wonder if they could be related to us."

"I hope not." Eliza sniffed and thumped toward the rocking chair in the corner. "They were *Englisch.*" She turned to Ruthy again, narrowing her eyes as she studied her. "You don't have *Englisch* relatives, do you?"

Before Ruthy could think how to answer this, Eliza sank into the rocking chair with a groan.

"Here's your coffee, Aunt Eliza." Waneta handed the cup to her aunt. "And here's the footstool." She brought the small stool from its place next to the wall.

As Ruthy poured herself a cup of coffee, she watched Eliza lift her left foot onto the stool with one hand and lean back in the chair, her lips pinched together. Raising the cup to her mouth, she blew on the hot liquid before taking a sip.

"Waneta," Ruthy said, sitting on the bench with her back to the table, "will you get a plate of cookies?" She took a sip of her own coffee, and watched Eliza's face relax as her body eased into the chair. The older woman appeared to be in much pain, but no complaints escaped, except for her gruff demeanor.

"You need to know up front that I don't approve of what my brother's done." Eliza took a cookie from the plate Waneta set on the small table next to her. "We could get along just fine without the expense of hiring someone from outside."

Ruthy kept a smile on her face as Eliza paused to take a bite of her cookie. Did the woman have any idea the hurt her words caused? Without a family of her own, Ruthy would always be an outsider.

"I told him I would take the little girls to live with me." Eliza spoke around her cookie, unaware of the crumbs that fell as she gestured. "Those two will never learn to be good wives, growing up without a mother as they are."

A small sound escaped from Waneta, who was sitting next to Ruthy on the bench. Ruthy glanced at her, but the girl's head was down, her bottom lip caught between her teeth.

"I don't think Levi Zook wants his girls to live away from him. Isn't your house quite far?"

Eliza grunted and shifted her bulk in the chair. "Not so much. It's only eight miles, and that's close enough to visit several times a year."

Waneta jumped up from the bench and went through the doorway to the front room. Ruthy heard her feet pounding on the stairway as she ran to her room and slammed the door behind her.

"Now, what's wrong with her?" Eliza gazed through the doorway where Waneta had vanished.

"I don't think she wants her sisters to live that far away." Ruthy took another sip from her coffee, and then set the cup on the table behind her. Irritation at this woman's callous behavior rose with each moment, and she didn't want her shaky hand to betray her feelings.

"Humph." Eliza took a bite of her cookie and inspected it as she chewed. "There's nothing wrong with making sure those little girls have all the advantages a mother can give them."

Ruthy clenched her hands together on her lap. "I'm sure Levi Zook has considered what his daughters need." She lifted her chin, looking at Eliza. She was beginning to understand why Levi was so anxious for her to stay here. "This family suffered a loss when their mother passed on, and it wouldn't help anyone to separate them now."

Eliza deflated in her chair, the corners of her mouth quivering. "*Ach,* you're right. I hadn't thought of that." With the bluster gone, Eliza was just a lonely old woman.

"Would you like more coffee?" Ruthy rose and went to the stove. Eliza wouldn't want a stranger to be a witness to her emotions.

"Ja, denki." Eliza sniffed, and the chair creaked as she shifted. By the time Ruthy refilled the two cups, Eliza was back to her old self. "You seem like a young thing to be taking on a job like this."

"Not so young. I'll be twenty-four this spring."

"Twenty-four? Why aren't you married?"

Ruthy flinched at Eliza's blunt words, but the other woman took another cookie from the plate and tackled it with relish. If she hadn't seen the vulnerable crack in Levi's sister a few moments ago, she might have run out of the room the same way Waneta had. But the downturned corners of Eliza's mouth revealed more than a demanding aunt who was used to riding roughshod over everyone around her. Something else made her very unhappy.

Ruthy considered this as she took another sip of her coffee. Eliza may be a lonely old woman, but that gave her no excuse to be cruel to her brother. Eliza wasn't going to bully this family while Ruthy was around.

"If I wasn't a *maidle,* I wouldn't be able to help this family, would I?"

Eliza raised her chin and regarded Ruthy through narrowed eyes, but Ruthy pressed on.

"If I wasn't around, your brother would need you to help, *ja?* Is that why you came today? To see if you could get me to run back to Lancaster County?"

The other woman's eyes narrowed further, and then a sudden smile broke over her face.

"You've got spunk. I like that. Maybe you will work out here."

Ruthy nearly dropped her cookie. Instead she brushed nonexistent crumbs off her lap. What was going on? A chuckle from the other woman made her look up.

"My dear girl, I'm not nearly as grumpy as everyone thinks I am." She tapped her knee with one hand. "Arthritis keeps me from getting around as I like, and sometimes the pain is unbearable. I try not to complain, but I know I can be short-tempered. I also know I stick my nose in where it doesn't belong at times, but I love my brother. He has a long row to hoe in front of him, and I was just trying to help."

Pieces fell together like a quilt top as Eliza paused to take a sip of coffee. Levi's crafty sister used her cranky attitude to get her own way, just as Laurette used her pretty face. Was this nothing more than concern for her brother and his family?

"Don't think I'm soft, though." Eliza's sharp eyes peered at Ruthy over the rim of the cup. "Levi's my little brother, and I'll take care of him just as I always have." She lowered the coffee cup to her lap and regarded Ruthy, her eyes narrowing. "You are much too young and pretty for this job, you know."

"What do you mean?"

Eliza's head tilted toward her. "We are to avoid the appearance of evil, but here you are, living in this house with a single man…"

Ruthy felt a cold lump turn in her stomach. "But I live in the *Dawdi Haus*. Surely that can't be construed into anything wrong."

"You know how people can talk, dear, and it only takes one comment to start rumors flying."

Ruthy concentrated on brushing a crumb off her knee as Eliza took another sip of her coffee. The woman was right. Even if she and Levi Zook avoided each other, her presence in this home could appear improper to anyone in the community. But what could she do?

As the other woman finished off her cookie, Ruthy caught a hint of a smile on Eliza's face, and the cold lump of dread turned to seething irritation. What a wily fox she was! Her attempt to bully hadn't worked, so she had changed tactics and had almost succeeded. Levi's sister didn't know her at all. *Daed* had always said she was stubborn as a mule, and she would keep her heels dug in. Levi Zook had hired her to be his housekeeper, and that's what she would be as long as he wanted her to stay.

Thumps and stamps from the porch told her Levi was coming in, so Ruthy rose to refill the plate of cookies and pour his coffee. How easily was he swayed by his sister?

Levi took a deep breath, his hand on the kitchen doorknob. He had put off facing Eliza for as long as he could, but now worry set in. Had she already succeeded in running off Ruth? Would he be searching for another housekeeper before the day was out?

Pushing the door open, he sought Ruth's face first. She glanced at him from the stove, where she was pouring a cup of coffee, her face pinched. At least Eliza hadn't reduced her to tears.

His sister, on the other hand, was settled into the rocking chair like a toad that had just snagged a fat moth. Whatever they had been talking about, it looked like he had come in just in time.

"Some coffee?" Ruth handed him a cup as she sat on the bench.

"Denki." Levi sat on the bench beside her and took a sip from the steaming cup.

"We were just discussing your situation," Eliza said.

"What situation is that?" Levi took a cookie from the plate Ruth had set on the table behind him and took a bite. A piecrust cookie, just like his *mam* had made. Ruth Mummert was full of surprises.

"A young girl, living in the same house as an unmarried man." Eliza leaned the rocker forward. "You know how that will look to the community."

Levi glanced at Ruth. Her face was growing red, but she tilted her chin up as she returned his look.

"I've done nothing against the *Ordnung,* sister. Ruth is no different than any other helper I might hire to work on the farm." Levi kept his voice sure and strong, but at the back of his mind a whisper of doubt crept in. What would the ministers say about this situation? After all, it wasn't what he had expected when he made the arrangement.

"I still think you should follow through on what we agreed."

All doubt disappeared.

"We never agreed to anything, Eliza. I am the head of this family, and I would never agree to send any of the children away."

Eliza drained her coffee cup and then looked at Levi. "You would if the ministers insisted."

She was right, of course. If the ministers decided it would be best if the girls went to live with Eliza, he wouldn't have any choice but to submit to their decision. He had hired Ruth Mummert to avoid this, but Eliza seemed intent on pursuing her plans. If only she had remarried when she had the chance twenty years ago, then she might have her own family and wouldn't be so interested in taking his.

Eliza planted her cane in front of her and hauled herself to her feet.

"I must be getting back. Susie needs milking on time, you know."

Ruth hurried to fetch Eliza's bonnet and shawl from the hook by the door. "You'll miss seeing the scholars. They'll be home in another hour."

"*Ne,* I can't wait that long."

Levi saw Sam peering around the door from the front room. "Sam, go ask Elias to hitch up Aunt Eliza's rig for her."

Sam edged past Eliza and then scooted out the door. His sister had never been friendly with the children, so why was she so insistent on raising Nellie and Nancy?

"We'll make the trip to see you next, some Sunday after the snow melts."

Eliza smiled as she pulled his sleeve until he bent down for her kiss on his cheek. "I may be seeing you sooner than that, little brother. You never know."

Levi walked with her to her sleigh. Elias held Ginger's reins as the horse tossed his head. The short rest in the barn had renewed his fire.

"That's a pretty feisty horse you have, Eliza. Are you sure he isn't too much for you?"

Eliza smiled at him from her seat as she wrapped a wool horse blanket around her legs. "Don't worry about me, Levi. I can handle him."

She nodded to Elias and he let go of Ginger's head. The horse lurched forward, but before they reached the end of the lane Eliza had him settled into a controlled trot. At the corner she turned Ginger neatly onto the snowy road and headed north.

Levi shook his head and reached back to massage his tense neck muscles.

"Did she ask you to let the girls come live with her again?" Elias asked, watching Eliza drive away.

"*Ja,* but it won't do her any good. I told her our family was staying together."

Elias turned to him, a younger version of himself. When had the boy gotten so tall?

"Is that why you brought Ruth Mummert here? To keep the family together?"

"*Ja.* With Ruth here, Eliza doesn't have any good reason for going to the ministers to ask for the girls."

Elias rubbed the back of his own neck. "I sure hope it works."

Chapter Six

Sunday morning dawned bright and crisp. By the time the sun rose above the horizon, the Zook family, plus Ruthy, were crowded into the family buggy on their way to Sunday meeting at John Stoltzfus's. Elias followed behind in his courting buggy. He and Waneta would be staying at the host house until after the young folks' Singing in the evening.

Ruthy sat on the front seat with Levi, Sam and Nellie scrunched between them. She pressed her knees together to keep from shivering, either from the cold or from being nervous about meeting this new church community. Since last week had been an off Sunday, this would be her first church service with Levi and his family.

"When will it be our turn to have church again, *Dat?*" Sam's words came out in puffs in the frigid air.

"Don't even mention that!" Waneta said, her teeth chattering as she sat with her other sisters and Jesse in the second seat. "It's so much work to have church."

"Now Waneta," Levi said, "you know you had plenty of help from the women the last time it was our turn."

"*Ja,* but they talked about you the whole time. I heard Minnie Garber say you should marry one of her daughters so your house could be taken care of properly."

Ruthy turned around and laid her hand on Waneta's knee. "You've done a wonderful job keeping house, and you have nothing to be ashamed of. Some people just don't think before they talk."

"*Ja,* daughter. Ruth is right." Levi gave her a smile that made her forget her cold toes. "Don't let Minnie Garber's words fester. Forget them and forgive her, and all will be well."

Waneta nodded. "You're right."

"So, when are we going to have church at home again?" Sam asked. "I want to show Johnny my calf."

"You don't have a calf yet," said David from the backseat.

"But I will when spring comes, won't I, *Dat?*"

Levi nodded. "You and Jesse will both have calves of your own to raise this spring."

"Will I have it before we have church?"

Sam wouldn't let go of a question until he got an answer.

"*Ja,* probably. It will be our turn to have church in May."

Satisfied, Sam settled back into his seat.

Martha leaned forward and touched Ruthy's shoulder. "Are you nervous about meeting all these people? They're all strangers to you."

Ruthy gave Martha a smile. "I'm trying not to be. You're right, I've never met them, but we're all part of the same church, aren't we? They're just brothers and sisters I haven't met yet."

"There are a lot of nice people in our district, aren't there, Waneta?"

Ruthy turned around to see a blush creep up Waneta's cheeks at her sister's words. Could there be a special young man Waneta was anxious to see?

Before long Levi's buggy was just one in a long line of black buggies heading west along the road. The fields here, only a few miles from Levi Zook's farm, were smaller, often with a creek dividing them and wooded strips following the path of the creek. Of all the things that were different between Indiana and Pennsylvania, the flat land around Levi Zook's farm was the hardest for her to get used to. She had been missing the rolling hills of *Daed's* farm, but this part of the district almost seemed like home.

Levi pulled to a halt at the top of the farm lane, where the buggies in front of them had stopped to let out their families. Ruthy got out with the children, ignoring the curious stares of the women waiting to enter the house. She had told Waneta she wasn't nervous, but she was glad she had the girls around her. She held Nellie's and Nancy's hands while Martha and Waneta stood behind her. Levi took his place in the men's line, one hand on Jesse's shoulder, the other holding Sam's hand. Ruthy didn't need to look around to know the older boys would be with their friends, being old enough to sit together on the front rows directly behind the ministers.

The woman in line in front of Ruthy turned to greet her. Holding a baby in one arm, the young woman's blue eyes twinkled from inside her bonnet, but she spoke in the soft tones appropriate for the day. "Good morning. It's always nice to see a visitor. My name is Annie Beachey."

Ruthy took the woman's hand and leaned forward to exchange the holy kiss, just as all the women in the line greeted each other. "It's so good to meet you. I'm Ruthy Mummert."

Annie gave her another smile, and then turned to face the front again as the congregation moved into the house. As she removed her bonnet, Ruthy reached up to check her *kapp,* but then realized that she stood out in this crowd. Not only was she a stranger, a visitor as Annie had graciously said, but her *kapp* was also the heart-shaped Lancaster County style. These women all wore stiff, cone-shaped *kapps.*

Never mind, she told herself. They all knew she was visiting today. Waneta could help her make a new *kapp* before the next church Sunday.

Ruthy followed Waneta to a seat, ignoring the curious looks that followed them. She and the girls filled an entire bench on the women's side, and she glanced over to see that Levi and the boys filled their own bench on the men's side.

Ruthy was relieved when one of the men sitting near the front started the singing at a signal from the bishop. She had let her mind occupy itself with thoughts about how these people would welcome her, but the familiar songs brought her back to the worship of God. She held the songbook for the twins, moving her finger along the lines of the *Deitsch* words so they could follow.

A month ago she had been at home, surrounded by her friends and celebrating Old Christmas. Everything in this meeting was different, but still so familiar. The hymns were the same, the prayers were the same, and the ministers followed the same lectionary, preaching on John the Baptist today. By the time the second sermon began, she'd forgotten everything but their words. She may be far from where she grew up, but she was still home.

After dinner Levi sent Elias and Nathan out to the buggy shed to check on the horses. The sun had come out during the morning service, but it hadn't tempered the cold at all. If anything, the air was even more bitter. There could be another storm coming. He took a cup of coffee with him and went to look out the front window.

John Stoltzfus came to stand at the window with him, looking through the bare maple branches toward the northwest sky.

"Looking for weather?"

"Just a feeling I have." Levi kept his eye on a shadow lying on the horizon. A cloud bank could mean snow.

"I see your new housekeeper arrived safely."

"*Ja,* she did. Her name is Ruth Mummert, from Bird-in-Hand in Lancaster County."

"I thought you had hired someone older."

Levi turned to John, the meaning behind his words becoming clear. "Believe me, I thought I did. There was a bit of a miscommunication, but she's working out well. The children like her."

John stroked his beard. "Your sister, Eliza, stopped by to see me the other day."

He should have known Eliza wouldn't let the matter rest. Sometimes a meddling sister was worse than having no sister at all.

"She's concerned about you, having an unmarried young woman living in your house."

A cold stone turned in the pit of Levi's stomach. He had never considered how Ruth's presence in his home might appear until Eliza mentioned it. "She lives in the *Dawdi Haus,* separate from the rest of us."

"This is thin ice, Levi. I know you would never want to show your children a bad example, and you would never take advantage of the situation, but things happen."

The vision of Ruth in the kitchen wearing nothing but her nightgown flashed through Levi's mind. John was right. Things happen when you least expect it.

"So, did Eliza suggest a solution?"

John laced his fingers over his stomach and looked out the window again. "She did, but I'm not sure I like it."

"She told you her idea to take Nellie and Nancy to live with her?"

John nodded. "It's a hard thing to contemplate separating children from their family, but she did have a point. Your children need a mother."

"*Ja,* they do. But I'm not having much success in finding them one."

Clearing his throat, John lowered his voice even further. "You know how much I had hoped my Ellie would accept your proposal."

"But that wasn't God's will." Ellie Miller had been a convenient choice, but he didn't love her. He would never have made her as happy as she was with Bram Lapp. "Now you can see why I hired Ruth Mummert, can't you? I had expected her to be older, since she was a *maidle* and willing to move such a long distance, but she's here now. I can't very well send her home again, can I?"

"I can see your point, but it's still something the ministers will need to talk over. As pure as your intentions may be, we must avoid the appearance of evil."

"I'll be sure to keep a distance between us. She's a great help to me, with the girls and all. I treat her no differently than I would a hired farm worker."

John gave Levi's shoulder a pat. "That's what I would expect. You'll let me know if anything changes?"

The stone turned again in Levi's gut. John was asking him to be accountable for his actions…and his thoughts. He would keep his distance from Ruth Mummert—he had to for his children's sake. "*Ja,* John, I will."

Levi's eyes followed John as he moved through the big front room, opened to twice its normal size for the church meeting. The older man stopped to talk to several men as he made his way toward the kitchen, including Bram Lapp, his son-in-law. The man who had married Ellie Miller last fall had become a good friend, but what would he think about this matter with Ruth? Bram had spent twelve years living an *Englisch* life in Chicago—he had witnessed much worse situations than this…but the people there weren't Amish. They weren't living under the *Ordnung*.

Ach, he was making a mountain out of nothing. Ruth was a lovely young woman. He ran his fingers through his beard. A young woman with the kinds of skills, strength and determination that made a good wife. He had to make sure he kept distance between them, for his family's sake.

Levi took a sip of his cooling coffee and stared at the cloud bank. If rumors started hinting that he had any romantic feelings for Ruth, Eliza would be sure to press the point with the ministers. He took another sip. He had to keep his children together, no matter what.

Ruthy was glad to take chubby Elias Beachey from Annie's tired arms. The six-month-old sat happily on her lap while she visited with her new friends.

"Was it hard to leave your home to come out here to Indiana?" asked Ellie Lapp, Annie's sister-in-law.

"Some." Ruthy shoved her mind away from thoughts of Elam and Laurette. "I miss my *mam* and *daed,* but it's an adventure, *ja?*"

"It certainly would be, caring for Levi Zook's ten children!"

"They aren't so much work. They're all *gut* children, and Waneta is such a big help."

Ellie nodded toward a quiet corner where Waneta was standing with a young man. "And with you to run the house, she may even have some time for courting."

Ruthy watched Waneta's face as the young man spoke to her. She remembered feeling that way when she was sixteen, when she and Elam first started courting.

"Do you know anything about that young man? Is he baptized yet?"

Annie laughed and Ellie smiled at Ruthy. "*Ja,* I know him. That's my brother, Reuben. He's nearly eighteen, and taking baptism instruction with Bishop. He'll treat Waneta well, don't worry."

"I thought Reuben had a special girl already," Annie said.

"He did. He was taking Sarah Yoder home from

Singings last summer, but this fall she decided she'd rather ride with a new boy from the Shipshewana district who has been coming."

"*Ach,* poor Reuben." Annie leaned over and jiggled the baby's foot.

"He was fine with the way it turned out. They had been friends since they were little, but he told me the spark just wasn't there."

Annie grinned at Ellie. "You mean the spark he sees when Bram looks at you."

Ellie blushed like a new bride, and Ruthy remembered that Ellie and Bram had only been married a couple of months before. "The way Waneta's looking at Reuben, I'd say he found it with her."

"How about you, Ruthy? Did you ever look at a boy like that?"

"*Ach, ja,*" Ruthy said with a smile on her face, but it was hard to get the words past the lump in her throat. "Hasn't everyone?"

"We'll just need to get busy and find a husband for you here in Eden Township," Ellie said.

"*Ach,* Ellie," said Annie, "the only single men are Roman Nafziger and Levi Zook, unless you count Bishop Yoder."

Ruthy saw the elderly bishop's shaking hands in her mind. Annie had to be joking.

"And you can hardly count Roman Nafziger, either," Ellie said. "He's older than *Dat.*"

"Then that leaves Levi." Annie nodded and leaned toward Ellie with a conspiratorial whisper. "We have our work cut out for us, there."

"Why?" Ruthy asked. "Levi seems like a nice enough man."

"He's nice enough, but…"

"But nice," Ellie said, finishing Annie's sentence. She gave Annie a glance that looked like a warning. "He's a nice man who needs a wife. Who knows? Ruthy may be just what he needs."

"Ja," Annie said. She regarded Ruthy thoughtfully, as if seeing her for the first time. *"Ja,* she may be just what Levi needs."

"Now don't start getting any ideas. I'm not going to get married."

"You're too young to settle for being a *maidle,"* Ellie said.

"I just don't plan to get married." Ruthy bit her lip. God had made that clear when Elam picked Laurette over her.

She was relieved when Ellie's and Annie's husbands chose that moment to gather their families for the trip home. She wasn't ready to explain her reasons yet, and wasn't sure if she ever would be.

Ruthy shivered as the family got out of the buggy when they reached the farm later that afternoon. The wind had turned to the northwest and it had a bite. She hurried into the house with the children and Levi, while the older boys took the horse and buggy to the barn. Once in the shelter of the back porch she was part of the friendly jostling as the children removed their coats and boots.

"Dat, can we make popcorn?" James asked.

"Popcorn sounds *wonderful-gut!"* said Nancy.

Ruthy waited until she saw Levi Zook's nod, and

then said, "I'll make the popcorn, James, if you'll go into the *Dawdi Haus* and start a fire in the stove for me."

Sam took her hand as they went into the kitchen together. "Don't go to the *Dawdi Haus* yet. Stay with us. *Dat* always reads to us on Sunday afternoon, and you can sit with me."

Ruthy glanced at Levi. He had avoided meeting her eye during the trip home from the Stoltzfuses', and hadn't joined in any conversations. She didn't want to intrude on the family's routine if he was uncomfortable with it.

Sam saw her glance and turned to Levi. "Please, *Dat,* Ruthy can stay with us, can't she?"

Levi didn't look her way as he gave his son a brief nod. "She can stay if she wants to."

"You want to, don't you, Ruthy?"

She looked down into the little boy's face. "*Ja,* sure. I'll make popcorn first, and then I'll be in."

Martha had already gotten a heavy pan onto the stove and was building up the fire. Ruthy went down the chilly hall to the *Dawdi Haus* and changed into her everyday apron.

An afternoon with the family would be fun. At home, the folks would be doing almost the same, sitting together in the front room. Sometimes they read together, but most often they sat and visited with whomever came by. She checked her *kapp* before going back to the kitchen and the warmth of the main house.

"Does Waneta often stay for the Singing?" Ruthy salted the fresh batch of popcorn Martha dumped into the clean dishpan.

"She went once or twice last summer, but no boy

asked to bring her home." Martha started another batch of popcorn. "I don't know what made her decide to stay today."

If Martha hadn't seen Waneta and Reuben talking together after church, Ruthy wasn't going to be the one to spoil the surprise.

"Maybe she heard someone special is going to be there."

"You could have stayed with Elias and Waneta, couldn't you?" Martha looked at her. "I mean, you're still young enough, right?"

Ruthy swallowed. Go to the Singing? *Ne,* she couldn't.

"I'd rather spend the afternoon here." She salted the popcorn again. "I enjoy the rest."

Nathan and James stomped their feet on the back porch floor as they came in, adding to the happy confusion of voices drifting into the kitchen from the front room. At home the house was quieter, with only Ruthy and her parents there, but in the Zook household noise abounded.

Ruthy smiled as she stirred melted butter into the popcorn. She liked it. She had always enjoyed visiting her cousins' large family when she was growing up—something was always happening, and it seemed that no one was ever wanting for company there. The spoon in her hand slowed, and then came to a stop. She and Elam had talked of having a large family, but now those dreams were dead. All of her dreams had died with Elam's betrayal.

She shook her head, dispelling the thought.

"Here's the cider," Martha said as David brought the

jug up from the cellar. "I'll take it into the front room and send Nancy and Nellie back for the cups."

"*Denki,* Martha," Ruthy said, dumping the last pan of popcorn into the dishpan. "We'll bring the popcorn in right away."

She followed Martha into the front room, where the children were gathered in a circle on the floor and Levi sat in a chair near the stove with his feet on a stool.

"Ruthy, you sit here." Sam patted the chair facing Levi's on the other side of the stove.

She hesitated, seeing a scowl on Nathan's face.

"*Ne*, Sam," he said, "that's *Mam's* chair."

"Nathan, your *mam* doesn't need it anymore." Levi's voice was quiet, but everyone in the room fell silent when he spoke.

Ruthy looked from Nathan's defiant face to Levi's sad one. She wasn't the only one who had lost dreams. The children's mother hadn't been gone long, and it wasn't her intention to take the woman's place.

"I'd rather sit on the floor. I can reach the popcorn better if I do."

Sam snuggled up to her as she settled on the floor between him and Nellie. The little girl leaned toward her and Ruthy put her arm around her shoulders. *Ach,* what a family. The little ones missed their mother's touch, but the big ones didn't need cuddling anymore. She would need to remember to tread lightly around their feelings.

Martha handed her a cup of cider and she settled in to listen as Levi opened the *Martyrs Mirror,* the story of the persecution of Christians in centuries past. When he didn't start reading right away, she glanced at him.

He was watching her with a look she couldn't fathom. Was he beginning to resent her presence the way Nathan did? Is that why he was so quiet on the way home from church?

When their eyes met, Ruthy quickly looked away, reaching for the big bowl of popcorn. As Levi started reading the story of the martyrdom of Ignatius, she found herself caught up in the familiar tale as if she had never heard it before. He instilled life into the ancient words, elaborating on the simple text until she felt as if she were standing in the Roman amphitheater with the brave bishop, the roars of hungry lions ringing in her ears.

Nellie shivered and Ruthy pulled the girl closer, laying her cheek on top of her starched white head covering. Glancing at Sam, she nearly laughed at the rapt expression on his face.

Levi mimicked the lion's roars as he neared the end of the story, and then his voice rang out with Ignatius's final words. She watched him, captivated by the changing expressions on his face as he told the story. He was a wonderful father to teach his children in this way.

He finished with a cacophony of lion roars as the poor priest was devoured at the end, and then was abruptly silent.

"Dat," asked Jesse from his spot on the other side of Sam. "What happened next?"

Levi looked around the circle, his gaze halting when he reached Ruthy. She felt her face growing red, until he finally finished the story.

"Ignatius fell asleep, happy in the Lord, a faithful martyr of Jesus Christ."

Nancy put her hand on Levi's knee. "That's where our *mam* is, *nicht wahr?* She's with Jesus?"

Levi's eyes filled with tears, and he looked away from Ruthy. *"Ja."* His voice was husky and he cleared his throat as he covered Nancy's hand with his own. *"Ja.* Your *mam* is happy with her Lord, just as the Bible tells us."

Ruthy's own eyes filled with tears as Nancy laid her head against her *daed's* knee. Beside her, Nellie sniffed. Pulling her handkerchief from her sleeve, Ruthy gave it to Nellie.

Levi cleared his throat and reached for the empty dishpan. "Are we out of popcorn already?"

Ruthy took the pan as she stood. "I'll make some more."

She put a smile on her face, but Levi wasn't looking at her. She fled to the kitchen, happy to leave the family alone. Why had she let herself be talked into joining them this afternoon? She would have done better to stay in her own rooms and take a nap.

As she measured popcorn into the heavy kettle, she felt small arms encircling her waist. It was Nellie.

"What is it?" Ruthy knelt down to look into the little girl's face.

"I just wanted to tell you I'm glad you came to live with us." Nellie sniffed again as she gave Ruthy's handkerchief back to her. *"Dat* used to get so sad."

"He seems pretty sad right now." Ruthy pushed a stray hair under Nellie's *kapp.*

"But he doesn't stay sad anymore. He said he'll read a happy story from the Bible next, as soon as the popcorn is done."

Ruthy smiled at Nellie, even as her eyes filled again. "Then we'd better make the popcorn, *ja?*"

Nellie nodded and ran back to the living room, where Ruthy could hear an animated conversation starting. Perhaps she did belong here after all.

Chapter Seven

The storm in the early part of the week had blown itself out by Wednesday, but Friday brought a frigid wind from the northwest and the promise of more snow. Ruthy shivered as she dressed for the day. Even though she stood as close to her little woodstove as she dared, the air in the *Dawdi Haus* was icy.

She opened the stove door and pushed the coals together, covering them with a blanket of ashes. They might last until evening, otherwise she would have to lay a whole new fire.

One last glance around the room showed that all was in order, and she picked up the lamp for the short walk to the main house kitchen. The room was warm, thanks to the fire already burning in the kitchen stove. It was thoughtful of Levi Zook to start the fire for her each morning.

After pumping water into the coffeepot and measuring enough coffee grounds, Ruthy started working with the sourdough. She'd make pancakes this morning instead of biscuits. That would be a treat on such a cold day.

By the time the family was sitting at table, Ruthy and Waneta had breakfast ready. After the prayer, she cleared her throat to get Levi Zook's attention.

"What is it?" He looked at her from the other end of the long table, before turning his attention to filling his plate again before she could speak.

"Today is marketing day, Levi Zook. Could Waneta and I take the buggy to the store?"

He shook his head as he poured tomato ketchup onto his eggs. "It's too cold today. I don't want the horses going anywhere, nor you and Waneta. The thermometer says three below this morning and the barometer is falling."

David whooped and James said, "You mean no school today?"

"That's right." Levi Zook nodded and took a bite of eggs. "I doubt the school bus will be running, so you boys can help Elias work in the barn today."

Ruthy swiftly went through the items on her marketing list. She could make do without them until tomorrow.

"Could Waneta and I use the buggy tomorrow, then?"

"There is a storm coming. I doubt we'll be going anywhere for the next few days. It's a good thing this is an off Sunday for church." Levi Zook took a swallow of coffee, then looked at Ruthy over the rim of his cup. "Is there something special you need?"

Something special? "Not really. I was going to get some more wool to make stockings, and I wanted to get a few groceries."

"*Ja,* well then, you'll have to make do with what we already have."

Ruthy nodded, trying to hide her disappointment.

She had been hoping to see what the store was like, and maybe meet some of their neighbors. She had forgotten this was an off Sunday for church, and she had been looking forward to the fellowship.

Breakfast cleared up quickly with the scholars at home to help. Ruthy put the girls to work on the upstairs bedrooms, Martha with Nancy and Waneta with Nellie. Working in pairs, the little girls would be good helpers to their sisters.

Ruthy started a pot of chili soup for dinner, knowing the family would need hot food on such a cold day. As she opened the jars of stewed tomatoes and kidney beans, she went through her mental list of pending chores. This would be a good day to go through the children's clothes and see what needed to be passed down and who needed new things made.

The rest of the morning was spent going through the girls' dresses. Martha's skirts were all too short, so they were handed down to Nellie and Nancy. Ruthy showed Waneta and Martha how to take in the side and shoulder seams so the dresses would fit the smaller girls.

"Nellie has the brown dress, and I have the green one for school," said Nancy, "but what about a for-good dress?"

"We'll have to make new ones for you, but I don't know where we'll find the material." Ruthy tried not to sound concerned as she pinned the hem of Nancy's new dress. The little girl stood on a stool, modeling the dress as Ruthy turned up the hem to fit her.

Martha smoothed the front of Waneta's blue dress that fit her perfectly. "I think *Mam* had some fabric up in the attic. She bought it before…"

Ruthy's eyes filled with tears as the girl choked on

the words she couldn't say. "Thank you, Martha. We can look for it together, *ja?*"

"Where is Waneta's new dress?" Nellie crawled up on Martha's bed next to her biggest sister. "She's giving hers to Martha, but who will give one to her?"

"Perhaps we can make one from the material your *mam* saved, if we can find it."

"Or there are *Mam's* dresses." Nancy twisted to look at Ruthy, pulling the hem of the dress out of her hands. "I know where they are."

Nancy jumped off the stool before Ruthy could stop her and ran out of the room. She followed Nancy down the staircase and around the corner to Levi Zook's bedroom. Ruthy stopped at the doorway.

"Nancy, what are you doing?" Waneta's voice came from behind her, and Ruthy stepped aside to let her pass.

"I saw them, in here." The little girl knelt next to a chest at the foot of Levi's bed and lifted the lid.

Before Ruthy realized what was happening, all four girls were staring at the dresses lying on the top of the contents of the chest.

"It…it smells like *Memmi.*" Nellie's voice was soft. She knelt down next to Nancy and reached out a hand to touch the charcoal-gray dress, folded neatly with the apron and *kapp* on top of it.

Ruthy hesitated in the doorway. She had never been in Levi Zook's bedroom. Stepping in the room would be intruding on the man's personal territory, but the girls had to be stopped before they went any further.

"Girls, close the lid and come out. We mustn't disturb your *daed's* things."

"I remember this dress." Martha's voice was a whisper. "*Mam* wore it when we went to church."

"I had almost forgotten what she looked like." Waneta lifted her eyes to Ruthy. "But I remember her wearing this dress."

"What dress?" Levi Zook's voice came from behind Ruthy, from the front room. "What are you doing?"

Ruthy twirled around, filling the doorway to his room. Would the girls close the lid before Levi Zook saw what they had been looking at? It tore her heart in two to see Nellie caressing her *mam's kapp* and the girls' tear-filled eyes. What would it do to their father?

He didn't look at her as he brushed past.

"I'm sorry. I didn't know what Nancy was doing when she came down here...."

"Waneta, girls, close that chest and leave. Now." His voice was quiet, but firm.

The girls obeyed, silently filing past Ruthy.

Levi Zook stood and leaned with one hand on the post of his bed, staring at the chest on the floor. Ruthy turned to leave him alone with his thoughts, but his strained voice stopped her.

"Wait."

She looked back. He sat heavily on the bed, his head in his hands.

"What made them come in here? What were they looking for?"

Ruthy cast back. What was it that had brought Nancy in here?

"We were passing dresses down to the younger girls, and there wasn't one for Waneta. Then Nancy said she knew where her mother's dresses were...."

Rising, he crossed the room to the door, his face red and twisted. "Just go." His eyes darted past her and then to the floor. "Just go. I need to be alone."

Ruthy stepped back as he shut the door in her face. Why hadn't she stopped Nancy before the girls opened the chest?

A sudden bang on the wooden door made her flee to the kitchen.

Levi kicked the twisted rag rug to the side with a growl and slammed his hand against the door. Why had the girls come in here? Why had Ruth let them? Did she have no control over herself?

Ach, he knew better than that. She hadn't even been in his room—only in the hall outside the door. The girls had been the ones to intrude, but he had never forbidden them to come in.

Sinking onto his knees next to the chest that held Salome's things, he laid his hand on the lid, the lid that hadn't been opened since the day she had died.

Until today. He rubbed one hand over his face, but the memory of his daughters' tearful faces remained. Opening this chest had been like opening a Pandora's box, releasing grief and sadness into the house all over again.

Was it wrong to save Salome's dresses and the few things he had found in her dresser drawers? He couldn't bear to just dispose of them as if she had never lived, had never been his wife, had never been the mother to his children.

He smoothed the top of the chest before lifting it. Salome's Sunday dress, *kapp* and apron lay on top. Underneath were her everyday dresses, and beneath them were her diary, letters from the round robin she had belonged to from the time she was Nancy and Nellie's age and a little faded dress—the first she had sewn for her doll when she was a child.

The sum of a woman's life in a little box.

All his anger evaporated and he closed the chest. Salome was gone and he missed her, but it was time to go on. It was what she had wanted, and what he intended to do. His children needed him.

He rose and walked to the window. Gray clouds met the horizon in an indistinct line of blowing snow. Through the fencerow he could see Salome's childhood home, sold now to *Englischers* since her parents were gone and her brothers had all moved west to Kansas. He had spent so many hours there as a child, playing with Salome's brothers, and then later while he and Salome were courting. Until she passed away last year, there hadn't been a day of his life that she hadn't been a part of.

He missed her. He missed her companionship, her laugh and her love for their children, but he wouldn't want to call her back from the blessed place where she was now. He hadn't realized how sick she had been. Since before Sam was born she had been wasting away, but he had blamed it on a difficult pregnancy, and then she had trouble recovering, until he finally had to admit her illness was more than a passing weakness. She faded away gradually, slowly, without realizing he was losing her until it was too late. She had suffered greatly in those last months while rounds of doctor visits and medicines had been useless. He would never wish that time back again.

Levi took in the room around him. He had kept his clothes on one peg, in one half of the dresser. He slept on one side of the bed. The room was waiting for another wife, another mother for his children. Would he ever find someone who could step into Salome's place?

The girls stood in the kitchen, their faces white and drawn.

"Is *Dat* all right?" Waneta asked as Ruthy came into the room.

Was he all right? She had never seen a man look as wretched as Levi Zook when he slammed the door in her face.

"He will be." Ruthy tried to smile to reassure the girls, but they only exchanged glances with each other.

Ruthy looked at the clock on the kitchen wall. "It's nearly noon. The chili soup is done, so why don't you girls set the table. Waneta, we can have bread with the soup, and Martha, if you would please bring up a jar of prune plums from down cellar, we can have a nice hot dinner."

Her face burned as the girls started their tasks and Ruthy hurried through the kitchen to the *Dawdi Haus*. Her rooms were cold, but silent and empty. She threw herself onto her bed and let the tears flow.

Why had she let the girls go into his room? They had intruded into Levi Zook's bedroom, pried into his belongings and disturbed his peace. He had every right to be angry with her, didn't he? But she had never seen a man act as Levi Zook had. Was this what grief brought a man to?

Ruthy's tears slowed as she considered his point of view. She was still a stranger, and yet she was watching his girls pry into his dead wife's things. She should have stopped them, she should have taken them away as soon as she saw what was inside the chest.

And yet, shouldn't the girls have reminders of their mother?

She rose from her bed, hurriedly splashing water to wash away the blotchy redness she knew the family would see when she went back to the kitchen. Drying her hands and face on the towel, she shivered. It certainly seemed colder than it had been this morning.

A knock sounded on the *Dawdi Haus* door as she adjusted the pinnings on her dress. The girls must need her help.

"*Ja,* I'm coming." She opened the door while holding her skirt in place with one hand, pins in her mouth and *kapp* askew, but instead of one of the girls, Levi Zook stood in the doorway, his hands in his pockets.

She hurriedly fastened the last of the pins into her waistband and straightened her *kapp* the best she could while he watched.

"I'm sorry to disturb you, but I wanted to talk to you while the children were busy."

"*Ja, ja, ja,* come in, please."

The man looked huge and out of place in the little *Dawdi Haus.* He looked around the room as he stepped in.

"It's cold in here."

"The fire is banked." Her words sounded foolish. Why was he here?

"I need to apologize to you." His face was tired, but all traces of his earlier anguish were gone.

"*Ach, ne,* Levi Zook. I'm the one who should apologize. I let the girls go much too far when they went into your room. It was unforgivable."

He had moved to look at her books on the side table, but turned at her comment.

"Unforgivable? Nothing is unforgivable."

Ruthy looked down and smoothed her skirt with her hands. "Some things are. Betrayal is unforgivable." Her voice shook. She hadn't meant to say that aloud.

Raising her eyes to Levi Zook's, she saw something there. Pity. Concern. Sadness.

"Nothing is unforgivable, Ruth. Our heavenly Father is ready and waiting to hear our repentance. We only need to turn to him."

Ruthy's heart felt cold and hard in her chest. He misunderstood, thinking she had been the one who sinned. But she had been the victim of Elam and Laurette's betrayal. How could she forgive what they did to her?

She tried to apologize again. "I am sorry for letting the girls intrude into your bedroom. If...if you think I shouldn't be working for you, I would understand."

He reached out to grasp her hand in his. "I was angry, and I shouldn't have been. I was afraid of what you'd think...what the girls would think... Is it wrong to save Salome's dresses and things? They're all I have to remember her."

Ruthy looked into his face. His eyes were shadowed, the anguish had returned.

"Not all, Levi Zook. You have her children."

Levi's eyes flashed open and he squeezed her hand.

"You're right. I could never forget her while I have the children, could I?"

Ruthy pulled her hand away and turned to the chair, where she had dropped her apron.

"Dinner is ready. You must be cold and hungry."

He stopped her with a hand on her arm. "One thing, first. I want you to take Salome's dresses from the chest and fit them for Waneta. I've laid them on the chair in the front room."

"But…"

Levi Zook continued as if she hadn't spoken. "I'll take her other things up to the attic. The girls will want to have them someday, when they're older."

Ruthy nodded. It was the right thing to do.

Sounds intruded from the kitchen. The boys had come in from the barn, bringing noise and laughter with them.

Levi dropped his hand from her arm. "I think it's time for dinner."

Ruthy looked into his eyes as she passed by him on the way to the kitchen. They were shadowed and red-rimmed, but held a peace she hadn't seen since she had met him.

Chapter Eight

The storm Levi Zook had predicted blew in that afternoon, with a sharp northwest wind whistling around the eaves and driving tiny flakes of snow against the windows in a relentless hissing.

Ruthy built up the fire in the front room so she could help Waneta and Martha make the needed alterations to their new dresses. The rest of the children played games on the floor near the stove while Levi took Elias and Nathan out to string a rope from the house to the chicken coop and barn. No matter how thickly the snow blew, the animals would need caring for.

"How long do you think this storm will last?" Ruthy squinted her eyes to thread a needle in the dim light. She had never experienced such wind at home.

"Sometimes it snows for a week," David said from the floor.

"It only did that once." Waneta was bent over her sewing and spoke around the pins held tightly between her lips.

"I remember one winter we couldn't go anywhere

for two whole weeks." James jumped David's checker and claimed it.

Martha looked up from the hem she was sewing. "Was that when those *Englischers* ran their automobile into the ditch at the end of our lane, and they ended up staying in the *Dawdi Haus* until the roads were cleared?"

"I don't remember that," Sam said, looking up from the farm he was building out of blocks.

"You were a baby then," David answered. "You didn't remember anything."

"Those *Englischers* were funny," Waneta said. "They were from the city, on their way to visit relatives. *Dat* said they didn't know any better than to stay home when bad weather threatens."

The sound of boots stamping off snow signaled the return of Levi and the boys from the barn and a glance at the clock told Ruthy it was time to start thinking about supper. She went into the kitchen just as Levi Zook opened the back door, letting in a stream of cold air.

"The wind is getting even stronger out there." Levi cradled the cup of coffee Ruthy gave him while the boys huddled around the kitchen stove.

"It must be getting colder, too," Ruthy said, opening the cookie tin and handing them around.

"Ja," Elias said, his voice shivering. "I was afraid the milk would freeze in the pails between here and the barn."

Levi sat at the kitchen table with his coffee while Ruthy took care of the buckets he had carried in. Elias was right—milk clung in frozen droplets around the rim of the pail.

"Will the animals be warm enough in the barn?"

"*Ja,* for sure. They'll keep each other warm." Levi finished his cookie and took another from the tin Ruthy had set on the table. "I hope no one was caught out in this storm, though. It would be dangerous to be out there tonight."

"Do you think that's a possibility?" Ruthy warmed up Levi's cup with fresh coffee. "Wouldn't everyone have known the storm was coming, like you did, and stayed home?"

"*Ja...*"

"What is wrong?"

Levi took a swallow of coffee. "I'm just a worrier, I suppose. This isn't a fit night for anyone to be out."

"If anyone is caught out in the storm, they would see the lights of a house, for sure, and find their way to shelter."

"You're right...." Levi didn't sound convinced as he sipped his coffee.

The boys joined the rest of the children around the stove in the front room while Ruthy opened jars of canned beef she had brought up from the cellar. She went through the supper menu in her mind. Beef and noodles, mashed potatoes, bread, crackers, pickles and the pies she and Martha had made yesterday would make a good meal.

"*Dat,*" Nathan said, coming into the kitchen. "Did we leave a light on in the barn?"

"*Ne.*" Levi rose from his seat and peered out the window next to the table, shielding his eyes against the light behind him.

"I thought I saw a light through the cowshed door."

"The snow is blowing so much I can't see...*ach,*

there. You're right." Levi shot a worried glance at Ruthy as he hurried out the door. "Nathan, you and Elias be ready to come out. Watch for my signal."

As the door slammed behind him, Ruthy moved to watch out the window with Nathan. Could a fire have started since the men had come in? *Please, God, let it be anything but a fire.*

Minutes passed. Elias joined Ruthy and Nathan at the kitchen window. Suddenly the slight glow they were watching went out and the cowshed door opened.

Ruthy's knees shook with relief. Levi was safe and there was no fire.

"Who is that with *Dat?*" Elias asked.

Coming toward the house were two figures. Levi was supporting a smaller man as they headed toward the house.

Ruthy turned to the children, who had all come in to see what was happening.

"That man looks cold. Martha, run into the *Dawdi Haus* and bring the extra quilt from my bed." She took another quick look out the window. "Waneta, will you start heating the beef for supper? And Nellie, please bring up another jar from the cellar. It looks like we have company."

"Who is it, Ruthy?" Sam asked. "Who's with *Dat?*"

Sam's question was answered as Levi reached the house. Elias opened the kitchen door and helped Levi guide the man to the chair at the end of the table. The look the *Englischer* gave Ruthy was shameful and apologetic. His cheeks were sunken and dirt darkened his pale skin.

Ruthy grabbed another cup and poured hot coffee into it. When Martha returned with the quilt, Levi took it and wrapped it around the man's shoulders while Ruthy ushered the children back into the front room.

"No one wants to be stared at by curious strangers. Let your *dat* talk to the man. You'll be able to see him later."

"But who is he?" Sam asked.

James fixed his eyes on Ruthy, his face hard. "He's one of those tramps, isn't he?"

"Tramp?" Nancy said, her eyes round as she watched James.

"*Ja,* he's a tramp. They go around and steal things—" he dropped his voice to a whisper "—and murder people in their beds at night."

Ruthy put her arm around Nellie before she could start crying. "James, where did you hear such a thing?"

"Tom Nelson at school told me. He heard—"

"It doesn't matter what he heard." Ruthy interrupted James's tale firmly. "A tramp is just a man who doesn't have a home. Some of them may be thieves, but most are only poor men who have lost their jobs, their homes and their families in these hard times. We'll treat him well, as the Good Book tells us to."

Ruthy patted James's shoulder. "You children go back to what you were doing while Waneta and I get supper ready. I'm sure we'll all hear the stranger's story if he wants to tell it." Suddenly remembering, she added, "Be sure to speak *Englisch* instead of *Deitsch* while he's here. We don't want to shut him out of our conversations."

Levi sat on the bench next to the stranger and pushed the cream pitcher and sugar bowl toward him while he reclaimed his own coffee cup and took a swallow. The man's hand shook so badly when he tried to lift the small pitcher that Levi reached over and poured it in the cup for him.

The man nodded. "Thanks." His voice was rough and dry. "I don't mean to be a bother. The barn is warm enough for me, if you'll let me stay there tonight." His eyes flickered up to meet Levi's, then down to his cup again.

"You're welcome to stay here. A man should be in a warm house in weather like this, not a barn."

"But your family…"

"My family will enjoy having the company."

The man lifted his coffee cup in both hands, keeping it steady enough to take a noisy sip.

"Now that's good coffee." He blew on the hot liquid and took another sip.

"There's nothing like hot coffee to warm you up from the inside out." Levi took another swallow from his own cup. The tramp's hands caught his gaze. The fingertips that emerged from the dirty wrappings he wore instead of gloves were black with grime, the nails broken. This man had been on the road for a long time.

Ruth came into the kitchen, giving him a reassuring smile as she joined Waneta at the stove. She had been prepared to give the man comfort even before he reached the house with their guest. Not very many women would have thought of a stranger's needs over their clean floor.

"Would our guest like to wash up before supper?" She glanced at Levi as she asked, and then smiled at the tramp.

Levi saw the shame that passed over the man's face

as Ruth spoke, shame she didn't see as he ducked his head away from her.

"Elias can show you to the guest room when you've finished your coffee," Levi said, trying to reassure the stranger.

Ruth said something to Waneta and his daughter started to draw hot water from the stove's reservoir. *Ja,* Ruth would make sure the extra room in the front of the house had everything the stranger needed.

Through the long, stormy weekend, the stranger, Jack, made himself useful where he could, going to the barn with Levi in the morning and afternoon and joining the family in the front room as they spent long hours playing games and reading while Ruthy sewed.

The man rarely spoke except to answer a direct question, until Sunday evening, after the storm had died down.

Levi Zook had just finished reading the story of the Prodigal Son from the Bible, translating the German into *Englisch* as he read. Listening to the familiar story in the unfamiliar language was like hearing it for the first time. Ruthy found herself thinking about the father in the story, rather than the son, like she usually did.

The father hadn't hesitated to forgive his son for what he had done, even though the son had turned his back on his family and his home.... Had Levi Zook been right when he said that nothing was unforgivable? Even a betrayal as devastating as Elam and Laurette's?

Ruthy shifted in her seat. This cozy room, filled with golden light and Levi's gentle voice as he told the story, pried at the icy wall shielding her heart.

Levi finished the story just as the clock chimed the hour for bedtime.

Jack cleared his throat. "The storm is over, so I'll be going on my way in the morning. But before the children go to bed, I have to tell you something." He sat forward in his chair, his head bowed as Levi Zook and the children watched him, waiting.

After a long minute, he spoke. His voice was strained, as if his story didn't want to be told.

"I haven't always been the way you see me now. My full name is John Davenport, but I've always been called Jack. I was born and raised in New York City. My father was an investor like his father had been before him. My grandfather invested in canals and railroads, and my father followed in his footsteps. They were successful. Very successful.

"My mother loved New York society. She was always attending one party or another. My brother and I rarely saw her."

Jack looked at the faces around him, his eyes wet. "We would have given the world for a family like you have."

He straightened up, wiping his hand across his eyes.

"When my father died, my brother took over the family business. He lived for it. He made more money in one month than my father had in his lifetime.

"And me?" He smiled. Ruthy had never seen such a sad smile. "I spent the money." He gestured at the Bible still in Levi Zook's hands. "I was that son in the story you just read. I spent money like it would never run out. I had friends, power, everything I wanted. I married the most beautiful girl around." His voice dropped. "We were happy. The gayest couple in town."

The room fell into silence. Ruthy heard the whisper of a log shifting in the stove.

"What happened?" James asked. "Why didn't you stay there?"

Jack held the boy's gaze. "My brother and I put our faith in money, you see? It was our lifeblood. We had never lived without it, never knew you could."

His gaze moved to the dancing flames in the stove. "When the stock market collapsed in '29, I heard nothing about it until I went to the office that afternoon. I found my brother there. He had committed suicide when he got the news."

Ruthy's stomach clenched.

"We lost everything. It was all gone. Every penny. My brother was dead, my wife left, the house was sold to pay debts, Mother went to live with her sister in Boston...." Jack ran his hands through his hair as if he wanted to tear it out.

Ruthy glanced at Levi—could he do something to help this poor man? But Levi Zook sat with his head down, his eyes closed.

"I wanted you to know my story because you've been more than kind to me. You didn't need to take in a lost soul like me, but you did."

Levi Zook put the Bible back in its place on the table next to him. "We only did as our Lord commanded." He looked at the man across from him. "Where will you go tomorrow?"

"I'll head west. I heard there's work in California."

"You won't go home?"

Jack looked into the fire. "I have no home."

"For sure your mother would want to see you again."

Jack shook his head. "No."

In the silent room, Levi Zook caught Ruthy's eye and nodded toward the children. *Ja,* it was bedtime now. She ushered the children up the stairs and they went without a word, subdued by the story they had just heard.

On her way to the *Dawdi Haus,* Ruthy glanced at the men in the front room. Levi Zook and Jack sat on either side of the stove, both their heads bowed. Levi was praying. Ruthy had often seen his head bowed in just that way. Before either of the men found their own beds, Levi would make sure Jack heard about the heavenly home that would never perish.

Ruthy made an extra-large breakfast the next morning. It may be many days before Jack was able to find a full meal again.

"There's one piece of schnitz pie left," Martha said as she took the platter of ham to the table. "Do you think Jack would like to have it?"

"Let's wrap it up and send it with him for his lunch," Ruthy said. "We can make ham sandwiches with some of these biscuits, too."

"Can I do that?" Nancy dropped the flatware she was holding on the table with a clatter and rushed up to Ruthy. "Can I fix his lunch?"

"After you finish setting the table." Ruthy sliced extra ham while Martha and Waneta put the rest of the breakfast on the table.

When the men came in from the barn, breakfast was ready. After the silent prayer, Jack gazed at the food on the table and turned to Ruthy.

"Thank you, ma'am, for this fine spread."

"We didn't want you to start out on your travels with an empty stomach."

"Well, there's no danger of that around here." Jack took the bowl of fried potatoes from Levi and piled them on his plate.

"Where will you head from here?" Levi asked, filling his own plate.

"I'll head out to the state highway and try to get a ride from someone going south. I've had enough of this cold weather." Jack grinned. "Somewhere around Nashville or New Orleans, I'll head west."

"What kind of work do you think you'll find in California?" Elias emptied the dish of potatoes and Ruthy rose to take up more from the stove.

"They grow produce out there year-round." Jack took a bite of his ham. "They always need workers to pick something or weed something or plant something."

"I read in my schoolbook that they grow oranges there." David stirred maple syrup into his oatmeal.

"Yep, you're right, young man. There are groves of orange trees, and oil wells."

"And the ocean?" David looked up from his oatmeal.

Jack's smile grew soft. "Yeah. The ocean. That's one thing I've missed about New York. Going to the seaside in the summer."

Ruthy exchanged glances with Levi. How had their talk last night turned out? She had hoped Jack would decide to go back home instead of to California.

When the meal was finished, Jack stood next to the door as they said goodbye, looking ill-at-ease.

"You don't have to go," Levi said. "Like I told you last night, you can stay here and work. I can't pay you, but you'll have a place to live and food to eat."

Jack glanced at the table and rubbed his belly. "It's a tempting offer, but no." He flashed a grin at Ruthy, a different man than had taken shelter in their barn three days ago. "I'm a traveling man, and it's time to be on my way."

With that he gave a little wave, and walked out the door, slinging a bundle with some extra clothes and Nancy's lunch over his shoulder.

"Will he ever find a home, *Dat?*" Jesse slipped his hand into Levi Zook's.

Levi shook his head, his wet eyes matching Ruthy's own. "I don't know, son. All we can do is pray for him. The rest is in the Lord's hands."

Ruthy watched Jack, a lone dark figure against the white snow, as he walked down the lane to the road. Would he remember the story of the Prodigal Son? Would he ever come running to his Father's welcoming arms? All he had to do was to repent and ask for forgiveness, and the Lord would welcome him.

The icy shield of her heart cracked as she realized the direction of her thoughts. The Lord expected her to forgive as He did.... He wanted her to forgive Elam and Laurette. *Ne, Lord, ask me anything but that....*

Chapter Nine

Ruthy hurried to get the ham-and-potato casserole in the oven in time for dinner. *Ach,* what a busy morning Mondays brought! But the morning's work was nearly done, with Waneta hanging the last of the washing while Ruthy fixed dinner.

As she slid the four loaves of bread into the second oven, Ruthy decided it was time for a short break with a cup of cocoa. By the time it was ready, Waneta would be back inside and ready for a rest, too.

Stirring the milk, sugar and cocoa on the stovetop, Ruthy counted the days she had been in Indiana. She had arrived on Tuesday, the twelfth of January and today was Monday, February eighth. Nearly four weeks. In that time they had weathered three snowstorms, the last one coming just two days after Jack Davenport had walked out of their lives. They had been snowed in for three days. Today was the first time Levi had let the children go to school since last Tuesday, and he had taken them himself in the sleigh, not trusting the *Englisch* school-bus driver.

So, four full weeks here, and the household routine was beginning to live up to her *mam's* standards. Levi appreciated her work, for sure. He often thanked her after the evening meal, or when one of the boys commented on a replaced button or mended trousers, but other than that he didn't speak to her at all. Was he sorry he had hired her and brought her here? *Ne,* it didn't appear so. But did her presence here remind him of the wife he had lost?

Ruthy moved the hot cocoa off the heat as she heard Waneta coming into the back porch. Now she was a different girl! Saturday afternoon Reuben Stoltzfus had come calling, even though many roads were still blocked with snow and no one else was visiting. He had spent the afternoon with them, and then driven Waneta to the young folks' gathering at the Beacheys that evening. Waneta's lighthearted humming had filled the house for two days.

"Everything is hung up." Waneta came into the kitchen with a smile as she saw Ruthy pouring the hot cocoa into waiting mugs. "The clothes will freeze in a hurry out there today."

"*Ja,* and dinner is in the oven. I thought we'd take a bit of a sit-down before getting the rest of the meal together."

"That sounds *wonderful-gut.*" Waneta took her cup to the table, and Ruthy joined her on the bench facing the windows.

Snow covered the barnyard, but bright sunshine made the farm look like a wonderland.

"Such a beautiful day, with that blue sky, *ne?*" Ruthy took a sip of her cocoa.

"Ja." Waneta turned her cup in her hands. "Ruthy, do you mind if I ask a question?"

"Of course not."

"Did you ever have a boy who…well, who wanted to spend time with you?"

Elam. Ruthy's heart clenched. Would she ever be able to think of him without remembering his betrayal?

"I did. Once." More than once. Elam had courted her for eight years.

"Did you feel like you could fly?" Waneta's voice was wistful as she gazed out the window, her chin on her hand.

"Ach, ja. Like I could fly over the clouds!" Ruthy laughed as she said it. She could remember those feelings, if she put the last year out of her mind. "And just why do you ask?"

Waneta's face reddened. "No reason, just…"

"Just that you enjoyed a certain young man's visit Saturday?"

"It was *wonderful-gut,* wasn't it? Did you see how he played with the little boys so sweetly, and talked to *Dat* about farming…." Waneta sighed. "Do you think *Dat* likes him?"

"Ja, for sure he does."

"He didn't look too happy when Reuben was here."

"Well, think about how he's feeling. Say he has a sweet heifer calf he's raised—bottle-feeding it, giving it the softest hay for its bed, protecting it from all kinds of weather. How would he feel if another farmer came by and asked him to sell that heifer calf? What would he do?"

"I'm no heifer calf, Ruthy," Waneta said, but she

smiled. "He'd want to know if the farmer would give the calf a good home. If he'd feed her well and keep her safe."

"*Ja,* for sure he would. Would he do any less for his daughter?"

"*Ne,* he wouldn't."

"Your *dat* loves you, and he won't feel right about any young man who comes to visit his daughters. It's Reuben's job to change his mind. If Reuben is the wise young man I think he is, we'll be seeing a lot more of him in the next few months."

"Is that what your young man did with your *dat?*"

"*Ach, ja.* Elam was at our house so often *Mam* set a place at table for him just like he was one of the family." He *was* part of the family....

"What happened?"

"What do you mean?"

"Why didn't you marry him?"

Ruthy felt her mouth quivering even though she tried to keep a smile on her face. "He decided he'd rather marry someone else." She stood quickly and took their empty mugs to the sink. "That's the way it happens sometimes."

"Perhaps you'll meet someone else. Someone here in Indiana." Waneta followed her to the sink to wash the dishes from their cocoa.

"I don't think so." Ruthy steadied her voice. "Sometimes God calls a woman to help others rather than have their own homes. That's why God brought me here, don't you think? This is the work He has for me."

Waneta dried the cups in silence while Ruthy scrubbed the pan she had heated the cocoa in.

"How do you know?" Waneta dried the pan while Ruthy took the perfectly brown loaves out of the oven. "Perhaps He brought you here to meet the husband He has for you."

Stomping boots in the porch told Ruthy the boys and Levi were coming in for their dinner. She hurried to open the quarts of beans to heat up, but her mind was still on Waneta's comment. Ellie and Annie had mentioned the same thing—that perhaps God had brought her here to find the husband He had for her.

She glanced up just as Levi Zook came in the door, laughing at something Elias had said, his face ruddy from the cold February air. When he saw her watching him, his laughter changed to a smile. A warm smile of greeting, just for her.

Levi sorted through the letters he had picked up at the post office in Emma when he took the children to school, letting Ruthy and Waneta set the table around him.

Ruthy moved back and forth as if he didn't exist, but he was aware of each movement she made. As the weeks passed, he appreciated her more than he thought possible. She cooked well, managed the housework without any complaint, worked well with the girls and treated the children like they were her own. But he wouldn't let his thoughts go any further.

He opened the bill from the feed store, but the paper could have been a blank sheet. His attention was captured by the efficient woman who leaned around him to place a casserole on the table. She had made herself a *kapp* that fit in with the ones the women in Eden Township wore, and had changed the tucks and folds of her dress also. He hadn't expected her to live according to the *Ordnung* here.

Was she happy? He didn't dare watch her closely enough to find out, but it seemed so.

"Ruthy," Sam said, sliding along the bench to make room for her, "sit by me."

"*Ja,* Sam." She smiled at him and let her hand rest on his head as she passed. "As soon as the food is all taken up, I'll sit next to you like I always do at dinner."

Levi stared at the bill, watching the numbers on the paper double and move sideways until the whole thing was a blur. Sam had liked Ruthy from the beginning, but he had caught the look in the boy's eyes as Ruth had caressed him. The five-year-old loved her.

And why not? Why shouldn't he love the woman who cooked for him and cared for him, and took the time to look at his drawings and listen to his constant stories?

He shoved the bill back into the envelope and leafed through the other envelopes.

"Ruth, there's a letter here for you."

"For me? I've been waiting for a letter from *Mam.*" Ruth dried her hands on her apron then reached to take it from him. When she glanced at the address her smile faded and she tucked it into her waistband.

"Is it from your *mam?*" Waneta asked as she set a plate of bread on the table.

"*Ne.* I'll read it later. It's time for dinner now."

Levi tried to keep his mind on his prayer, but the look on Ruth's face as she tucked that letter away wouldn't leave his mind. Instead of thanking God for his food, he found himself praying for Ruth. Whatever was in the letter, she wasn't looking forward to reading it.

"Moolah is nearly ready to calve, *Dat,*" said Elias when the prayer ended. "She's been pretty restless all morning."

"You put her in the calving stall?"

"Not yet, but I will after dinner."

"I want to watch when she has her baby," Sam said, his mouth full of bread. "Can I, *Dat?*"

"It won't be this afternoon, son. You can watch when it happens, unless it's in the middle of the night."

Ruth put a spoonful of green beans on Sam's plate and took some for herself. "Will she be all right?"

"Moolah? *Ach, ja.* She's had several calves already, and never has trouble with the birth." Levi took a piece of bread from the plate as it was passed and reached for the rhubarb preserves. "Did you want to watch, too?"

Ruth reddened as he waited for her answer. She hadn't been to the barn since her first day when she had confronted him about the children. The weather had kept all the girls inside the last couple of weeks.

"I helped my *dat* with the calving at home, and I thought I could help with Moolah if you needed me."

Levi thought of the long hours spent in the barn waiting for a calf to come. Salome would never come to the barn to watch a calving, and that had been fine. Women belonged in the house with the children, not sitting with him in the barn during the long hours of the night. He shifted in his chair as he had a sudden vision of sitting alone with this woman, talking together the way he and his sisters used to when they lived at home. What a good companion she would make…. But *ne,* she was his housekeeper, nothing more.

"I don't think I'll need the help." He didn't look at her at he spoke, but he could tell his words had hurt her.

She turned from him to Sam. "What did you do to help your *daed* this morning?"

As Sam launched into a long tale of the chores he had helped with, Levi remembered it had been Ruth's idea for Sam to start learning to chore in the first place. *Ach,* and she had been right. He took another bite of casserole as he turned this thought over in his mind. She had an instinct for what the children needed. Even with the older boys. She treated them as men, not just boys who needed the same care their little brothers did.

Levi let his gaze rest on her as she listened to Sam talk. She nodded as he explained how to feed the cows, her face interested, although this must be old news to her. She smiled often, he realized. Some might say her mouth was too wide, but he thought it added to her beauty.

This was ridiculous. He didn't need to be staring at his housekeeper and thinking about her looks. He turned to his meal, concentrating on each bite. If he let Ruth take a place in his thoughts, then who knows where they would lead? John Stoltzfus hadn't said it outright, but it was plain that a young woman living here could appear wrong. There was nothing to worry about—they were conducting themselves properly— but if he let his thoughts stray, the wrong actions could follow right on their heels.

Ruthy didn't have a chance to look at her letter until after the dinner dishes were washed and Waneta went out to check the drying laundry. She sat in the small wooden rocking chair in the kitchen, left there from the days when Levi's wife had been ill and needed to sit often during the day.

She put her feet up on the footstool and pulled the envelope from her waistband. She had recognized the handwriting immediately. How many letters had she and Laurette exchanged over the years?

The familiar rounded script brought tears to Ruthy's eyes. She missed her *mam* and *daed,* but Laurette had been her dearest friend. She hadn't spoken or written to Laurette since that day in September when Elam told her they were getting married. Her beau and her best friend.

What did Laurette have to say now? What could she say? She and Elam were wed and expecting their first child. The man who should have been Ruthy's husband, the child that should have been hers.

Ruthy pulled a hairpin from her *kapp* and inserted it in the envelope flap, but hesitated. What did Laurette have to say that she couldn't have said last fall? Or worse yet, what if the letter were only full of news of Laurette and Elam's life together, sharing every detail of her life just as all her letters had through the years?

Ruthy smoothed the envelope on her lap. Ever since Laurette's *mam* had died when they were both eight, Laurette had been more of a sister to her than a friend. Living just down the road, it was easy for her to drop by their house whenever she grew tired of her *daed's* company.

Laurette had known how much Ruthy loved Elam, but had still accepted his invitation to ride with him the night Ruthy had missed the Singing because of a cold. After that, Laurette had told her about her new beau, her first ever, but had never told Ruthy the boy's name. Meanwhile, days went by with Elam making excuses not to see her—and all the time he and Laurette...

Ruthy covered the envelope with her hand and set the chair rocking with one foot. Would she forgive Laurette if she asked?

How could she? Laurette had stolen Ruthy's only chance to be a wife and have a family. She would live as a *maidle* her entire life, like Aunt Ella, *Daed's* sister, moving from one family's house to another, only staying until she wasn't wanted or needed anymore, and then traveling on to the next house.

Just like she would stay at Levi Zook's house only as long as she was needed.

Leaning her head back against the edge of the chair, Ruthy closed her eyes, worn out by the morning's work. Life was easier at home, for sure, with only three people in the house, but as much as she missed her home, this house was so pleasant to work in. It would be a sad day when Levi married and didn't need her anymore.

Ruthy let her imagination see Levi Zook's new wife in the kitchen, sitting in her chair at table, talking with the children, laying her hand on Levi's shoulder as she placed his coffee cup on the table in front of him...imagining the feel of Levi's broad shoulders under his cotton shirts, his smile as he turned his warm brown eyes to catch hers, his soft *denki* meant for her ears alone...

Ruthy's eyes flew open. Where had that thought come from? What was she thinking of? The man practically ignored her, for heaven's sake. He never spoke directly to her unless she asked him a question, avoided looking in her direction whenever they were in the same room together and spent most of his time in the barn. In the evenings, if she joined the family in the front room, it was because one of the children insisted, not him. As far as she could tell, he didn't even like her, let alone have the kind of feelings that would cause him to look into her eyes.

Ruthy pushed the letter back into her waistband and rose from the chair, glancing out the window toward the barn as she did. *Ach,* why did her thoughts always stray to him? She was nothing more to him than…than a cow who provided the milk his family needed.

Pulling the mixing bowl from the cupboard, Ruthy scooped an egg-sized lump of lard and a cup of sugar into it. Making a batch of oatmeal cookies would get her mind off Laurette and the life she had left behind in Pennsylvania.

She paused before cracking an egg against the side of the bowl. *Ja,* and off that Levi Zook, too. She hit the egg against the rim of the bowl with one hand, cracking it open as her *mam* had taught her. Another egg followed the first, and then Ruthy started beating the lard and eggs together with a wooden spoon.

What would *Mam* think of Levi Zook? She would compare him to Elam, of course. Where Elam was a boy, Levi Zook was a bear. Where Elam's blue eyes grew soft and dreamy as he gazed at her, Levi's brown eyes were sharp, avoiding hers whenever he could. Where Elam teased girls until they cried, Levi gathered his little daughters onto his lap and tickled them with his beard. Where Elam had betrayed her…what would Levi have done?

Ruthy's spoon slowed in the bowl, the eggs, lard and sugar beaten into a creamy yellow mass.

A man like Levi Zook would never betray anyone.

Chapter Ten

Moolah's first bellow stopped Levi's feet on the stairs. After a day full of unending work, he was ready to fall into his bed, but the day wasn't over yet. He had just tucked the little boys into their bed and given each of his girls a kiss. It was time for his last check on the barn, but Moolah's second mournful cry warned him this could be a long night.

The cow had been safe in the calving pen and seemed calm as he and the boys did the evening chores. Her labor hadn't started yet, but that had been almost four hours ago.

"Dat," said Elias from the top of the stairs, "do you want me to go out to check on Moolah?"

"Ne, son, you go on to bed. I'll go see if she needs anything."

Levi heard another bellow as he went through the kitchen to the back door. She sounded alarmed at something. He shoved his arms into his coat and grabbed his hat. The path to the barn led through snow at least two feet deep, but it was well-packed. The stars shining on the white world gave him all the light he needed as he hurried through the frigid night to the warm cowshed.

Lighting the lantern kept on a nail by the door, he walked past the sleepy cows to the calving stall. Moolah was standing in the far corner with her head down and back hunched. He turned the lantern toward her head and she stared at him with white-ringed eyes.

"Moolah, good girl," he murmured to her, opening the gate to the stall and walking toward her. She shied from his approach, moving to the next corner with a halting step. "*Ach,* Moolah, what trouble have you gotten yourself into?"

She let him approach and he ran his hand along her side, feeling the muscles of her abdomen tighten as a contraction gripped the Holstein. Moolah humped her back and kicked, bellowing again in her pain. Something was wrong. Very wrong.

He ran his hands over her distended stomach, trying to feel the calf through the unyielding wall of flesh. Every other time Moolah had calved, the little one had been born easily and quickly and Moolah hadn't seemed to notice the discomfort.

She moved to the other corner of the pen again, her steps halting. She nearly lay down on the straw bed, but then struggled back to her feet.

Levi knew what had to be done. He had seen his father reach inside the cow's birth canal to assess the problem in a difficult calving, but he had never done it himself. His hands, so strong when handling his team of six Percherons, were too large to attempt what Moolah needed without causing more pain than what she was going through now.

Scratching at his beard, he watched as Moolah suffered through another futile contraction. He had to rely on Elias, he had no choice. The boy's hands were small enough, but could he talk his son through the job when neither of them really knew what they were doing? He had to take the risk. Without this calf, without Moolah, his family would suffer.

"She's having trouble, *ne?*"

The woman's voice startled Levi. Ruth opened the gate and slid into the stall beside him.

"*Ja,* she's in trouble."

Ruth looked at him, her blue eyes nearly black in the dim stall. "If the calf is turned wrong, they'll both die."

"I know. I was just going to get Elias to help."

"Has he ever done this before?"

"*Ne,* but I can't do it. I'm afraid I'd hurt her."

Ruth looked at his beefy hand holding the lantern above his head. The light shone on her face, casting a golden light on her flushed cheeks. "I've helped my *daed* deliver calves many times. I can try."

Moolah groaned as another contraction gripped her. The cow was weakening. If he didn't do something soon, he would lose both of them.

Levi's face was cast in shadow and unreadable. Would he let her help, or would he send her back into the house?

Another bellow from the laboring cow wrenched an exasperated nod from him. "All right. What do I need to do?"

Ruthy hung her shawl and sweater over the gate and pushed up her sleeves. Standing behind Moolah, she pulled the cow's tail to one side. As another contraction started, the small calf's nose appeared, only to retreat once the contraction subsided, sending a wave of dread through Ruthy. Was the poor thing still alive?

"It looks like the calf might have a turned leg. Maybe both." She looked at Levi again. "We need to reach in and straighten the legs, and then the calf can slide out."

Levi hung the lantern from a nail protruding from the beam above his head. His face was pale in the light. "I've seen it done, but…" He lifted his big hands, shrugging. "I'm not sure I can do it."

"I can try, if you can hold her head still."

Levi nodded and Ruthy eyed the cow again. Moolah was the biggest Holstein she had ever seen, much bigger than *Daed's* Guernseys. She found soap and water in the milking parlor while Levi lit and hung some more lanterns. The more she scrubbed her hands and arms, the more nervous she got. Why did she tell Levi Zook she could do this? If she were wrong, or if she weren't strong enough to help this poor cow, then the family would lose a valuable animal.

Moolah bellowed again and kicked the side of the calving pen.

"Is there anything else you need?" Levi Zook's strained voice told of his worry. Did he doubt her ability, too?

"I'll need a bucket of lard, and a length of stout chain, or rope, in case we have to pull the calf out." Ruthy went through the procedure in her mind, remembering all the possible outcomes, as Levi disappeared through the door.

Moolah was still standing in the calving pen, but she didn't relax between contractions as a cow should. By the time Levi returned to the barn, Ruthy knew what course to take.

"First I need to find out exactly what's wrong." Levi nodded, waiting for her instructions. "Hold her head still and talk to her. It will help if she can rest between contractions."

Ruthy scooped up a handful of lard and greased her left arm up to the elbow and past it, waiting for the contraction to end. As Moolah's muscles loosened, she inserted her hand into the birth canal. She felt her way past the head and pushed past the neck to the calf's legs. Just as she thought—they were both turned back along the calf's body instead of lined up along the nose as they should be. She pulled her aching arm out. *Daed* had always told her to check the cow with her left hand to save the strength in her right for the real work.

"I think everything will be fine, but we need to move quickly." Ruthy started greasing her right arm with the lard. "I just need to bring the two front hooves forward, and it'll slide right out."

Levi Zook nodded, his face green in the lamplight. What would she do if he fainted while she was working?

"I need you to hold her head. She won't like what I'm doing, and she may try to get away from me. You have to keep her still."

Levi nodded again. "*Ja,* just be quick about it."

Ruthy braced herself and forced her right hand past the calf. She found one hoof and, cupping it in her hand, brought it forward alongside the nose.

She found the second hoof just as another fruitless contraction started, gripping her arm in a vise. Ruthy closed her eyes and gritted her teeth, the only way she knew of to withstand the intense pressure.

"Are you all right?"

Opening her eyes, she saw Levi holding Moolah's

halter with one hand and reaching toward her with the other.

"*Ja, ja, ja.* I'm fine." She gasped as the calf struggled, nearly slipping the second foot out of her hand. "Just waiting for the contraction to end. Don't let go of her head."

As the contraction subsided, Ruthy brought the second hoof forward and lined it up with the first. When the next contraction came, the calf's nose, cradled between the two soft hooves, followed her hand through the birth canal. Moolah gave a straining push and the little heifer dropped to the soft, straw-covered floor.

Ruthy backed up until she was leaning against the side of the pen, and Levi joined her, letting a tired Moolah tend to her new calf.

"That was *wonderful-gut,* Ruth. You did just the right thing."

Ruthy nodded. Levi Zook's praise brought heat to her cheeks. Her arms were trembling from the exertion of manipulating the calf.

"I must wash up...." Ruthy reached for her sweater and cape, but both hands were covered in grease and slime.

Levi plucked one of the lanterns from the beam above them and led the way to the basin in the milking parlor. Warmth from the cow shed kept the water from freezing, but it was still cold. By the time Ruthy had washed her hands and arms again, her teeth were chattering. Her dress was filthy, but cleaning it would have to wait.

The entire time she scrubbed in the freezing water, Levi stood silently, holding the lantern. He watched her, she saw as she glanced at him once, like Moolah had watched her calf as it struggled to stand. What was he thinking?

"Are you going to stay with the new calf for a while?" Ruthy dried her hands on a piece of sacking she found near the basin while Levi threw the wash water outside.

"*Ja*. I want to make sure she's eating well." Levi didn't look at her, but led her back to the warmth of the cowshed and the calving pen. "You could stay…." He bit off his words, as if he hadn't meant to say them.

"I really should get back to the house." She put her arms into the sleeves of the sweater Levi Zook held for her. "Morning will come awfully early tomorrow."

"It's already tomorrow." Levi's voice was soft as he settled her shawl over her shoulders. "It's past midnight."

Ruthy shivered one last time as Levi turned her to face him and drew the shawl closed in front. He stood, unmoving, for a long minute, his eyes dark. Ruthy thought he was leaning toward her. If he kissed her, what would she do? At that thought she turned toward Moolah and her calf, breaking the moment.

"She's a fine heifer calf, Levi Zook." Ruthy struggled to keep her voice light, normal.

Levi leaned on the gate of the calving pen next to her, closing the gap she had tried to put between them. "God was good to us, tonight." His voice was rough and he cleared his throat. "Without your help, we could have lost both the heifer and our best milker."

"We make a good team when it comes to delivering calves, Levi Zook." She smiled at him.

Levi laid his hand on her arm and leaned closer, his own smile warm. "*Ja*, we do. A good team."

The calf stood once, and then fell into the straw.

Ruthy watched Moolah give the calf an encouraging lick, then the calf stood again and started searching for the teat that would give her the sustenance she needed. A calf needed its mother from the very first minutes of life.

"God makes families, even for animals, doesn't He?"

Ruthy wasn't aware she had spoken aloud until Levi Zook grunted his agreement.

"He does. It's part of His care for us."

Ruthy glanced at his profile in the lantern light, suddenly sorry she had mentioned it. With Levi Zook still grieving for his wife, her comment would be a sad reminder, but he only grasped her hand more firmly and pulled it so her arm rested entwined with his as they watched the calf until it finished eating and dropped into the soft straw bed, sound asleep.

Levi blew out the lanterns and they left the cows in the quiet barn.

In the dark kitchen, Ruth gave him a whispered "Good night" and slipped through the *Dawdi Haus* door. Levi padded across the kitchen toward his own room and bed, too aware of the short night ahead. Morning wasn't far off.

He dropped his trousers and shirt on the floor and crawled into his cold bed, shivering as he waited for warmth to gather under the quilts. When Salome was still alive, they would keep each other warm on nights like this, but *ach,* would she ever complain when he climbed into bed after being up late like he was tonight. He chuckled at the memory.

Ruth was right. God was so good to put people in families, but would he ever know the joy of a wife again?

As his mind drifted toward sleep, the night's events replayed in his mind. What would he have done without Ruth Mummert there? She was…like his right hand. The memory of her presence warmed him even now. He drifted to sleep with the feel of her arm entwining in his.

In spite of the short night, the morning's work had to be started on time. As Ruthy entered the kitchen, Levi was already kneeling in front of the stove, coaxing the fire to wakefulness.

"If you're running late, I can start the stove."

"Ne, denki." He paused to blow on the embers and added a handful of tinder. "I'm almost done here. If I leave the fire for you to start, that will just delay my coffee."

As Ruthy reached past him to take down the coffeepot, he stood, bumping into her. If he hadn't grabbed her arms to steady her, she would have fallen back, but instead found herself held close to his broad chest. She laid her hands against his shirt front to keep from falling against him.

"Are you all right?" he asked. His voice was low, with the same intimate tones he had used in the barn last night. Ruthy's stomach fluttered.

"Ja, I'm fine. We shouldn't try to stand in the same place—there isn't room enough for both of us."

"I don't mind."

Ruthy looked into his face. *Ne,* she hadn't been dreaming last night. Levi's eyes were warm as he held her close. She didn't move until she heard young men's feet on the stairway and she pulled back.

"Breakfast will be ready by the time you get back from choring."

"You won't forget the coffee this time?"

Ruthy picked up the coffeepot and waggled it in front of him.

"*Ne,* I won't forget your coffee."

Levi stared at her, holding her with his gaze as firmly as his hands had held her seconds ago. "Ruth, I…"

"*Dat,* did Moolah have her calf?" Nathan asked as he burst into the kitchen with his brothers.

Levi smiled before he turned to his sons.

"*Ja,* we have a new heifer in the barn."

"Whose turn is it to name her?" James asked as the three boys and Levi closed the door to the porch behind them and their voices faded.

Ruthy rubbed her arms where Levi's hands had left the burning of awareness behind. Elam's touch had never set her skin afire the way this man's did.

She worked at the pump to start the water flowing, and then filled the coffeepot and set it on the stove. Condensation formed on the sides of the blue enameled pot as heat from the stove met the cold metal and evaporated in an instant. In an instant everything had changed.

Ne, not an instant, but in a night. She would never look at Levi Zook the same way again.

Levi leaned against the side of the calving stall, watching Moolah with the new heifer calf. Even though her start had been rocky, the calf was bright and alert in the midmorning light, standing close to Moolah's sturdy side.

He turned as the door of the cowshed opened. Ruth walked in with a thermos. He had forgotten to go into the house for his coffee break, but she remembered. *Ja,* he thought again, he had done a *wonderful-gut* thing when he'd brought Ruth Mummert here.

"How is the new little one doing?" Ruth pulled a clean cup from under her shawl and handed it to him while she unscrewed the lid of the thermos.

"She's doing *wonderful-gut,* thanks to your help." He held his cup steady as she filled it with steaming coffee, the cream and sugar already added.

"It's all those hours I spent with *Daed* in the barn, I guess."

"You said he runs a dairy farm?"

"*Ja,* he and my brothers together. The boys are all married and have families of their own. They live on adjoining farms and have forty cows all told. But with the three of them working together with *Daed* they have plenty of hands for the milking."

"He has Holsteins?"

"*Ne, Daed* breeds Guernseys. He says they have the best quality milk."

Levi glanced at the woman next to him. She was watching the black-and-white calf with a wistful smile on her face. Was there anything he couldn't talk about with her?

"I've heard of Guernseys, but everyone around here has Holsteins. What makes their milk better?"

"Higher butterfat, almost as high as a Jersey's, but with quantity closer to a Holstein's. *Daed* says with Guernseys we have the best of both worlds."

Levi took a sip of his coffee. What would happen if he crossbred his Holsteins with a Guernsey bull?

"I brought some cookies, too." Ruth pulled a tin box

out from under her shawl. What else did she have hidden under there?

"Ach, denki." Levi took two cookies and popped one into his mouth.

Ruthy laughed. "I had better get the rest of these to the boys before you eat them all."

"Ne, don't go yet." Levi put his hand on her arm, stopping her with his touch, but then drew his hand back. It was all he could do to keep from letting his hand travel up to her shoulders and draw her close to him.

"I… I just want to say *denki* for being willing to help last night. We might have lost both Moolah and the calf if you hadn't been here." And if she hadn't stepped forward just when he needed her.

Ruth shrugged slightly, her hands full of the cookie tin and the empty thermos. "Moolah needed help and I knew what to do. It was nothing."

"Ne, it wasn't nothing. Most women would never step out of the house on a cold night, and yet you stayed out here until both the cow and calf were out of danger. I appreciate that."

Ruth turned her face up to his, her blue eyes gray in the dim light of the barn. Levi stepped close to her, his arm going around her waist without thought. She leaned her head onto his shoulder as he drew her close. It was only a brotherly embrace, nothing more. He leaned and laid his cheek on her *kapp.*

A brotherly embrace never felt this good….

Ruth jumped in his arms as a man cleared his throat behind them.

Ach, ne… Levi turned to see Deacon Beachey standing in the door of the cowshed.

"Elias told me I'd find you in here," the older man said, "but he didn't tell me you were occupied."

Ruth ducked her head, her cheeks bright red. "Good morning, Deacon." She turned to Levi, avoiding his eyes, and took the empty coffee cup after tucking the thermos under her shawl. "I'll just take the rest of these cookies to the boys."

Deacon Beachey stood silent as Ruth went into the barn and closed the door behind her. Levi's gut broiled with disgust at himself. Of all the people to come in when he had weakened... The deacon's job was to make sure the *Ordnung* was being followed, and the man had seen he and Ruth in a position that would be hard to explain. This would be reported, for sure. What would happen to Ruth's reputation?

"I heard there was a young woman living here that you aren't related to, Brother Zook."

Brother Zook. This was an official visit.

"*Ja,* that's right. I hired a housekeeper from Lancaster County."

"I take it that young woman is her."

"*Ja,* Deacon. Ruth Mummert." Deacon had met Ruth at the last church meeting. This formality turned Levi's blood cold.

"John Stoltzfus defended you. He said there was no harm since she lives in the *Dawdi Haus,* separate from the family, but I have to wonder, considering what I just witnessed."

Levi shrugged, helpless in his own sin and thoughtlessness. "I have no excuse. I meant to give her a brotherly hug, to thank her for her help, but..."

Deacon Beachey stepped close to Levi, his voice

quiet. "Is this the first time you have touched her in this way?"

Levi's mind rushed back to the kitchen this morning. He could tell himself he had only tried to keep her from falling, but the truth of it... He shook his head in response to Deacon's question. The truth of it was he felt a rush of...something...when he was close to her. If he closed his eyes, he would see himself pulling her closer.... A desire he hadn't known existed sputtered with a growing flame—a desire for more moments like the one after the little calf had been born, when he and Ruth were working together. A partner, a friend...

"Deacon, I have not sinned. I have done no more than touch her arm and give her that one embrace...."

"Levi, remember what Christ said, 'If you look at a woman with lust in your heart, you have committed adultery.' If you have not sinned outwardly, that is good. But where have your thoughts led you?"

Levi turned to watch the new calf, now lying prone on the soft hay, Moolah standing over her, chewing her cud. God knew where his thoughts were leading him. His desire for Ruth was to be more than a partner and friend.

"Should I send her away?"

"Would that be the best thing to do?" Deacon Beachey stroked his gray beard, watching Moolah and the calf. "We need to consider her feelings, and your children, too."

"The children love her."

The deacon turned. Nothing could be hidden from this man.

"Only the children?"

Levi rubbed his forehead. How did he end up in this mess?

"*Ja,* for sure. Only the children."

They both watched the calf settle into the trusting sleep all newborns enjoy.

After long minutes, Levi cleared his throat. "I'll have to tell her to go back to Pennsylvania."

"That would leave you right back where you started, wouldn't it?"

"*Ja.*" Back to Waneta working too hard. Back to the lonely evenings watching his children's sad eyes. Back to Eliza demanding he send the younger girls to her.

"Would she be willing to marry you?"

Levi snapped his gaze back to the deacon. "Marry her?"

"Haven't you considered it? Would she make a good mother for your children? Does she seem happy living here?"

His mind raced. She would be a *wonderful-gut* mother, and she seemed to enjoy her home here. What more did he require for a wife? "I can ask her."

"Then do. But take heed, Brother Zook. Sin crouches at your door, and you are setting the example for your children. Marry the woman, or you will have to send her away."

"*Ja,* Deacon, I know."

Levi watched the deacon leave, but his mind was on Ruth. Would such a young, beautiful woman consider him for a husband?

He turned back to Moolah, scratching her between the ears as she moved closer to him. What did a woman like her expect from marriage? When he'd married Salome, neither of them expected to love each other at first. It was a good match. She was a hard-working, faithful girl, and he had this farm. Love came later, for sure it did, somewhere in those hard years after the twins were born, and before she got sick. He knew he loved her as he watched her suffer through her illness, and as he said goodbye to her. They had a comfortable love, one that would have lasted all the long years of their married life.

But this Ruth Mummert…he felt things for her he had never felt for Salome. Was that love, also? If it were, it was like a fire that warmed him and threatened to burn him all at once.

What would his life be like, married to Ruth Mummert? She was opinionated, for sure. He had never met a woman with stronger opinions, but she didn't stop there. She acted on those opinions. He had never heard of a woman working in the cowshed the way she had last night.

On the other hand, he had never met a more feminine woman, either.

Would she marry him? He was so much older than her, and all he had to offer was hard work.

She thrived on the hard work, but would she rather have a younger man?

Levi sighed and patted Moolah on her boney shoulder. All he could do was ask.

Chapter Eleven

Waneta had dinner well in hand when Ruthy came back into the house, with bread cooling on the counter under a cloth and stew simmering on the stove.

"*Denki,* Waneta. It smells *wonderful-gut* in here."

"Did the boys like the cookies?"

"For sure they did."

Waneta hummed as she rolled out a piecrust.

"Waneta, do you mind if I go to the *Dawdi Haus* for a bit? I didn't get much sleep last night, and I think I could use a rest before dinner."

"*Ja,* for sure. Sleep as long as you like. I'll get dinner for *Dat* and the boys and keep yours warm if you're not up in time."

"*Denki.*"

Ruthy went to her own little house, took off her shoes and fell onto the bed. She must be tired, that's why Levi's actions had unsettled her so. The way he had held her in his arms made her feel so safe, so protected.... But that isn't what she should expect from him. He was her employer, nothing more. She had to remember that.

Ruthy pulled the quilt over her and closed her eyes,

but sleep refused to come. Opening them, she looked around the room, willing herself to relax into sleep, but instead the letter from Laurette caught her eye. She had stood the envelope against the hairpin holder on her dresser, and Laurette's distinctive writing held her gaze.

She had to read that letter sometime, and it might as well be now, when sleep refused to come. She stood at the dresser, looking at the address while she removed her *kapp* and brushed out her hair. Perhaps if she went through the usual bedtime motions, she would be able to sleep. She took the letter back to her bed and burrowed under the quilt again.

Dear Ruthy,

I was so sad to hear that you moved west. I'm sorry we haven't been friends lately, and I know it's because of Elam, but I hope you can forgive me and think of me with sisterly love as you used to.

I wish I had some funny story to tell you, or some good news to share, but I can't think of anything. I have been so sick lately, and it takes all of my strength just to cook dinner. When Elam is away, I don't even do that.

We had such a cold spell after you left that I didn't even leave the house for a week. Elam left the gate to the chicken house open in the middle of the cold weather and we lost all six of the hens to a fox. Elam was sorry about it, of course, but now we have no chickens and no eggs.

Last week felt like spring was nearly here with a warm wind from the south and sunshine. I went outside for the first time in weeks and sat in the sun. It felt good until the clouds blew in.

I don't know what I'd do without your *mam*. She came twice a day while Elam was away last week. She even cooked dinner for me and scolded me because I hadn't been eating my vegetables. Don't tell her, but I don't eat them because they don't stay down. I lose nearly everything I eat, but I know that's normal for someone like me. Sometimes I wonder why people have babies, if this is the trouble they cause.

You must write and tell me about the family you're caring for. Your *mam* said your letters sound like you're enjoying your job caring for those ten children. I couldn't believe it when she told me! It makes me tired just to think of it. But with all those children, you must have some funny stories to share.

Please write back, dear sister. I know I hurt you terribly, and I'm so sorry. My greatest wish is to hear you say you can find it in your heart to forgive me.

I must close so your *mam* can take this letter to the mailbox for me.
Hoping to hear from you soon,
Your friend, Laurette

Ruthy's eyes filled with tears. Laurette had a husband, a baby on the way and now Ruthy's own *mam*.... What she wouldn't give to be held in *Mam's* arms, just for a minute, and Laurette was right next door, where *Mam* could drop in at any time....

Throwing the letter to the floor, Ruthy turned her

back on it and buried her head under her pillow. Hot tears trickled across the bridge of her nose.

She wouldn't cry. She wouldn't. She had wasted enough tears on Laurette and Elam. Jealousy burned hot, hardening the icy shell around her heart into brittle crystal.

Laurette wanted her forgiveness? She wanted their friendship to continue? It was too late. Too late. Ruthy could never forgive what Laurette had done to her.

Ruthy slept through the noon meal, waking to a room dim in the late afternoon dusk. She had never slept like this during the day when she wasn't ill, but her head ached as if she were. Sitting up on the side of the bed, she saw Laurette's letter, white against the dark floor. She swallowed hard, fighting back the tears that threatened. She had work to do.

Rising quickly, she twisted her hair into a bun and adjusted her *kapp*. She slipped into her shoes and hurried through the passageway to the main house.

The kitchen was full of noise, with Waneta, Martha and the little girls chatting as they prepared fried ham and potatoes for supper. Sam's face lit up when he saw Ruthy and came running to her.

"Ruthy, I saw her! I saw the calf! And it's my turn to name her!"

"*Ach*, Sam, that's *wonderful-gut*. What name have you chosen?"

Sam's face fell. "I wanted to name her Ruthy, after you, but *Dat* said *ne*."

Ruthy laughed, the gloom of the day vanishing at Sam's words. "*Ach,* your *dat's* right. At home, we never name our cows after people we know."

"But why not? It's a good name, isn't it? And I love her as much as I love you."

Warm tears sprung into her eyes as she put her arm around the little boy's shoulders. He would never know how much his simple words meant to her. "If you named the little cow Ruthy, and then one day told your *dat* you were going to feed Ruthy, how would he know if you were talking about her or me?"

"*Ach,* that's right." Sam's worried brow cleared. "I'll have to name her Buttercup, then. That's the name of Johnny Lapp's cow, and she's real nice." He took Ruthy's hand. "It's all right to name her after another cow, isn't it?"

"*Ja,* that's fine. You've chosen a *wonderful-gut* name."

"Ruthy, do you feel all right?" Waneta's concern showed in her voice.

"I'm fine. I just didn't get enough sleep last night and needed to catch up. You girls have supper nearly ready. Is it that late already?"

"For sure, you slept a long time."

"What can I do to help?"

Supper was on the table before long and the family sat in their seats, falling into silence as Levi sat in his chair and cleared his throat. He looked at Ruthy, his brown eyes soft in the lamplight, then around the table at the children.

"I have something to confess. I've neglected our evening prayers since…well, for the last year or so. I want you children to forgive me, and we'll start again tonight."

"For sure, *Dat,* we forgive you. You needn't even ask," said Elias.

"Denki." Levi cleared his throat. "Before bed we'll gather in the front room…and Ruth, if you'd like to join us…"

She raised her eyes to look into his. *"Ja,* Levi Zook, I would be happy to."

He smiled at her, and she thought maybe she hadn't imagined how she felt when he had held her in his arms earlier.

Levi sat in his chair next to the stove with the family Bible and the *Christenpflicht*—the book of prayers. After Deacon Beachey had left the barn that morning, he had considered what marriage to Ruth Mummert would mean. Not only her company and her partnership in the family work, but he also craved having a future to look forward to again.

Ever since Salome had become ill, he had only lived from day to day, running the farm and raising the children the best he could. When he had thought to marry Ellie Miller last year, he hadn't considered much beyond the convenience of having someone to take over the household responsibilities and the care of the children.

Marrying Ruth would mean more than seeing his family complete with both a mother and father again— he would have someone to share his journey…and he would share hers. More children would come along, if God blessed them in that way, and the family would grow. That was a future to work toward.

By the end of his day of musings, he had begun to look forward to marrying Ruth very much.

But could he convince her? She treated him kindly, but more as a sister would her older brother. He had never really courted a woman, since he and Salome had known each other from the time they were children. How could he make marriage look appealing to a young woman like Ruth?

The first step to start moving the family forward again and making Ruth feel a part of it, he had decided, was to go back to leading them in morning and evening prayers. Before Salome died, he had followed the same pattern his father had, reading a chapter from the Bible and one of the prayers from the *Christenpflicht* at each prayer time.

The children gathered in the big front room, arranging themselves near the stove. Ruth sat between Sam and Nellie on the floor, as if she were one of the children.

"Ruth," Levi said, "take the other chair. It must be uncomfortable on the floor."

She glanced at Elias, and then said "*Ne, denki.* I'll sit on the sofa."

Ruth crowded on the sofa next to Jesse, and Sam followed her, climbing onto her lap. She cuddled the boy close and put her other arm around Jesse.

Levi looked around the room from face to face. His children. The Lord had blessed him so greatly.

"At the close of this day, let us turn our hearts and minds to our Lord Jesus Christ." Levi opened the old German Bible to the gospels and started reading from the first chapter of John. "'In the beginning was the Word....'"

Reading to the end of the chapter, Levi was struck again by the beauty of the words. How had he neglected this for so long? He closed the book and reached for the little *Christenpflicht,* turning to the first prayer. "'O Lord, almighty God and heavenly Father...'" He read slowly, letting the words of the martyred forebears find their way into the children's hearts. As he finished the prayer, the room was silent for a few minutes before anyone stirred.

"Denki, Dat." Waneta was the first to speak, her voice thick with emotion. "I didn't realize how much I missed our family prayers. We haven't done it for a long time."

Levi glanced at Ruth. She sat with her cheek leaning on the top of Sam's head, watching the fire in the stove. What was she thinking?

The clock struck the hour and he shifted in his chair.

"Ach, children, it's off to bed. The little boys are half-asleep already."

"Dat, can I check on Buttercup?"

"You go on to bed, Sam. I'll look in on Buttercup when I'm out checking the others. I'm sure she's fine."

Waneta herded the younger children up the stairs and the others followed her, leaving him and Ruth alone in the front room. She tucked her feet up on the couch and rested her head on her hand.

"What are you thinking about?"

She started, as if she had forgotten he was still in the room. *"Ach,* I was just thinking how nice it was to hear the scripture read. It reminded me of home, and made me wonder what the folks are doing tonight."

"Do you miss them? Your family and your friends?"

"Sometimes. I'm thankful for letters. When I get a letter from *Mam* it's almost as good as talking to her."

"Was yesterday's letter a good one?"

Ruth's smile disappeared as she stared at the stove. "That one wasn't from *Mam.*"

Levi moved from his chair to sit next to Ruth on the

sofa. He had to be closer to her to ask what he needed to ask.

"Deacon Beachey's visit today wasn't just a social visit."

Levi studied her profile in the lamplight until she turned to face him.

"Did he come to talk to you about me for some reason?"

"It was about you, and me. I never thought having you work and live here would be a problem...."

"But it is? Because we were—"

"Ja." Levi interrupted to keep her from saying the words. His fists clenched at the memory of holding her in his arms, and he longed to move closer to her, take her in his arms again, protect her from what he had to say. "It seems that Deacon thought we may be living in an inappropriate way."

Ruth's cheeks flushed as she turned away from him and started to rise from the couch. He stopped her with a hand on her arm. "Don't go. I told him the truth."

"But that wasn't good enough, was it?" Her voice was soft, resigned. "It doesn't matter what we do or don't do, it's the appearance, isn't it?"

"Ja." Levi sighed with the word, but didn't move his hand from her arm. "He wanted me to send you home, but I can't do that."

Ruth shot him a look. "Disobey the deacon? How can you do that?"

Levi ran his hand along her arm and grasped her hand. "He had an alternative to sending you away." He swallowed. This wasn't the way to ask her to marry him, but he didn't have time to do it right. "We could get married, and then everything would be proper...." His voice failed him.

They both stared at the stove, listening to the sounds of the children drifting down from the second floor.

Finally Ruth stirred. "*Ja,* it would be proper." She took her hand from his and rose, wrapped her arms around her waist and walked closer to the stove, standing with her back to him. "Why would you want to do this?"

Why? His mind flashed with visions of holding her in his arms, talking together, sharing their lives together, but when he looked at her ramrod-straight back, the words wouldn't form. Would she even welcome his embrace? His kiss?

"I need you to stay. I want you to stay."

She turned to face him, her eyes shadowed in the lamplight. "Why, Levi Zook? Why do you need me to stay? Why would you marry me to keep me from leaving?"

What could he tell her? He wanted her, but more than that, he needed her to keep his family together. He cast about in his mind for reasons—what could he say that would convince her?

"I... Well, there's Eliza. She still wants me to send Nellie and Nancy to her."

"It would break their hearts to leave you."

Levi nodded. "With you here, they have a mother, do you see?"

Ruth turned back to the stove, her shoulders slumped. "*Ja,* I see. That's a good reason, I suppose."

A thrill of hope ran through Levi. Would she agree to be his wife?

"We would make a good family—you and I..."

"And the children."

"Of course." Levi sighed. This conversation wasn't going the way he had wanted it to, not at all. Why couldn't he tell her how she made him feel? She continued standing with her back to him, shutting him out.

When she spoke, her voice was soft, as if she were talking to herself. "I would be able to stay here. I would have a home, *ja?*"

"This would be your home, with me. With us." Levi rubbed his hand on the back of his neck. She spoke as if she expected him to make her leave…but that was the alternative the deacon had given, wasn't it? If she refused, how could he watch her walk out of his home? Out of his life?

"I will consider what you said, Levi Zook."

He stood, moving behind her, but before he could take her into his arms, she sidestepped away from him.

Levi clasped his hands behind his back to keep from reaching out to her. "There isn't anyone else, is there? Someone back in Pennsylvania waiting for you?"

She shook her head, her arms crossed in front of her. "Not anymore."

Of course she had been courted by another man. A woman as beautiful as Ruth Mummert didn't remain single without a good reason, but whoever it was had bruised her heart.

"If there is any possibility of him claiming you…if you still love him…"

"*Ne,* he's in the past. It's over." She rubbed at her cheeks with the heel of one hand and took a shuddering breath. "If we did this, if we married, I would want to remain in the *Dawdi Haus.*" She didn't look at him as she spoke the words knifing into his heart.

"Not live as man and wife?"

She looked at him then, her eyes dark as a lake under stormy skies. "I would do this for the children and for a home, Levi Zook, if you ask me, but God has called me to remain single. I would love your children and be a mother to them, but I don't think I could be anything more." She looked at the floor, holding her bottom lip between her teeth. "Let us both take some time to think about this, *ja?* Make sure it is what we should do."

"We'll think about it." He wanted to shake some sense into the woman. Did she think he could be content with a wife who lived in another part of the house?

"Good night, Levi Zook." Ruth brushed past him to the kitchen.

"Good night." But he spoke the words to an empty room.

Ruthy fled to the *Dawdi Haus,* shutting the door behind her. If there were a lock she would lock herself in.

What kind of proposal was that? He wanted to marry her so he wouldn't need to send his children away?

But he didn't say he loved her. After last night in the barn, and the look in his eyes this morning, she had thought she saw feelings there…but she had to be mistaken. He had the opportunity to tell her how he felt, but he had only rambled on about Eliza…and the children…and not one word of love.

Even if he had told her he liked her and love would come later, then perhaps she would consider it. But a marriage only for his convenience? *Ach, ne,* never!

Ruthy undressed quickly in the chilly bedroom. The bed would warm quickly after she tucked in the towel-wrapped brick that had been warming on top of the stove since Nathan had started the fire after supper. She slid under the covers, thankful for her long underclothes and thick flannel nightgown.

As the warmth spread, she relaxed under the quilts, but her mind stayed wide awake. She had slept too long this afternoon. She let her mind play back over the events of the day, lingering on those moments when she had felt so close to Levi Zook. Would marriage to him be so bad?

She could welcome his love so easily. Elam's claim that he loved her paled next to what Levi's love would be like. Elam was a boy, and his love had been a battle that ended in her broken heart. But Levi was a man— honorable, truthful, loyal to his family....

Too loyal, it seemed. Was he really willing to marry her only to keep his children together?

Marriage was not a thing to be taken lightly. Once they were married, only death would part them, and there was no doubt he would honor that promise.

Perhaps that was the reason—perhaps he still loved his first wife and couldn't love another.

Ruthy turned in the bed, letting the warmth lull her into sleepiness.

If he loved her... Her thoughts went to the feel of his arm around her waist, the comfort of her head on his shoulder. A shudder went through her as her mind strayed to what might have happened if Deacon Beachey hadn't come into the cowshed at just that moment. Would he have tightened his embrace and held her closer? If he loved her, she would have welcomed his protective arms around her.

Elam's embraces had always been pressing, pushing for more closeness. He persisted in asking her for kisses, even though she told him she was saving their first kiss for their wedding day. Every buggy ride with him had been a struggle, and she longed for the day when he would have a right to claim her.

Sleep fled as the memory of their last few rides together rushed into her mind. She had been relieved that he had been content with holding her hand, thinking she had finally convinced him to wait for the wedding they had planned for the fall. But now she knew he had stopped pushing her because Laurette was giving him everything he had been asking Ruthy for. He hadn't needed her anymore.

She turned restlessly in the bed, kicking the covers into place.

Why had she given Levi those conditions, that if they married she would continue living in the *Dawdi Haus?*

Ach, she knew. Her long courtship with Elam had shown her what loving a man was like. Marriage left no room for her own wants and needs, but she would spend all her time caring for a selfish man and his children. Elam had never thought of her wishes, but only his own. Could she expect Levi would be any different?

Her eyes filled with tears. Of course Levi was different. Everything about him was different from Elam… but marriage? Surrender herself to him? Become his alone?

Could she bear to have children with him if it were only his duty? She had already given up all hope of having her own children when she had resigned herself to being a *maidle.* Would living in the *Dawdi Haus* after a wedding ceremony be any different than what she had now?

Ja, one big difference. She would have a home for

the rest of her life. This house, not just the *Dawdi Haus,* but the main house, too, would be hers. She would have a home, children to love and a man to cook for.

She would have a purpose, a community, a family. She would belong. No more the solitary note. She pictured the children marrying, having grandchildren, family dinners… She would have a family of her own to share all the joys and sorrows life would bring.

What more could she want?

Ruthy kicked at the smothering covers. What more could she expect?

Chapter Twelve

Levi slid into the welcome warmth of the cowshed, chilled after the short walk through the frigid evening. The cold was always strongest this time of year, just before they could expect the first thaws in late February. He lit the lantern hanging on the nail just inside the door and started on his nightly round.

The milk cows, Milly and Kitty, didn't move as he walked past their pen. They both lay in their straw bed with their legs folded under them, eyes closed and chewing their cud. Moolah was up in the calving pen, standing over her sleeping calf. He stopped to rub the cow's forehead.

"You did a good job, giving us a heifer calf, Moolah. Good girl." He grinned at his own words. Wasn't it a silly thing to be talking to a cow?

He went on through the door into the barn cellar, shining the light into each horse's stall, and then into the pigsty. The animals looked at him with sleepy eyes, used to his nightly visits. All was well.

He retraced his steps to the cowshed, pausing to give Moolah another pat. Was it just last night that he and

Ruth had worked together to help the cow past her crisis? He had held no thought of marriage than beyond a passing whim, but ever since Deacon Beachey's visit this morning the idea had taken hold of him. His first thought had been that marriage to Ruth would solve his problems, but the more he considered the idea, the less he thought about anything but what a *wonderful-gut* wife she would be.

And then she had given him her conditions.

Could he live with her, knowing that in the eyes of the church they were man and wife, but at home they were no closer than brother and sister? Could he go through the motions of every day knowing he had the right—but restrain himself from even kissing her?

Levi leaned on the top rail of the calving stall, his shoulders slumped.

He could hope she would change her mind, that her feelings for him would grow, but what if they didn't? There had been someone else…that nameless man back in Pennsylvania. She claimed she no longer loved him, but why else would she consider a marriage like the one she had proposed? Could he marry her, knowing she loved someone else? Could he love her…?

Levi rubbed his forehead, willing the tension to leave.

Did he love her? If he did, it was nothing like the easy camaraderie he and Salome had shared. When he was with Ruth, he wanted much more than friendship, but was that love?

Levi gave Moolah a last pat, then blew out the lantern and replaced it on its hook. He pulled his coat tighter and braced himself for the cold walk back to the house. He looked up at the dark bedroom windows. The children were all in bed. The only light shone from the lowered lantern he had left in the kitchen. Even the *Dawdi Haus* windows were dark.

Was Ruth sleeping, or was she lying awake, thinking of his proposal?

In the kitchen, he blew out the lamp, ready to go to his own bed, but the door to the *Dawdi Haus* drew him. Standing in his stockings, the cold seeping through to his feet, he struggled with the temptation to lay his hand on that doorknob.

If they were married, would he be able to resist the temptation to go through that door?

If they didn't marry, even on her terms, would he be able to let her leave, knowing he would never see her again?

Ruthy couldn't meet Levi's eyes during breakfast the next morning. She kept her attention on the meal and the children as Levi ate silently at the other end of the table. Elias and Nathan discussed the coming planting season while the girls teased Martha about a boy at school. James and David ate quickly, trying to fill their bottomless stomachs while Sam and Jesse, on either side of Ruthy's end of the table, had their own discussion about their continuing afternoon game.

What would the children think if she married Levi? The younger ones would welcome her, she knew that, but Elias still resented her taking his mother's place in the kitchen. How would he feel if she married his father? Would he and Nathan join together against her? She would hate to be the cause of division in this family.

On the other hand, isn't that what would happen if she and Levi didn't marry? She let her gaze rest on

Nellie, sitting on the other side of Sam. She was a sensitive girl, such a contrast to her twin, Nancy. Being separated from her *dat* would be terrible for her. She looked farther down the bench to Nancy, on the other side of Martha from her twin. Taking these two girls from their family, even to live in their aunt's loving home, would change them.

"Ruth," Levi said, his deep voice carrying through the children's chatter, "is there more coffee?"

"*Ja,* for sure." They could be alone in the room, for all the attention Levi's request garnered from the children. Using her apron to protect her hands from the hot handle, Ruthy took the coffeepot from the stove. Levi moved his cup to the edge of the table so she could pour more easily, but as he did his eyes sought hers.

Ruthy struggled to keep the pot steady, to keep the hot coffee pouring into the cup, but his gaze unnerved her. What was he thinking of? Did he still think it would be good for them to marry?

The cup full, Ruthy glanced at his face. His eyebrows were raised in a question over his brown eyes, but he only said, *"Denki."*

She took the pot back to the stove, knowing his gaze followed her across the room. Sure enough, as she walked back to her seat, he watched every step.

After the Bible reading and morning prayers, Levi, Elias and Sam went to work in the barn while the scholars went out to the end of the lane to catch the bus. Waneta cleared the table, humming as she worked.

Ruthy dipped water into the dishpan from the stove's reservoir and then took the bar of soap from the shelf above the sink, shaving bits into the hot water with a knife.

"We're nearly out of soap," Waneta said as she set the pile of plates next to Ruthy on the drain board.

"How much is left?"

"There are only three bars down cellar...." Waneta stopped and wiped at her eyes with the hem of her apron.

Ruthy put her arm around the girl's shoulders. "Waneta, what's troubling you?"

"I just remembered, those are from the last batch *Mam* made...." Waneta sniffed and took out a handkerchief she had tucked in her sleeve. "She made an extra big batch that year. I think she knew she wouldn't be making any more for us, and wanted us to have enough to last...."

To last until someone else came who could take over that chore.

"We'll ask your *dat* if there's enough lard to make more. I saw a bucket of ashes on the back porch, *ja?*"

Waneta dried her eyes. "*Ja,* we always save the ashes. Maybe we can borrow lard from someone until we butcher."

"We'll plan on making the soap after this cold spell passes and we have fine soap-making weather." Ruthy tried to keep her voice cheerful, to help Waneta look forward rather than back to the loss of her mother.

She must have been successful, because Waneta gave her a smile. "I'm so glad *Dat* brought you here, Ruthy. I could never do this alone...."

Ruthy almost laughed at the thought of Waneta relying on her as a teacher. She had never made soap without her own *mam,* but she had to start sometime. "When you're a married woman you will."

"*Ja,* but that won't be until after I've made soap a few times with you."

Ruthy gave Waneta's shoulders a squeeze. "Even when you're married, we can still do chores like this together. You can bring your little ones and the twins can care for them while you and Martha and I make soap."

Waneta laughed at this. "That sounds like a *wonderful-gut* plan. By then, Martha will be married, too. We'll make a family frolic out of it." She turned, taking Ruthy's hand in her own. "But will you be with us that long?"

"Perhaps. It's up to your *dat.*"

"I know. I've been hoping…"

"What?"

"It's none of my affair, but Martha and I were talking about how *wonderful-gut* it would be if you and *Dat* married." Waneta paused, her eyes on Ruthy's heated face. "Only if you wanted to, of course, but we'd love to have you for our new *mam.*"

"I couldn't take your *mam's* place…."

"*Ne,* but we see the way *Dat* looks at you. He needs to be happy again."

"Your *daed's* happy. He's always laughing with you children."

"*Ja,* but he's still lonely."

Lonely in a house full of children? Ruthy swished the soap flakes in the dishpan as Waneta went to bring more dishes from the table. *Ja,* she could see being lonely even in this full house. Waneta was *wonderful-gut* to talk to, but Ruthy also enjoyed meeting the other women closer to her own age at Sunday meetings. She could spend more time talking to Levi when the children weren't around, like they did last night after the children had gone to bed....

Ne, not like last night. Alone in the front room, they were too close, too intimate.

But isn't that what it would be like if she married him?

Ruthy attacked the pile of dishes. She needed to talk to Levi, to find out what he was thinking. If she hurried, she would have a few minutes before starting dinner.

Levi took a sawhorse into the stall with Badger, the near horse in his team of Percherons, and the gentlest horse he knew. Grooming the gelding was a big job, but if Sam were going to learn, Badger was the horse to learn on.

"All right, son." Levi lifted Sam up to stand on the sawhorse. "We'll start with the curry comb. Take it and make circles through Badger's hair, like this." Levi swirled the comb through the horse's long winter hair. "There, now you try it."

Sam took the curry comb in both hands and pushed it back and forth on Badger's neck.

"In circles, son. Try again."

Elias opened the gate of the box stall. "Ruthy is in the cowshed, looking for you."

"All right. Can you take over here? After he's done currying this side, show him how to do all the brushing but the feet. You know how ticklish Badger's feet are if you don't use the right pressure."

"For sure, *Dat.*" Elias moved into the stall, taking Levi's place next to Sam.

Ruthy was leaning over the fence of the calving stall, scratching Moolah's face. She turned as Levi opened the door from the barn, her face red from the cold. Levi's pulse quickened at the thought of marrying this beautiful woman, even on her terms.

"*Hallo,* Ruthy."

"Buttercup is getting so big already, isn't she?"

"She's doing very well. Nice and healthy."

They both laughed as the little heifer bobbed her head at the attention and backed under Moolah's belly. Levi stepped close to Ruthy and reached over to pat Moolah's neck.

"Elias said you wanted me. Have you been thinking about what we discussed last night?"

"*Ja,* I've been thinking a lot, and I've been wondering what you've been thinking."

"Ruth, I need you here…."

"For the children."

"*Ja,* for the children." Levi sighed. She would marry him for the children, but would she ever learn to love him? He glanced at her, so young and beautiful. Could she ever come to love an old man like him? But he couldn't send her away. "For the children, but also because if we didn't marry, you wouldn't be able to stay with us, and I don't want you to go."

She turned to face him. "Why not?"

"*Ach,* well, you're a good cook, and the children like you…." She turned away from him and scratched Moolah between the ears. She was disappointed with his answer. Could he tell her he liked the way she smelled as she leaned close to him to fill his coffee cup? How he liked the way she felt when he held her in his arms? His mouth was dry as cotton.

"I will marry you, Levi, if you accept my terms."

Her terms. He scratched his beard. She wouldn't

choose to live in the *Dawdi Haus* if she thought she could ever love him. Could he take this step into marriage with her on the chance she might change her mind later?

He watched her lean over the fence, coaxing Buttercup to come nearer. He wanted to break down this wall she had put up between them, to be able to tell her how he felt. Would that barrier break down with time? As they lived and worked together for the rest of their lives?

Combing his fingers through his beard, he knew the decision had already been made. He had to take that chance.

"*Ja,* Ruth, we will marry on your terms. I'll go to talk to Bishop about it this afternoon, and we can tell the children tonight, after supper."

She nodded once, then turned and left him standing in the cowshed.

"You're what?" Elias's words burst from him.

Ruthy ducked her head at his shout. Of all the children, Elias had been resenting her presence the most, and now the news of the upcoming wedding brought that resentment into the open with a vengeance.

"Elias, calm down." Levi's voice was firm, but quiet as he faced his oldest son.

Ruthy glanced at the other children, all of them staring at their brother. Levi's news had brought smiles and exclamations from all of them—except Elias and Nathan. She watched Levi as Elias dropped his gaze, his dark face stormy and defiant.

"You can't marry her, *Dat.* She has no right to be here in the first place, and now..."

Ruthy's heart wrenched as Elias looked from face

to face around the table. So much a man, and yet a boy. Why did he resent her so much?

"Elias, you may not speak in such a way about Ruth."

Elias stood again, his face twisted in an effort to make his point. "She doesn't belong here, *Dat. Mam* is your wife, not her."

With that, Elias pushed past Levi to the door, banging it behind him as he went out into the night. Nathan stood to follow, but Levi stopped him with a motion.

"Let him be, son. Give him some time, and then I'll talk to him."

Nathan sank back onto the bench, but turned to watch Elias's flight to the barn through the window. The other children sat in silence.

Levi looked at Ruthy down the length of the table, his eyes reflecting the helplessness she felt. What if Elias never accepted her?

"We'll let Elias sort out his feelings. I'm sure he'll calm down."

"*Ja,* you're right." But Ruthy knew how strongly a sixteen-year-old could hold on to his resentment. Elias may never forgive her for intruding in their family.

Levi put a smile on his face and reached over to pat Waneta's shoulder. "How about the rest of you? What do you think about Ruth living here with us always?"

"I think it's *wonderful-gut.*" Waneta took her *daed's* hand and gave Ruthy a smile that eased the sting of Elias's rejection.

"Me, too, *Dat,*" said Martha, her eyes glowing. "It will be *wonderful-gut* to add to the family. It's been so long since a baby came to live with us."

Ruthy felt her face grow hot and she took a drink to cover her reaction to Martha's words. Of course the children would expect a baby. How could she tell them not to?

"Martha, don't you think we've had enough babies in this family?" James's voice was filled with disgust as he regarded his sister across the table.

Ruthy smiled. Eleven-year-old boys wouldn't look forward to a new baby the way their sisters would.

"We don't need to worry about babies right now." Levi stopped any arguments before they started. "The wedding won't be for several weeks. Bishop suggested we have the ceremony on the last Tuesday of the month, so we have plenty of time to adjust to the idea."

Waneta turned to Ruthy. "Will your *mam* and *dat* be able to come?"

Ruthy smiled at the thought of seeing them again. "I hope so. I'll be writing to them tonight to tell them about it."

Jesse stuck his fork into his cherry pie. "You can marry Ruthy, *Dat,* as long as she makes pie for us."

Even Nathan laughed at this.

"Wedding or not, it's time to get dishes done and homework started." Ruthy stood and started gathering the plates from her end of the table.

"Ruthy." Sam grasped her sleeve and tugged her down to his level. "When can I call you *Mam?*"

Sam had whispered his question, but the others had heard him and waited for her answer. Ruthy looked at Levi, but his eyes were on the spoon he had stuck in his coffee cup. Waneta's eyes were wet, and she dabbed at them with her handkerchief.

Ruthy held the little boy close and looked in his face. "As soon as Bishop says we're married, then you can call me *Mam.*"

She was rewarded with a pair of arms thrown around her neck and a sticky kiss on her cheek. Her eyes stung as she held him tighter. She may never have a *boppli* of her own, but God had given her these children to love. *Ach,* what a blessing!

As Ruth settled the children at the cleared table to do their homework, Levi followed Elias out to the barn. He was a good boy, growing into a fine young man. Some fathers had trouble with rebellious young people, but Elias had never gone against anything Levi had said or wanted—until now.

Levi found his son in the box stall with Champ, the new driving horse. The three-year-old was spirited, but was making progress in his training. Elias had done much of the work with him under Levi's direction, and the horse responded well to the boy.

Not the boy—the man. Elias was young, but a man in most ways. He would soon be taking baptism classes and courting some young woman. Did he have his eye on a particular one yet? But before any of that happened, Levi had to get to the root of this outburst against Ruth.

Elias glanced at him as he leaned on the side of the stall, but kept on with his grooming.

"How is Champ doing with his kicking?"

"He still hates to have his feet handled." Elias picked up the horse's front hoof, patted the bottom and then set it back on the floor of the stall. "But I do this a couple times a day, and he seems to be getting used to it."

The horse turned his ears back when Elias moved to a rear foot, but didn't kick.

"Where did you learn that?"

Elias straightened and ran his hand along Champ's back. "I don't know. I just thought of it, I guess."

"You have a way with horses, son. It's a gift."

Elias moved to Champ's head and straightened the forelock as the horse nudged his pocket. "*Ja*, Champ, there's a carrot in there." He pulled a chunk of carrot out of his coat pocket and gave it to the horse.

If only he could be as understanding with Ruth.

"Champ has come a long way since we first bought him last fall." Levi moved into the stall on Champ's other side.

"*Ja*, he has." Elias patted the horse's cheek. "He was a pistol at first, wasn't he, *Dat?*"

"A big surprise after Maddie."

Elias turned to Levi. "Maddie just wore out. She was a good horse."

"*Ja*, she was."

"You can't expect Champ to take her place so easily." Elias moved quickly to defend his horse. "He's young and green, but he's learning quickly. By spring he'll be as good a driving horse as Maddie, for sure."

"But he'll never be another Maddie."

Elias snorted. "I wouldn't expect him to. No two horses are alike."

"No two wives are alike, either, Elias."

Elias froze and Levi waited, letting his words sink in. Elias picked up the curry comb with a jerky movement and started in on his grooming. "She'll never be my *mam*."

Levi sighed and kicked at the straw littering the floor. "*Ne*, son, she'll never be your *mam*. You don't need a *mam* so much anymore, almost grown as you are. But the little ones need her."

Elias leaned his arms on the horse's back and stared at Levi. "What about you? Do you need another wife?"

Levi's memory filled with the feel of Ruth in his arms. Not just another wife. He needed her.

"I do, Elias. God didn't make man to live alone. He made us to be yoked with a companion, a wife."

"You have me, *Dat,* and Waneta and the others. Why do you need her, too?"

Levi gestured to the other stalls surrounding them. "We have Badger and Drift, Pokey and the others. Why did we need to buy Champ?"

"That's different. Badger and Drift and the others are draft horses, and Pokey's just a children's pony. None of them could be a driving horse like Champ."

"It isn't that much different. The horses all have their roles to fill. Waneta has been trying to fill your *mam's* role for too long, but we all need someone older, more suited for the task. God has sent us Ruth."

Elias leaned his forehead against the horse's back. "I think I see what you mean."

"Elias, have you forgotten Maddie, even though she's gone and we have Champ instead?"

"I'll never forget Maddie."

"You'll never forget your *mam,* son, whether I marry Ruth or not, and neither will I."

Elias raised his head, his eyes wet, but the face looking at Levi was a man's face. "I'm sorry, *Dat.* I'll tell Ruth I'm sorry, too. If you think she'll make a good wife for you, and a good *mam* for the little ones, that's good enough for me."

"*Denki,* son." Levi's voice came out rough and he cleared his throat. "Someday you'll understand better, I hope."

"I think I already understand why you want a new wife."

"You do?"

Elias grinned at him and went back to currying Champ. "Because I know how much I like Ruby Zigler."

Levi grinned back. Elias only had the slightest idea of the joys marriage could bring.

Ruthy set the sponge for tomorrow's bread as the scholars worked at the table, the only sound coming from the turning of a page or the scratch of a pencil on paper.

She would have never thought a house could be this peaceful with so many children. Salome must have been a *wonderful-gut* wife and mother.

And Levi was a *wonderful-gut* father.

As she went through the evening routine of *redding* up the kitchen for morning, Ruthy felt a new sense of ownership. This was to be her stove, her mixing bowls, her wooden spoons.

Ne, she would get new ones and keep these back to send on with the girls as they married and set up housekeeping. Each should have something of their *mam's* to take with them, just as she had the few kitchen things her *mam* saved for her.

Her busy hands slowed as she wiped the counter for the final time. Who would she pass those things on to when the time came? Without a true marriage to Levi, she would never have her own daughters.

She rinsed the rags a final time, and with her work done, she sat in the small rocking chair and picked up her knitting. Before long, Levi would return to the house, the scholars would be done with their studies and it would be time for evening prayers. She would need to continue to step carefully around Elias's feelings, but the other children were anxious to welcome her into the family. Other than that one cloud, she could look forward to years of joy in this home.

Ruthy concentrated on the pattern of stitches to turn the heel of the stocking. *Ne,* there was more than one cloud on the horizon. With only friendship between them, would Levi grow tired of her? Once the children grew up, would her companionship be enough to make their marriage last? Or would they end up as two strangers sharing a house?

The stocking's heel turned under her needles, smooth and perfect. That's how things turned out when you followed a pattern. Whoever wrote the pattern had a plan in mind, and if you followed the pattern, the end result was perfect, every time.

God's plan for marriage was perfect, wasn't it? Ruthy pushed away the fly buzzing in her thoughts. There were plenty of examples of marriages in the Bible where the two people didn't even know each other, and they had good marriages, didn't they?

She and Levi were friends, they liked each other, they knew they worked well together...wasn't that enough?

It had to be enough.

Chapter Thirteen

"It looks like we're going to have good weather the next few days." Levi's words carried over the clatter of breakfast dishes being cleared and feet pounding on the stairs as the children hurried to finish getting ready for school.

"Ja?" Ruthy stacked bowls and gathered spoons into an empty serving dish. He stood at the window next to the kitchen table, adjusting his suspenders as he peered at the lightening sky. She paused to watch him, taking just a little longer than necessary. His brown hair held tints of red in the morning light, and she had never noticed what a well-shaped nose he had....

He turned around so suddenly he almost caught her staring. "I think we need to visit Eliza today. It's a good day for the drive, and we can stop at the store in Middlebury to pick up the replacement parts for the cream separator and other things you've been needing."

"I'll make sure the children are ready." Ruthy started stacking plates. Levi was right, they would have to tell Eliza about the wedding sooner or later, and the sooner the better, before she heard the news from someone else.

"The children can stay here." Levi stacked the plates on his side of the table and passed them across to her. "The scholars will be at school, and Waneta and Elias can look out for the farm and Sam. You tell Waneta and I'll hitch up Champ. We'll leave right after the school bus comes."

Ruthy took the plates to the sink where Waneta was getting the dishpan ready. "I'll go braid the girls, and then I'll be down to help with the dishes as quick as I can. Your *dat* wants to visit Aunt Eliza today." She laughed at the stricken look on Waneta's face. "Just the two of us—you, Elias and Sam can stay here."

"Ach, es gut...." Waneta went back to drawing water from the reservoir. "Not that I wouldn't be happy to visit Aunt Eliza..."

Ruthy gave her a quick hug. *"Ja,* I know. It might become an uncomfortable visit once your *dat* tells her about the wedding. You'll be all right on your own here? You don't need me to stay behind and let your *dat* go by himself?"

Waneta laughed. "You're not trying to get out of going, are you? We'll be fine here for a day."

By the time the dishes were finished and Ruthy had put on her thick stockings and warmest flannel petticoat, Levi was waiting for her with the buggy. As she climbed in he made sure the warming pan was next to her feet and laid a clean horse blanket over her lap.

"It isn't as cold today as it's been, but it will take us a couple hours to drive to Eliza's."

"This is fine. *Denki.*"

Levi drove down the long farm lane and turned north on the county road.

"We won't be able to court the way young folks do,

but we should try to get to know one another better before the wedding."

Ruthy glanced at him. He looked as nervous as a young man driving a girl home from his first Singing.

"You're right. This is a good time to learn to know each other better. You can start. Tell me about your family. Is Eliza your oldest sister?"

Levi talked about his six sisters and how he had been a surprise addition to the family when his mother was in her forties. "*Dat* had given up on ever having a boy, and then I came along. Eliza was already married, and *Dat* had considered giving the farm to Eugene, her husband, but he didn't want to."

"Why not?"

"The folks over in Middlebury have always been a bit freer with their *Ordnung* than we are here in Eden Township. Eugene had some pretty liberal ideas about things like using tractors for farming instead of horses, but then changed his mind. He knew if he went too far afield, *Dat* would never give him the farm. But then he died young, leaving Eliza a widow. By that time, I had come along and the problem was solved."

"How much older is Eliza than you?"

"She was twenty-five when I was born, and Eugene died just a couple years later. They never had children."

"And she never remarried?"

Levi gave a short laugh. "*Ne,* not Eliza. She's always been a bit too independent."

"And your other sisters?"

"They're all married and have families. Three of them live in the Shipshewana district, one moved to Iowa with her husband about twenty years ago, and you've met my youngest sister. She's Nellie Graber, Mose Graber's wife."

"*Ja,* I remember meeting her."

Levi had turned west while they talked, and now pulled Champ to a stop at the state highway while a truck lumbered by.

"I'm afraid Eliza gave you a pretty hard time the last time you saw her."

Ruthy shook her head. "*Ne,* not too bad."

"You stood up to her. She likes that."

The truck passed and Levi hurried Champ across the road. Ruthy snuggled closer into her shawl, wishing Champ would go a little slower. Levi and Waneta were both right. She wasn't looking forward to seeing Eliza again, but when she married Levi, they would be sisters-in-law. They didn't have to be friends, but they needed to come to some kind of understanding.

"What do you think she'll say when you tell her about the wedding?"

Levi reached over and covered her mittened hands with his big leather glove. "I don't know. I hope she'll be happy for us, but she can be awfully stubborn at times."

Ruthy turned her head so she could see his face past the sides of her black bonnet. "She does love you. She only wants what is best for you."

Levi pulled his hand back to turn Champ north at the corner. "*Ja,* I know. But usually her idea of what's best is the only thing that matters to her."

When Ruth fell silent, Levi glanced her way. She was watching the side of the road and chewing her lower lip. Suddenly she shivered. Did he really have to drag her all the way to Middlebury to put her through another visit with Eliza? It looked like she was dreading this errand as much as Waneta usually did. But if Eliza heard about the wedding from someone other than him, she'd never forgive him.

"Are you cold? I should have brought another blanket."

"Just a little," she said, her breath puffing out in a cloud.

"Move over a little closer to me." Levi shifted the reins to his left hand so he could help adjust the horse blanket as she scooted close enough to touch him, but not quite.

"You need to sit closer if you want to get any warmer."

She moved a little, just enough that the edge of her shawl brushed his sleeve.

After a few more miles, Levi turned west again and could see Eliza's house in front of them. He nodded toward it. "That's Eliza's place, there."

"It looks like a cozy little house."

"*Ja.* She sold most of her farm soon after her husband died, but kept the house and a few outbuildings. She was the school teacher until the state changed the laws a few years ago. Once they put stiffer requirements in place, she had to quit. She finished eighth grade, but now they require teachers to have more education."

"She lives here all alone?"

Levi nodded. "I think she likes it that way, or else she would have married again."

As they drove in the lane, Eliza came out of the chicken coop, juggling a basket of eggs and her cane in one hand while she latched the chicken house door.

Levi pulled up to the hitching rail at the end of the back walk and got down from the buggy, reaching up to give Ruth a hand. "I'll blanket Champ and then I'll be right in."

Ruth gave him a shaky smile, but turned to greet Eliza as she picked her way across the snowy yard.

"*Hallo,* Eliza. How are you today?" She went forward to take the basket of eggs from Levi's sister.

"Well enough." Eliza greeted Ruth with a nod, then turned suspicious eyes on Levi. "*Hallo,* Levi. What brings you here today?"

"It's such a nice day, and Ruth wanted to get out a little bit." Levi hoped Ruth would forgive him for stretching the truth. "We thought we'd come over and visit with you for a little while before we go on into Middlebury."

"Middlebury? Isn't that a bit out of your way?"

"A bit, but Varns and Hoover is the only store around that carries the parts for my cream separator."

She held his eye, waiting for him to waver the way he did when he was a child. But he didn't need to let her bullying bother him anymore. Levi winked at her and she backed down, turning to Ruth.

"Well, come in and have some coffee, unless you want dinner…"

"*Ach, ne,* don't go to any trouble. A cup of coffee will be fine." Ruth took Eliza's arm and walked toward the door of the house with her. "We won't be staying that long. We need to run our errands and return before the scholars get home from school."

Levi slipped a blanket on Champ and fastened the straps. But by the time he had followed the women into the house, Eliza had already said something to put a troubled frown on Ruth's face.

"Ruth tells me the children are doing just fine." Eliza set a cup of coffee on the table.

Levi sat in the chair and glanced at Ruth. She stared at her own cup. "*Ja,* for sure everyone is doing well."

Eliza sat in the chair on the opposite side of the table with an exaggerated sigh and took a sip of her coffee.

Levi cleared his throat. "I have some news for you, Eliza."

"Ruth has already told me you aren't here to make arrangements for Nancy and Nellie to come live with me."

"*Ne,* we aren't." Levi hesitated. Eliza was headstrong and blind to the facts. If she still held out hope of the girls coming to live with her, how would she react to his news? "Ruth and I are getting married, so there will be no need for you to take them in."

Eliza turned her cup in its saucer. "I see."

"We hoped you would be happy at the news." He glanced at Ruth. She turned her own cup, staring at the brown liquid.

"Isn't this quite sudden? After all, you've only known each other for a couple months."

Levi fought to control his temper. His sister had always been able to prick at his conscience when he felt guilty. *Ja,* he and Ruth had come to this decision quickly, but hadn't Eliza been the one to force it?

"It is only because—"

"It's because of the children," Ruth interrupted. "It wasn't right for them to continue on with me as only a housekeeper when they need a mother so badly...."

Eliza stood, knocking her chair back. "And I'm just an old woman no one needs, *ja?*"

Levi held out his hand to calm her. "Now, Eliza, no one has said that."

"No one needed to say that, Levi. I'm not wanted. You can marry this stranger if you want, but I'm not going to be around to pick up the pieces when your home falls apart." She turned and limped into the front room.

"*Ach,* Levi Zook, what have I done?" Ruth's hand was over her mouth and her eyes were wet with tears.

Levi took her other hand in his. "It's nothing you've done. It's me, and Eliza's own blind stubbornness. She'll get over it."

Ruthy stood, looking for her shawl and bonnet. They needed to leave. Eliza would never forgive her, they could never see her again. How could this happen, that in trying to keep Levi's family together, she would cause a rift between him and his sister?

"Ruth, sit down." Levi tugged at the hand he still held. "We must stay and talk this through with Eliza. It won't take long for her to come to her senses." He drained his coffee cup.

Taking her chair again, Ruthy glanced into the front room. Eliza was pacing between the two windows facing the road, never looking their way. If Levi said they needed to stay, they would, but she would much rather leave and forget she had ever met this irascible old woman.

When she turned back to Levi, he was smiling at her. He still hadn't released her hand.

"I have a feeling you've never met someone quite like my sister."

"*Ne,* I haven't."

"She blows up quickly, but she gets over it just as quickly. I learned long ago to be patient when dealing with her. She can be maddening, but eventually she'll realize she has hit a brick wall and won't get her own way this time." Levi squeezed her hand. "You know, sometimes you remind me of her."

"Me?" How could he say such a thing?

"*Ja.* You're both stubborn women who are bent on doing things your own way."

Ruthy felt her face grow hot as she turned away from him. He was right.

He tugged at her hand until she looked at him again.

"I don't mind at all. I love my sister, as irritating as she is sometimes. I think that may be why I like you so much."

The thump of Eliza's cane on the wooden floor signaled her return to the kitchen.

"Levi, you take yourself out to the barn or somewhere. I want to talk to Ruth alone."

Levi gave Ruthy's hand another squeeze and then left. As he pulled the door closed behind him, the sound was like a shot in the still house.

"Eliza, I…"

Eliza raised her hand to stop Ruthy's words.

"Let me say something, and then you can talk." Eliza sat heavily in her chair. "My brother is a very deliberate man, so the suddenness of this marriage took me by surprise. He isn't one to make a decision like this lightly." Eliza held Ruthy's gaze with her own. "I know he's doing it only so I won't continue to ask for him to send Nancy and Nellie here. He wants to keep you living on the farm with him, and the only decent way to do it is to marry you. Am I right?"

Ruthy nodded. There was no way to answer the woman without hurting her feelings further.

"I'm an old woman, Ruth."

"You're not that old…."

"The arthritis makes me old. Levi is right." Eliza waved her hand around her small house. "This is no place for two lively girls, as much as I'd like to have them here." She sighed, slumped in her chair. "I try to fight it. I try to make myself believe it isn't too late for me to have a family...." Her voice drifted off and Ruthy shifted in her chair. Would she ever figure out Eliza's swiftly changing moods?

She took a drink of her coffee, and then gave Ruthy a sad smile. "I know why Levi wants to marry you, but why do you want to marry him?"

Ruth took a sip of her own coffee. It was cold. "I love the children, and I like living in Indiana...."

"Why did you come here, Ruth? What did you leave behind in Lancaster County?"

Ruthy looked at Eliza. Could she trust this woman enough to confide in her? "I left because there was no future for me at home."

"So you decided to be a *maidle*."

"I didn't decide. God made my calling clear through someone else's actions."

"But now Levi comes along and you don't need to be a *maidle* anymore. You can have a husband and children. A family just waiting for you to step in."

Ruthy shook her head. "That isn't how it is at all. You make me sound like some desperate girl who was jilted at the altar and is now grasping at any straw that comes along."

"If that isn't how it is, then tell me. Why do you want to marry my brother?"

Ruthy took another swallow of her cold coffee. "There was a man at home that I was planning to marry...."

"Ahhh…" Eliza leaned back in her chair.

"He… Well, he married someone else."

Eliza remained silent.

"He married my best friend. They had…betrayed me in the worst way."

Eliza nodded. "And you couldn't stay at home, alone and unwed, while they were happy with each other."

All the hurt and anger rushed back as Ruthy thought of the last time she had seen them, so smug and joyful with each other.

"*Ne,* of course not." She raised her eyes to Eliza's. "Would you be able to do that? Would you have been able to forgive them for what they had done?"

"I'm not the one God placed in this situation. You're the one who needs to make the decision to forgive them."

"I don't think I can. It isn't that easy."

Eliza snorted. "Of course it isn't easy. Life isn't easy. It's hard and only gets harder until we reach our heavenly home." Eliza stood and took her empty coffee cup to the sink. "But God gives us family and friends to make the journey easier."

Ja, Eliza was right. When she could forget about Elam and Laurette, she was thankful for the life she had. Even a future with Levi, with a man who didn't love her, held hope…as long as she kept that black memory at bay.

"Does Levi know you were going to marry someone else?"

"I told him there had been another man, but that it was over between us."

"So now we're back to my question." Eliza took her

seat at the table again. "Why do you want to marry my brother?"

"He…he's a good man. He's honorable and faithful. He loves his family. He's kind…."

"*Ach,* Ruth, you could be describing your favorite dog! Tell me—do you love him?"

Ruthy squirmed in her chair. Did she love Levi Zook?

Eliza threw up her hands and slumped back in her chair. "You young people are going to be the death of me. If you don't love him, how can you think of navigating through all the things life will bring you?"

"I know I like him, and I think I can learn to love him."

Eliza nodded, satisfied. "And does he love you?"

Ruthy shook her head. "I don't think so. He still loves his wife, doesn't he?"

"What makes you think he doesn't love you?"

"He never tries to…" Ruthy faltered. How could she share such intimate details?

"He never tries to what?"

"He's never kissed me."

Eliza laughed. "I wouldn't worry about that. I've seen the way he looks at you. The kissing will come."

"*Ne,* I don't think so. He's only marrying me so his children will have a mother."

"So why did you agree, if you're not sure you love him?"

"A *maidle* has no home." Eliza nodded and Ruthy went on. "You are alone, but you have a home, a place where you belong. A *maidle* belongs nowhere and to no one. When I marry Levi Zook, I will be needed and loved by the children. I'll have a purpose in my life and a permanent home."

"And when the children grow up and leave? What will you have then?"

"I'll still have a home. That's more than I would have if I never married."

"But you said God called you to stay unmarried...."

"Until I met Levi, I thought that was true."

Eliza sighed, shaking her head. "I can tell you're both determined to see this through, but let me tell you one thing. I'm going to tell Levi that I will no longer ask for any of his children to come here, if he chooses to marry or not."

"You're satisfied that I'll be a good mother to them?"

"I'm satisfied that my brother will do anything to keep those children of his away from me."

Ruthy cringed at the raw feeling in Eliza's voice. "That isn't what he's thinking at all. He just wants to keep his family together."

"He wants it enough to marry a stranger, *ja?*" Ruthy sputtered, but Eliza held up her hand. "*Ne,* don't carry on so. Even if Levi is only marrying you to provide a mother for his children...well, many have married for worse reasons." She struggled to her feet and Ruthy rose with her. "Let's go tell him he doesn't have to marry you. Maybe he'll throw you over and you'll be able to marry someone you really love."

Chapter Fourteen

Levi didn't throw her over.

He had come out of Eliza's barn when he saw them emerge from the house and listened to Eliza's news without a word. He only continued removing Champ's blanket and folding it, and then turned to Eliza when she had finished.

"After all this time, all the worry you've put me through, you've decided you don't want the girls?"

"You know I only wanted what was best for all…."

Levi raised his hand to stop her words. His face was stormy, his breath blowing clouds in the frosty air. Ruthy thought he had been angry the day the girls had found the chest of their mother's clothes in his room, but she had never seen him like this.

"You always want what's best for you, Eliza. You've caused heartache for my children, sleepless nights for me and forced me to pursue marriage with a woman I didn't love."

Ruthy recoiled from his words. She knew he didn't love her, but to hear it so bluntly nearly brought her to tears. She stumbled to the door of the buggy and climbed in.

"Levi Zook, how dare you…"

"How dare I? Eliza, one day you'll regret your high-handed ways." Levi shoved his wide-brimmed hat more firmly on his head. "You're invited to the wedding. It will be on the last Tuesday of the month. Until then, goodbye."

Levi climbed into the buggy and slid the door closed with a bang. Backing Champ until he was far enough to turn without running Eliza down, Levi guided him down the short drive and then onto the road. He slapped the reins on the horse's back, urging him to the quick trot Champ loved.

Ruthy sat as far away from the man as she could on the narrow bench seat. He thought there was still going to be a wedding? After that outburst? She could marry a man who might grow to love her someday, but she wouldn't marry a man who resented her presence even before they took their vows.

"Take me home, Levi Zook." She forced down the tears that threatened to turn her into a sobbing mess.

"What do you mean?"

"I mean I want you to take me home."

Levi slowed Champ and pulled him to a halt at the side of the road.

"Did my sister say something to upset you?"

Ruthy turned so she could see his face. "Your sister? *Ne,* Levi Zook. You don't remember your own words?"

"I… *Ach,* I was too harsh with her." He pulled off one glove and rubbed his hand over his face. "I was so angry with her, I didn't even think…" He stopped and looked at her. "You don't think I would ever treat you that way, do you?"

The tears pushed against the lump in her throat. Ruthy looked away from him. "You said she…she forced you to pursue marriage with a woman you didn't love. I know you don't love me, Levi Zook, but I don't want you to feel like you're forced to marry me."

"I made a mess of things, for sure." Levi slapped the reins on Champ's back, pulling the horse into a U-turn on the road. "If you misunderstood me, then I know Eliza did, too. I have to go back and apologize to her."

"You think I misunderstood you? You were pretty plainspoken from what I could tell."

Levi glanced at her. "When I said that I was talking about Ellie Lapp."

"Bram's Ellie?" *Ja,* now she remembered Waneta talking about her father wanting to marry Ellie.

"Before Bram moved here, everyone—at least my sister and Ellie's parents—thought we were the perfect match. Her husband had died, I had just lost Salome, and we both had children we needed to raise."

"But you didn't marry."

"We didn't get very far along that path. I don't think she likes me very much."

"You don't feel forced to marry me? Doesn't what Eliza said change the situation?"

Levi turned to her. "You mean about not asking for the girls to come live with her anymore?"

"She thought you might not feel the need to marry me if she stopped putting pressure on you. You could just hire another housekeeper…."

"Why do you think Eliza would change my mind? She might have been the reason I started looking for someone to come and help us, but she isn't the reason I asked you to marry me."

"But when you first asked me…you said you wanted to keep your family together…."

Levi combed his fingers through his beard, staring out the windshield. Champ trotted on.

"I had more than that one reason for asking you to marry me, Ruth."

Ruthy's hopes fluttered, then stilled. He didn't love her.

"Your children still need a mother, I suppose."

"*Ja,* they do, but there's more than that. I like you, the children like you. You've brought something to our home that has been missing…."

Fixing her eyes on the snowy fields at the side of the road, Ruthy fumed. Did the word *love* have no place in this man's vocabulary?

"I don't want to live without you, Ruth." Levi took her mittened hand in his until she turned so he could see her face. "I want you beside me for the rest of my life."

Ruthy gave him a quick smile, and then turned to face forward again. He liked her, he wanted to be with her. It wasn't love, maybe, but she could live with what he was offering. If he decided he loved her later? She would face that when the time came.

By the time Levi unhitched Champ and turned him into his box stall late that afternoon, he was exhausted. Eliza had accepted his apology quickly, as he knew she would, but the strain still wore him down. When would he learn to curb his tongue when he spoke to his sister?

Ruth had been quiet for the remainder of the trip. Even their stop at the store in Middlebury had failed to arouse any enthusiasm, except one time. While he was paying for the new skimming disks for the cream separator, he noticed she paused at a display of wash-stand bowls and pitchers. She had reached out to finger one with a delicate blue-flower decoration, and then pulled her hand back as if she were afraid to admire it.

That image had stayed with him all afternoon. Would she like something like that? It would make a nice gift for her. Something for her to remember their wedding day.

What kind of wedding would it be, though, when he couldn't even tell her how he felt? When his mind went back over their conversation in the buggy, he wanted to kick himself. He liked her? The children liked her? Why couldn't he say what he wanted to? That she brought light into his home, that he thought she was beautiful, that he... He couldn't bear the thought of marrying her on her terms, and he couldn't bear the idea of not marrying her at all.

Glancing at the house, windows glowing in the soft dusk, he sighed. A wall stood between them, a wall that shouldn't be between two people talking of marriage. But he couldn't get over it or past it, and he would never be able to go through it unless she let him. Until then, he could be patient. He could wait.

Ruthy steeled herself for the questioning she knew was coming. Bishop Yoder needed to confirm that she was a baptized church member, that she was marrying Levi of her own free will and that she had nothing in her past that would prevent her from entering this marriage.

Her stomach turned as Levi pulled Champ to a stop outside Bishop's house. While her feelings concerning

Elam and Laurette wouldn't prevent her from marrying Levi, she hated the thought that she would need to bring them up. If asked, she had to tell the bishop and Levi why Elam had thrown her over for Laurette when she would rather just forget the whole thing ever happened.

She followed Levi out of the buggy and up the walk to the front door. Bishop lived in a little *Dawdi Haus* on his son's farm, separate from the main house and outbuildings so that people who came to him for counsel would have some privacy.

After knocking on the door, Levi reached for her mittened hand and gave it a small squeeze. The gesture calmed her nerves. Did Levi know how hard this interview would be for her?

The door opened and Bishop motioned them in. "Good evening, good evening. Come and sit down. I expected you to come by." The old man caught Ruthy's hand as she walked past and she looked into his eyes. "I'm so glad you have come to live in our community, Ruth Mummert."

"*Denki*, Bishop. I am, too."

Levi had already taken a seat at Bishop's square table in the center of the kitchen, and Ruthy sat across from him.

"You're here to talk about your coming marriage?" Bishop sat carefully in his chair, settling himself on a cushion and leaning his cane against the table.

"That's right." Levi glanced at Ruthy, and when she nodded in agreement he went on. "Last week when I asked you to announce the wedding, you said you wanted to talk to both of us before we went any further."

The bishop turned to Ruthy. His kind face and gentle smile put her at ease, and she answered his questions one by one. *Ja,* she was a baptized member of her church in Bird-in-Hand and planned to continue her membership here in Eden Township. *Ja,* she was entering into this marriage willingly.

"No reservations?" Bishop Yoder peered at her closely.

Ruthy glanced at Levi. He was studying some imperfection in the table's wood grain, as if he were waiting to hear her answer.

"Ne." Ruthy shook her head. "No reservations."

"Before I ask this next question, I must tell you Levi has already shared with me that you were to marry a young man in Pennsylvania, but that agreement has come to an end."

Ruthy nodded. *"Ja,* that is right."

"Are there any sinful actions or thoughts from your past that need to be repented of before entering into this sacred union?"

Ruthy's tongue dried into a stiff board. "I…" She looked at Levi. He was looking at her. Waiting for her answer. She would never forgive Elam and Laurette, but was that a sin? It was as a drop of water in an ocean compared to what she had suffered as a result of their actions.

"Ne, Bishop, I have no sin I need to repent of."

Ruthy heard Bishop Yoder ask Levi the same questions he had asked her, but her thoughts were on her statement. She hadn't been asked to share any details of her past with Elam, and she hadn't sinned against anyone, so why did her words keep echoing in her mind like some loose gate banging in the wind?

Finally Bishop Yoder was satisfied, and closed their time together in a prayer. Ruthy closed her eyes, but the old man's words flew past her without resting. She took a deep breath and let it out slowly. She was just nervous about the approaching wedding. It had nothing to do with her feelings about Elam and Laurette.

When Bishop Yoder made the announcement of the coming wedding at the end of worship on Sunday, the women sitting near Ruthy hardly waited for the word of dismissal before turning to her.

"*Ach,* what a surprise!" Ellie Lapp reached over the children to give Ruthy a hug. "I had a feeling you were just the right one for Levi, but I didn't know it would happen so soon."

Annie Beachey had to settle for a handshake of congratulations as the other women crowded around to extend their best wishes for her happiness. Ruthy gave up trying to match names with faces and let herself enjoy the welcome.

Elizabeth Stoltzfus enveloped her in a motherly hug, and Ruthy clung to her for a brief moment. "Levi is such a *gut* man," Elizabeth said, holding Ruthy at arm's length and smiling at her. "I hope both of you will be very happy."

Ruthy felt her face go red as she glanced across the room at Levi, who was shaking hands with the men of the church. "*Ja,* he is a *wonderful-gut* man. *Denki.*"

After dinner, Annie and Ellie pulled Ruthy into a quiet corner.

"The last time we met for church, you let us go on and on about how you and Levi would make a good match, and you never gave us a hint of what was happening," Annie said, hitching little Elias up on her hip.

Ellie watched her as she tried to come up with an

answer for Annie. "I don't think you had any idea Levi would ask you to marry him, did you?"

She put a hand on Ruthy's arm, and the gentle gesture sent Ruthy's stomach rolling again. What would these women think if she told them Levi didn't love her, but was only marrying her to provide a mother for his children? She had seen the way Ellie's husband looked at her, and Annie's husband was just as loving in his attention to her. Was it wrong for her to marry Levi when she longed for the kind of marriage her friends had?

"You've talked to Bishop Yoder about this, *ja?*" Ruthy nodded in response to Ellie's question. "And you've spent enough time with Levi to know you want to marry him?" Ruthy nodded again. "And you've prayed for God's direction?" Ruthy nodded once more. "Then you'll be fine, and before long you'll stop feeling like you're being led to an execution."

"How did you know?"

Ellie laughed. "For one thing, it's written all over your face. Before my wedding, both weddings, I felt like I was coming down with the flu." She patted Ruthy's arm again. "Don't worry. You'll feel better when it's all over."

"And then life just gets better and better." Annie jiggled her baby in her arms and smiled at Ruthy.

Ruthy turned to greet another woman, and caught sight of Levi across the room. He towered above the men around him as they shook his hand, congratulating him. Would life with him get better, just as Annie said?

Just then, Levi looked up and caught her staring. A slow smile spread on his face before he was pulled away by Bram Lapp. Ruthy's face grew warm as she bent to receive the holy kiss on her cheek from Miriam Miller.

The older woman patted her hand and moved away, and Ruthy looked back at Levi. For the first time since he had suggested they marry, she felt like they had made the right decision.

Chapter Fifteen

Sam bounced from one foot to the other on the train platform in Shipshewana, jumping in and out of the shadow cast by the overhanging roof in a game to beat the dripping water from the roof.

"It would be warmer inside, Ruth. Do you want to wait there?"

Ruthy shivered as she pulled her cape more closely around her, but shook her head. "I'm too anxious to see them. Out here I'll be able to hear the train even before we can see it."

Levi laughed. "*Ja,* for sure you're anxious to see your *mam* and *dat.* You've been away for nearly three months."

"And they're anxious to meet you and the children, too." Ruthy turned to look at Levi. Ever since they had agreed to marry, he had changed. He was more relaxed, his eyes sparkled more. In the evenings he told the children stories so funny he would set them all to laughing so hard the little ones would end up sitting helpless on the floor.

But other times she would catch him looking at her

with an unfathomable, sad look in his eyes. Was he haunted by his wife's memory as they prepared for their wedding? Or was he sorry he didn't withdraw his proposal before it was too late?

He had that look in his eyes now as he watched her. The early spring sunshine turned his beard to reddish gold, framing his sad smile. "Do you think they'll like me, Ruth? They won't think the less of me for keeping you here so far from them?"

"*Ja*, for sure they'll like you, Levi Zook. Who wouldn't?"

"Do you like me, Ruth Mummert?" His voice was soft, the words meant only for her.

She smiled at him and laid her hand on his arm. "I wouldn't be marrying you if I didn't, now, would I?"

Levi laid his hand over hers, the wistful look on his face disappearing. "I hope you'll always like me."

"There's the train!" Sam's shrill voice was drowned out by people from the waiting room crowding onto the platform.

The steam engine rolled past the station, hissing loud bursts of steam, the wheels squealing as brakes took hold. The mail car went by, and then the passenger cars rolled to a stop. Ruthy searched the windows for *Mam,* knowing *Daed* would keep her sitting until the train came to a complete halt.

Sam grabbed Ruthy's hand. "Do you see them? Where are they?"

"Be patient, Sam." Finally, she saw *Mam* in the last car. Ruthy waved to her and rushed to the door where the conductor was lowering the steps for the passengers. She kept Sam's hand in hers as Levi followed.

Mam's face beneath her bonnet hadn't changed at all,

and *Daed* loomed over her tiny frame as always, carrying their bag in one hand. Ruthy melted into *Mam's* arms.

"It's so good to see you."

Mam patted her back as she held her. "It's hard to believe it's only been three months since you left." She pushed back to look up at Ruthy. "You look good, daughter. They must be treating you well here."

"*Ja,* they are." Sam tugged at Ruthy's shawl and she put her arm around his shoulders. "This is Levi Zook and his son, Sam."

Daed shook Levi's hand, measuring him with his look. "It's good to meet you. We were surprised to get Ruthy's letter telling us about the wedding."

"It's good to meet you, Ezekiel." Levi looked toward Ruthy, still holding *Mam's* arm. "I'm glad you were both able to come."

Daed's eyebrows raised above his glasses. "I hope you aren't rushing into all this too quickly."

Levi glanced at Ruthy, and she rushed to head off *Daed's* questions. "We can talk about that later. Let's get home. Waneta will have dinner all ready for us."

While *Daed* sat in the front of the buggy with Levi, Sam wiggled in between Ruthy and *Mam.*

"When Ruthy marries *Dat,* you'll be my *grossmutti, ja?*" He grinned at *Mam,* waiting for her answer.

Mam glanced at Ruthy over the boy's head, and then put her arm around his shoulders. "*Ja,* I'll be your *grossmutti.*"

"I've never had a *grossmutti* before."

Mam laughed. "I hope I'll be a good one for you."

"*Ja,* Johnny Lapp says they make the best cookies."

When they reached the farm, Ruthy took *Mam* and

Daed inside the house while Levi and Sam took care of Champ and the buggy. As Ruthy hung her bonnet from the hook on the back porch, *Mam* took her by the shoulders and spun her around.

"Ruth Mummert, what have you done to your *kapp?*"

Ruthy reached her hand up to make sure the pins were in place. "It's the kind they wear here, *Mam*. Waneta helped me make new ones."

Mam shook her head at the difference, but Ruthy had become so used to the Indiana style, she didn't notice it anymore. Still, she thought as she followed *Mam* into the kitchen, the Lancaster County *kapps* looked so soft and homey. Just the sight of the heart-shaped *kapp* covering *Mam's* gray hair brought back the pangs of homesickness she thought she had conquered.

The kitchen met *Mam's* approval, Ruthy saw. Waneta had a late dinner well in hand, with the table already set and a ham coming out of the oven. After introducing them, Ruthy led the way through the front room to the spare bedroom at the front of the house.

"I hope this room will be good for you."

Daed put the satchel on the floor and walked over to the window. *"Ach, ja,"* he said. "I'm surprised Levi had an extra room for us, as large as his family is."

"This room has always been for guests." Ruthy smoothed the quilt she had stretched out on the bed that morning, remembering Jack, their last guest. "But you could have Levi's bedroom if you think this one might be too chilly. He's made himself a place in the barn until after the wedding. Bishop thought it would be best."

Daed gave her one of his measured looks while *Mam* sat on the bed and took Ruthy's hand. "Before any more time passes, we need to know why you and Levi have hurried this wedding so much. You can hardly know each other." She pulled Ruthy down to sit on the bed next to her. "Elam broke your heart, I know that. Is that why you're marrying Levi? To run from Elam? Or is there another reason?"

Ruthy looked from *Mam's* worried face to *Daed's* frown. She had always been able to share everything with them, but would they understand the reasons she couldn't fathom?

"I know you're worried that something inappropriate has happened, but it hasn't." *Mam* squeezed her hand, but let her continue. "After Elam, I didn't think I'd ever marry. Sometimes God calls women to be single, doesn't He?" *Mam* nodded and *Daed* turned to look out the window as he listened. "The church—the deacons and Bishop Yoder—thought it was unsuitable for me to live here with Levi without being married, even though I live in the *Dawdi Haus*."

Daed turned to her. "You must have given them some reason to think there might be a problem with it."

Ruthy felt her face heat as she remembered the day Deacon Beachey had found them embracing in the barn. "*Ne,* not really. It was more because we are both the right age to marry, and because, well, we like each other." She glanced at her parents' unsettled faces. "Like brother and sister, not in any way that could be wrong…"

"And there are impressionable children to consider," *Mam* said.

Daed clasped his hands behind his back and rocked from his heels to his toes. "So, I think I see what's happened. You're living in the *Dawdi Haus* and Levi is living in the barn. Meanwhile, he has ten children who need a mother and he wants to live in his house again, so he asked you to marry him."

Ruthy nodded. "*Ja,* that's part of it."

"You've been counseled on this by the bishop?"

"*Ja, Daed.* Both Levi and I have talked with him."

Mam squeezed her hand again. "Do you love him, daughter?"

Ruthy hesitated. She thought she did, but was it right to love a man who would never love her back? "*Ja, Mam,* I do. It isn't the same as with Elam. Levi is a good, honorable man who loves his children and would do anything for them. I know we'll have a good marriage."

Daed smiled as he patted her shoulder. "That's good enough for me, then. Some marriages have started out with less than what you have. We're just glad he hasn't taken advantage of you in some way."

"You never have to worry about that with Levi."

"And the children?" *Mam's* worried look hadn't left her face yet. "Are you ready to be a mother to ten children who aren't your own?"

This question Ruthy could answer without hesitating. "I already love them so much." She looked down at *Mam's* hand holding hers. *Mam* had lost so many babies before Ruthy was born, but always said she was content with the four God had spared to them. "You know every child is a blessing from the Lord." *Mam* nodded, her eyes moist. "God has given me ten *wonderful-gut* children to raise. See how He has blessed me already?"

Mam leaned over to gather Ruthy into a hug. "We had better get out to the kitchen and help Waneta with dinner."

* * *

With only five days before the wedding, and one of those a Sunday, Ruthy, *Mam* and Waneta worked hard to prepare all the food needed for the celebration.

"We're only expecting about two hundred guests, since it's winter. Levi's sister from Iowa won't be able to come, but his sisters from Shipshewana and Middlebury won't have any trouble making the trip." Ruthy put the last cookie sheet full of snickerdoodles in the oven.

"It's the same with your brothers. They couldn't leave the dairy farm to make the trip." *Mam* packed cooled cookies in boxes to store in the cellar until Tuesday.

"How many brothers do you have, Ruthy?" asked Waneta.

"I have three, and all of them are older than me. They're all married and have families. *Mam* has fifteen grandchildren back in Bird-in-Hand."

Mam smiled at Waneta. "And by next Tuesday, I'll have ten more."

Waneta smiled back. "And tomorrow the women are coming to help clean the house. That will be fun."

"Are you sure you aren't just looking forward to the young men who are coming to help get the barn ready to shelter the extra horses?" Levi had told Ruthy that Reuben was planning to help out on Saturday.

Waneta blushed. "I don't know what you mean."

Mam and Ruthy both laughed.

"Waneta, if you can finish up the cookies, I have something I want to show Ruthy."

"For sure, I can."

"What is it?" Ruthy asked as she followed *Mam* to the front bedroom.

"Shhh…" *Mam* closed the door behind them and

lifted a large box with rope handles onto the bed. Ruthy had been curious about that box ever since they picked up *Mam* and *Daed* at the train station yesterday.

"When you and Elam started courting," *Mam* said as she worked at the knots in the rope, "I made a wedding quilt for you." She opened the box to reveal a beautiful red-and-white mariner's compass quilt.

"Ach, Mam..." Ruthy's eyes filled with tears. Such a beautiful quilt for her and Elam? What would she ever do with it now?

Mam lifted the quilt out of the box and set it on the bed. In the bottom of the box was another quilt, the same pattern, worked in blue and white.

"After Elam and Laurette…well, I just couldn't give you that quilt, so I started another one." She lifted the blue-and-white quilt out of the box and unfolded it on the bed.

Ruthy stepped forward to finger the beautiful quilt. Every stitch done with loving care by *Mam* and the ladies of her church in Bird-in-Hand. Her eyes filled with tears.

"This one is for you and Levi, although when I started it I had no idea what your husband's name might be." She folded the edge back and picked up the red quilt again. "When you said in your letter that Waneta had someone special, I thought you might want this quilt to put aside for her wedding someday."

"That's a *wonderful-gut* idea. Waneta will love it."

"And when I get home I'll start on quilts for all those other grandchildren you're giving me."

"Ja, I'm sure Elias won't wait too long before he's married, too."

Ruthy helped *Mam* fold the quilts again, putting the

red one in the bottom of the box. She could imagine Waneta's face when she surprised her with it someday.

"I wanted to talk to you about something else while we were alone."

"Ja?"

"It's Laurette."

Ruthy retied the rope on the box and pulled the knot tight. "What about Laurette?"

"She's heartbroken because you haven't written to her."

Ruthy set the box back on the floor and shoved it into its place with her foot. She could have kicked it. She didn't want to talk about Laurette.

"I haven't written because I don't know what to say."

"You could tell her you forgive her. You don't know how hard it was for her to write to you and ask for your forgiveness."

Mam sat on the bed and patted the spot next to her. Ruthy hesitated, and then joined her. She couldn't say *ne* to her.

"How can I do that, *Mam?* She and Elam destroyed my life…."

"Did they?" *Mam* sighed. "Laurette is very unhappy, and I can't help but think you would have been just as unhappy married to Elam."

"I'm sure she's only bothered by her guilty conscience." The words sounded cruel, even as Ruthy spoke them. "I'm sorry, *Mam.* I shouldn't have said that."

"Laurette does have a guilty conscience. We've talked for many hours about what happened last summer, and she wishes she could take it all back. But that's only part of her problem." *Mam* sighed again and fingered the fabric of the quilt they were sitting on. "Elam has turned out to be… Well, he isn't a good husband, and I don't think it has anything to do with either you or Laurette."

"What do you mean?"

"He leaves Laurette alone for days at a time while he disappears. When he comes back he refuses to say where he's been. The church leaders have talked to him about taking on his responsibilities, and he promises, but then a few weeks later he takes off again." *Mam* shook her head. "Meanwhile, poor Laurette is having a hard time with the baby coming, and no husband to help her."

Mam reached out and grasped Ruthy's hand. "God forgive me, but I can't help being glad Laurette is the one who married Elam and not you. And I do need to ask God's forgiveness for rejoicing in Laurette's difficulty." Mam pulled a handkerchief from her sleeve and wiped her eyes.

Ruthy sat, thinking about *Mam's* words. *Ja,* for sure Elam was young and thoughtless at times, but surely he would have settled down once he and Laurette were married. It must be Laurette's fault that he was acting like this—Ruthy remembered many times when Laurette grew shrewish when things didn't go her way.

"She needs you, Ruthy. She feels so alone. All the time, growing up, you two were best friends, and now you won't even talk to her."

Ruthy stood and walked to the window, looking out on the white fields. "I can't, *Mam*. She betrayed me, and I can't forgive that."

"You must, Ruthy, for your own sake if not for hers. Bitterness will eat at you until you become consumed with it. You must forgive her."

Ruthy rubbed at a bit of dust on the windowsill. *Mam* was right about the bitterness. She could feel it in the back of her mind like a dark, brooding shadow. But when she was talking with Levi, or working in the kitchen, or playing with the children, it disappeared. As long as she stayed busy, she didn't need to think about it.

And anyway, forgiving Laurette was out of the question.

Chapter Sixteen

Ruthy turned over in the warm bed. She should get up. Breakfast needed cooking, chores needed doing and...*ach!* She sat up in bed. It was Tuesday. The wedding was today.

She lit the lamp and quickly drew on the new green dress *Mam* had made for today. Gathering her hair into a long coil, she pinned it in place and then settled her *kapp* over it. It should be her husband's privilege to unpin her hair tonight...but not for her and Levi. After the wedding, their lives would go on as they had the last several weeks.

But was she right? Was it fair to Levi to continue to be his housekeeper rather than his wife?

Ruthy jabbed a pin into her waistband and pricked a finger. She stuck the sore finger into her mouth to keep blood from dripping on her new dress.

Ne. Ne, it wasn't fair to Levi. It wasn't fair to her, either, but she had made her bed and now she must lie in it. *Ne,* she hadn't made her bed. Elam and Laurette had. If things had turned out differently, she would have married Elam last fall.

She hurried through the breezeway between the *Dawdi Haus* and the kitchen. Levi had already been in to start the stove. Ruthy glanced at the clock on the wall. Four o'clock. They were both up early.

Before breakfast was cleared away, the helpers started coming. Bram's Ellie and her mother, Elizabeth, were the first to arrive, and before Ruthy could even finish greeting them, three more buggies drove into the farm.

Mam directed the whirlwind of activity while girls flew everywhere, preparing the dinner that would cook in a slow oven during the three-hour service. Ruthy was glad to keep busy, but every once in a while she found herself staring out the window toward the yard, where the men were working, bringing the church benches into the house through the front door. What was Levi thinking this morning?

Just before nine o'clock, a commotion in the yard brought everyone to the windows. Eliza had arrived and her horse reared in protest as she tried to stop him at the house. Boys rushed out of the barn to help calm the feisty animal, and Eliza climbed down from her buggy as if nothing were amiss. She took Ginger's reins from Nathan and brought the horse's head down to hers. The animal calmed down and followed Nathan to the barn.

Next to Ruthy, Waneta shook her head. "Only Aunt Eliza would be able to handle a horse like that."

Elizabeth Stoltzfus chuckled. "Only Eliza would want to."

"Ruthy," *Mam* said softly, "it's time for you to change your apron. Bishop will be here soon."

On an impulse, Ruthy grabbed Waneta's hand.

"Come help me. You can make sure everything is straight."

They went into the *Dawdi Haus,* Waneta giggling as they entered the silent front room. "I didn't think I'd ever want to have church here again, but this is so much fun, isn't it?"

"It is, with everyone here and working together. It should be a good day." Ruthy paused as she untied her apron. "I think I know which part of the day you're looking forward to the most. It's the Singing tonight, *ja?*"

Waneta blushed. "*Ja.* There's just something so romantic about a Singing after a wedding. Everyone is so happy for the new couple, and even the boys have weddings on their minds."

Ruthy slipped her new apron on over the green dress. "Even Reuben?" She smiled. Waneta was bubbling with joy and it was a pleasure to see.

"*Ja.* Even Reuben."

Waneta helped her tie her apron and tucked a stray hair under her *kapp.*

"Am I ready?"

"You look ready to me. Do you feel ready?"

Ruthy hesitated. This step was irreversible. Once she said her vows to Levi, she would forever be Levi Zook's Ruthy. She looked into Waneta's eyes, so different from Levi's that she knew they must be from Salome, Waneta's mother.

"I'm ready to become your *daed's* wife, Waneta, but are you and the others ready for me to be part of your family?"

Waneta hugged Ruthy, and then stepped back. "*Ja.* We're all so happy you're to be our new *mam.*"

"Even Elias and Nathan?"

Waneta laughed. "*Ja,* even them."

Ruthy whooshed out a breath and then laughed along with Waneta. "Well then, let's go. We mustn't keep everyone waiting."

Levi forced himself to sit quietly on the bench, Jesse on one side and Sam on the other.

When he and Ruth had spent their time with Bishop during the first hymn, he thought she looked scared. Terrified. Or maybe just nervous. But she had listened carefully to Bishop's counsel on marriage, and had answered his final questions with a steady voice. He had only been able to give her a quick smile before they took their seats in the congregation again twenty minutes later.

He glanced over at her, beautiful in a new dress. Her *mam* sat on one side of her, and Eliza sat on her other side. A welcome sign of support.

If she looked his way, he could give her another smile, or a nod…something to show her how happy he was that this day had finally arrived. But she kept her eyes on the minister, as if this were just any Sunday morning service.

Finally the sermons ended and it was time for him to step forward with Ruth, the Bram Lapps and Waneta and Elias stepping forward as the two couples who would be their witnesses. The vows Bishop read weren't hard for him to assent to. He would gladly care for her in sickness. He would learn to love her, and bear patiently with her. He would never be separated from her until…his throat thickened as he thought that one of them would have to endure the final separation of death. Was he selfish to hope he wouldn't have to travel that path again?

After making their vows, Ruth turned to go back to her seat, glancing quickly at him. He tried to give her a smile, but she turned away too quickly. As he joined the rest of the congregation in the final kneeling prayer, Levi prayed for Ruth's comfort. He prayed she would never regret marrying him.

Dinner lasted well into the afternoon. Levi and Ruth sat at the corner table set apart for the newly married couple and their friends. Waneta and Elias sat with them, even though the rest of the youth were acting as waiters for the crowd, who ate in three sittings.

Partway through the meal, Sam and Jesse came running up to them.

"We can now, can't we, Ruthy?" asked Sam. He pushed past Waneta to stand next to Ruth's chair.

"You can what?" Ruth put one arm around both boys, squeezing them together.

"We can call you *Mam* now, *ja?*"

Ruth turned to bring Jesse closer. "Now you may call me *Mam*."

When the boys went off with their friends, Levi reached under the table to take her hand. "*Denki*. They have been waiting for a long time for their new *mam*."

She took a handkerchief from her sleeve and wiped her eyes. "I've been waiting, too, Levi Zook." She sniffed, and then laughed. "I don't know why I'm crying. This is a happy day, *ja?*"

He squeezed her hand where he still held it, out of sight of their friends and family. "This is a happy day. They're tears of joy, aren't they?"

Ruth nodded, but her chin trembled. Levi turned to

greet Matthew Beachey as he walked up to the table, but kept hold of her hand. He had to make sure she knew how much he appreciated her. How much this marriage meant to him and his family. How much he hoped she would make her home here and be happy.

Matthew moved on to shake Bram Lapp's hand and to say hello to Ellie. Bram leaned over and put his arm around his wife's shoulders as they talked, and Levi caught the loving look in Ellie's eye as she looked up at Bram. They were true partners.

He glanced at Ruth again, and she was watching Bram and Ellie as well, with a look of longing in her eyes. He looked away before she caught him watching her.

They had a long way to go before they would have a loving marriage like the one he hoped for, like the one Bram and Ellie had. Would Ruth be willing to work toward that same goal?

This is not how she had expected to spend her wedding night.

Levi paced from the tiny kitchen to the front room of the *Dawdi Haus* and back again while Ruthy kept her hands occupied with her knitting.

"You don't have to go to the barn, Levi, you could sleep on the floor in here." But she wouldn't get any sleep knowing he was just on the other side of her bedroom door.

"*Ne, denki.* As soon as I know Ezekiel and Naomi are asleep, I'll head out to the barn."

"At least you'll be able to move back into the house tomorrow, after they go back home."

"*Ja,* that will be good." Levi stopped his pacing and

stood in the center of the front room, watching her. "Are you sorry we did this?"

Ruthy glanced up at him, careful to keep a cheerful smile on her face. "*Ne,* Levi, I'm not sorry. We both have what we want, don't we? The children can stay together, and I'll be a good mother to them. You'll have your family and I'll have a home. We'll grow old together and watch our grandchildren grow up. It will be a good life and we'll be content."

Levi rubbed his beard and Ruthy concentrated on her knitting as he continued to stare at her.

Did it matter if he didn't love her? What would he say if she told him he didn't need to keep those conditions she had imposed? If she asked him to stay with her in the *Dawdi Haus* on their wedding night?

Would she continue to see Salome's shadow every time he looked at her, or would he eventually learn to accept her? If things were the way they should be—if he loved her—would he be content to spend this night in the barn, away from her?

Levi spun on his heel and paced into her little kitchen, and then back into the front room again. "They must be asleep by now. I'll say good-night."

Ruthy didn't look up as he went out the door to the connecting breezeway. He had left. Her wedding night, and she was knitting socks for a man who didn't love her. She wrapped up her needles in the stocking and tucked them into her knitting basket. Blowing out the light, she walked into the kitchen and looked out the window toward the barn. A sliver of light showed through the door of the cowshed, where Levi had made a bed for himself in an empty stall.

She watched until Levi blew the lantern out, and then

went to her own cold bedroom. Lighting the lamp, she took off her *kapp*. As she turned toward the dresser to put the hairpins away, she saw it. Sitting on the washstand were the blue flowered bowl and pitcher she had seen in Middlebury.

Levi. He was the only one who could have put them here. When she had seen them in the store, their delicate beauty had captured her heart, and somehow Levi knew.

She reached out to stroke the blue flowers. Elam would never have done something so thoughtful.

Levi turned in his straw bed, knowing from the restless movements in the cow pens that morning wasn't far away. His body ached from the uncomfortable bed and the knowledge that he had the right to share his wife's bed last night.

What had induced him to accept that woman's conditions for a marriage like this? He thought being near her every day, to talk with her, share his life with her and raise his children with her would be enough, but after this one night he knew it wasn't.

The sight of her sitting in the lamplight of the front room in the *Dawdi Haus* flooded over him once more. He wanted to hold her, to talk with her, but he would never be able to stand the possibility of her rejection. Leaving the *Dawdi Haus* tonight had been hard enough, and he couldn't risk watching her turn away from him forever.

Levi turned again, and then gave up trying to go back to sleep and stood, brushing the straw from his clothes. He walked to the door of the cowshed and prodded it open an inch or two, just enough to see the kitchen window. *Ja*, the lamp was lit. She was there making his coffee. The thought made the aching in his back ease a bit. She liked him, at least, and perhaps love would come. He could be patient.

Chapter Seventeen

Spring came overnight, it seemed. Ruthy first noticed the red clusters of buds on the maple trees one breezy Monday morning as she and Waneta hung clothes on the line. Two weeks ago, when the house had been filled with the warmth of friends and family celebrating their wedding, the world outside had still been trapped in the icy stillness of winter. But now, even with the gray skies, there was the smell of thawing earth on the wind and Ruthy couldn't quench the wild, light feeling bubbling up inside her.

When a gust whipped one corner of a sheet out of her hand, she watched helplessly as it flapped above her head.

"Grab it!" Waneta said, her own hands full of a flapping dress. "If it gets away we'll have to wash it all over again!"

The sheet drifted toward her in the fitful breeze, almost within reach of her outstretched hand, but the next gust blew it straight into the air again, pulling it loose from the clothespins anchoring the other end to the clothesline.

"*Ach,* there it goes!" Ruthy ran after it, knowing it was too heavy to go far, but she groaned as it caught on the fence of the cow pen, the bulk of the sheet in the hoof-pocked mud. She reached for the corner still clinging to the wooden fence rail, but before she could grasp it, it slid into the mud with the rest of the sheet. She stepped up on the bottom rail and leaned down into the pen, but it was too far out of reach.

"Having some trouble?" Levi had stepped out of the cowshed door and was watching her. She didn't need to see his face to know he'd be laughing at her predicament.

"The sheet blew away. Can you help me get it out of the mud?"

He waded through the slime in his rubber boots and gathered up the muddy cloth. It was wetter than when it had come out of the wringer and streaked with black mud where it had lain on the ground. Levi held it up.

"You're sure you want this?" His brown eyes sparkled in fun.

"*Ja,* I want it. I have to rewash it and get it hung up again."

"You could come in here and get it."

What possessed that man? Ruthy glanced down at her leather shoes, fine for wet grass or a gravel drive, but they would be ruined if she went in the pen.

"You know very well I can't come in there, Levi Zook. You bring that sheet over here this minute." Frustration made her voice squeak at the end, and she heard a giggle from the clothesline behind her. Waneta was enjoying this standoff.

"What will you give me if I do?" Levi stepped closer to the fence, holding the muddy sheet away from her.

"I'll have you know, Levi Zook, if you don't give that to me, I'll feed your dinner to the pigs."

Levi came a step closer and stopped, inches away from where she still stood on the fence. His eyes twinkled, but he dropped his voice so it wouldn't carry to Waneta. "You wouldn't feed my dinner to the pigs. You would never waste good food that way."

"You don't think so?" Ruthy's frustration melted away as he drew even closer, her breath catching as his eyes drifted across her face and rested on her lips. "I wouldn't hesitate if…if I…" This man was her husband, and she had never kissed him. She tore her gaze away from his face and focused on the sodden mass hanging forgotten from his grip. "I wouldn't hesitate if you refused to give me that sheet."

Gaining her composure again she looked back at him. The teasing look was gone, his eyes soft. He reached up with one gloved hand and barely stroked her cheek with the side of his finger.

"I'll take the sheet up to the house for you. It's awfully dirty and heavy."

"*Ja, denki.* It's time for your morning coffee, anyway." She stepped back to the ground and turned away, her cheek burning where he had touched her. Waneta had finished hanging the wash and was nearly back to the house with the empty basket. Ruthy turned back to Levi. "Waneta made some coffee cake, too. It's fresh out of the oven."

Levi smiled at her. "Just the thing. *Denki,* Ruth."

Ruthy hurried into the house, knowing he watched her as she went. If she didn't avoid encounters like that, how could she keep from showing him how much she wanted his love? Since the wedding, she had been careful to only see him when some of the children were nearby—at mealtimes and in the evening. She always busied herself in the kitchen after the children went to bed, and went to her *Dawdi Haus* while Levi was in the barn for the last check of the night. Their routine had been working fine. Their lives were comfortable. He kept to his chores and she did hers...until this morning.

Levi stared after his wife as she disappeared around the loaded clothesline.

His wife.

He turned to pick his way through the muddy pen to the door of the cowshed. *Ja,* his wife in name only. He had never so much as kissed her, but he had nearly done it this morning. As she had hung on the fence, the wind blowing tendrils of hair into her face, her cheeks pink with the cold, the morning light giving her a golden glow, he wanted to. He would have, if she had lingered one more minute before turning away.

But it was only his imagination that made him think she would welcome his attention like that. She had kept a careful distance from him ever since the wedding, clearly showing her desire to keep their marriage friendly, but separate. She was more like a sister than a wife.

Levi let himself into the back porch, setting the dirty sheet on the wash bench. Through the window in the kitchen door he could see Ruth and Waneta, chatting as they prepared his morning coffee. Ruth gave Waneta a one-armed hug as they laughed over some comment and she caught sight of him. The glance was too long. He couldn't tear his eyes away until hers dropped, and he pulled off his muddy boots.

Ne, not a sister. She would never be a sister to him, but yet, she wasn't his wife, either.

Levi hung up his coat and hat, brushing his fingers through his hair and beard. He poured water from the waiting pitcher into the enameled tin washbasin, grabbed the soap and plunged his hands into the basin. The water was warm. Ruth had gotten warm water ready for him again this morning. Just one of the many thoughtful things she was always doing for him.

The warm cinnamon smell of coffee cake enveloped him as he opened the door.

"Here's your coffee, *Dat.*" Waneta placed a cup on the table as he sat in his chair.

"*Denki,* Waneta. The coffee cake smells *wonderful-gut.*"

"Where are Sam and Elias? Weren't they coming in?" Ruth put the pan of brown sugar crusted cake in front of him, setting his mouth to watering.

"I told them it was time. Maybe they didn't hear me."

"I'll go call them again," Waneta said. She was out the door before Levi could stop her.

Ruth brought her own cup of coffee to the table, placing it in her usual spot that left room for Waneta on the bench next to Levi.

"Ruth, why do you sit so far away?" Levi pointed to the bench at his elbow. "You can sit closer to me. I won't bite."

Ruth gave him a glance that said she thought he just might bite, but moved her cup and sat near him.

Levi helped himself to a piece of cake. "The children are starting to wonder why we don't sit near each other more, being newly married and all."

"I suppose we should act like we enjoy each other's company, *ja?*" Ruth sipped her coffee.

"Well, we do, don't we?"

She looked at him. "We do what?"

"Enjoy each other's company. I like being with you, talking with you. I wouldn't have married you if I didn't."

"I suppose." Ruth took another sip of coffee. "You should call me Ruthy, too, like the children do. Everyone calls me Ruthy except you."

"Ruthy." Levi tried the name. He had never felt free to use it before. When the children had used the name, it seemed like they were close friends, but for him...it was intimate, closing the distance between them. "And you must call me Levi."

She straightened in her seat. "I do call you Levi."

He pointed his fork at her. "You have never once called me Levi since you met me. You always call me 'Levi Zook.' What wife calls her husband by his full name?"

A pink blush started in the center of her cheeks as a ray of sunshine broke through the overcast late winter sky and shone through the window, lighting her face with gold.

She was so different from Salome. He hadn't had much experience with wives, and he had thought Salome was nearly perfect. Irreplaceable. But here was Ruth... Ruthy. His words to Elias from a while back came to him. She wasn't Salome, but she was the right woman for him now. What was that Bible verse? There is a time for every season? A time for every purpose under heaven?

He grasped her hand where it lay on the table between them. Nearly as large as his own, her hand was all feminine grace and red, chapped knuckles. The hand of a woman who wasn't afraid to work, who cared for her family with little thought to herself.

"Levi…" His name escaped from her mouth in a whisper.

Waneta's and Elias's voices drifted in to them as boots thudded on the back steps. Ruthy tried to withdraw her hand from his and started to slide down the bench to make room for Waneta, but Levi didn't let go.

"*Ne,* sit by me." He smiled, rubbing the back of her hand with his thumb.

She returned his smile, but moved her hand away as the three children entered the kitchen, bringing fresh air and loud voices to interrupt their stolen time together.

Levi sipped his coffee, watching Ruthy's blushing face as she cut pieces of coffee cake for Waneta and the boys. It was a step closer, and he was patient. That wall she placed between them was softening, melting. Love would grow, he was sure of it.

Waneta came back into the kitchen after hanging the rewashed sheet on the clothesline just as Ruthy put the chicken casserole into the oven.

"It's so windy today! The clothes we hung out earlier are nearly dry already."

"That's *wonderful-gut.* It helps wash day go so much faster when we have a warm breeze like this."

Waneta picked up a knife and started scraping the carrots Ruthy had laid out. "Spring seems like it's nearly here on a day like today."

"*Ja,* for sure."

"You and *Dat* seem to be getting along."

Ruthy pried the lid off a jar of applesauce and glanced at Waneta. "Of course we're getting along. Why wouldn't we?"

"It's just that…" Waneta's face reddened. "You still live in the *Dawdi Haus, ja?*"

Ruthy's face grew warm. She should have known Waneta would notice.

"Elias thought it was because you didn't like each other much. After all, there was no talk of marriage until after Aunt Eliza was here. We know she went to Bishop, and you only married because he told you to, and because otherwise the girls would have to go live in Middlebury."

"It's hard to explain, Waneta. Your *Dat* and I like each other, and we married because…" Ruthy's mind turned over the feel of Levi's warm hand holding hers. Why had they married? "Because I love you children, and I couldn't continue living here without being married…" Why did it all sound so contrived?

"I think you got married because you love each other." Waneta finished peeling the carrots and started cutting them into chunks. "You may not admit it, but I've seen the way you look at *Dat* when you don't think anyone will notice."

Now the tips of Ruthy's ears were burning. "It takes more than one person's love to make a marriage, Waneta." She had to change the subject. "Did you have fun with Reuben yesterday afternoon?"

Waneta's face lit up. "*Ach, ja.* We went to visit his sister Sally, and the Bram Lapps were there, too. We had a fun time playing a game of Parcheesi and then Sally made popcorn. Reuben has a *wonderful-gut* family."

"I didn't hear Reuben's buggy until nearly one o'clock

this morning. Surely you weren't playing Parcheesi and eating popcorn all that time." Ruthy kept her voice light, teasing Waneta. *Ja,* for sure now she was blushing as red as Ruthy felt.

"Well, we went to the Singing, and then he took me for a ride."

Ruthy put the bowl of applesauce on the table. "It must have been awfully cold in that open courting buggy of his."

Waneta couldn't hide her smile, and busied herself with the carrots. "I wasn't cold at all."

"Do we need to start thinking about another wedding?"

Waneta blushed even redder as she put the carrots in a pot with water. "Reuben says he won't talk about marriage until I've joined church."

Ruthy smiled and gave Waneta a hug. "That is one smart young man."

A knock on the front door made Ruthy look at Waneta. "I've never heard anyone knock on the front door."

"Maybe it's another tramp, looking for some food. They'll be coming by more often as the weather warms up."

"Well then, Waneta, you go bring him around to the kitchen and I'll get something together for him."

Ruthy slid the pan of biscuits into the oven next to the casserole and hurried to the cellar for some cheese. If the tramp had come any day but Monday, she could offer him some fresh baked bread this time of day, but he would need to make do with what they had. She sorted through the cheeses on the shelf. There had been two wheels when she came two months ago, but one had turned bad and she had given it to the pigs. The partial wheel that was left was moldy in places, but it would have to do. She cut the moldy rind off and was able to slice enough good cheese to make a sandwich. Making cheese was another project for this spring, after the grass was growing and the cows were giving more milk.

She wrapped the cheese in a clean cloth, found a couple of good apples and started up the cellar stairs. The biscuits and cheese would make good sandwiches, and the apples could go in his pockets for later.

When Ruthy opened the door to the kitchen, Waneta was checking the oven.

"Ruthy, we have a visitor, all the way from Lancaster County. He says he's a friend of yours."

An Amish man was sitting in Levi's chair at the table, a cup of coffee in front of him. Ruthy's knees quivered as he turned with his usual lazy smile.

Elam.

Chapter Eighteen

For sure, Elam had to stay for dinner. For sure, he had to sit next to Levi, exchanging news and stories while Ruthy sat at the end of the table next to Sam, trying her best to overhear what the men were talking about.

"*Ja,* it's been plenty cold this winter, but not too much snow," Elam said, helping himself to another biscuit. He leaned forward in his seat to catch Ruthy's eye and held up the biscuit. "Your biscuits are just as good as they've always been, Ruthy."

"*Denki.*" He could take that biscuit and get right back on the train home. What was he doing here, anyway? Ruthy was thankful Elam had introduced himself to Levi as a friend of hers, without mentioning that he had been the man she had nearly married. That they had spent the last eight years courting. That he had told her he loved her countless times before marrying her best friend.

"So, what brought you to Indiana?" Levi settled back in his chair and Ruthy rose to get his coffee.

"The farmer I work for wants to buy a bull he saw

advertised in *The Budget,* and sent me out here to look it over. I knew Ruthy lived here, so I thought I'd drop in and say hello."

Levi glanced at her as she set his coffee in front of him, his eyes worried. Had he noticed how much she did not want Elam here?

"Ruthy's parents told me about the wedding." Elam looked at her as he said this. "I was surprised you married so soon."

"You shouldn't be." Ruthy struggled to keep her tone even, her face calm. "Levi is a *wonderful-gut* and honorable man." Everything you aren't, Elam Nafziger. "How is Laurette doing?"

Elam stared at the coffee Ruthy set in front of him. "She's fine, I guess, except she feels poorly most of the time with the baby coming anytime now."

Ruthy's stomach flipped. She didn't need the reminder of how soon after their wedding Laurette's baby would be born.

"She'll feel better once it's here, then, *ja?*"

Levi took a sip of his coffee, watching her closely. "That's been my experience."

Ruthy took her own cup to her seat while Waneta put a tin of cookies on the table for dessert. She struggled to keep her face calm. It was for sure a good thing she was married to Levi now. Her future was secure, at least.

Dinner over, Waneta cleared the table. "Ruthy, you and Elam will want to visit. I'll do the dishes, and Sam can help."

"*Denki,* Waneta."

Ruthy saw Levi hesitate before going back out to the barn with Elias. He should stay and visit with their guest, but it seemed he was content to leave her alone with another man.

She led Elam to the front room, but rather than taking her usual place at the end of the sofa, she sat in the chair across from Levi's—the chair where she usually declined to sit out of respect for the children's mother. But she would need some of that woman's strength to face Elam the way she was feeling right now.

Elam lounged in Levi's chair, crossed his ankle over one knee and regarded her with eyes crinkling in the corners as he smiled. "Well, Ruthy-girl, look where we've ended up."

"What do you mean?"

"Look at you." Elam waved his hand around to take in the spacious front room, the house sprawling around them. "Levi seems to be doing pretty well, and you've moved into a ready-made family. Life seems to be turning out well for you, after all." He placed both feet on the floor and leaned forward. "You've forgiven me, haven't you?"

Ruthy wiggled her toes inside her shoes. Forgiven him? She could never forgive him, in spite of what *Mam* said, and what she had been taught as a child—forgive your brother, no matter what his sin against you may be. It's what the Lord desires. . . .

"Elam, you know I can't. You ruined everything, you and Laurette." Tears stung as she looked at her hands in her lap, at the stove between the two chairs, anywhere but at Elam Nafziger. "You betrayed me, Elam. You betrayed my love, and everything we had planned." All the hurt of the last months boiled, trying to force its way out, but she held the lid firmly on that kettle. It wasn't the Amish way.

Elam played with the hem of his trouser. "You can't blame me for everything that happened." He rubbed at the leather sole of his shoe.

"Are…are you and Laurette happy?"

"How can we be? Married life is harder than I ever thought it would be. Laurette has been so sick and complains about everything."

"Does she…does she ever talk about me?"

"I don't know. She talks about everything and everyone. I know she wishes you'd write to her."

Elam picked at a spot on his trouser leg. Sam's delighted laughter drifted into the front room as he and Waneta played a game while they worked. Ruthy's mind took this in, but she couldn't move past the icy wall that kept her from feeling anything for either Elam or Laurette. Did she even care they were unhappy?

"I wish you'd say something, Ruthy. I want us to be friends…."

"What can I say?"

He lifted his eyes to meet hers. "Say you still love me." He whispered the words, as intimately as he had all those evenings in his courting buggy. "Say you don't love him, you only love me."

"How would that help anything, Elam?"

"I'd know there's something that wasn't ruined. I'd know you still care for me."

She had never seen how selfish he was before, thinking only of himself. Had he been that way when he was courting her?

"I'm married now, Elam. Even if I did feel that way, it wouldn't make any difference."

Elam's eyebrows shot up. "You don't love him, do you?"

Ruthy shifted in her chair, her face growing hot. "Of course I do."

"Then he doesn't love you."

She couldn't answer him. How could she, when he had guessed the truth?

"I think you had better leave. Tell Laurette I..." Ruthy swallowed. She missed Laurette so much, but could things ever be mended between them? "Tell Laurette I think of her often."

"*Ja,* all right."

"When do you go back to Bird-in-Hand?"

"Next week. I have some business in Fort Wayne."

Ruthy shot a glance at him. "I thought you told Levi you were here to look at a bull."

Elam shrugged. "Mr. Millhouse thinks so, too. But I'll tell him the animal wasn't worth the money. Meanwhile, I'm meeting friends this weekend."

"What kind of friends? What are you involved in, Elam?"

He grinned at her. "Let's just say the bishop wouldn't like it." He leaned closer to her. "I'm making a name for myself playing my guitar. You'd be proud of me."

Ruthy looked away. "I'd be proud of you if you followed the church and lived up to your commitment to Laurette."

Elam snorted. "You'll think different when I've made it big. Then everything will be going my way for once." He stood up, adjusting his trousers. "I'll come by next week before I head back to Pennsylvania."

"You won't need to come back here." Ruthy stood, smoothing her apron.

"You're sure? Not even to say goodbye?"

Ruthy pressed her lips together. "*Ne,* not even to say goodbye."

Elam made his way through the kitchen, waving to Waneta and Sam, and then left. Ruthy went to the window facing the lane and barnyard to get one last glimpse of him. She rubbed her forehead, trying to ease the ache away. Elam may be gone, but the door he had opened was swinging wide. The truth of her hard heart toward both Elam and Laurette lay behind that door, and try as she might, she couldn't close it again.

Must she live the rest of her life with this icy rock of hatred lodged in her heart?

Levi hated leaving the house with Elam there, but the man had obviously come to talk to Ruthy, not him. He went to the tool bench to get a hammer, and then started on the mindless job of checking the nails in the cow-pen fence. It was a chore he had planned to give to Jesse after school, but if he took care of it now, he'd be outside, where he could keep an eye on the house.

How close were Elam and Ruthy, anyway? She had said he was her friend's husband, but the look on both their faces hadn't gotten past him. There was more to their relationship than that. Was he the man she had told him about? The one she had planned to marry?

He whacked on each nail in the fence post, whether it looked loose or not, each whack getting harder as he thought of his wife talking with another man. A young man. A man her own age, from her own town. A man she had once loved. Perhaps a man she still loved.

Ach, they were both married. Ruthy wouldn't go back on her marriage vows, would she?

He hit the next nail head with the hammer so hard he dented the wood.

Had their vows been binding anyway, if they never went further in their marriage than to stand before the church? Should he have insisted they live together as man and wife? Would that have bound her to him more closely?

Levi leaned his arms on the top of the fence and looked over his shoulder at the house. He had Ruthy's promise to live here and to be the mother his children needed so badly, but he had ignored his own need. He needed a wife—a wife he could trust.

When the door opened and Elam stepped down to the drive, Levi busied himself with the hammer again. Elam waved and got into his borrowed buggy. He was gone. Levi looked toward the house, hoping he wouldn't see her, but there she was. Her face pressed to the window was twisted in grief, and his heart wrenched.

Ruthy drew back from the window, leaving him alone in the afternoon wind. It had turned to the north. He hunched his shoulders inside his coat and went into the barn, where harnesses were waiting for his attention.

By suppertime, when Levi went into the house for the evening, Ruthy seemed like she had forgotten her visitor. She talked with the girls as they filled the table with dishes of macaroni and cheese, pickles, beets and bread, her voice just as gay as ever, but when she caught his eye as he walked through to the front room he saw the shadowed pain in her eyes. Dark violet and haunted, her look was a silent plea.

Levi went into his bedroom, now emptied of everything that would have reminded him of Salome, but still with nothing of Ruthy's. It was a man's room, barren and plain. He found the pair of slippers Ruthy had knitted for him and slipped them on. She had been right, he thought as he gazed at the brown felted wool covering his feet. He hadn't worn out a single pair of stockings since she had made these. Each child had their own pair, brown or dark blue, and Ruthy saw they were worn whenever shoes or boots weren't.

It was only one of dozens of little changes that had happened since she had come to them. He fingered the blue-and-white quilt on his bed. She had made his bed every morning since the wedding, where before he had just thrown the covers up over the pillow and left it until evening. But now when he came in after a day of work, his room was always neat and tidy. Orderly.

What did she think of when she was in his room? Did she hurry through the task, anxious to be done with it, or did she linger, thinking about him?

What would he do if he lost her now? He rubbed his hand on the back of his neck. That Elam Nafziger had a place in her heart, for sure, but did *he?* Was there anything he could do or say to keep her with him if she had her heart set on leaving him?

Gott im Himmel, what a burden already filled his heart at the thought of it! When Salome had left…when she died, it was like the passing of an old friend, the mother of his children. She was everything home was meant to be…. Salome had been dear to him, and her love was like a banked fire in the stove, always there, always welcome, always ready for whatever he needed.

But Ruthy… She was like the flash of a morning sunrise, fresh and new every time he saw her. How could two women be so different?

Levi stood up and walked to the window where the last light of the day turned the lowering clouds orange on the gray. The farm fields stretched out to the south, their flat surface broken by the fence row a quarter mile away. All he asked for was order, to live as God called him to live, with his wife and family looking to him and to their Lord. But what could he do if Ruthy wanted to rebel against him, against their marriage vows?

Woo her.

The words echoed in his mind.

Court her.

He had never courted her before their wedding, there hadn't been time. But now—did he dare, if her heart belonged to another? How could he risk her rejection when his need for her was so overwhelming? If she rejected him, he would be devastated. But if he didn't make some effort and she still rejected him, would it be any worse?

He had to try.

Ruthy loved sitting with her little boys during evening prayers. Sam and Jesse had missed a mother's touch for so long, and they snuggled next to her on the sofa each evening. How long would it be before they decided they were too old for this? Then who would cuddle with her?

Ach, no one. Sam was the youngest, and would always be the youngest. Levi had his children. Surely he didn't want more now that his wife was gone. Ruthy would just need to gather up as much love as she could from these boys before they grew up.

Levi finished reading tonight's prayer from the *Christenpflicht* as they all kneeled together in the front room. The words of the prayer echoed in Ruthy's mind as she rose and took her seat again. It had reflected on God's blessings of the day that was closing. A day of blessing? All she could remember was Elam's words. He was tempting her, trying to get her to deny her vows.

She glanced at Levi in his chair next to the stove. She had made her vows to an honorable man, and he was the man she belonged to. He had loved his first wife, but he had put the past behind him. Removed her things from his room and welcomed her into the family in Salome's place.

She would never give into Elam's temptation. She would never betray Levi the way she had been betrayed.

Sam shifted and looked up at her. "*Mam,* will you tuck us in tonight?"

"Doesn't Waneta do that?"

"*Ja,*" Jesse said, his voice sleepy, "but she's always in a hurry. You wouldn't leave until we said our prayers, would you?"

Ruthy leaned down to kiss the tops of their heads, first Jesse and then Sam. "All right. You go put your sleeping clothes on and I'll be up in a couple minutes."

Both boys jumped off the sofa and ran for the stairway door. Levi chuckled as he watched them.

"I think their sleepiness has fled already."

Nellie scooted into the spot next to Ruthy where Jesse had been. "After you tuck the boys in, would you tuck me in, too?"

"And me?" Nancy spoke from her spot on the floor at Ruthy's feet, looking up at her.

"*Ja,* for sure. I'll come to your room as soon as I finish with the little boys."

Nellie reached up to give her a kiss on the cheek and

then followed the rest of the children up the stairs, leaving Ruthy alone with Levi. She usually went into the kitchen to set the bread sponge at this time, while Levi went to make his final check on the barn, but she had promised the children.

"They love you, Ruthy." Levi laid the *Christenpflicht* on the small table next to him with his Bible.

"And I love them, too."

"You're a *wonderful-gut* mother to them."

Ruthy caught her bottom lip in her teeth. "I'm sure I'm not as good for them as Salome. They lost so much when she died."

Levi rose from his chair and sat next to her on the sofa. He took his hand in hers and held it closed in both of his. "You're not the same as Salome, that's true. But they love you for who you are."

Ruthy shook her head. Would Levi ever love her for who she was? "I'm only second best, I know."

Levi was silent. He turned her hand over in his and stroked her palm with his thumb. Then he spoke so softly she had to lean toward him to catch his words. "You aren't second best to me."

She looked up into his eyes. Warm, soft, trustworthy, honorable. Was he only trying to make her feel better?

"Salome was a *wonderful-gut* wife and mother." Levi lowered his eyes to her hand as he continued to stroke it. The gentle motion softened that hard place in her heart that Elam's visit had exposed. "We had known each other since we were babies, Salome and I. Our *mams* were best friends and neighbors, so we were together almost every day while we were growing up. She was a good friend, always kind and understanding."

Ruthy gazed around the room, still filled with memories of this woman she would never meet. She had looked like Waneta, she knew, and she had heard snippets of memories from the children, but she had never seen Salome through Levi's eyes, the man they had both married.

"We married very young, as soon as we were old enough to join church." He shrugged and squeezed her hand. "I had never thought of marrying anyone else. She was always there."

Catching a drift of what he was trying to say, Ruthy had to ask the question. "Did you love her?"

"*Ja,* for sure I loved her, but…" He reached his hand up to her cheek, turning her toward him. "But she was steady, warm. I loved her, but you aren't Salome. What I felt for her was nothing like what I feel when I look at you."

His words crashed against the hard rock in her heart. Ruthy felt her heart beating so fast she was afraid it would run out of her chest. She stood up, her mind blank. What was he telling her?

"The children are waiting. I must go and say goodnight."

He released her hand and his face shuttered closed. His eyes were no longer as warm as sunshine on rich garden soil, they were black and closed in the lamplight. "*Ja,* and I must go check the barn."

His voice was gruff, but he didn't look at her as he went through the kitchen to the back door.

What had she done? Why couldn't she respond to him when he was so gentle? All she needed to do was to welcome his words. Let him learn to love her.

She sank back on the sofa, her fingers and toes cold even though the room was warm. The wretched feeling

Elam had brought with him expanded until it threatened to fill her whole being. She fought it down, struggling to regain control. The children were waiting for her to tuck them in, hear their prayers, kiss them good-night, just like her mother had all those years at home.

She longed for the comfort of *Mam's* presence tonight.

Ruthy headed for the stairs and the waiting children. Their own *mam*. That's who she was now—their *mam* and Levi's wife. She loved her life. The children and her work brought her joy, and she was content with the home God had given her.

As Ruthy's foot hit the bottom step, the muffled slam of the back door sounded through the house. Levi was gone, on his way to the barn. She paused, pulling her bottom lip between her teeth to control its quivering. She couldn't bear his disappointment. Why didn't she respond when he reached out? What if he offered his love? She leaned against the stairway wall, clinging to the bannister. She would do anything to hear him say he loved her,

One foot after the other, she climbed the steep, narrow stairway. Then why was she afraid to let him get close to her? Blood rushed in her ears, roaring against the icy wall enclosing her heart. She stopped on the fifth step, pushing the persistent nudge away. She knew the answer to her question. Nothing would change until she forgave Elam and Laurette. But she couldn't…she just couldn't.

Chapter Nineteen

Levi didn't look at Ruthy at breakfast the next morning, but he caught her hand in his as she placed his coffee in front of him, giving it a brief squeeze before releasing it.

With a kitchen full of family and the noise they made, it was the only way he could ask her to forgive his behavior last night. He had bolted out of the house like a skittish rooster.

He had moved too quickly, he realized that. She wasn't ready to hear how he really felt about her, and yet all night thoughts of her had filled his head, chasing sleep away. His bed had never felt so empty. But he was a patient man. God would open her heart to him, he was sure of that, and it would be in His time and His way.

He sipped his coffee and listened to the children's conversations. To his left, Martha and Waneta whispered together over Nancy's head, most likely about some boy, the way they were giggling. Nellie concentrated on her oatmeal, while on her other side Sam had finished his cereal and was digging into his scrambled eggs doused with ketchup.

Levi took the jar of ketchup from Elias and poured it over his own eggs and potatoes. He glanced up at Ruthy as he did it, enjoying the look on her face. She had never heard of eating eggs this way until she came to live here, but she soon learned to put a jar of ketchup on the table at breakfast. That didn't stop her from showing him what she thought about the practice, though. He took a bite and winked at her.

Ach, she was pretty when she blushed like that.

"*Dat,* when will you start the plowing?" James asked. His face was eager, and Levi knew why.

"Not for a few weeks yet, son. The fields are much too wet, you know that."

"But you need my help today, don't you?"

"James, you're not getting out of school today. You only have a few years left, and then you'll be home to help full-time." James's face fell. "But when I do start the plowing, I'll need your help, for sure. Both you and Nathan, whether it's a school day or not."

"Me too, *Dat?*" Nine-year-old David looked at him even though he got a sharp nudge from James when he asked.

"*Ne,* son, not this year. This is James's first year. You'll be able to help with the plowing after you turn eleven."

At the end of the bench, Jesse looked at James with wide eyes and Levi chuckled to himself. The boy was watching his older brothers grow up before his eyes. But soon enough Jesse would be the one looking for a courting buggy and shooting up out of his trouser legs. They grow up fast. Too fast.

Levi finished his eggs and sausage, mopping up the last of the ketchup with a biscuit. After the Bible reading and morning prayers, the family would scatter, most to school, while he and the boys would go out to their work in the barn and Ruthy and Waneta would stay in the house.

What a difference from only a few years ago when there were so many little ones! Salome would fall into bed exhausted at the end of each day, but what joy filled her eyes each and every night as they shared the day's events before falling to sleep. He missed having little ones around. Would he ever be blessed with more children?

He glanced at Ruthy, sitting quietly at the other end of the table while she waited for him to begin. She looked up, gave him a tremulous smile and then turned to silence the little boys before they started a new conversation. The restlessness he had been feeling turned into an ache of longing. Did she ever desire more children? Her own little ones?

Patience. He would wait patiently until the time was right. She would come around.

The scholars hadn't been home from school for long that afternoon when Ruthy heard the boys shouting in the yard.

"What in the world is that?" Waneta looked up from the table where she had been cutting some trouser material.

Ruthy looked over the curtains. A man was walking up the lane from the road—an *Englischer*. He waved at the boys running toward him.

"It's Jack Davenport! He's come back."

Waneta joined her at the window. "Do you think he'll stay for a few days like he did last time?"

"I certainly hope so. We put clean sheets on the bed in the front room after *Mam* and *Daed* went home, *ja?*"

Ruthy opened the back door while Waneta quickly gathered up the sewing things and put them away. The man walking toward the house with Levi was a changed Jack. He wore new clothes, and his face was clean and shaven.

When he saw her waiting in the doorway, he covered the last few feet of sidewalk with a bound. Standing on the step below her, he took off his hat. "Good afternoon, Mrs. Zook. I hear congratulations are in order."

Ruthy looked over Jack's head at Levi's beaming face. "Thank you, Mr. Davenport. I'm so glad to see you again. Please come in for some coffee."

"Oh, yes, ma'am." Ruthy stepped back as he walked into the kitchen. When he reached the middle of the room, he turned in a circle, breathing deeply. Then he grinned when he saw the family watching him. "There's nothing that smells so good as your kitchen, Mrs. Zook. I've surely missed it while I've been away."

Supper was filled with lively conversation as Jack told them about his travels to California.

"Did you see the ocean?" asked James.

"I sure did. Went swimming in it, too."

"In the winter?" Sam's eyes were round as he gazed at Jack.

"Sure enough. It's warm there all year round. But the most important thing—" Jack turned to Levi "—is that I found a church there. I'm not a homeless wanderer anymore."

The table blurred as the emotion-strained words worked their way to Ruthy's heart. That was the difference in Jack.

"Why did you leave, then, if you found a home there?" Elias leaned forward in his seat.

Jack smiled, looking from one face to the other. "My home isn't in California. I have a heavenly home, just like your father told me about. It took a lot of thinking and the teaching of a good preacher to understand what he meant, but the Lord finally got through this thick skull of mine. I had to come by and tell you."

"Where are you going now?" asked Nathan.

Jack looked down at his plate, and then back at Nathan. "I'm going back to Boston, to find out if my mother is still alive." He cleared his throat. "I've been gone for eight years, and I'm not sure what I'll find when I get there, but if Mother is still there, she deserves to know what happened to me."

The rest of the evening passed quickly, and after the children were in bed, Levi, Ruthy and Jack sat in the front room, sharing the last of the pie from supper.

"Will you be able to stay a few days?" Levi scraped the final crumbs of the cherry pie from his plate with the side of his fork.

"I'd like to, but no." Jack set his plate on the side table. "I can't stay anywhere too long. There's this urge to get home that keeps pushing at me." His voice dropped. "I'm afraid I'll be too late."

"Is there something wrong? Is your mother ill?" Ruthy's voice caught.

Jack shook his head. "I have no idea. It isn't just that I haven't gone back to visit, I haven't been in touch with Mother or anyone. As far as they know, I'm dead."

"Why? Why would you let them think that?" Levi leaned forward in his chair.

"I guess I was too ashamed." Jack didn't look at either of them. "At first, I was ashamed at what I had done. I had squandered our family's money…and I've asked myself over and over if there was something I could have done to save my brother. And then Mother…" Jack broke off. His shoulders shrugged. "Mother told me she never wanted to see me again. She blames me for all of it, I know."

Ruthy ate the last bite of her pie and set the plate on the table next to her chair. Jack was too ashamed to even ask for his mother's forgiveness?

Levi looked at Ruthy, then back to Jack. "For sure, she can't blame you even now, can she? Don't you think she would be glad to see you again?"

Jack shook his head. "I don't know. But I'm willing to try."

Ruthy looked at Jack's clean-shaven face, his handsome profile. All of the signs that he had been a troubled man were gone, but it still took all of his courage to ask his mother's forgiveness. After all these years, would she be able to see past her own hurt and anger to see how sorry he was for what had happened? Surely she wouldn't hold the past against him now.

"My life is so much better now than it was a couple months ago," Jack said. "But there's still this one thing… I need my mother's forgiveness. That's the most important thing to me right now. But it's so hard to ask when I know how much I hurt her."

Ruthy's fingers suddenly grew cold in the warm room. Wasn't that almost the same thing *Mam* had said about Laurette? Had Laurette gone through the same anguish as Jack when she wrote to her, asking for her forgiveness?

Watching Jack's face, the shadowed look in his eyes,

the icy wall surrounding Ruthy's heart cracked. *Ach, Laurette, what have I done to you?*

She knew what she must do. She must write to Laurette tonight, before it was too late.

Ruthy held her breath as she lifted another scoop of litter from the henhouse floor and headed for the door. Her eyes smarted from the ammonia, but once out in the fresh air she could take a deep breath again. This was her least favorite of all the spring chores, but it was over quickly.

"Do you think the chickens are thankful when we clean their house for them?" Waneta whooshed out her breath as she followed Ruthy to the compost heap with her own load.

"Chickens are so scatterbrained, I doubt if they even notice." Ruthy set her pitchfork into the soft ground of the dormant garden and wiped her forehead with her sleeve. "We have a nice warm day for the work though, *ja?*"

"*Ja,* for sure." Waneta poked around on the other side of the compost heap with a stick. "Look here! The rhubarb is beginning to come up."

Ruthy joined her and spied the curling leaves as Waneta moved winter debris aside with her stick. "For sure, spring is here to stay."

"And before we know it, the asparagus will be coming up."

Waneta went to the far side of the garden while Ruthy laughed. "*Ne,* you know we won't see asparagus until at least May."

"You're right." Waneta straightened up and tossed her stick away. "But I get so anxious. There's nothing like fresh asparagus." She looked past Ruthy and shaded her eyes against the afternoon sun. "Someone's coming. It looks like your friend who was here on Monday."

"Elam?" Ruthy turned to follow Waneta's gaze. For sure, there was Elam, alighting from the buggy and striding up the back steps to the door. He pounded on it, and then looked around to the barn, finally sighting Ruthy by the garden. Ruthy's heart sank. What could he want?

"Ruthy," Elam said as she met him at the edge of the garden, his voice broken. He handed her a yellow paper. "It's Laurette…"

Ruthy took the paper from him, a Western Union telegram. Her hands shook as she read the brief message. *Wife dead. Baby fine. Come home.*

Laurette…

"Ruthy, you have to help me." Elam's face was white, his eyes dark and flat. "What am I going to do?"

Laurette was dead? She couldn't be…she couldn't.

"Come with me. I can't go back alone." Elam grabbed for her hand, clung to it. "Please, Ruthy."

Go home? Now? "Levi isn't here, and I have to talk to him first."

"The train leaves in just over an hour. Ruthy, please…"

She looked at Elam, his face desperate. Laurette was gone, but Elam needed her, and she had to make her decision now.

Ruthy turned to Waneta. "I must go home, they need me there. Will you explain to your *daed?* I'll only be gone for a few days, maybe a week…." Waneta broke into a trot to follow her as she hurried into the house. Elam went before her to open the door.

"*Ja,* I guess. Martha and I can do the work while you're gone."

Ruthy stopped in the kitchen and gave Waneta a quick hug. "I know you can. You'll take good care of your *daed,* just like you did before I got here." Elam stood in the doorway, his hat in his hands. "Give Elam something to eat while I pack my bag, *ja?*"

She hurried to the *Dawdi Haus* and pulled her bag out from under the bed. She folded her good dress, put in her extra *kapp* and her hairbrush and then fastened the carryall. Satisfied the *Dawdi Haus* was orderly, Ruthy hurried into the kitchen again. Waneta had made sandwiches and put them in a bag. Ruthy threw on her shawl and bonnet while Elam took her bag to the buggy. She kissed Waneta's cheeks.

"You take care of yourself and the family, *ja?*"

"*Ja.*" Waneta's eyes were wet. "You hurry back home."

"For sure, I will. As soon as I can."

With a glance at the clock, Ruthy gave Waneta one last hug. "That one is for the rest of the children." She ran out to the buggy where Elam waited, barely taking her seat before he had the horse off down the road toward Shipshewana.

Chapter Twenty

"She said she'd be gone a week at the most," Waneta said, spreading butter on slices of bread as she made sandwiches.

Levi put seven apples into the lunch basket, followed by some cookies in a tin box. Martha wrapped each sandwich as Waneta finished it and he stacked them at the top of the basket.

"But it's been more than a week," Martha said.

"Lots more than a week." Jesse carried his plate to the sink.

Levi closed the lunch basket and handed it to Nathan as he went out the door into a pouring spring rain with the others just in time to meet the school bus at the end of their lane. Without Ruthy, the morning routine was gone. This morning, like every morning since last Tuesday, had been chaos.

He poured himself another cup of coffee and sat at the table while Waneta started on the dishes. Elias had Sam with him in the barn where they were starting the chore of cleaning out the cowshed for the spring. He should be out there helping them, but he didn't want to move. After his coffee was gone, he took a sip.

"When do you think she'll be back?" Waneta opened the reservoir and ladled hot water into the dishpan.

"I don't know." Levi rubbed his eyes with one hand. "That's all she said when she left, that she'd be back?"

"Elam gave her a paper to read, and then she told me she had to go home."

With him. She left with Elam. The reminder made him burn all over again.

Levi drained his cup and took it to the sideboard with the rest of the breakfast dishes.

"You're doing a *wonderful-gut* job taking care of us while she's gone, Waneta."

"It isn't the same without Ruthy—without *Mam*." Waneta kept her head down as she swished the dish rag around each plate. "How long do we wait, *Dat?* Should I go after her?"

"*Ne,* daughter. We know she'll return when she can."

Levi stepped onto the porch and shrugged on his coat. He clamped on his hat and hunched his shoulders against the rain as he made the journey to the barn. He waved to the boys working in the cowshed and then went on to the workshop door.

He shook the rain off as he stepped in and shivered at the chill. Lighting a fire in the small stove, he took his seat on the stool at the workbench. He picked up the harness he had been soaping the day before, but kept his gaze out the window. Every day this week he had sat here, waiting for her to return, except after dinner when he drove into Shipshewana to meet the daily train from the east. The train she might be on.

No letter, no message, no Ruthy with her face pressed against the glass window watching for him on the platform.

He was a fool to wait, thinking he had time to court her. He should have told her he loved her. He should have insisted that she live as his wife, not his house-keeper. He should have done something to keep her from going.

Levi stared down the lane toward the road, the harness forgotten in his hands.

It had been eleven days since she had left. Eleven days. What should he do? Go after her?

He needed advice.

Leaving the harness, he banked the small fire in the stove and went into the barn. He brought Champ out of his stall and hitched him to the buggy. Elias came into the barn as he worked.

"*Dat?* We've done as much as we can in the cowshed today. Should we start on the plow?"

"*Ja,* you know what to do. Look it over, grease the moving parts, and make a note of anything that needs replacing. I'm going to John Stoltzfus's, and then to get the mail. I'll be back after dinner."

The rain let up some as the horse trotted down the muddy road, but a drizzle remained as he pulled into the Stoltzfus barnyard. Levi tied the horse to the hitching rail and went into the barn. John was repairing his manure spreader.

"A good rainy-day job, *ja?*" John said, laying down his grease pot and wiping his hands on a rag.

"*Ja,* for sure."

"Would you like to come in the house for some coffee? Elizabeth has some pie."

"*Ne, denki.*" Levi shifted. He didn't want to have

this conversation at all, but for sure not in front of anyone else.

John looked at him closely. "What's on your mind, Levi?"

"It's Ruth. She went back to Lancaster County for a visit, but I haven't heard from her since she left."

"You could write to her family. She's staying with them, isn't she?"

Levi glanced at John. If he wanted the older man's advice, he'd have to tell him everything.

"I don't know where she's staying. A man came from Lancaster County to visit one day, and then a few days later he showed up again. I wasn't at home, and when I got back I found she had left with him. She packed everything in her bag and left."

John sighed and rubbed the back of his neck. Levi couldn't look at John's face, afraid of the condemnation he'd see there—condemnation for the woman he had married.

"Did she say anything? Leave a note for you?"

"She told Waneta she'd be back in a week at the most."

"Do you have reason to think she's not coming back?"

Levi thought of the possessive look on Elam's face the day he stopped by their home. The man knew Ruthy, probably better than Levi did, and he was the one who had taken her away. Had they run off together? Abandoned this man's wife and family as thoughtlessly as Ruthy had abandoned them?

"I don't know, John. I wanted to ask what you think—should I go to Pennsylvania? Should I go look for her?"

John looked at him, compassion in his eyes. "If it was my Elizabeth, I would. I know she wouldn't stay away without word unless there was a good reason. I would go to find out what's going on."

Levi nodded, looking at the floor. "I don't know how long it will take, and it's almost time for the spring plowing...."

"Don't worry about that. I'll give your boys a hand if you're not back in time."

Relief washed through Levi. He had a plan, action he could take. He shook John's hand. "*Denki.* I'll leave on tomorrow's train, and I'll keep in touch."

Ruthy lifted Grace from her cradle, a bottle of warm milk ready for the hungry baby. She sat in the rocking chair and snuggled the little mite close. Even so simple a thing as feeding a baby was comforting. She rocked the chair gently.

"Is she still eating well?" *Mam* asked from her own chair where her hands were busy with her knitting.

"*Ja,* she guzzles it down like a bum lamb." Ruthy smiled as Grace sucked on the bottle, her dark eyes locked on Ruthy's face.

"Two weeks old tomorrow." *Mam* paused in her knitting to count stitches.

Two weeks since Laurette had died, leaving Grace alone.

Ruthy had arrived the next day with Elam. He had taken one look at the baby, too small, born too early, and handed her to Ruthy.

"You take her," he had said. "I don't know what to do with a baby."

Mam had been with Laurette when she died. On

the bedside table, Ruthy had found the letter she wrote the night Jack Davenport had been to their house. She hadn't been too late. Laurette knew she had forgiven her before she passed on.

So *Mam* and Ruthy had brought the baby home, and they had nursed the frail little girl together. Now she was thriving, if still a bit too small.

Ruthy held the baby close, breathing in her fragrance, and searched her face for something of Laurette in her. The shape of her nose, perhaps. And she definitely had Laurette's chin, determined and a bit pointy. Her eyes were still a mystery, but as much as Ruthy searched, she found very little to remind her of Elam. It was as if he was as distant from this baby in looks as he had been since she was born.

Grace finished the bottle and Ruthy lifted her to her shoulder to burp her. With every little thing she did to care for this baby, the icy wall in her heart broke down. With every diaper change, every bottle, Ruthy had Laurette in her thoughts. If she had only answered Laurette's letter earlier—if only she could have shared Laurette's hopes and dreams for the baby—but no one had guessed that Laurette wouldn't live to see her daughter.

"Have you heard from Levi?" *Mam* asked.

"Ne." Levi and the children seemed so distant now that she was home again. She longed to go back, but what would she do with Grace?

"Should you write to him, tell him what has happened?"

"Ja, I should. But I don't know what to say. Elam hasn't been by to see Grace at all. I know he wanted

me to care for her, but for how long? Once he gets over his grief, surely he'll want her back."

"Will he be able to raise her on his own?"

"I don't know." Her Elam, the boy she had planned to marry, had been adventurous and carefree. At the funeral he had looked like he was lost in a swirling maze with no end.

"I'm going to lie down for a bit." *Mam* folded her knitting and put it in her basket.

"Once Grace is asleep, I may lie down myself."

Mam made her way to the bedroom and Ruthy patted the baby's back as she rocked her, listening to her soft sucking sounds as she found her fist. She closed her eyes, letting the chair's motion and the soft baby sounds relax her. Once Grace burped, then they could both take a nap.

At the sound of a knock on the door, Ruthy rose with the baby still on her shoulder.

Passing from the front room to the kitchen, she stopped short when she saw Elam standing on the other side of the screen door. He stood on the step, his clothes rumpled and his hands dirty. He rubbed them on his trousers as he saw the direction of Ruthy's gaze.

"Hello, Elam. Where have you been? I've been worried about you."

"Ruthy, I need to talk to you."

"*Ja,* come in. We have some pie left from dinner."

Elam looked past her into the kitchen, and then glanced to the barn.

"*Ne,* I want…"

Grace stirred on Ruthy's shoulder, catching his attention.

"I thought you could come to my house…to see

what I got ready for the baby." He shifted his feet and glanced at the barn again. "You can make sure I did things right."

Ruthy hesitated. When she and Elam had been courting they had taken many walks down the farm lane between the fields and through the woods to Elam's farm, but now they weren't courting. She was Levi's wife. "I'll come outside to talk with you, but I can't go far. The baby will need changing soon."

"Bring it along." His feet shifted again, and this time he peered past her, into the house. "I have diapers. I mean, Laurette got things ready, right?"

"I need to tell *Mam*...."

Elam shook his head. "You don't need to. We won't be gone that long."

She hesitated again. Elam didn't seem to be in any condition to be taking care of a baby, but maybe she was just being too protective. With *Mam* napping, she didn't want to disturb her. She could go with Elam and be back before *Mam* awoke. She'd even be back before *Daed* returned from her brother's farm down the road.

She nodded, and Elam stepped back so Ruthy could come out. He took her free hand and led her to the path that led behind the barn and across the fields toward his house. Once they got past the chicken coop to the pasture fence, out of sight of the house, he slowed his pace.

"I'm glad you're here, Ruthy. I need you so much."

"I'm happy to be able to help. The baby is so sweet. I'm calling her Grace—I know that's the name Laurette would have chosen for her."

Elam waved his hand, pushing away her words. "I don't care what you named the baby." He turned as he walked, grinning at her. "You're a good *mam* for her, for sure."

Ruthy smiled, remembering how Grace fixed her eyes on her face while she fed or talked to the baby. "How could anyone not love her? She looks more like Laurette every day, you know."

"I don't want to talk about Laurette." Elam pulled at her hand, hurrying her across the back field, leaving the worn path and heading toward the woods.

"Where are we going?" Ruthy tried to pull her hand back, but he held it tightly. "This isn't the way to your house."

"It's…it's a shortcut I made. You'll see."

He led her into the woods and then turned again, heading in the direction of his house.

"Elam, I can walk better if you let go of my hand."

"I'm not letting go of you." He grasped her hand tighter, making her wince. "I'm just doing what I should have done before you ever left us. Before I ever started going out with Laurette."

She tried to dig her heels into the soft dirt, but he pulled hard. Grace protested, and Ruthy stopped struggling to keep the baby calm.

"What do you mean?"

Her stomach churned when he turned to her, his eyes almost glowing in the shadowed woods.

"I never loved Laurette, just like you don't love your husband." Ruthy started to protest, but he squeezed her hand tighter. "We could be happy together, couldn't we? Just like we planned?"

Ruthy tried to pull back. She had never seen Elam like this, his face flushed beneath the short beard. Both of his hands grasped at hers, tightening as she tried to pull away.

"Elam, think about what you're saying. I'm married, and whether I love my husband or not, nothing will change that. It's too late."

"*Ne,* don't you see? We could move away from here and start over again. No one would know where we went." He grinned then, with the same enthusiasm he had shown when they had discussed their future together all those years they had been courting. "I'm making a name for myself in the hootenanny show in Wheeling. They think I could make it big in movies, just like Gene Autry. We could go to Hollywood and start a new life together out there."

Ruthy's feet turned cold. "What do you mean? You're singing on the radio?"

"Yeah." He used the *Englisch* slang she had always avoided. "I'm really good on the guitar...."

"You're talking about leaving the church."

"Of course." He moved closer to her and she recoiled. "As far as the church is concerned, you'll always be married to that old man, but that doesn't matter to us, does it? You know we'll be happy together."

"Elam, I will never do what you're asking. I would never forsake God for anyone, even you." Ruthy's breath caught as a sudden thought swirled through her mind. "What about Grace? Would you take her away from our faith? Would you want your daughter to grow up outside the church?"

Elam's face grew harder as she spoke. "Ruthy, you don't think any of this really matters, do you? What matters is you and me." He pulled at her hand again, hurrying her along. "We will be happy together, I know we will."

"*Ne,* Elam. I can't, I won't leave Levi and our family." She tried to resist him, but he was too strong for her. "We will never be happy if you do this thing. You can find another girl who would be glad to marry you. You can have more children, brothers and sisters for Grace."

"That's not the kind of life I want, Ruthy. I'm not spending my life scratching in the dirt for a few potatoes. I'm going to make it big, and I want you to come with me."

He pulled at her again as they reached the top of a rise. Below them, at the edge of the woods, was a truck. When they reached it, he opened the driver's door, pushing Ruthy inside in front of him. She got into the truck, knowing that the only way to get away from him now would be to fight him, and Grace could get hurt. Maybe, somehow, she could talk some sense into him.

The truck started up with a roar, and Elam put it into gear. He sped up quickly, and Ruthy sat, helpless, as he drove her farther and farther from her home.

Chapter Twenty-One

Levi hopped off the wagon that had brought him to the Mummert farm from Bird-in-Hand, waving *denki* to the farmer. Even the *Englischers* knew Ezekiel Mummert, and he had no trouble finding a ride from the train station.

Brushing off his trousers and straightening his coat, he took in the farm in front of him. From the cozy, white frame house to the lofty dairy barn behind it, the entire place spoke of a hard-working farmer. But was Ruthy here?

When he knocked on the side door, Naomi came rushing to answer it, but she stopped when she saw it was him.

"*Ach,* Levi! Levi!" Her face crumpled into tears.

Dropping his bag on the step, he pulled the screen door open and grabbed Naomi before she collapsed onto the floor.

"What's wrong? What has happened?"

Ezekiel appeared in the doorway to the front of the house, his shoulders slumped.

Levi helped Naomi to a chair at the kitchen table. "Is Ruthy here? Have you seen her?"

His father-in-law shook his head, taking a seat next to his wife and cradling her in his arms as she wept. "She has disappeared. She's gone."

Levi took the chair across the table from Ezekiel, looking into his face, trying to understand.

"She was here?"

"*Ja,* until this afternoon. I was visiting our son, and Naomi was asleep. When she woke, Ruthy was gone, along with the baby."

"What baby?"

He listened as Ezekiel told him the story of Laurette's death, the baby Elam had apparently abandoned, and how, until this afternoon, everything seemed to be going well.

Levi pushed himself away from the table, pacing back and forth in the kitchen. She had been here. If he had been a day earlier... But perhaps she had gotten word of his coming and had run away from him?

Ne, that couldn't be. But where was she? Where would she have gone?

"Did she pack her bag? Take her things?"

Naomi shook her head. "*Ne,* nothing in her room has been touched. She didn't even take a bottle for the baby, or a blanket."

"You've looked all over the farm?"

"*Ja,*" Ezekiel said, nodding. "The barn, the outbuildings, the fields...even the well. There was no sign of her anywhere." The older man rubbed his hand over his face. "Our sons are coming, to help with the search. She can't have just vanished."

"Was she worried about anything? Expecting anyone? Did she have any plans?"

Naomi sniffed, controlling her tears. "She was worried about you, that she had been away too long, but she didn't want to leave until she knew what Elam was going to do."

Elam again. "Why did she need to wait for him?"

"He had asked her to care for the baby, and then left. But we thought sure he was coming back to his farm and his daughter. She didn't want to leave the wee little thing without knowing what kind of home Elam was going to give her."

The door burst open as three men came in, all the same height and build as Ezekiel. They could only be Ruthy's brothers. After a quick introduction, Matthias, the oldest brother, stuck his hands in his suspenders.

"We need to start looking off the farm. Could she have gone to a friend's house?"

"*Ja,* that could be." Ezekiel named a few friends, and the two younger brothers ran out the door, ready to call on those families.

Levi couldn't get Elam out of his mind. "Could she... could she have gone to Elam's?"

Matthias nodded. "She could have." He shot a look at Levi. "You'll come with me?"

Levi nodded and they headed out the door.

"We'll check quickly, and then come back here. Someone needs to stay here in case she shows up again." Matthias waited until he got an answering nod from Ezekiel, and then set out at a jog.

He led the way along a path that passed behind the barn. "This isn't a good welcome for you, to find Ruthy missing."

"I only want to know what's happened. To know that she's safe."

"And the baby, too. She loves that little bum lamb of hers. She'd do anything to protect her."

Levi nodded as they jogged along. He could imagine Ruthy's fierce devotion to her friend's baby. Matthias picked up speed as they came to a field, passing a side trail that led toward a stand of timber. Levi stopped to look up the trail. Bruised grass showed someone had passed that way recently.

"Matthias," he called. The other man turned around.

"Ja," he said, nodding as he examined the trail. "Someone has been this way today. Let's follow this and see where it takes us."

Just inside the edge of the woods, Levi stopped to pick up a rag that had been caught on a bramble. Not a rag, a diaper that had been used as a burp cloth. He held it up to Matthias.

"It looks like she's been this way. Are there any other signs?"

Matthias pointed out some scuff marks in the dirt, and they continued following the path to the top of a rise, and then down to the edge of a road. The trail ended there.

Levi paced along the edge of the road and back.

"She got into an automobile." He rubbed the back of his neck. Where could she be? And why?

"Not just her. She wasn't alone." Matthias pointed to the scuff marks. "There were two people here."

"Does Elam have an automobile?"

Matthias nodded. "He has a truck. He claims it isn't his, but too many have seen him driving it for him to be able to deny it."

"Do you… Do you think she went with him willingly?"

The other man gave him a level look. "How well do you know your wife?"

Levi shook his head, helpless. "I thought I knew her, but…"

"I know my sister. If she left with Elam, she had a good reason. She has the baby with her, and I wouldn't be surprised to find out she's protecting her, at all costs."

Levi was sick. What kind of danger could she be in? Then a nagging suspicion flooded his thoughts—what if she weren't in danger at all? Could she have gotten into that truck willingly?

Dashing his hand across his face, Levi tried to wipe the thought away, but it persisted. It couldn't be true, could it? Not his Ruthy.

Ruthy sat in the corner of the truck's passenger seat, as far from Elam as she could. Grace slept peacefully, but for how long? And then what would she do? She had no clean diapers, no bottles, nothing to take care of the baby.

Elam hadn't stopped talking, but she had stopped listening. His talk of going to California, making it "big in Hollywood"—whatever that meant—alarmed her. He couldn't be serious, could he? Was he going to drive all the way there?

Ruthy chanced a sideways glance at Elam. His eyes on the road, he drove with his left hand on the steering wheel, gesturing with his right. He was animated and excited, not noticing her discomfort.

He drove on back roads, where the houses were scarce. Eventually they would come to a town, though, and she might be able to find help. Would anyone notice an Amish woman in a truck?

Elam drove around Lancaster, avoiding the city, but once they crossed the Susquehanna River, Ruthy was lost. She had never been this far from home except by train. The afternoon was waning, and Grace was beginning to stir. Her diaper was soiled and it was near her feeding time.

"Elam." He didn't respond, so Ruthy raised her voice. "Elam?"

"What?" He barked the word. He never liked being interrupted.

"Grace is going to be hungry soon, and she needs a diaper change. Is there somewhere we can get some milk, and something to use for a diaper?"

He glanced over at her and the baby. "Yeah, I guess we have to. We'll stop at a store when we come to a town. You gotta speak English, though. That way they'll think we're Mennonite and won't think twice about the truck."

Elam was still speeding along back roads with no town in sight when Grace's crying turned to screaming. Ruthy tried to keep her quiet, but the baby was hungry, and there was nothing she could do to pacify her. Elam drove faster and faster along the gravel road, but there was no town, no store, not even a farmhouse. Finally he skidded to a stop by the side of the road.

"I can't stand that noise." He pounded on the steering wheel and yelled, "You've got to make her stop, or I will."

"She's hungry," Ruthy shouted back at him. Grace's crying filled the cab of the truck. "She won't stop until she gets something to eat."

Elam reached under the seat, pulling out a dirty bottle with brown liquid in it. "Give her some of this. It'll keep her quiet."

Ruthy moved the baby as far away from him as she could. "That's whiskey. I won't give her that. She needs milk."

He eyed the bottle, and then the baby, and stuck the bottle back under the seat.

"If the brat's going to be this much trouble, then leave her here. I only wanted you to come, anyway."

"Leave her here?" Ruthy echoed his words without thinking as she looked out the windows. The road they were on went between two empty fields. She couldn't see a house anywhere.

"Yeah. Just put her by the road. Somebody will find her." He shifted his leg and the engine roared.

"You can't be serious. She isn't a piece of baggage or an animal that you can leave behind when it becomes a bother. She's helpless. She needs someone to take care of her."

Elam glowered at her, his brows dark and heavy over his eyes. Had she ever loved him? Or had he changed so much in just a few short months?

"Then you get out with her."

Ruthy looked around them again. It was getting dark and the road was still deserted.

Elam reached across her and lifted the door handle.

"Go on. Get out. You won't leave the brat here, and you can't take it with you, so get out. It was a mistake to think this would work. I'll do better on my own."

She got down from the truck, Grace screaming in her ear. Elam pulled the door shut and gunned the motor. Red taillights disappeared in the dust kicked up by the truck, and he was gone.

Chapter Twenty-Two

Levi accepted the cup of coffee someone handed him and took a sip of the bitter liquid. Ezekiel, Naomi, Matthias and the rest of Ruthy's family sat around the kitchen table, exhausted and defeated, while some of the neighbor women worked to feed the searchers.

Two days. It had been two days and there was still no sign of her. It seemed every Amish family from Lancaster to Ephrata had joined in on the search, but there had been no glimpse of Elam's truck, Ruthy or the baby.

With nothing more to discuss, no more ideas to pursue, they sat silently. Naomi worried a handkerchief in her hands, turning and twisting it over and over.

When the sound of an automobile drifted through the open window, Levi and the other men jumped up to look out the window. Two men in uniforms were emerging from the white vehicle. The state police.

No one had informed the police of Ruthy's disappearance, had they? How did they end up here?

Levi followed Ezekiel to the front door. The policeman who knocked looked at a card in his hand. "I'm

Officer Charles, this is Williams. We're looking for the Nafziger residence."

Ezekiel stepped back so the two men could come in. "Elam Nafziger is our neighbor, on the next farm east. Have you been there?"

"Yes, but no one is around. The place looks empty."

Ezekiel exchanged glances with Levi.

"Why are you looking for him?" Levi asked. "Is there some kind of trouble?"

The policeman cleared his throat. "Is there someone we could talk to? Next of kin?"

"Elam is a widower, and his parents passed on several years ago." Ezekiel shrugged his shoulders. "I suppose I'm about as close to him as anyone. Why do you ask?"

The policeman handed the card to Ezekiel. "There was an accident, and the man carrying this driver's license was injured. He was wearing Amish clothes, but he had been driving a Ford truck. Could this be the same Elam Nafziger?"

Ezekiel rubbed at the blood on the card with his thumb. "He was injured, you say? Will he... Will he survive?"

Officer Charles nodded. "We think he'll be fine, eventually. He has some broken ribs and a concussion. He'll have to stay in the hospital for a while, but he should recover."

Levi stared at the card in Ezekiel's hand. If Elam had been in an accident, what had happened to Ruthy?

"Was there anyone with him in the truck?" Levi's voice cracked and he cleared his throat. "A young woman? A baby?"

The policeman looked at him, his eyebrows up. "No, he was alone. Was someone supposed to be with him?"

Levi looked at Ezekiel, waiting until the older man nodded. *Ja,* it was time to ask for help, even from *Englischers.*

"My wife... We think she was with Elam in his truck."

The policeman shook his head. "We didn't find any evidence that anyone else was involved in the accident. Either she wasn't with him, or she left the vehicle sometime before."

"Where did it happen?"

One of the policemen went back to the car for a map, and everyone gathered around the kitchen table as they spread it out. Officer Charles stuck a thick finger on a spot on the other side of the Susquehanna River, southeast of York.

"It was out in the middle of nowhere. He had gone off a bridge into a culvert. That's why the wreck wasn't spotted right away."

"So if Ruthy was with him, before the accident, she must be somewhere in here." Levi drew his finger along the crooked roads between the spot Officer Charles had pointed out, across the bridge in Columbia, and back to Lancaster.

"Then let's start looking." Matthias grabbed Levi's shoulder. "You and I can take my buggy and we'll search the roads all the way to the site of the accident."

"You won't cover much ground in a horse and buggy," Officer Charles said. "We can use our cruiser, and we'll contact other state police in the area. We'll need a description of both the woman and the baby."

"I'm going with you," Levi said. "I have to find her."

Officer Charles nodded, and Levi grabbed his hat and coat off the hook on the wall.

"We'll go together," Matthias said.

Levi grasped Matthias's arm in thanks. He could use the help of a brother on this search. The two of them squeezed into the backseat of the police car and Officer Williams started up the motor. Soon they were traveling faster than Levi would have thought possible. Lancaster flashed by in a haze of automobiles and buggies, and they were in open country again.

"We'll be crossing the river soon, and then we'll be in York County." Matthias spoke *Deitsch,* close to Levi's ear so he could be heard above the noise of the motor.

Levi nodded, and Matthias grasped his arm. "You have nothing to worry about. We'll find Ruthy and the baby."

When Levi only nodded again, Matthias leaned closer to him. "There's something else wrong, isn't there? Something you wouldn't tell *Mam* and *Daed.*"

Rubbing his hand over his beard, Levi considered how much he could tell Matthias. Over the last couple of days, the two of them had grown closer than he could have been with a brother of his own.

"Ruthy and I… Well, our marriage isn't all it could be."

Matthias nodded. "I thought that might be the case, when she showed up here with Elam."

"If…when we find her, I don't even know if she will want to come home with me. Ever since Elam stopped by our house three weeks ago, she's been different."

Matthias looked out the window, then turned back to Levi. "Did Ruthy tell you about Elam?"

"Was he the man she had planned to marry?"

"Elam courted her for years. Ruthy never would look at any other boy, from the time they were in school together. It seemed strange to me that years went by and Elam never got any closer to marrying her. I also didn't like the way he acted. He joined church at eighteen, but he never seemed to be part of it. Kneeling on the outside, but standing up on the inside, if you know what I mean."

Levi nodded. He had known others who had only made the appearance of joining church, but without a real love for the People or God.

"Then it was announced that he was marrying Laurette. Ruthy had no idea they had been dating, even though Laurette was almost part of the family since her *mam* died when she was so young. When it got out that Laurette was in the family way... Well, it was a hard way to find out that the two of them had been sneaking around behind her back all summer. Something seemed to die inside my sister."

"And that's when she saw my ad in *The Budget*."

"Ja." Matthias fell silent. They both watched out the window as the car sped across the bridge. The river stretched out beneath them.

"When she came back, after Laurette died, I saw a difference in her. Even though she was grieving for her friend, there was a joy that I hadn't seen since she was a little girl. I think it's because of you. She married you, and she loves her life. When she talked of her family in Indiana, she mentioned the children, but mostly it was 'Levi did this' and 'Levi did that.'"

Levi smiled in spite of his worry. He could hear her telling Matthias about the farm and the work there.

"If Ruthy went with Elam, there's one thing I know.

She didn't go willingly. He would have had to force her to go with him."

Levi glanced at Matthias. Ruthy's brother gave him a grim smile and squeezed his arm again. "She loves you, Levi, not him. She wouldn't leave you."

A knot that had been growing tighter inside his chest with each passing hour loosened with Matthias's assurance. They would find her, and he would take her home.

Another truck, but this one wasn't being driven by Elam. Between Ruthy and George, the farmer who was driving, sat Margie, the farmer's wife. Without their help, she wouldn't have known which way to turn after Elam left her by the side of the road. But they had taken her in after she had stumbled into their farmyard on that nightmarish evening two days ago.

Margie, a woman about *Mam's* age, had clucked and scolded like a mother hen, feeding Grace, finding some old diapers she could use, and finally bedding them both down in the spare room.

George hadn't been able to make a trip into town yesterday because of trouble with one of his sheep, but first thing this morning they set out for York and the police station there.

"I don't want the police involved," Ruthy had said. "I just want to find a way to get home."

George had held up his hand to stop her protests, his bushy gray mustache wiggling back and forth. "We need to tell them what happened to you. Your folks will be worried, and the police can get you home lickety-split."

So here she was, in another truck. Margie fussed over Grace as Ruthy thought about her next move. To get home to *Mam* and *Daed,* that had to be first. They must be worried to death about her, and at the same time they would be constantly praying. Had they asked the neighbors to search for her? Did they have any idea what had happened to her?

But then the next thing would be to go back to Indiana. To Levi. To her home. Now that she had been able to forgive Laurette and the icy rock that had taken over her heart was gone, it was time to start fresh with her husband. She loved him. The weeks away from him had softened her heart, for sure, but when she compared Elam to Levi…she didn't know how she could have ever loved Elam.

She had honored and respected Levi ever since she met him back in January on that snowy train platform, but somewhere along the way, love had crept in. She had to tell him she loved him. Perhaps, someday, he would come to love her, too.

George drove the truck into the outskirts of York, a huge city compared to Bird-in-Hand. Ruthy stared at all the automobiles on the streets and the tall buildings in the center of town. George parked the truck in front of a gray limestone police station and escorted them in.

He led the way to a high desk where a balding man in a police uniform sat. Ruthy forced herself to be calm. She wasn't used to dealing with so many *Englischers*.

The man behind the desk peered at Ruthy. "Well, what do we have here?"

Ruthy was glad when George spoke for her. "This girl has been separated from her family and needs to get back to them. Is there some way she could get a ride to Lancaster?"

The policeman smiled. "I think I can do better than

that. There are a couple of gentlemen here looking for her. They came in a few minutes ago, wanting to file a missing persons report on a woman with a baby, and their description fits her to a *T*."

Following the policeman down the hall, Ruthy wondered who the men could be. Elam? Or could it be *Daed?* Tears filled her eyes when she turned into an office and saw Matthias in front of her. He grabbed her in one of his bear hugs, lifting her off her feet.

"*Ach,* Matthias, how did you come to be here?"

"Not only me, Ruthy. Look who I brought with me."

As Matthias set her down, he spun her around as if they were playing "pin the tail on the donkey." Reaching out to grasp something, anything, to keep her balance, a familiar hand reached out to steady her. Levi?

She looked up into his face, and couldn't keep the tears back any longer. Even in front of all the people in the tiny office, Levi pulled her into his arms, letting her cry on his shoulder, holding her as if he were never going to let her go.

Chapter Twenty-Three

"How will we get home from the train station?" Ruthy asked, jiggling Grace on her shoulder.

Levi glanced out the window at the familiar Indiana landscape flashing by. "I sent a telegram to Elias when I bought the tickets back in Lancaster. If he got it in time, he'll be there to meet us. If not, we should be able to get a ride from someone."

"It will be good to get home."

Home. Even though he had only been away a few days, Levi felt the pull of his own kitchen, his own barn, his own bed. His family together. His stomach still clenched when he thought of how close he had come to losing Ruthy—what would he have told his children? But God had been watching over them, for sure.

"Here, let me hold Grace for a while. You must be tired." Levi reached for the baby, ignoring the stares of the Amish man across the aisle. It didn't matter that men didn't take care of babies. He did. He had taken care of his share of diapers and colic when his first two babies had been born, and he found he liked it. Grace would get just as much attention from him as he could give her.

He laid Grace on his chest and hummed under his breath. She settled in against him, mesmerized by the sound, as he cradled her tiny body in his hands. Such a wee mite of a thing, and yet it had been all he and Ruthy could do to keep her content on the train ride.

Levi glanced at Ruthy, and she smiled at him. "You have a way with little ones."

"I've had a lot of practice."

"*Ja,* you have."

"You have a way with babies, too, Ruthy, and with the older ones, as well. You always know just what they need."

"I always dreamed of having a big family. Lots of children…" She stopped and bit her lip, turning away from him to look out the window.

Levi leaned close to her, speaking so his words wouldn't carry to the other passengers. "So why did you put those conditions on our marriage? If we really lived as man and wife, we could be blessed with those children you wanted."

Ruthy turned to him, her eyes dark. "I didn't want to take Salome's place. I know you still love her, and I didn't want you to feel obligated… I know I'm not the woman you would choose to be your wife."

"Why not?" Levi's voice rose with his question and the man across the aisle glanced at them. He leaned close to Ruthy's ear, his cheek brushing her *kapp.* "Why wouldn't I choose you?"

Ruthy blushed. "I know I'm not attractive. You married me because I was available, and your children needed someone. I know you still love Salome, and I don't blame you. She must have been a wonderful wife and mother."

Grace had gone to sleep on Levi's chest. He shifted her so he could hold her with one arm while he turned Ruthy's face toward him with one finger. "Don't ever think you're not attractive." She tried to look away but he kept her facing him. "And you're right, I still love Salome, and I always will. But that doesn't have anything to do with us." He moved one finger to caress her cheek, then shifted his hand back to straighten the sleeping baby. "If there's anything I learned the last few days, it's just how much I need you. How much I love you."

Ruthy's eyes widened as he spoke, and a smile flashed, but then disappeared. She lowered her eyes. "Elam told me the same thing, Levi, and look what happened. How can I believe you?"

Levi felt rising anger against the man who had thrown this woman away like an old sock. "What Elam did was foolish and wrong, but I'm not Elam. I would never do anything to hurt you. You're my wife, and you will be for the rest of our lives." He lowered his voice again and took her hand in his. "I'm just glad I've been given a second chance to show you how much you mean to me."

She smiled again at his words, a smile that remained as she squeezed his hand in response and leaned her head against his shoulder.

Ruthy took Grace from Levi as the train approached Shipshewana and he gathered their bags. He kept meeting her eyes every few minutes, and once he even winked at her, sending shivers through her. Was this what it felt like to be truly married?

When the train came to a complete stop, Levi carried

the bags down the aisle to the door at the end of the car while Ruthy followed him with Grace.

"There's James," Levi said, bending to look through the window. "It looks like Elias got my wire."

Ruthy hurried behind Levi, anxious to see whomever was waiting for them on the platform. Levi stepped out of the car into the circle of his children and Ruthy watched, drinking in the sight of their reunion. All ten children had come to meet the train, and Ruthy couldn't wait to hug each one of them.

"What does *Mam* have?" Nancy asked, noticing Ruthy waiting on the steps.

"Children, I want you to meet your new sister." Levi helped Ruthy step down and they were both surrounded by the children.

"A new sister?" Jesse asked, his eyes wide.

"Where did you get her?" Nellie asked.

"Nellie, you know where people get babies," David said, and pushed past her to get a better look at the baby.

"But, you weren't..." Martha's face turned red. "I mean, this is a surprise, isn't it?"

"Let's all go and get in the buggy," Levi said, herding them all away from the train and the group of curious onlookers. "You'll all hear the whole story."

After they all crowded into the big family buggy, Ruthy watched the children's faces as Levi told them how Grace's mother had died, and her father had given the baby to them to raise. She was thankful he didn't say anything about Elam's actions after that, but focused on how much Grace needed them.

"Grace is our baby now," Levi said, "and she's as much of a gift from God as all of you were."

The children all nodded as Levi spoke, but Sam

leaned over Ruthy's shoulder. "I only have one question."

"Ja?"

"If you were going to get a new baby, why couldn't it be a boy?"

"I know why she's a girl," Nellie said. "With Grace we have five girls and six boys. We're almost even now."

"It's all right, Sam," James said. "It's good to have some of each. It's more fun that way."

"Well, just make sure the next one's a boy."

Levi looked sideways at Ruthy as the children talked about names for the next baby, but didn't make any comments as they continued home.

Ruthy watched the farms go by. Every one that she could name the owners of brought them closer to their own home. When they reached the farm and Levi pulled into the lane, Ruthy gazed at the big house with one addition leading into the next, all the way to her little *Dawdi Haus* tacked on the end.

Not her *Dawdi Haus* anymore. Butterflies danced in her stomach as she realized tonight she would not be sleeping in her own bed, but in Levi's, as his wife. She gazed at Grace's face, peaceful in sleep. It would be *wonderful-gut* for Grace to have a sister close in age.

"Tomorrow's a church Sunday, *ja?*" Ruthy turned slices of ham in the frying pan while Grace slept in the cot Levi had brought down from the attic when they had arrived home.

"Ja," Waneta said. She hummed a familiar tune as she opened a jar of pickled cauliflower.

"And I think someone's looking forward to the Singing tomorrow night."

Waneta glanced at her and smiled. "Ruthy... I mean, *Mam*..." She blushed and then turned back to putting the cauliflower into a dish next to the pickled beets. "I always look forward to the Singings."

"But more now that someone special brings you home afterward, *ja?*"

"What do you mean?" Martha asked, slicing potatoes. "I thought Elias always brought you home."

"*Ne,* not lately." Waneta's smile grew broader. "Elias has been taking someone else home now."

"So, who have you been riding with?"

"Can't you guess, Martha?" Ruthy said, putting the ham on a plate on the back of the stove to keep warm while she dumped the sliced potatoes into the big frying pan.

"Is it Reuben Stoltzfus?"

Waneta turned bright red. "Now you keep quiet, Martha, or I'll start telling stories on you."

Martha clamped her lips tight as she lifted a stack of plates out of the cupboard and took them to the table.

Ruthy stopped stirring the potatoes and gave Waneta's shoulders a hug. "He's a *wonderful-gut* young man."

"I think so, too." Waneta hugged her back. "I was afraid you weren't coming back when you were gone so long. I wanted to go after you and bring you home."

Ruthy stirred the potatoes again, turning the crisp brown sides up while the pale sides sizzled in the bacon grease. "I'm sorry I left in such a hurry, but I was so upset about Laurette...."

Waneta glanced at the cot near Ruthy's chair where Grace lay. "God knew what He was doing when He took you back there, didn't He? Who else would be as good of a *mam* to Grace than you?"

"I never thought of it that way." Ruthy stirred the potatoes again, remembering that terrible train ride to Lancaster with Elam, knowing it was too late to ask for Laurette's forgiveness. "I only felt like I had let everyone down—you, your *daed,* Laurette…"

"But it turned out right anyway, didn't it?"

"Ja." Ruthy gave Waneta a smile as Levi and the boys came in for supper. *"Ja,* everything has turned out just right."

When Ruthy came back downstairs after tucking the little ones in for the night, she paused at the bottom step, drinking in the sight before her. Levi sat in his chair in the circle of lamplight, holding Grace as he held her bottle for her and sang a hymn in his quiet, rumbling voice. Ruthy sat on the end of the sofa near Levi's chair and watched him until Grace finished her bottle.

"I'll change her and put her to bed," Ruthy said, standing up.

"Ja." Levi caught her hand as she bent to take the baby. "I'll check the stock, and then I'll be in. No *Dawdi Haus* tonight?"

"Ne, no *Dawdi Haus."* Ruthy smiled at him as he kissed her hand.

Ruthy took Grace into Levi's bedroom…their bedroom. She had put her clothes in the dresser drawers that afternoon, and hung her Sunday dress on the hook behind the door. Levi had made room for Grace's cot next to the dresser along the wall at the bed's foot.

Ruthy changed the baby's diaper and then lifted her to her shoulder. Taking a few minutes to make sure she had no gas would help all of them sleep better tonight. With that thought, Ruthy glanced at the bed. How many times had she smoothed the quilt over Levi's bed, tucking in the edges to make it neat and orderly, and wondering what it would be like to sleep there with her husband?

Grace gave a burp and relaxed into sleep. Ruthy laid her in the cot as the bedroom door opened. Levi stood in the doorway, watching her, the lamplight throwing his shadow on the wall next to the door. Ruthy shivered. She trusted Levi, but Elam's betrayal still haunted her. She couldn't shake the feeling that he would never go any further than standing in the doorway looking at her—that perhaps he would want her to move back into the *Dawdi Haus* after all. Could he really want her for his wife?

Levi stepped into the room and closed the door. "Ruthy, if you're here waiting for me every night like this, I may have to give up checking on the stock."

"You'll have to go back and check them again. I'm not ready for bed, yet."

Levi leaned back against the door. "*Ne,* I'm not going anywhere. I've been waiting for weeks to watch you brush out your hair, and you aren't going to cheat me out of that tonight."

He stepped close to her, but she still couldn't quell the lingering doubt. "Do you really think you could ever love me?"

"Ruthy, I would never have married you if I didn't, and the more time I spend with you, the more I like you." He took her in his arms, pulling her close, kissing her cheek, and then her jawline. "You're my wife. I love the way you love the children, I love the thoughtful things you do for me, I love the order and peace you've brought to our home."

She pulled back, looking straight into his eyes. "You love the things I do, Levi, but do you love me?"

He smiled, pulling the pins out of her *kapp*. "Ruthy, I think I've loved you ever since that first day when you came storming into my workshop, insisting that I tell you how many children I had. You were so beautiful." He took off her *kapp* and fumbled with the pins that held her hair up until it fell, cascading down her back. Levi lifted its weight in his hands, running his fingers through it.

"I wasn't beautiful. I had just spent hours on the train and we were talking in the barn. What on earth was beautiful about that?"

Levi brought a handful of her hair to his face and breathed in the scent. "You laughed. That's when I knew our home could be happy again. You brought laughter and love back when we had forgotten how." He kissed her cheek again, and then her eyebrow. With each kiss Ruthy's knees grew weaker. "When did you first know you loved me?" He whispered the words into her ear, sending chills down her back.

Ruthy smiled, remembering. "When I saw how you cared for Jack, even when he was at his worst." Levi's kisses trailed down her other cheek and she took a deep breath. "That's when I knew you were a man worth loving."

Levi stopped kissing her and pulled back, his eyes looking deeply into hers. "Be my wife, Ruthy, please?" She nodded and he leaned in, claiming her lips in a kiss.

* * * * *

WE HOPE YOU ENJOYED THESE **LOVE INSPIRED**® AND **LOVE INSPIRED**® **HISTORICAL** BOOKS.

Whether you love heart-pounding suspense, historically rich stories or contemporary heartfelt romances, Love Inspired® Books has it all!

Look for new titles available every month from Love Inspired®, Love Inspired® Suspense and Love Inspired® Historical.

Love Inspired®

www.LoveInspired.com

Love Inspired®

Save $1.00

on the purchase of any
Love Inspired®,
Love Inspired® Suspense or
Love Inspired® Historical book.

Available wherever books are sold, including
most bookstores, supermarkets, drugstores
and discount stores.

Save $1.00

on the purchase of any Love Inspired®, Love Inspired® Suspense
or Love Inspired® Historical book.

Coupon valid until June 30, 2017. Redeemable at participating retail outlets in the
U.S. and Canada only. Limit one coupon per customer.

Canadian Retailers: Harlequin Enterprises Limited will pay the face value of this coupon plus 10.25¢ if submitted by customer for this product only. Any other use constitutes fraud. Coupon is nonassignable. Void if taxed, prohibited or restricted by law. Consumer must pay any government taxes. Void if copied. Inmar Promotional Services ("IPS") customers submit coupons and proof of sales to Harlequin Enterprises Limited, P.O. Box 3000, Saint John, NB E2L 4L3, Canada. Non-IPS retailer—for reimbursement submit coupons and proof of sales directly to Harlequin Enterprises Limited, Retail Marketing Department, 225 Duncan Mill Rd., Don Mills, ON M3B 3K9, Canada.

U.S. Retailers: Harlequin Enterprises Limited will pay the face value of this coupon plus 8¢ if submitted by customer for this product only. Any other use constitutes fraud. Coupon is nonassignable. Void if taxed, prohibited or restricted by law. Consumer must pay any government taxes. Void if copied. For reimbursement submit coupons and proof of sales directly to Harlequin Enterprises, Ltd 482, NCH Marketing Services, P.O. Box 880001, El Paso, TX 88588-0001, U.S.A. Cash value 1/100 cents.

® and ™ are trademarks owned and used by the trademark owner and/or its licensee.

© 2017 Harlequin Enterprises Limited

LIINCICOUP0317R

Get 2 Free Books,
Plus 2 Free Gifts—
just for trying the Reader Service!

Returning to her Amish community, Lizbeth Mullet comes face-to-face with her teenage crush, Fredrik Lapp. As he builds a bond with her son and she falls for him all over again, will revealing the secret she holds turn out to be their undoing—or the key to their happily-ever-after?

Read on for a sneak preview of
HER SECRET AMISH CHILD *by* **Cheryl Williford,**
available April 2017 from Love Inspired!

"Lie still. You may have broken something," Lizbeth instructed.

His hand moved and then his arm. Blue eyes—so like her son's—opened to slits. He blinked at her. A shaggy brow arched in question. Full, well-shaped lips moved, but no words came out.

She leaned back in surprise. The man on the ground was Fredrik Lapp, her brother's childhood friend. The last man in Pinecraft she wanted to see. "Are you all right?" she asked, bending close.

His coloring looked normal enough, but she knew nothing about broken bones or head trauma. She looked down the length of his body. His clothes were dirty but seemed intact.

The last time she'd seen him, she'd been a skinny girl of nineteen, and he'd been a wiry young man of twenty-three. Now he was a fully matured man. One who could rip her life apart if he learned about the secret she'd kept all these years.

He coughed several times and scowled as he drew in a

deep breath.

"Is the *kinner* all right?" Fredrik's voice sounded deeper and raspier than it had years ago. With a grunt, he braced himself with his arms and struggled into a sitting position.

Lizbeth glanced Benuel's way. He was looking at them, his young face pinched with concern. Her heart ached for the intense, worried child.

"*Ya*, he's fine," she assured Fredrik and tried to hold him down as he started to move about. "Please don't get up. Let me get some help first. You might have really hurt yourself."

He ignored her direction and rose to his feet, dusting off the long legs of his dark trousers. "I got the wind knocked out of me, that's all."

He peered at his bleeding arm, shrugged his broad shoulders and rotated his neck as she'd seen him do a hundred times as a boy.

"That was a foolish thing you did," he muttered, his brow arched.

"What was?" she asked, mesmerized by the way his muscles bulged along his freckled arm. It had to be wonderful to be strong and afraid of nothing.

He gestured toward the boy. "Letting your *soh* run wild like that? He could have been killed. Why didn't you hold his hand while you crossed the road?"

Don't miss
HER SECRET AMISH CHILD by Cheryl Williford,
available April 2017 wherever
Love Inspired® books and ebooks are sold.

www.LoveInspired.com